THE BORDER

By the same author

THE BORDER

Elaine Feinstein

Hutchinson
London Melbourne Sydney Auckland Johannesburg

Hutchinson & Co. (Publishers) Ltd

An imprint of the Hutchinson Publishing Group

17–21 Conway Street, London W1P 6JD

Hutchinson Publishing Group (Australia) Pty Ltd
PO Box 496, 16–22 Church Street, Hawthorne, Melbourne,
Victoria 3122

Hutchinson Group (NZ) Ltd
32–34 View Road, PO Box 40–086, Glenfield, Auckland 10

Hutchinson Group (SA) Pty Ltd
PO Box 337, Bergvlei 2012, South Africa

First published 1984
© Elaine Feinstein 1984

Set in VIP Sabon by
D. P. Media Limited, Hitchin, Hertfordshire

Printed and bound in Great Britain by
Anchor Brendon Ltd, Tiptree, Essex

ISBN 0 09 156320 8

For Ruth Padel

WALTER BENJAMIN, born Berlin 1892, died Port Bou 1940. German-Jewish essayist of genius. Major work includes criticism of Baudelaire, Karl Kraus and Franz Kafka. Posthumous admirers, such as Hannah Arendt and Gershom Scholem, have disagreed about the weight of mysticism and Marxism in his thought.

Part One
SYDNEY
9 September 1983

'All sorrows can be borne if you put them into a story or tell a story about them'
Isak Dinesen

— A glass of tea? Or maybe a little schnapps?

The old woman's hair was arranged carefully about her perfectly shaped skull like skeins of beige silk. As the boy hesitated, she chuckled, and rose briskly on her neat, stick legs to bring over two glasses and a bottle of cognac.

In profile she looks like an eagle, the boy thought. Eighty-three, was she?

In her turn, he was scrutinized critically.

— A handsome young man. Such a lot of black curly hair. And good, narrow hips.

The boy marvelled at the way she had enclosed herself in a piece of Central Europe, as if she had conjured the walnut chest, inlaid tables, and curving velvet button-back chairs into place; or perhaps transported them with infinite care, to be reassembled in Australia, like the wooden house of the first Governor General in Melbourne. When she put a porcelain plate before him, with a plain yellow cake upon it, the aroma of nutmeg and cinammon rose to his memory as if he had spent his own childhood in Vienna or Budapest.

Which he had not.

She seemed to guess his thoughts, although hardly answering their direction.

— A pity Frederick married so very *Californian* a wife. It has kept us apart, I think. What a fortune to have grandsons, at least, who resemble the child he was. Now. Tell me about yourself. Saul, isn't it? And you are a historian.

— At Oxford.

— Good. England is not much admired here, but I know

better. Is Hans' work read in England now? Is he remembered? He is translated in America, I know; but it would have mattered more to him to be read in London and Paris.

    – I have read him in German, said the boy.

    Her eyebrows rose.

    – And do you find him good? I cannot read his poetry you know. It is a kind of blindness. Music, yes. Some paintings. But not poetry.

She patted his hand, as he sipped his cognac; and he smiled. An easy, lazy smile that lit his grey eyes and brought a sigh to the woman watching him.

    – You live in another world now. Probably no better, but at least different. Well. It's a long haul from Europe. It was kind of you to come and see an old woman. I wonder what draws you. Oh yes, I know *you*, young man, more than you suppose. You are not a philanthropist. You are curious. Why?

She poured two more glasses of brandy, and her eyes grew black as she lay back comfortably.

    – As a historian? Don't you find writers always have something of the vampire about them? Guiltless, naturally. But sucking the marrow bones of the rest of us none the less. Where else would they find the sweetness they need?

    – You knew Walter Benjamin, said the young man, hesitantly.

The old woman put on her spectacles and sighed: Of course we knew Walter. A little. In that terrible French city we had gone to for refuge. How should we not know another one of the hunted? And Hans admired him.

    – On the train, said the young man: South of Perpignan.

    – Nobody travelled by train. It was not a practical plan, said the old woman sharply: In June, we broke down in Quercy, between the Dordogne and Lot. Hah. Where to begin our history of disastrous choices! For we had choices, there is no question in my mind as to that. The road forked so many times, and always we went up the wrong turning.

Supposing in 1937, for example. Supposing I had looked out of the window and said quite simply. Of course. It is obvious. It is what we both want.

She shifted restlessly in her chair.

– You must do whatever you like, I said instead, reasonably. So many choices women force upon men. Out of cowardice. Or perhaps everything is fixed and inevitable.

Do you know what today is?

– Somebody's *birthday*, he guessed.

She looked amused.

– A kind of birthday, she agreed: A New Year's Day.

The boy looked out of the balcony window down upon Rush Cutters Bay, where the yachts danced on the silver waters, and the high towers with reflecting orange glass in their windows rose behind them. What vegetation he could see was evergreen and confusing.

– You mean it's Spring? he asked.

But she had moved on.

– All my life Hans used my thoughts as he used his own pain. How can that be excused? He put out a travesty of my spirit into the world. And before the ink was dry, people were questioning me: Is it really true? You were so cross. So disobliging, so cruel?

She shrugged.

– We did not speak to Walter at Port Bou; but his correct little moustache, and tin glasses stick in my mind. Well. Who knows? Who gives up, who endures, who fails and forgets, what saves one man in the pit and sends another to his pistol? What kills? The answers to such mysteries are locked in our very cells; or else in each childhood either endured or enjoyed. They remain mysteries.

The boy looked disappointed, and said: I hoped there might be more. Some manuscript, some poems, letters perhaps?

– You have been spoiled by women, she sighed: Already I feel reluctant to disappoint you. And did I say there was nothing? Hans once said to me: I should never have turned to you for insight. You've always been locked into a world of cause and effect. And it is possible. I offer no opinions. *But*, if you would like to look in a briefcase, I shall be glad to give it to you.

The boy was startled: I shall be enormously careful, he began.

– A gift, the woman repeated vigorously: It is my gift to you. Because you are beautiful, and who knows otherwise if I should ever have seen you, living here as I do in this antipodean wilderness?

Part Two

HANS WENDLER'S DIARY

'To the lover the loved one appears always as
solitary'
  Walter Benjamin

VIENNA: 1938

1 January

I do not usually keep a diary. But since my tongue catches on every consonant, as I try to explain my life's perplexity from a couch, my poor analyst has suggested I begin to do so in writing. Something certainly must be done to break through the new and terrifying block I have developed about lecturing in public. Very well. The matter is too serious to refuse even the most dubious remedy. The last two lectures of my course in the Philosophy of Art had to be cancelled altogether. It cannot be long before my stammering terror is publicly exposed next term; I cannot prolong the excuse of laryngitis forever.

Needless to say, the whole idea of turning to an analyst springs from my wife Inge.

2 January

Inge has a warm heart. I know. I have always known. But Inge's warm heart has never been much use to me. Sensitivity would have been preferable. I had every reason to believe I was marrying a woman of sensitivity. Interested in poetry. Language. And discussing such matters seriously. I was mistaken.

Now I've heard it said that women lose interest in sex when they get married. I can't say that for Inge. But certainly she lost interest in talking to me. In me altogether, perhaps, I should say. Except as something to cling to at night, and you might say the same for a hot water bottle. She has stopped seeing me, really. I could be a pile of clothes or papers for all the attention she gives me. I should explain:

17

she is very grand in such matters, and has always believed herself far above domestic work.

Not, of course, that she is lazy. Most of her energy goes, indeed, into work. *Her* work. That is, her own arcane, incomprehensible work in particle physics.

I am told she is highly regarded as a research scientist. Well, I have no means of discovering whether that is true or false. I regret to say that science has never excited me in the least. Anyway, she is a scientist, which is unusual enough in a woman; and possibly a distinguished figure in her field. I, on the other hand am a poet. Not a bad poet. There was a time when my work was highly regarded; but I am no longer vain enough to hope for much acclaim. How can anyone know? Poetry. Who believes in it? In any case, I keep myself going in a variety of part-time jobs, which bring little honour.

I cannot altogether blame Inge's impatience with the whole class of behaviour which is thought of as literature. In our corrupt modern age it may well be some dangerous fantasy land, where people can live out, like voyeurs, a life they would be afraid to lead. And if art is only talking about itself, what could be more pompous? Is it any wonder intelligent people have given up taking any writer seriously? Novelists are no closer to the sharp edge of life than poets.

My own books were doubtless too obscure to be thrown on any fire, but the silence that surrounds them is all the deeper.

3 *January*

Today I watched a young girl carrying her stack of books and settle at the table across from my own. My intense gaze must have woken her to my presence for she looked up. She looked straight at me. And then, she smiled a sad, tender smile. Filled with some loneliness I could only guess at. She was too young to be lonely, I thought, returning her smile.

And felt a thrill of disturbance that was not so much erotic as spiritually engaging. Tenderness. It was altogether missing in my life. And here was a young girl – I doubt if she is more than twenty-five, smiling tenderly at me. Only at me.

I hardly looked at her body, which was sensibly dressed for cold weather. It was her face that ensnared me. Gentle creature, I thought: how I wish I had someone to care for and protect. I could accept the blind or the lame or the sick, if their faces bespoke such sweetness.

Such a deep need. In the bend of her soft neck over her book, I sensed a solitary nature like my own, with the same necessity to love deeply and share thoughts with a fellow spirit.

4 January

Inge is the best friend I have in the world. Is it my fault that I no longer take much pleasure in making love to her? Take no pleasure is wrong, perhaps; the pleasure of the body is always functional; necessary even; but remote. There is no shiver of true desire in our approaches; no lyricism at the moment of submission; no transport in her evident delight. It is not simply domesticity as such. If I am to be honest, these thoughts of mine go back to our earliest encounters. We enjoyed a sibling passion. There has always been something almost incestuous in our love. We have become too close, with the years. Partly because she protects me? Perhaps. But truly she does not feel like a mother, not even a bad mother. We are too alike; we are evenly bad at the business of providing for one another's needs. And I have to fight to make her accept the most banal propositions; I spend myself in such arguments. She questions, turns, *destroys*, everything I say. Her logic is relentless; I cannot match her, even when I'm altogether certain that I am right.

Inge has never understood how different a human being I could have been, if she had not exacerbated even the *mildest* attempt at aesthetic discussion. She once tried to tell me, poor bewildered creature, that she *too* needed encouragement in her worldly ambitions. But why should I not behave as other men do, why should I not be permitted to say I want this done, or that. Why am I alone in being denied the god-given licence to grumble?

Her family disapproved of me, naturally; but they were even more opposed to her scientific work.

They were a wealthy family, whose women were supposed to lace themselves tightly in silk and do good works with any energy they had remaining. When I first stepped over the threshold of their shining home, and took in the Biedermayer furniture, the collection of Hungarian folk art, the sheer wasteful grandeur of the apartment, I remember a sensation of overwhelming envy.

To say my family were poor in those days is to convey nothing. Everyone was starving. But my mother had no knack with food or money, and my father liked to gamble at cards, which indeed he often did at the Jewish social club round the corner. In the nature of things he must surely *sometimes* have won but we saw no pfennig of it. And when he lost, he shamelessly took whatever money there was in the house.

That he was out of work was no shame. Millions were out of work. Still, the bitterness in him fed on that. He was a man who had wanted to work hard, and had nothing to which he could turn his hand. Even in good times, he would have worked for any firm that employed him.

Inge's family must have shared the trouble of those days. But her mother was a shrewd woman. She kept a clean house, and made good soup out of vegetables. Who knows how some people manage better than others? Which is not to say that any member of Inge's family showed much interest in things of the mind and spirit.

I should never have had the nerve to propose marriage myself; it was Inge who took a wild fancy to me. At that time she loved music, film, theatre, even poetry; she would listen to me read aloud for hours. I could not understand quite why she seemed so determined to marry me.

Now I think she deliberately chose someone to whom she could feel of use. To whom she could offer a hand in rescue. And that, beautiful as she was, she shared some of the same terrible insecurities that I did. Being a poet and being a woman made us equally outsiders. We could not fit in any Biedermayer household.

And so we set up on our own; and remained intimately dependent on one another in spite of our very different spheres of activity. I was much more notably successful at first than she was; and she seemed to take great pleasure in it. Little enough she bothers now about what is happening to me. Or what is happening in the Faculty.

She sails on fearless, or so they tell me. And I deal with the schemers about me as best I can. She no longer has the time to care, perhaps. First it was the child, then her new job. I carry on working, nevertheless. My first lecture for the next semester is written as always; but I cannot touch the pages without trembling.

7 January

A late developer, of course. A sickly child, not delicate, which suggests a fine spirit, but simply subject to every germ that proliferated in my wretched home. And, no doubt of this at least, ill fated in my father. Red-faced, disappointed bigot, he used his malign tongue on every one of us. No one could have tried harder to sabotage my academic career. I learnt to smile from mother. A fake sweetness in my case; I cannot remember her well enough to be sure. In any case, I learnt the ease of seduction young. And if Inge was not precisely my physical type, she was handsome enough. It was the strength of her love that caught me; or I should hardly have chosen such an extraordinary woman. If indeed I chose at all. In my own defence, there was no sign then that she was to become eminent at anything.

9 *January*

My analyst is not pleased with my notes, though I thought them frank and open, not to say gross in part. I was a little ashamed of them. But he only wants to know about my mother and father.

There is nothing neurotic, I want to say, about hating a father like mine. I was beaten by broom handles, leather belts, and horny red hands more often than I can recall. His anger was always surprising to me. He was a butcher by trade; a thick-set, high-coloured man with a spade beard. Once it was for listening to the radio. I think it was French poetry; my father decided inexplicably that it was sent from the Devil.

My mother was from Poland, I believe, with surprisingly blonde hair and blue eyes. It is strange, now, when I visit her grave I can remember few examples of tenderness from her during my childhood. But then, my father was a brute to her above all. He had her in tears every night. Perhaps it was a substitute for sex?

I think very rarely of my family and never see them now.

10 *January*

I have always steered clear of politics. Any man who is not frightened of what may happen these days, is a fool. And further. All violence terrifies me.

Only yesterday, I was standing at the No. 5 bus stop with Stefan, a young pupil of mine, who has recently left his wife and children and is living like a wolf in any place he can find. He has no money whatsoever; and the thought of lending him some had just struck me, when he pointed across the road towards Heidi, his new blonde mistress. It must have been about five o'clock; that strange time, when shops flood the wet streets with reflections of their own electric splendours, and yet there is still an uneasy light from the sky itself.

As we watched, a young man we both knew joined her, and she greeted him with an innocent enough kiss, as far as I could judge. But Stefan went quite white with rage.

– The bitch! He screamed, and I could hear in his voice how long he had spent over his afternoon coffee with brandy: It's a deliberate humiliation.

From the rails at the other side of the street, a tram arrived, blue sparks above it; but he strode across nevertheless. For a moment the tram hid the pavement altogether. Then I heard the bell, and the grinding rails as the tram moved away. And I saw to my bewilderment that Heidi was lying on the ground in front of Stefan who would not allow her to regain her feet. As I stared, a passing stranger tried to restrain Stefan; and received a blow in the face for his trouble. I could see his broken spectacles fall to the ground and blood pouring from his eyes.

– What are you doing? I yelled angrily. I could do no more, for the traffic was too dense to cross the road. And so I had to watch another vicious kick to the girl's head, and God knows what other damage would not have been done if a policeman had not sauntered on to the scene.

By the time I reached the brawl, the policeman was writing notes in a book, while the girl sobbed miserably on the wet ground. Whatever he had been asking her, she agreed, and her answers seemed to satisfy him. My pupil turned his indignation on the policeman.

– What does any of this matter? She is a whore. Putting her filthy tongue into a stranger's mouth. Right in front of me.

– Calm yourself down, the policeman suggested, without any of the indignation I might have expected. It was as if the

23

hatred men feel for women, even those they have wronged, was too commonplace to pursue. Catching my eye, he hesitated and, almost as if apologizing, added: Everyone quarrels when they are drunk.

When I described the incident to Inge, her glacial contempt quite unjustly accused me of doing less than I should.

12 January

Perhaps if Inge knew some of the difficulties I have with Kurt we would be closer. I mean, however much they were predictable, ill judged, all my own fault. What has happened to me through Kurt is none the less a betrayal.

Among the rest of the preposterous ill-paid nonsense I spend my life upon, one, small enjoyable hour is the class I give in Ethics as part of the University Department of Fine Arts. The Director must once have read my early poems, I believe. For three years now, I have been able to enjoy a small, but regular stipend, for a decent, honourable chore.

The class itself was undeniably a little stodgy. (Students with more talent would have been put into the Professor's class.) So when a young son of an old friend of mine presented himself to me, I was entirely flattered. He had few qualifications, but his mother had been talented; a clever actress. And I was happy to have him in my class.

He was very much like his mother as I remembered her; narrow-featured, with jet black eyes that glittered with a malice which was, for some reason, attractive rather than alarming. At least, I found it so at first; before I understood what was happening.

My stammer (at that time little more than a slight hovering over certain difficult words) was never remarked upon by the students. For my part, I was delighted to welcome an eloquent student. I did not see how he threw my own sober, honest sentences into shadow beside his brilliance. In plain terms, he decided to seduce my class from me; and it was through him I first heard ripples of laughter that were no longer tolerant but antagonistic.

14 January

I have never had much faith in miracles; though Inge claims it is the poet's province. But today I must confess I opened my mail and revised that opinion. Some group has read an early poetic play of mine and wants my permission to stage it in Paris. It is true no money is mentioned; and for all I know the group is drawing audiences of less than a dozen. I looked the play out again, however. Yes. It has a certain style, an edge, some tang of the sketches so successful at the *Simplicissimus*. And, of course, there are many German émigrés in Paris now.

15 January

I have looked at the letter again, and I am by no means sure that anything definite has been proposed. Inge claims that the French use subjunctives only as a form of politeness. But I have been betrayed by her optimism before. Why is she so sure of everything when she is so often wrong? Even if I were cautious for no other reason, her unquestioning delight would be sufficient reason for alarm. After all, who is to say it is not a trick? I searched all morning for the envelope in which the magical letter arrived, to make sure at least it had been posted in France. In some insane fit of tidiness, it has been thrown away. Inge says she looked very closely at the postmark before giving it to me. She cannot understand why I don't believe her. I was forced to cancel the first seminar of the term.

16 January

I have formed the clear intention of not replying to the letter. If it's a serious offer, they will know how things stand in Vienna now. An Austrian passport deserves to be zealously guarded.

17 January

Inge left yesterday. She will be away ten days at a Scientific Congress in Berlin, which I must say seems selfish, considering my condition.

I looked at her closely, my Inge, with her amber eyes and aquiline face, and speculated. Was she perhaps contemplating a little sexual adventure? I could hardly blame her. Women age so much more unfairly than men. At forty, she was still in the prime of her life; and fidelity is not much valued in our circle. There is something too straitlaced in her, however, some cowardice which would probably prevent her responding boldly. I know she is lonely in her own way. But then. It was her idea to send the child away to America, last July; the very day after Germany promised not to interfere in Austrian afairs. I suppose she must miss him terribly. I cannot say I feel so strongly. To tell the truth I shall be quite pleased to have a few days alone.

I took her to the station; and on my return, to my astonishment, there was another letter from Paris. Well, the offer seems to be serious. For some reason, which I cannot altogether fathom, I was pleased that the offer had come to me in Inge's absence. Why do I feel so much more excitement? It is my offer. Not our offer.

I shall send her a telegram with the news nevertheless. She will be pleased and proud. I'm a child! She could perhaps investigate a little. They claim to number some of Brecht's own group among them.

8 February

I went in to work at the Library as usual.

12 February

So our Chancellor Schusschnigg has paid a friendly call on Hitler. And yet everything remains normal. No one seems particularly alarmed, even the few outright Jews who remain in the University. An exception is Gerhardt Brandt, who has quietly applied for his US visa. As a physicist, of course, he will have no difficulty. But for a poet; it is a kind of suicide.

Am I making a fuss? Gerhardt is remarkably plausible, I am haunted by his simian face. He assured me that everyone in the Jewish community at least could read the cards now; the little tea party had included enough jackbooted generals to spell out Hitler's true meaning. And how could we trust any government that contained von Seyss-Inquart?

I said I hardly knew what he meant. Though of course I knew the name as the leader of the Nationalist Opposition.

– You will see, he nodded.

– Schushnigg is an academic, I began.

– Exactly. Which is not what is needed to deal with Hitler.

He then told me some gossip of how Hitler had treated his so-called friend and ally. I did not see how he could know so much, and said so.

Everyone is preoccupied with his own private agony. It is common knowledge that Gerhardt will soon be removed from his post as a radical.

13 February

I can no longer disguise the fact that Kurt is trying to destroy me. Why? Why? I cast my mind back to my dealings with his mother. It is true we were one-time lovers; but it was not a passion that went deeply on either side. For a moment, I

27

wondered whether he suspected I was his true father? Could his mother have suggested as much? But the dates would be wrong.

Yesterday, I determined to make a real attempt to grasp the nature of his hostility. I invited him to the Reiss Bar in one of the streets of Karntnerstrasse. The bar is all shiny mahogany, red leather and chrome. He grimaced when I suggested the rendezvous: A place of whores, he said.

– Not in the middle of the day. We can sip a liqueur. Talk, I pleaded.

– Very well, he agreed indifferently.

There was only one waiter; and no girls, I was glad to see. Upon our arrival the waiter put on the radio which played light music of depressing sweetness.

Well, I had planned everything I was going to say. That there was no truth that I could see in the letter Kurt had recently written to the Director. In what sense could my lectures be said to undermine the morale of the class? It was true I had some difficulty in speaking clearly; but surely nothing I said could be construed as polluting young Austria? Looking at him across the table, I felt my confidence dwindle. I drained my first schnapps to give me courage; while he still looked down at his, thoughtfully.

– Have I harmed you in some way I don't know? I began abruptly and not at all as I intended.

Kurt only smiled at me.

– Personalities don't come into it. You are polluting our homeland, he said.

My neck froze at the newspaper phrase.

– Pollute? How so?

He wagged his finger at me, like a Swiss burgher.

– We shall have no more mongrels soon.

– Inge, I began.

– I am not talking about your wife.

As soon as he said that I was afraid to probe further. The knowing malevolence in his eyes seemed too formidable.

28

I wanted to ask his own politics; and did not dare. I voted for Schusschnigg; whom did he favour?

– What are you asking me to do?

– You should leave, he said, still smiling.

– You want my post. Is that it? I shouted. I shouted mainly because it was only the sudden burst of anger that had freed my tongue at all.

– I have been ill, I said sombrely.

– Illness is something we shall have no time for, he said.

And I still had no idea whether he was speaking for a group on the left or the extreme right. I was too frightened to ask.

He rose, leaving his brandy untouched. When I was sure he had left the bar altogether, I furtively exchanged glasses. But even the brandy could not prevent me shaking.

14 February

Today my analyst wrote to cancel our appointment. He says he is ill; but I have a different theory. In our last session, he was decidedly inattentive. (And I had a most interesting dream; very rare for me. My dear dead mother had turned into a black owl, and hooted a warning from a tree.) It is true the man asked to see my diary but I had the distinct impression that he leafed through without much consideration.

I am not a fool, and do not propose to confide all my thoughts to my analyst. Damn him, I found myself thinking with a peculiar sense of liberation. At least, I shall be spared his strictures this week.

It would not bother me in the least if I stopped seeing him altogether. My professor confided to me only the other day that no one believes in psychoanalysis any more and whispered they might soon be outlawed as quacks.

I remember when Herr von Neurath, the German Foreign Minister, came to visit Vienna last year. I stood in the crowds to watch. He was such a reassuringly silver-haired gentleman, a German aristocrat as one likes to think of them; I was only sorry that Inge was not at my side to witness his descent. I was a little surprised when he greeted our waiting Austrian diplomats with a brisk 'Heil Hitler' and the Nazi salute; but I suppose it is by now a mere figure of speech. I confess his rising arm disturbed me as much as the enthusiastic crowds that responded. But Austria is not Germany, whatever these thugs may like to believe.

15 February

Today. How shall I describe today? I rose with my extraordinary sense of freedom still with me, and walked out into the wintry Vienna streets towards the Library. The sky was blue, and the whole world had a crisp, glittering beauty. The snow sat in the crotches of the cherry trees like blossom. I felt clean and young and filled with poetry.

And then, who should join me at my sunlit table but the very girl I have been staring at so intensely for the last few weeks. And it was she who spoke first.

It was a young, sweet voice, as tender as her face; and the pleasure was so intense that for a moment I did not catch the words, delivered as they were in French.

Thinking herself misunderstood, she repeated them in German: You have been watching me. I suppose you remember where we met?

I had no such memory; but I could feel my lips open sweetly in a smile. Perhaps the whole world was about to begin again?

Naturally I did not refuse the simple occasion for intimacy she offered.

– You will let me buy your tea? And perhaps an apple pie?
– I never eat much, she said.

It was what I expected her to say. Food was a gross, Biedermayer passion. My only worry was the excitement, and the effect it might have on my uncertain voice control.

Speak to me again in French, I wanted to say; because my heart was squeezed with the kind of poignant joy I remembered most sharply from French films. German was a hard language, and it did not suit her gentle tongue.

– Will you let me know your name?

– Hilde, she said promptly.

– At my age I forget names.

She laughed: But you can't be more than forty.

At this I could feel my back straightening, and I probably put up my hand to straighten my hair and touch my tie. It was a pity Inge had forgotten to collect the dry cleaning before she left. At least she could have left me the ticket. How unfair that I should be in an old jacket and trousers.

Inge is not a willing creature. I remembered her face with a certain sadness. Partly to assuage a sense of what I wanted. I thought particularly of that myopic bewildered stare she turns on me when she is crossed. Her friends have described her eyes to me as mournful, or even warmly loving. Well, every man must meet the eyes he sees, and they are not often turned in warmth and love upon me.

My fault, you will say. Well, I do not deny the brutalities in my own behaviour. I don't deny I have been, shall we say, *unfeeling*, myself. A man has to be taught to feel, if he comes from a home like mine.

Partly to cure my nervousness, I selected a good piece of Schwarzwald cake; and then cursed myself for such gross overeating. To my surprise, Hilde said as much immediately, as if we were in telepathic communications.

– A handsome man like you should not allow yourself to become overweight.

I found myself smiling at her mischievously.

– Sometimes it is necessary to celebrate. She looked sad at that, and it occurred to me that she was someone of whom I knew nothing at all; for all I knew her parents might have been whisked off in the middle of the night. Perhaps there had been a lover's quarrel. I looked at her hands. There was

31

a simple gold band on the forefinger of her right hand. She was married, I guessed. It was no answer to feeling unhappy.

The urge to comfort the girl was so powerful that I was furious to find a friend of mine taking a seat at the table with us. He was, moreover, a brooding fellow from the South, and a friend of Inge's too.

– How is the new book of poems going, Hans?

– Slowly. As ever, I replied, my spirits drooping a little. I had almost forgotten the book I am supposed to be preparing.

– Did you read of the happenings last night? he asked.

I was momentarily surprised. My friend is not much of a newspaper reader normally.

It seems there was a public rally outside the Parliament buildings to protest against the number of foreigners trying to escape over our frontier.

– Criminals, in flight from Germany, he said. His eyebrows rose as he called them *criminals*; but I did not respond to the implied irony, even though his eyes sought mine with a desperation, that reminded me of *Ostjuden* huddling in their slums. On any other day, I would have tried to reassure him; but it was impossible in front of Hilde. Luckily, he got up soon and left, without much of a friendly word in farewell.

And then I turned and looked into Hilde's eyes; which were as pale as muscat wine; and to my own astonishment I began to confess everything to her that was making me unhappy. My father seemed a good place to begin. And it turned out, miraculously, to be an affliction she shared with me. She, too, had been beaten by broom handles and leather belts; she, too, had lost her mother young.

There and then, sitting in that cold, ill-lit room, I confessed to my speech impediment. I even admitted to my terror of giving the first lecture of the term.

– You could practise it with me, she murmured.

– In your flat? She smiled and nodded. We did not speak of Inge; but she must have known I was married.

16 February

Chaque époque rêve la suivante.
Michelet

So I began to read my paper aloud to Hilde, who sat adoringly at my feet. My voice was fluent and steady.

– The ruins of modernity, I said. And she sighed and looked up as if what I spoke had been transfigured into a sensuous lyric. I paused, and almost without thinking put a hand on her soft, baby-clean hair. Inge's hair was crinkly under my hand, like a monkey's, I often thought unkindly; just as her face was tinged with yellow and there was always something indoor and sour about her whole person that the heavy perfumes she preferred seemed only to enhance.

And here was a snub-nosed girl of twenty-five with her yellow hair against my thigh, looking up at me and understanding all the ideas I had tried out so often on Inge, to find them falling dead at my feet.

The girl could not have heard what I read to her with more delight if it had been a love poem. I was not stupid. I could feel my penis rising as I read (so near her hair, so close to those adoring, uncoloured pink lips). Her idolatry was intoxicating; and if I continued to read the paper rather than bending there and then to make love to her, it was because there was something so deeply sensual in our sitting together it was as sweet as copulation.

I knew we would exchange souls. I had a boundless trust in the consequence of such love. And I loved everything about her room, which was different from my own. I never liked the smell of any house we lived in. With such certainty of joy only a moment's thought stayed me. I had an appointment with the Director early the following morning and would need clean clothes. (Later it struck me as an act of extraordinary prescience that Hilde had clean underclothes and a shirt of my correct size laid out ready for me. Marvellous creature.)

– Grandiose and grotesque, I concluded. And for a moment, looking down, I wondered if, after all, it was the woman in her I had stirred.

– Wonderful, she breathed: So lucid, so brilliant.

It came to me with great precision that I had never been understood so clearly by Inge in the whole of our marriage.

18 February

Inge arrived home. To my horror, she looks ill and shaken. At first, she would say nothing except that Berlin had frightened her. Uneasily, I wondered if rumours of my behaviour had reached her. I hoped not; I don't know why, but it seemed important.

She sat smoking a cigarette; and I offered her a brandy. Only then did she begin to speak, in a shrill, frightening voice. I thought she must have taken leave of her senses. Berlin was relatively calm, she insisted; there were still Jewish shops open on the main shopping streets, and although there were many yellow stars, things had not been as bad as she feared.

But her cousins had been picked up.

– For what?

– As Jews, she said.

I laughed. Her family had been baptised Catholics for nearly a century. It was a comic blunder. She flinched at my laughter.

– Supposing I took a job in Paris? Would you come with me?

– You can't be serious.

– Listen, she said: Both my mother's parents are buried in Jewish holy ground. That is enough for the Nazis.

34

– Well, enough for what?

– To be taken away, to be put in a camp, perhaps abused. There are worse rumours. And what of your own roots, Hans?

I was very angry: I hope you won't throw my parents' origins in my face.

– Hans, I have always known you didn't wish me to speak of it. I have always avoided the subject. But surely now you can see we must be honest, at least with one another? Your mother came from Poland. I have always known your origins, Hans. Why do you imagine I am the only one?

– I am altogether German, I shouted: What should I do in Paris?

– As much as you do here.

– Why should we run away like cowards?

I should be leaving Hilde behind, I realized suddenly, and perhaps that gave some genuine conviction to my voice.

– Well, Hans. We should not be the first to leave. Thomas Mann left long ago; and Hannah Arendt; and Brecht.

– I am not a left-winger.

– As a writer, exile is difficult, she said. Then sighed.

For a moment, I thought she might be suspicious, after all. Then I saw her eyes were filled with tears.

– You are not a fool. You must see the danger. I had not expected you to be so brave. Very well. If you wish it so, we will stay.

She bent over to kiss me, and I drew in an acrid breath of smoke and cognac.

– Good night.

19 February

Inge is once again a whirl of activity, suspecting nothing. There are so many kinds of betrayal.

Spice. Inge has always found spice in others, and not in me. It does not matter that it isn't erotic. She gives them her energy, and nothing is left for me. Long ago, as I stopped writing poems, as I began to wither and die, she watched indifferently. Now I have begun to write again, she observes no change. I feel as full of poems, as if my new love drew them from me as easily as she draws my passion. I am not ashamed. Sex is not the only kind of infidelity. And when I question Inge about her lunches with friends, she finds only petty curiosity in my interest. Wrong. And bitter. Jealousy is an emotion a man may forgive; it has its place, its dignity, it leaves a man whole and hard. But an interest in gossip?

She understood nothing; her own infidelity went too deep. She couldn't help it, couldn't help me. As my life dwindled, as I became a hack journalist, whose poetry no one remembered. How easily she went on saying, 'But I love you. Only you.'

Now I hold Hilde in my arms, and I do not need that love. I am returned to life. And the source of creation.

20 February

Inge and I listened to Hitler for the first time broadcasting on Austrian radio. Thundering Seig Heils! greeted his arrival as we had expected. But then he devoted most of his speech to the economic miracles achieved under his stewardship. He barely referred to the Jewish question; there were no denunciations of Bolsheviks either.

– Well, I said, as if confirmed in my opinions. Neither of us could deny the feeling of relief. When I met Brandt later in the day, I made a great deal of the news that Bruno Walter's contract with the Vienna Opera had been renewed for a year.

22 February

For the first time I stayed out until nearly morning, without any explanation to Inge. We spent a long while talking. I remember saying to Hilde: How did I waste the first forty years of my life without you?

– Now we shall be happy, the girl encouraged me.

– You will not love me long.

– As long as we live, she said quietly: How she has hurt you, that arrogant bitch of a wife. Why?

– No, I said: Not arrogant.

– She doesn't see you, she has left you alone following her own career.

I shifted uncomfortably, because she had picked up my criticism just a shade too easily, and I was anxious, thinking of Inge alone at home.

– I have also made her miserable, I said at length: She is a kind of human being you don't understand, my love. She is genuinely without calculation.

– How appalling, she said: And without the slightest care for you.

– We neglected one another equally, I tried to explain.

– Look at her clothes. The way she stands. Her joy in her celebrity.

– She doesn't think like that.

– You'll be telling me next she is good, murmured my beloved Hilde.

– Yes, I said, relieved: That's it. She is.

To my horror, I found Inge was still awake as I let myself in. Dressed and awake and yet bleary, as if she had spent the night pacing.

– My God, what has happened? I asked stupidly. She flung her arms round me, and sobbed as if her heart would break.

– I thought you were dead.

– Look, you don't usually wait up for me. How could I guess? I remonstrated practically.

– Hans, I have given in my resignation to the lab, she said: I have been here all day waiting to tell you. And then, as I

waited through the whole evening, I became convinced.
They would take out my foolishness on you.

– Resign? I held on to the only bewildering word I could
make out of the blur of her speech.

– They have appointed a monster in place of Brandt. I
have resigned in protest.

– And Brandt?

She seemed to collect herself, then her eyes looked me
over closely.

– Where *have* you been? she asked me directly.

– Talking.

– Until six in the morning? She asked me.

– Yes.

She raised her eyes incredulously.

Suddenly I was desperately tired.

– Come, she said softly, and we went to bed and wound
our arms about each other.

My heart banged uncomfortably. In my mind, I turned
over what I should tell Hilde.

23 February

A restless weekend. As far as I can tell, Inge has decided to
let the matter of my night away from home pass without
further comment. A great relief, but I wish Hilde understood how important *caution* is to me now. One or two of
my men friends have already hinted that they know more of
my affairs than I guess. Worse, Kurt dropped in to deliver an
essay which he particularly wanted me to read. (Damned
boy. Why should his respect still flatter me?) And as he left,
he too murmured something about Hilde's wild past. Something dangerous and political and quite invented I dare say.

24 February

I looked at myself for a long while in the mirror, and tried to imagine how Hilde could prefer me to admirers close to her own age. If my old therapist had not disappeared, I would have put the matter to him quite frankly. One piece of good fortune: The University does not seem to question my absence for the moment.

25 February

Inge is agitated today both about friends in France, and others returning to the Soviet Union. It is rumoured Brecht is among them. Her own hope in Russia died with the Moscow trials; but some people are endlessly gullible. But she still puts some faith in French Socialism. She argues it is now a question of Trade Unions in France, and that social reform is the order of the day. Don't I approve of better hours, paid holidays and so forth? The danger in her eyes comes always from the Right: Action Française. The Catholic literary intellectuals.

– Why literary? I would have liked to ask.

– Listen, she said. And told me more about the well-springs of hatred; the Mouvement Anti-Juif Continental, the weekly *Gringoire*, not to mention *Candide*, and what more suitable name? That villain Voltaire. As if anyone would condemn Voltaire for one idiosyncratic prejudice.

– I don't know what is best, she said: At least the French hate the Germans. All this year the mood has been growing darker in Paris.

– Mark my words, she said: By next month we shall have Germans in Austria. Hans, please. Let us leave while we still can.

I was tempted, not so much by her arguments; but by the thought that, after all, I should not arrive altogether a nobody. Not only was my play to be performed, but the group were happy to pay me a sizeable fee. On the other hand, I did not want to leave Hilde.

– Why don't you go ahead now? I suggested.

39

I swear I was not thinking of getting her out of the way, but allaying her anxieties. But even as I promised to follow, as soon as I could arrange something, her mouth closed into a tight line.

— I don't agree it is a good idea to separate.

— This would not be a separation in the ordinary sense, I said smiling.

— A separation is a separation. I know you, Hans, she said.

And for a moment I realized that it was true, in a sense, but what Inge knows is only the *worst* in me, the pettiest and the least interesting.

— Do I grudge you your women friends? I asked.

— How is that to the point? she glared at me. It was an old story.

— To be sure, in this world there is no eternal love. Even ordinary faithfulness is out of the way. Perhaps women sustain one another against that knowledge, that vulnerability. But there is nothing erotic in my friendship with women, said Inge sullenly. I knew it was true. Her narrow figure, slim hips, and proud head attracted other women; but she had never wanted their love.

It was a fantasy of mine that there was something masculine about her. But if there was any truth in it, it was not a matter of hormones. She knew more than other women; she seemed too strong. And she earnt a man's wage.

When I was angry, I sometimes searched her top lip, which even in her forties was unmarked by hair, and accused her of plucking out the evidence.

Today, I tried to soothe her. She is losing weight, I observed.

She coughed several times and found difficulty catching her breath.

— It will be my death, she said. Without explanation.

26 February

Disturbed today. On my walk to the library I passed a figure that seemed half-familiar to me; as if, in another context, I might even know him very well. The man had grey hair, and an overcoat of brown herringbone tweed, belted at the waist with a knot of string. Under his arm he was carrying several rolled newspapers. The shabbiness of his clothes suggested madness more than poverty. And his little eyes darted about as fiercely as the arm that held the newspapers was pressed to his side.

He seemed to be walking with a determination not to fall apart; and this impression was increased when, to my surprise, he reached the street where a few cars were parked close by the old police station. In spite of the filth and rust that must have spattered his coat, he forced his old body tight up to the wall. I could see he was panting a little, and was a little afraid he might actually stick half-way and have to be dragged out. But he pulled his chest in, and his belly, and his face reddened with the effort and then he was through. And then I recognized him. He was my old analyst. Something terrible had certainly happened to him. I did not risk finding out what it was.

27 February

How shall I live this down? How shall I bear it? Today I attempted to give my second lecture. It goes without saying that I had brought not only comprehensive notes, but also the most varied and widely drawn quotations to read, just in case I found myself undergoing the terrible vocal paralysis of the preceding term. My pulse rate was high, but all began well enough, though I saw Kurt in the audience, grinning, as if waiting for my collapse.

There was a slight breathiness in my voice such as might accompany ordinary nervousness. But I felt confident enough to make the traditional request for hands to be held up by those who found me inaudible.

I then began to read a quotation from Spinoza, my head poised over the page so that every period should be correctly pointed, and every word enunciated as it should be. I only lifted my head at the end of Spinoza's paragraph.

And what did I see then but a forest of hands. They extended, not only from the back three rows where the acoustics are admittedly tricky, but up to the very first bench. For one moment, I had the exact sense of being caught up in a dream. On stage in an opera perhaps (I cannot sing a note), or in a foreign play; or perhaps in some familiar piece, where the action leads up to my speech but I have forgotten.

I laughed, a little feebly.

And then I saw Kurt's face. And some of his friends were standing in the gangways. They stood there, with arms folded, and waited, until every arm in the room rose into what was more or less the Nazi salute.

I wanted to say many things. Simple things. For example, that it is forbidden to stand in gangways. The University expressly forbids it. That Spinoza (if such was their objection) had been cast out by his own community. But no word came out of my lips.

It must have been then I noticed Hilde, who was sitting on the bench below Kurt.

It looked to me as if, when he leaned forward, his hand touched her head. Of course, it is impossible to be sure, because it was at that precise moment I pitched forward in a dead weight down the steps of the podium, and crashed into the blackness.

I am writing this from my hospital bed. Inge brought in my diary without comment. I cannot tell if she has read it.

– Luckily, it is your left arm that is broken, she said.

Can she really be so unfeeling?
They have told me I shall be home in a week.

28 February

Two things have bewildered me today. Hilde has left for
France with no more than a note saying that she loves me as
passionately as ever; and when can I join her? This has
frightened me more than anything yet.

Inge saw my pale face, and imagined it had something to
do with our neighbours; the Bratsky family, who completed
their arrangements for leaving yesterday. I was sorry for
them, they looked so pale and wretched. Of course. Bratsky
lost his University post. Something political, it is said. They
say Bratsky has been secretly transferring funds to a Swiss
bank account for years. Although they have been our neighbours these last ten years I feel little in common with them.
Why do these people cling so to their religion? As if it hadn't
been proved time and time again that God takes no care of
anyone.

Inge seems to be disproportionately distressed. In fact, I
am just a little worried about her. She has lost more weight,
and has no appetite. I blame her quixotic gesture. It makes
no sense; and endangers both of us. Inge said drily: It is as
well we were once a family with two incomes.

She has not mentioned leaving Vienna again, I'm glad to
say. The general consensus, even among outright Jews of my
acquaintance, is that Hitler cannot last much longer. Even if
those who might have kept him in check have failed; now he
is going to extremes, the people never will follow him.

1 March

A blowy day, with few signs of Spring. I had arranged to
take Hilde to Switzerland this weekend. Unlike Inge, who
has no real interest in anything outside major cities, Hilde

43

loves Nature as I do. We had planned to meet again on neutral territory for a short walking excursion, which she has called off. She was rather mysterious about her reasons. I pressed her, for some reason; the face of Kurt was present very vividly to my mind as I stared into the black telephone. But she seemed genuinely surprised. The reason has to do with only herself and me. I don't know why my heart sank at the phrasing. I did not know how to explain how much I would prefer if she kept our relationship secret; but it seemed mealy-mouthed to do so.

When I asked Inge if she would (since the hotel is booked) like to come away for a weekend to Interlaken with me, she burst out crying. I was appalled. Apparently, she took the offer as a serious renewal of love. Perhaps, in part, she was right. And indeed as we walked through the Spring grass, the turf bouncy under our heels, and I watched Inge striding ahead with an impatient spirit, I *did* acknowledge how deep an affection I felt for her. It occurred to me then, that, whatever happened, I could not manage without her. Hilde was one thing; and this was another. I could not manage without either or them. I would have liked to say as much, when we were in bed, in our mountain chalet. Inge lay open-eyed, staring at a gathering storm about the ice peaks above us.

– Blue lightning, she murmured.

– You are my true family, all the family I have ever had, I exclaimed.

And then she was silent for a long time in the dark, and I did not know what she was thinking.

We prolonged our stay for a week. I realized that, as much as anything else, I did not want to return to Hilde's news.

3 March

We came home to a pile of mail; one in Hilde's handwriting. I put it first to one side; then in my pocket, in the hope it would escape Inge's attention.

Then I went anxiously in to the lavatory to read Hilde's letter. To my enormous relief, there was no sign of the crisis she had suggested over the telephone. Was it possible I could plan to take the evening train to Paris on Tuesday?

I came down again, feeling freer; and caught a glimpse of Inge's face, as she proceeded stolidly to open her own letters, one after the other. There is something archaic about that expression, I thought; an archaic strength, as if she had an Egyptian in her family tree.

Her eyes looked up as they felt mine upon her; and I dropped my own before the inquiry in their gaze.

Part Three
INGE WENDLER'S DIARY

'Natural guilt . . . befalls man not on account of action and decision but through idleness and hesitation'
  Walter Benjamin

PARIS: 1938

3 September

Hans has been so elated by the success of his play, that he walks like another man. He strides about our rooms, whistling, as if he owned the whole world; as if our friends still in Austria were not being horribly abused and tormented. I don't grudge him the happiness, but I resent the frivolity. When I say so, he laughs and says: Write more letters, Inge. Perhaps you will find a job, after all.

I write letters every day. It has not been easy. We are thought of as aliens, here in Paris; there were too many physicists from Germany already. To be German, and a woman, and now to be counted as Jewish: these are handicaps.

And whatever rewards Hans' play may have brought him, the money was no fortune; and I am told the piece will be taken off any day now. Our savings, which I was lucky to get out of the country, cannot last forever. When I say as much, Hans nods, and seems to know; but his thoughts are elsewhere. He is living in a dream.

We arrived in Paris only days before the *Anschluss*. Chance, Hans calls it. It is possible. He has no idea what it would mean to apply that principle to the universe I once investigated daily. When I try to explain, he falls into bored preoccupation. He has never understood the relevance of magnetic fields to the God in his poems, never seen any relevance to the human heart in the laws by which the atoms move. And yet he asks himself whether we are creatures with whom God is amusing himself, as if at a dice.

I have spoken to enough refugees from Germany now to

understand what horrors we escaped. People who left Germany six years ago still speak of their experience with fear.

And then, from the personal point of view, I am happy whenever I think we have left behind whatever entanglement my poor Hans had found himself so caught in before we came away.

6 September

Hans' friend, Hilde, has found us a cheap room in the Marais with some Jewish friends of hers. Convenient as it is for the moment, I gather she herself is living in some splendour near Les Invalides. Not for the first time, I wonder why she has chosen to run away from the Nazis. I have satisfied myself she is not even partly Jewish.

Someone, certainly, is supporting her. I observe it is the latter suggestion which produces spasms of indignation in him.

These days I do not even dare to cry.

10 September

I am grateful that I brought the letters from our son Frederick with us. It was an impulse rather than foresight. They were so painful to me, those first bewildered letters from his twelve-year-old pen: resentful, fearful, unexpectedly bossed by my cousins in their Los Angeles suburban home. How strange he found American schooling. How he was unused to being at the bottom of the class. To hear music ridiculed by quite intelligent children; to be so lonely, so terribly in need of love.

It used to squeeze my heart every time I looked at them. Only this year did he begin to write coolly, and often in English.

Hans used to blame me for sending him away; but even if I never live to see him again (and these last few days I have been choking with some bronchitic infection, I cannot imagine how I will get through the winter) even then I rejoice to think he has been released from this European dungeon. Because, for all the pleasure Hans takes in it, and for all the splendours of its gay heart, Paris as we live in it is a dungeon.

I have sent Frederick our new address, but so far there has been no word.

10 September

I like the district: cobbles, narrow streets, continuous bustle, unfamiliar smells. A butcher's shop round the corner sells goods, cheap offal, even spleen; I wish I had room enough in the gas stove to cook it as it should be prepared.

The attic room is small, with room for only one desk. Yesterday rain brought down the plaster over the bed. I wash clothes in the sink downstairs; it's not such a hardship. The other lodgers are friendly; many of them refugees as bewildered by their situation as we are.

12 September

Last night, we went to see a group of German students in *Faust*. A marvellous play. Hans has often explained all its ambiguities to me. Tonight he seemed fascinated. Particularly by the girl who plays Margarita. Certainly she is a particularly beautiful actress. They are all students, none of them more than twenty-two or twenty-three. Afterwards, we went to the theatre backstage, which we can do as members of the University. It was Hans' idea; I wanted to please him, but I was tired. I said so.

— When are you *not* tired? When were you *ever* young? he demanded: I want to have a drink at the bar and see if that girl is as sensitive to speak with as she seems on the stage. You can go home if you like.

As I sit shuddering, at the wall, I watch the ease with which he picks her up. No stammering in these situations I thought bitterly. No fear, even as he looks at her first shyly, then slyly; soon he buys them both a drink. For twenty minutes or so, he turns all the benevolence of his face upon her. That night, as we were dropping off to sleep, he said: 'I have never loved you enough, and that is what I am being punished for.'

– Punished? I asked, puzzled. But he is asleep and doesn't answer.

16 September

I do not know what to do about Hans' *affaire*, which continues, he maintains, only as friendship. The pain of it puzzles my head.

– Why didn't you tell me? I asked.

– I didn't want it to spoil our love, he said. I could only gaze at him with incredulity.

– It's over, he said: I promise you.

– Really? I wanted to believe him. There was enough in the newspaper to frighten us into closeness again.

– Look at what has been happening in Vienna! They have old women mopping up streets. And such delight in looting and rape. Always rape.

He sighed. But I could tell the shadow that crossed his face was from another threat.

– Have you arranged to see her again? I asked him, evenly.

– See who?

I knew he understood, and shrugged. So that he was forced to reply.

– Yes. Listen. Trust me. Will you trust me?

I didn't see what sense it made but I nodded.

– Surely you can trust me for one night?

My heart ran cold again.

– To be out all night?

I hated to be alone in the flat, and of all times now.

– Not alone of course, he reassured me: Look, I'll arrange for my brother to call round, he has sent his wife to England. Such a graceful woman you know. A mistake . . .

I murmured something: *Why* all night?

– Trust me. Believe me.

Almost I did believe him.

– She can do us terrible damage.

– Politically?

– Perhaps.

– How? Is she *mad*? Or what?

– A little mad, he said: Please. Think of this as some little lie you might tell me about the butcher's bill to keep me happy. When you do that it is to protect me, isn't it?

– You are going to *her*, tonight, to protect *me*? *How*?

– Trust me.

Suddenly I didn't believe him at all. I said: What worse can she do? You don't deny she is your mistress.

– Worse. Much worse. Darling.

Reluctantly I let him go, and with him the whole peace of my mind.

His brother came late and hungry, and expecting more than the cold supper I had provided. I could hardly bear to talk to him. In dim lights, the resemblance to Hans was close enough to disturb me; but I did not see what else there was in the world to talk about.

He on the contrary was filled with gossip. Did I know that? And that? And had Hans and I yet taken the necessary steps for?

We have done none of these things; poor improvident creatures and I was glad to see him go.

Hell. I am in Hell. I suppose he is with her now. And I don't know and can't know, what is really going on, or what is the nature of this terrifying power which he so fears, and which he will not even put into words. To protect me? How many more grey nights, sleepless and waiting must I bear with the question that he will never answer.

Dear Lord, what is to become of us? Does he know how frightened I am? He says that *I* am real, and I haven't lost him, and yet. What does he tell *her*? What has he promised *her*? She has summoned him to her and he obeys. What are they doing? Does he not, frankly, find it more entertaining with her? Will she bind him to her with sex, and youth, and lively conversation?

– I'm slowly disentangling, he says.

Why slowly?

When at last he returned, it was morning again and I had begun to cry with a wild abandon I knew must be close to madness.

– Must you do that? he asked.

There are women who can look enticing when they weep, but my own animal abandon frightened me as well as repelling him. What if I lost my senses altogether? How could such a situation be coped with?

– There, there, he said awkwardly. And I heard the falsity in his voice: We'll work out something, you'll see. Some compromise.

– Never, I shrieked. Never. I won't be condemned to that.

And then I began to moan: What's to become of me? What's to become of me?

Hans appears to me now to have been the centre of my life all the time. Not my work, as I had imagined. How could he not know the difference in me?

When I tried to explain as much, he looked sardonically upon me, and inquired whether my work was now going as badly as his own once had.

I am too cowed to provoke further cruelty.

16 September

Things can't go on like this.
And yet the remedy is worse.
Worse than this torment of fear and waiting?
Yes, since *loss* is what I fear, and loneliness.
How can I leave without him?
Such sweetness to remember his arms around me.
His comforting whisper.
Even if I don't believe the comfort.
Do people recover from such pain, or are
they damaged forever?

17 September

A hot night. Impossible to sleep. Hans is not usually out so late without phoning.

The rehearsal must have ended long ago. Even if he went on talking with the keener actors. Why do I go on sitting here? It is because I am afraid to go to sleep, and wake alone. . . .

18 September

Today I lectured at the Sorbonne on Niels Bohr. I have barely slept, and must look like a gargoyle. I was not sure I could even face so many unfamiliar faces; to move from a chair takes more energy and will than I can muster. And yet, the lecture was an amazing success. The taste of the applause lifted me for a moment, like alcohol; and yet, stupid and pointless as I know it to be, I could not linger. I dashed away from my friends to catch the Metro back to Hans. So he should not feel alone?

He has no such worries about me.

Or is it, as his eyebrows suggest, to make sure he is at home? I am ashamed of my own obsession.

21 September

I have lab space now, following a letter from Brandt (who is in New York). It does not much hearten me. Hans and I are moved further apart as soon as I begin to work.

It is strange how our situations have changed. Once, he seemed only to be interested in squeezing some *pleasure* out of life: in consuming theatres, galleries, books, lively people. And now, suddenly, all that has become frippery, and all that counts for him is his writing.

And I, who once grudged the time to accompany him into the cafés he loved, and the galleries he enjoyed so much more than I did; I, who thought all these years that the true centre of my life was work, can barely face the task of lifting a pencil. I force myself to go into the laboratory; but I am only pretending. No one is deceived except Hans. I know now that, all the time, I was in some sense working for *him*. To impress him? Not precisely, though perhaps I had once hoped for that. But yes, in some sense to have him admire me. It was *his* admiration I craved; and I do not know if I can bear life without it.

27 September

He will not let me question him. He will not let me react naturally in any way. I have to swallow my fear and my rage or else he will not come home at all. I know that in some womanly piece of myself from my adolescence. I made one attempt to explain the severity of that demand.

But as soon as he began to feel the blackness and bitterness rise in me, he moved towards the door. Hans, what am I to do with my rage if you won't let me speak it out? It will kill me. I shall be the one that dies, not you, you old hypochondriac. He paused only to ask whether I had made any further inquiries about visas.

– How many visas?

– Three. Naturally.

I had indeed begun to make inquiries, but the impudence of using me to find a visa for Hilde choked me.

– It is still possible, of course, in theory, but we should not count on it. In any case, it will be too late for me, I could not help adding bitterly.

– So you mean – if I can't love you enough, then you won't help me? he asked directly.

I hesitated: It's hard.

– Then I won't leave, he said simply.

– It is the crudest form of blackmail, I sobbed: I have tried to trust you.

1 October

Last night I behaved shamefully. Without dignity. I deliberately came home early, and waited for Hans to leave. To see where he went. He had claimed to have met some marvellous new friend, a man called Walter Benjamin, whose ideas inspire him with a new sense of purpose. He said he was to meet him at a café. Little as I know we can afford it, I took a cab to follow his. And watched him sit down at a table (with Hilde, certainly, but also with another man). I was almost disappointed, as I dismissed the cab. Why? Did I want fresh evidence to convict him?

I watched the three of them. They were so animated and full of joy as they talked, I sat and watched them from my corner across the street, with tears pouring down my face.

When they all rose to shake hands in farewell, Hans and Hilde left together.

Thank God I had the self-restraint to go straight home, since, absolutely contrary to all my expectations, Hans returned only minutes after I did.

He was full of the talk he had been enjoying.

– Magical. A Marxist who is not a materialist. He has come to grips with all the horrors of our time. Even the

57

horrors of Nazism. And he has a whole library of which I know nothing to help him. Imagine. He uses the Kabbalah. The work of an old theologian like Abulafia. He laughed at me when I drew back from my own Jewishness. I didn't even know there was a Jewish mystical tradition.

– And even if there is? I responded sharply.

– I understand you, he replied, mercifully: It was what I said myself. But the point is that this man knows Brecht. Writes about him knowledgeably. He has read everything. And yet. He has this other face, which makes me read my own differently.

– And your face, too. He kissed me.

I can only take in, that, for some reason, our lives are entwined closely as a result of that meeting. It is almost as if, a book-list, and a few holy names, and sacred texts, have led him to forgive me for my Jewish grandparents. Perhaps it will even lead him to forgive his own father, as one rotten apple fallen from a fine tree?

I can only thank God I followed him no further.

4 October

Hans loves me.

His lips are warm, and his tongue is in my mouth, and I am not dreaming. He calls me lovely, blesses me. I am radiant with happiness. Fearless.

5 October

In my relief, I spent this morning walking about the *Marais*. It was as if, only now, with the warmth of Hans' love once again around me, I could spare the attention to observe, among the bustle on the Rue des Rosiers, the stalls of fruit and shoes, the piles of fish, the pedlars from Kovno or Kiev who filled the pavements with a babble of energy. Even the shops in the walls seemed to bulge out into the streets. I must have been blind or asleep; today I woke to find myself in the heart of Asia.

And that is not all I have missed. There are strange archways, too, through which I stare at secret gardens and statues moulded with a baroque loveliness that reminds me of Vienna. I can see as much without pain. The tight clamps in which I have been living for so long seem to have released me. I flow out into the world about me now with avid curiosity. Museums do not usually excite me. (It was something which long came between Hans and I.) This morning, almost as if in celebration of our new-found closeness, I took a few tentative steps into the Musée Carnavalet, which had once been the house of Madame Sevigné. Hans must have once given me some account of her life, since I could not remember reading any of her books; and it was for a time an unexplained pang that pursued me among the splendours of her carved chairs and glittering clocks. Then I recalled the unthinking, monstrous passion she had felt for her daughter; and with that memory, a flicker of my own early morning dream. There had been some childhood glimpse of Frederick, with his arms out, calling for me, as I drove off resolutely to the laboratory. Did I cry then? I am crying now, as I think of it.

Frederick. My only son. Though I must remember, when I asked him about it, only six months later, he claimed to have no memory of my desertion. His impudent face opened into an uneven grin; the charm of it mocked me. His mockery and his confidence were alike precocious, and I loved them equally. Even now, I only have to close my eyes and his whole childish presence is there. Black eyes, solemn in their concentration upon some piece of balsa wood sculpture. Or black hair flowing in the wind as he climbed some dangerous peak to pose, his thin, precisely balanced body, as if defying us to fear for him. He was always an artist. An artist, or a pianist, or perhaps a chess player of genius. The school could not be sure.

59

As the memories crowd back upon me, I marvel again at the insanity of sending him so far away. Only my crazy terrors of these last months have kept out the longing for him; with the first release from that pain, another knowledge rushed in to take its place. Not exactly anxiety.

I think of him at six, at the piano, his feet too short to reach the pedals, playing Mozart, Beethoven, Chopin. How much I hoped from him, how much I took from his gaiety. His spirit was the gaiety of our house. And his courage. At six, he outfaced bullies with his nimble wits. My own cowardice made me plead with him to placate rather than tease. But it is not his nature. He reminds me of my own father, who never bent his head to anyone in his life. Yet Frederick is so much more frail. My father was built like an ox; and Frederick is delicate boned. His wrists are thin. When he came back bruised from fighting, my heart was squeezed with a sense of his fragility. It is part of his beauty, which seems to spring neither from Hans nor myself. And yet there is nothing feminine in his carriage. He holds himself bravely. Like a matador, I often thought; prepared to take on the whole world with a sweep of his cloak. And by the same token, he was much the most fastidious of any of his class in his choice of clothes. Taking him to a tailor was an ordeal; where Hans could not have been more casual in his choice of clothing.

Was our closeness unhealthy? At least, Hans was never excluded. How could he be, when so many of Frederick's chief joys were those he had given the boy? Hans could play the violin and sing; it was he who had taught Frederick to sight read. They spent hours in the music room together. And their affection for one another gave me pleasure.

And yet it is true I was more dependent on the boy than Hans was. Hans had another kind of magic in his life, the pleasure in his own creation which my own work in a laboratory could not give me. In any case, gaiety was his element; he lived in it. Perhaps his example gave Frederick the secret of inner joy. He understood how much I was dependent on other people always: colleagues in the laboratory, recognition, awareness of what contributions I had made. Both of my men seemed free of such obsessions. Just as neither of them seemed to need, as I did, to belong to a team.

If there were quarrels over the child, they were always on questions of order which concerned Hans. I suspect he saw discipline as a way of freeing the child from the inheritance of his own family. He meant so well; yet I could not help interposing myself between him and the boy; could not help trying to protect him, as I felt it. And yet Frederick himself made no objection. I know it enraged Hans; because it was an echo of the way his father had punished his mother. The worst he could imagine for himself was to become like that. And by my resistance I could tell I was in danger of putting him into that role. How long ago it seems. And my fatal mistake was my attempt to placate Hans by suborning Frederick's charm to offer him. Soon he became impatient with it, saw through it, and began to look for duplicity. Some mistake I must have made; for their love for one another soured on absurd arguments.

Hans began to worry that the child would waste his talents, for all his wonderful perkiness; always, and in everything else an optimist, this he was not prepared to leave to chance. And so we quarrelled. How it hurts me now to think that we could ever have quarrelled!

When we had the chance, the one chance, in the one and only life I have ever believed in, *why* did I deny Hans the decent ordinary home he demanded for his son?

For there is a sense in which I felt we were a little above such concerns. Our ambitions put us above them. And Hans, in particular, since I always saw him, as it were, in the vanguard of our family fame, even if my stubborn muscles provided the bedrock of our fortunes.

How is he now, our Frederick? I think of him. Tenderly at

61

ease with all animals. The appointed caretaker of all the potted plants that abounded in our house. Green-fingered, so that an avocado pip would sprout for him into a tree. Where is he now, and how does he remember our old voices over his childish head?

It is a long while since I have wept for anyone but myself. Now I weep to think of him, imagining him as an orphan, imagining his loneliness. Or perhaps even these tears are selfish, and what I dread most is his forgetfulness.

When Hans came in that evening I burst out: we have lost him. Frederick. We have given him away to strangers. And he watched me oddly.

– It was wisdom to send him away.

– You opposed it.

– You were right to persist.

And he took me warmly in his arms, and soothed away the fears in my heart.

6 October

The morning was so brilliantly blue and sunny that we decided to breakfast expensively at a small café at the corner of our street. I have never tasted such delicious coffee; never relished the melting of butter into croissant in the same way. And the trees astonished both of us simultaneously. I do not usually observe the changing of nature, except as Hans once teased me, through a microscope. Now it seems to me that Parisian trees are actually a different green from our old familiar Viennese varieties. Even their approaching autumn has only increased their loveliness.

– I always said you should read the poets, he smiled.

– But the books you put in my hands never spoke of trees, I protested: Verlaine, Mallarmé, Apollinaire, René Char. I only remember the names.

– But Char writes of vegetation. He is a lush poet.

– Well, my French is not good enough I suppose, I confessed, without anxiety.

– What hours such a confession would once have taken to force from you, he exclaimed.

I perceived myself on dangerous ground.

– Perhaps.

– Don't answer mechanically like that. It is a way of dismissing what I say.

My heart began to stir and beat heavily, and I bit my lip. When he saw as much, a recognition of what he was risking seemed to touch him also, and he leant forward to recover my hand with one of his.

– Frederick loved poetry, I continued bravely: You taught him to do so.

– Yes, he replied.

But I could see that the thought of Frederick no longer had the same power over him as it had yesterday.

Whereas I was much troubled by a nightmare I recognize now I have had before. Frederick has been caught stealing a musical box. It is one of those so charmingly made in Czechoslovakia or Hungary, where it is possible to watch the moving parts going around. It is familiar in some other way too; inlaid with mahogany or rosewood. I think it is perhaps something from my parents' home.

Why should Frederick steal such an object? For I can see that he is indeed responsible for the theft. There he is, in some American desert town, with the box behind his back, being threatened and still outfacing his questioners. His stance is belligerent and a little sulky. He is being threatened by unknown adults; police, not relations. Adults who keep asking my own question:

– Why? again and again.

He never admits the crime, and, at last, a man brings out a leather thonged whip with which he proposes to punish him.

63

My cry of horror wakes me, as I think it may have done before. As I try to explain the horror of the dream, and at the same time make sense of it (for after all it was to escape whipping, or worse, that we sent him far from the barbarities of Europe) I am not at first soothed as I expected. Instead, Hans reminds me of how often he had called my attention to the boy's dishonesty. Appalled at his insensitivity, I realize I am still inside the dream, that I have *not* woken up! Or *cannot* wake up. And when at last I do, I am bathed in a villainous sweat as though in the grip of a fever. Hans is still deep in his own sleep; and I snuggle gratefully against him, waiting for the full morning light to come round to our window, and wondering what my mind intends me to understand by such a vision.

8 October

This morning I woke feverish. Sweat pours down every limb, gathers in the hollow between my breasts and runs down my face. My breathing also is alarmingly shallow and fast; Hans says I must have an infection, but the sweating may have more to do with a lack of oxygen in my blood. In times of tension, my mother often presented the same symptoms. Hans teased me. He hoped I was not going to become like my mother, for whom he had no great liking.

For the first time it comes through to me clearly that I may easily die without ever seeing Frederick again. The thought is so overwhelmingly painful, that, even though I know it is the very worst thing for my condition, I abandon myself to great sobs of grief.

Self-pity. Self-indulgence. I know. And yet it is as if my body will not obey my will. Tears choke me. And my mind presents febrile visions of my son in different guises. He is nine. One foot up on a footstool, playing a lute and singing. Mischievous eyes denying the angelic perfection of his voice. Then he is running home through the snow, a bundle no larger than a small piece of hand luggage, muffled to his eyes. I watch him fall down in front of me, unable to catch him. I look into his clear eyes. He refuses to cry. His courage hurts me.

– What will become of Frederick if I die, I call out to Hans.

Hans says: Don't be silly. Lie calmly. I will call a doctor.

He is frowning. But I cannot tell why he is worried for me. I know my face is red and puffy with grief. But, usually, he takes my toughness for granted. Finds my hypochondria faintly irritating. Today, he seems to be taking my illness very seriously, and another little clutch of fear touches my heart.

I'm finished. I'm finished. I have been destroyed by everything that has happened.

As the terror rises, I can hardly breathe. My chest hurts too much even to speak. Only hot tears continue to trickle down my cheeks.

I shall never see Frederick again.

I know it.

About half an hour later, Hans returned with a doctor from the flat below, who is also a refugee from Vienna. He will take no money; and insists on giving me sulphonamides nevertheless, which must be very expensive. Then he sent Hans away so he could talk to me.

I burst into tears as I tried to tell him my fears.

He listened seriously. Then he began to talk about his own son. He and his wife know very little about what happened to him, since he was first dragged out of his class at the University of Heidelberg two years earlier.

They try to hope he may only be suffering privations in prison; and that his health is not altogether ruined. His eyes tell the true terror. He no longer believes his own son is alive.

Hans brought me up hot milk with some tang of alcohol in it. He is protective. Calming. He reassures me: the decision to send Frederick away was the only sensible choice we could have made. I let him say 'we', because it reduces my own sense of lonely guilt, even though we both remember well how the decision had been taken after many battles.

– My brave Inge, he says: you will recover. You must recover. I need you. Don't you know how much I need you?

The warmth of his words, the milk, and the pleasantly aniseed-flavoured liquor send me into a luxuriant, pleasant doze such as I cannot remember enjoying for months. Perhaps years. Whenever I wake, with a start, Hans is still there at my side. He has a small bedside lamp on, and he is reading.

Sleepily, I ask him: what is the book?

– A typescript. Of Walter Benjamin's.

So we pass the night.

By the morning, I was in normal health; though still bothered with phlegm in my lungs.

– How strong you are, Hans greets me.

I wanted to get out of bed, and help him make our rudimentary breakfast. But he would not hear of it. He is as tender to me as if I were a child myself. I wonder if he, too, is thinking of Frederick. When he brings me my pills and another hot drink, I study myself carefully in the glass. Lying against the pillows, and still a little weak, my face has lost some of its tension, and I can just catch the old fleeting resemblance. The same ambiguously flecked eyes, roughly curling hair. I once became used to the ease with which other parents recognized me as his mother. And though I had never particularly rejoiced in my face, the strength in my features was excellent in a boy. Without vanity I could see that what might be ponderous in me would be handsome in him.

Hans has gone out this afternoon. The pills have made me dozy, and I slept without anxiety. Before he had returned home, I was out of bed (for all his protests). My throat was free, my cough gone.

– You are trying to impress me, he accused, but I could tell he was only teasing.

We are happy, I discover, wonderingly.

9 October

As for my brief joy! This evening we went to an early party in the sunlight of Erlichman's patio. Iced champagne. Hans looks so young, so triumphant. Leaving, I say as much proudly; and he smiles, with just a touch of complacence 'So. Would you let me have an adventurous life?' Drily I reply: 'I wouldn't have any choice.'

He finds that a grudging response, and our mood of friendliness vanishes as if it had never been.

Tonight Hans dreamed that a man had damaged his penis, and he was afraid that it would not heal.

10 October

There is only one thing for it. We must meet. All of us. I cannot go on with this unexplained threat hanging over us. I asked Hans if the girl would come round to supper.

– I have a right to meet her.

– I cannot see what good can come of that, he replied.

– I want to understand her, I said.

And my real motives? I think I wanted to put Hans in a position where he could not say one set of things to me and another to her.

– You are precipitating a crisis, he groaned, as if guessing as much.

– No.

– How can it go well?

– She is the girl who found us this room, I know that much. And I think I met her once at Mass before we left Vienna: Won't you arrange it?

Reluctantly, he agreed.

12 October

I felt very confident I could handle the girl, and whatever threat she presented. It was only a matter of facing her with our true situation surely? All day Hans tried to dissuade me.

– I'm not sure this is a good idea. I don't *feel* it's going to go well.

– Why not?

There was a long pause.

– Are you afraid I'll get hysterical? I won't. I promise to be perfectly calm.

– Not exactly hysterical.

– What then?

– I don't fancy it. I think we should call it off.

I don't know why, but his reluctance made me all the more determined. I should be on my home territory. I could handle everything, I thought.

– What time is she coming?

– Please, he said: I want you to think about this. I can't see what good it can do.

A little bead of sweat began to form on my upper lip, and I wiped it away. I longed for a strong drink, to steady my hands. There are important things I don't know, I thought. Hans is saying as much.

– Don't say anything about me, will you? he asked: That will make her see me as feeble. Or finished.

– Of course not.

He too was pale and wet-skinned.

– You look very nervous, I said brightly.

– Well, darling, you must realize. At the beginning of a relationship. You say things. You don't always know where it is going. You won't talk *coarsely* about her? I should have to defend her then, wouldn't I?

14 October

She sat in my room, radiant with confidence.

– We have to rid ourselves of all these bourgeois ideas of property, she said: No one belongs to anyone, as if he were a thing.

Her face was broad, and flat-nosed; not exactly pretty, perhaps, but healthy-looking, and young.

– Here you are foreigners, refugees. Can you not smell the stink of defeat in France? It will need a Revolution to save her. A war might help. Might at least temper her energies. She might emerge from any nightmare strengthened.

– War means dying. Many people die. A whole generation, sometimes. How can you want war? Still less Civil War? Are you a Communist? I asked stupidly.

– I am proud to be so. That is how I know, the terrible, possessive love you feel for Hans will only stifle him. You must let him go free. Let him do what he likes. Relinquish your hold over him. His soul is dying in your hands.

– What about *my* soul? I demanded energetically: Why do I have to connive at anything that breaks *my* human spirit?

– If you loved him, you would want him to have anything that makes him happy.

– You are suggesting I accept you as a kind of official mistress? But isn't that exactly the self-indulgence the old France you mention stinks of?

– There *is* an altogether more important struggle, said Hans.

– We are only a part of it, the girl insisted. Of course, I don't know if I can make Hans any happier than he has been with you.

– Have you known one another long enough, even to wonder *that*? I asked crisply.

– A year.

– You were away, surely. Much of that year.

– There was hardly a day when we didn't speak. On the phone, at least.

My heart cringed with the pain.

– I see.

– Darling, you aren't saying enough? Hilde turned to Hans.

And Hans was smiling all the time, always that familiar sweet smile I loved so much, but given to her, the stranger: You see, there is more pain here than you imagine, Hilde. You must be gentle.

And even then, I did not really doubt his love, until I heard the soft voice he used to say goodbye to her. It was a family voice. They were close. I could no longer pretend.

15 October

Hans has begun work on a new play. He says it concerns the historical dimensions of Nature. I do not understand a word of it. He is taking it round to his typist tonight with a great deal of excitement.

– What excites you?

– The whole phantasmagoria of the nineteenth century.

Yes, I thought, the ghosts and the voices, those I can hear. The myths and the lies: I can put my roots down into that holy mud any time I want. Those who are dead and those who will die and those who will smell long after the New Europe is built over them.

– How can I look to you for strength? he muttered before leaving.

Strange how he loves the modern; as if this whole century has not delighted in exhuming prehistory. It is almost a deliberate regression, isn't it. To childhood.

20 October

A letter today from Frederick. It is cheerful, and I should have been made happier by it. But I could hear the distance

in his voice. He is forgetting us, I thought. He is making his
own life, and adjusting; soon he will not only behave like a
little American boy he will feel like one, and even if we meet
again soon he will look strangely at me, as if I were a
peculiar foreigner.

The thought made me fall to the floor and weep. Hans
found me there, but I didn't care. I didn't care about anything else but the distance between myself and my only son.

He watched me with surprise as well as horror.

– Inge. What is it?

– It is Frederick. I have made a mistake. I have made a
mistake. I did not know it would break my heart, I wept.

– You? You are like steel, was all he said, turning on his
heel.

From this, I gather something new has happened, but
cannot guess what.

21 October

Hans has been telling me the news from Germany. He is
nearly distraught. Why? The news is bad (looting and bait-
ing, and extraordinary sadism) but his misery looks as if
something closer to home is disturbing him. All Jews of
Polish extraction have been deported over the Eastern border; and, as the Poles refuse them, they have to inhabit a
no-man's land in sickening conditions. Perhaps this hurts
him.

And yet. It is a terrible thing to say, but I have only ever
seen him look so wild-eyed about disasters which involve
himself. His stammer, which we had almost forgotten,
returns as I try to question him.

29 October

Hans has just told me that Hilde has been asked to return to
Moscow. She is uneasy about it, as well she might be. Both
Hans and I know of loyal Communists who returned in
1937 and then disappeared without trace. Hans is afraid to
suggest she stays on in Paris, however, since the arm of the
NKVD is long enough to reach her, even there; and her
disobedience would certainly provoke some disciplinary
action.

My one fear is that Hans might decide to go with her. I
suspect she has been pressing him to join her.

Much may be forgiven to those who bring converts.

5 November

7.00 a.m. Hilde has left for Moscow. Hans accompanied her
as far as Le Havre, where she is taking the boat across the
Baltic. Every minute today I have been afraid I should hear
he has decided to leave with her. He has taken all our
money. What will I do if he decides to throw his lot in with
her completely?

1.00 a.m. Not so. Praise God. Hans has returned to Paris.
But he looks at me with pink eyes filled with hatred, as if
their separation in some measure is my fault.

I have a sense that I will be punished for being a factor in
his decision to stay.

7 November

Something terrifying has happened. A seventeen-year-old
boy, Herschel Grynszpan, who is at present living in Paris,
has been driven out of his mind by the fate of his parents
herded into a camp near Zbonszyn. He has shot and fatally
wounded one of the Secretaries of the German Embassy,
Ernst von Rath. The indignation in Paris has swelled to the
most terrifying proportions. And it isn't only the French that

are behaving disgracefully. The leaders of the Jewish Community here are themselves among the first to insist on his foreign origin.

10 November

The news has begun to come through of reprisals taken against Jews still living in Germany. I can hardly believe what is happening. It is like an apocalypse. Synagogues razed to the ground. Shops burnt. Thousands arrested. Hundreds killed.

We listen to the news together, alongside the sycophantic mouthings of our Western leaders.

– You see? I should have gone with her, says Hans.

I renew my attempts to contact my old friend Brandt to beg his help for a visa to the United States. But the pressure on that haven is by now so strong that they have put up barriers against us. It is very difficult to imagine them listening, even to Brandt, when one imagines how many important men in their midst have the direct ear of the President. And even people with the strongest protectors in the States are failing to get visas.

– I was a coward. I should have gone with her, said Hans before we went to sleep.

England should be easier, I think. But the walls are there too.

11 November

Hans said this evening: I had a drink at a café with that Walter Benjamin again. He spoke of Palestine. He has never done so before, with Hilde present. Zionism! It's pretty alien to me. And the Arabs are probably as dangerous as Europeans.

– Whatever makes you consider it? I asked the man.

– I can hardly stay alive on what I earn here, he said.

He is in such dire financial straits that I lent him a little of our money. In return, he offered me one of his death capsules, from which I turned in horror.

I listened to all this with attention. Perhaps Palestine is not such a bad idea? In Hans' dream there is no threat to France. Not even to Czechoslovakia. I remember the plebiscite we were promised in Austria that was called off at the last moment.

There are worse things than dying; we knew that too. And if, in Paris, you cannot hear the shouts of *Juda Verreck*; thousands of voices are waiting, as in Germany. The whole of Europe is contaminated with the same hatred.

Yesterday we had another letter from our son. It is difficult, but not yet impossible for us to join him. I long to do so. If I were close to him, I could even bear the terrible gap that is growing between Hans and myself.

22 November

Hans no longer believes Hilde is alive. Many loyal Communists who returned with her have been shot. I laughed at him.

– Who would go back to be shot? Clearly, she did not believe anything like that herself, or she would scarcely have returned.

– Those who don't obey orders can be shot here, he repeated quietly.

I was still incredulous.

– Is this what you had been protecting me from?

– In a way. She has been working with several intelligence services.

25 November

He has received his first letter from Moscow. His joy is open and unashamed.

Nothing has separated us more.

Part Four

HILDE DORF'S LETTERS TO HANS WENDLER

'The face of the "angel of history" is turned
towards the past . . . but a storm is blowing from
paradise . . . the pile of débris before him grows
skywards'
  Walter Benjamin

MOSCOW: 1939

12 January

My love, I want you to know how well I am here. And *happy*. (Or would be if I did not long for you every moment of the day!) This city, with its frozen mountains of snow everywhere and the dull grey ice of its river, and the gutters – well, it *all* suits me! As if I were the Brunnhilde you liked to call me, and not just your poor little Hilde who misses you so much.

Don't worry for me. Above all, *don't* believe all the lies in the Western press. We have fresh garlic here. And lemons. And I never felt more healthy in my life. I have a good job. They found it for me right away. I work in the German section of one of the big State Publishing Houses here. Not translating yet; though I am working hard at my Russian. But even if I am only typing, it is amazing how interesting and different everything seems here. I had no idea Germany was producing such a fertile stream of healthy work.

Of course, I can't live near my work. Only very important party officials, or famous musicians, or writers, live there in special flats. I live right outside Moscow – almost in the forests – in a wooden house. It's like a fairy tale. And you need not worry I am cold. In the office, the radiators pour out heat.

I am even beginning to save money. It is easy here. Rents are so low, and heating so cheap. If you could *only* summon the courage to join me, I could even buy you a ticket.

You must know I never forget you, and never shall. Be *very* careful, my darling, you are watched, as you know. And not among friends.

All my love,
Hilde

77

February, 1939

My love. No word from you. Is it possible the French are so *mean* they stop all post to the Soviet Union? The stupid French pigs, as if I didn't know what you would be saying without paper and ink! All the same I look in my box every day hopefully. Do write!

My situation has changed a little. But for the *better*. One of the other girls who work in the Publishing House has a boy friend who is a member of the Writer's Union; and they have moved into a flat quite close to the Tretyakov Gallery. There is a room they don't need! So imagine my good fortune. She has asked me to move in with them.

So now I live in Moscow itself, and can walk along the river banks, and go to the Museums, and see the walls of the Kremlin for myself. There is nothing in the world to be afraid of here; if only I could persuade you to join me, I should be happier than at any other time in my life. You cannot think how people value writers here. If you came, you would be a *celebrity*! The other day I saw Pasternak walking along in his huge belted coat, and everyone nudged and pointed him out to me. Can you imagine that happening in the West? I know the rumours, but they are not true; I saw him myself walking along the riverside.

Won't you believe me and join your still lonely and always loving,

Hilde

April, 1939

Still no word from you, my love, and I am beginning to worry about you in that horrible capitalist prison. You cannot know how many Poles are flooding into Moscow at the moment. Many of them are Jews, and such things can be said freely here, did you know that, Hans? There is a whole section of this very Publishing House devoted to the translation of Soviet writers whose first language is Yiddish. I am told there is a great tradition in it; and that the Soviet Union is proud of them. What more different from the world I have left! Oh, have *done* with it, Hans, and join me here!

I *do* worry for you. Are you writing? I fear your silence may mean you are not. You *must* write poems Hans, it is your work. Every one has to work. And yours is to write plays and to make poems. Another trouble: your voice. Has that silly voice impediment returned now that you no longer have your Hilde to tease you and soothe you? Reassure me.

I know you love me; but this silence is terrible between us. Write many, many cards and letters just so that I know you are well. Or at least alive. And have not forgotten me altogether.

Hilde

30 April 1939

My love,
Sometimes strange things happen, don't they, unbelievably strange like the happenings in a dream, that mean something to one person and nothing at all to another. Perhaps one day we can meet and talk about what is happening.

But I have a horrible premonition that we shall not meet again. That something has already happened to you. Or *has* happened. Or will happen to me. Nonsense, I know. I try to shrug it off, but without a word from you, it is very hard. My friend has quarrelled with her boyfriend. And he has disappeared. She doesn't know what to make of it.

For God's sake write. You can't *know* what it is like to feel that Spring is coming and there are still so many miles between us.

A lot of things can happen. Please.

Don't forget me altogether.

Hilde

Moscow
2 May

Dearest, I have been alone all week in this huge flat. Perhaps it will seem absurd, but I regret so much moving into town from my fairy-tale hut in the forest. I try so hard to remember your face, and your smile. If only I can think of you clearly enough and hard enough and truly enough I am sure I shall be safe. I wish you were here to hold me!

One surprise. I met Kurt here in the street yesterday. Do you remember Kurt? I don't think you liked him very much. Perhaps you thought he might once have been my lover. As if any such thing in the past could matter once we were together. He has changed. Looks thin, and his jacket quite threadbare.

He has nowhere to live, and has been spending the last fortnight with a cousin who is unfriendly and suspicious. She hardly knows him, so I suppose it is understandable.

For old times' sake, I said he could move into the room that is now unoccupied; though I joked: It has an unlucky history.

He sees your photograph on my wall, but so far hasn't made any comment upon it, which I find tactful of him, don't you? In the circumstances.

But he is away a great deal, and the silence here still presses in on me.

Still no word from you, Hans.

Hilde

Part Five
SYDNEY
20 September 1983

'Death is not punishment but atonement'
  Walter Benjamin

– So what happened? asked Inge's grandson.

– To Hilde? She was arrested some time in early May on charges of spying for France. Sentenced to fifteen years' hard labour. Which she served in full. And survived, said Inge Wendler.

– But Hans? I have translated the poems, by the way. You should look and see if you approve.

– How can I know?

– Tell me what happened to Hans?

Inge sighed.

– That is a long story. And like all stories can be told many different ways. Sometimes I see it one way, sometimes another. Today I see it sadly. As if we came up together to a point in time where all our past miseries could have been eliminated and with a little more trust we *might*, just might, have avoided all the pain. Today it seems unnecessary, what happened. But sometimes it seems to follow with a kind of crooked logic. Inexorable.

– But the facts, the boy demanded impatiently.

– Facts. And you call yourself a historian? Very well. I will tell you how I see the story today.

When the letters stopped arriving from Hilde, I experienced an enormous relief. Even the outbreak of war could not prevent my optimism returning. I had no problems with the Nazi–Soviet pact. It was no more appalling to me than the English and French betrayal at Munich.

But I worried obsessively about Hans. It takes time for trust to return, and I never learnt to renew mine.

He was writing constantly. Secretly. I no longer knew where he went at night; if he returned late, I did not dare question where he had been. And, since, for all his efforts, he saw none of the work of this period published, he always returned painfully unhappy. There was no consolation I could offer, and my attempts at comfort often brought back an ugly stammering stream of abuse. Some days he hated me; perhaps because he imagined my heart was now at ease; while he continued to suffer.

My heart was not at ease. How could it be? It has never been at ease since. I could not understand his anger. And he never expressed guilt towards me.

In my mind, his sudden rages sprang from a resentment at his choice of me rather than Hilde. I hardly dared inquire into that. I know now it was altogether more complex; then I thought it was my apparent facility in returning to work which made him hate me. Yet how else should we have had the money to eat?

In that year that built up to the war we were already thought of as enemy aliens. Worse, as émigrés, probably hoping to push France into a war nobody else wanted. Why should France fight for the Jews? as many thought. Hans read Céline with his own flesh shrinking in horror; and once showed me a passage from L'Ecole des Cadavres, where Céline speaks of the French disappearing body and soul from the place like Gauls, if there was to be a new war.

When war came, naturally, the French police arrived the next morning at our room, and Hans was taken away to be interned.

I was left at liberty, one of the very few times I have found being a woman fortunate. It gave me a little time. In Hans' face I read his hopelessness. He was already resigned to death. He had not yet shaved; and when I pointed this out, they courteously enough refused him the chance to do so. To this day, I can see the white fuzz of hair coming up through his skin.

We kissed then as if we were saying goodbye; and my heart lurched with the love I felt for him. Desperately, I rushed about inquiring where he had been taken; upon what charge; and what French friends we had who could help establish that Hans was no Nazi.

When he was released, towards the end of October, I was afraid at the change in him! His arms made no response to my embrace; and there was no solidity to his lips under my kiss.

I had lost my own job in the interim, but it no longer seemed important. I knew in my bones that it was essential to leave Paris; Hans resisted me. He resisted passively. But his passivity won. Because if he would not come, there seemed no sense in leaving.

We were deeply in debt by the time the Germans crossed the Maginot line in June. All of us, poor creatures that we were, now owed even the cheapest cut of horse meat to the charity of our neighbours. And when it was clear that the German troops were flooding over the whole of France, we set out South with whatever we could find. Your father had two briefcases; I had some sentimental treasures – your father's letters – my father's watch, and a wedding ring, which I supposed could be used to pawn in an extremity.

We set out on 10 June. And it looked as if all of France were making the same pilgrimage. People moved in every possible conveyance; mostly walking, with pitiful bundles clogging the roads. But there were carts, milk floats, horses, bicycles. And every so often we were shot at by wandering enemy planes.

All trains were impossible. We were at first lucky in sharing a stolen French car; bought with the sale of my father's fob watch, to a rogue dealer, who knew the car could not possibly take us more than a hundred miles.

– Merde, one of our friends exclaimed when the car finally gave out.

Hans, who had said so little for months, got out of the car

85

with the rest of us, and shook his head. It confirmed his worst fears. We were not intended to escape. We did not deserve to.

   — We must find a place to hide, I insisted.

   — You are stupid, he said: Who will hide us?

But we found our own barn, and lay there; in my case more frightened by the noise of dogs than any other sound. I have never trusted animals.

   — You *still* loved him then? interrupted the boy listening to the story, as light faded through the windows.

   Inge stared.

   — Of course. He is the only man I ever loved, she replied: But I understand your question. So many months ago I had been forced to accept what was involved in loving him. It is possible to love passionately and not be blind. He was not so much cowardly as careful in his learning from his experience. His life had been ruined from the moment we left Vienna; the brief success with his play in Paris was a coincidence of that emigration. What future could there be for a German writer in France? And gradually I understood more. In his grief for Hilde, there was always an element of disappointed vanity; but it was a generous grief, also. He was utterly without calculation. Hilde made no offer of fidelity; and he could not have expected it from her. I see you still find the depth of the bond I felt for him puzzling. It is unfashionable, I suppose, in your generation, where people marry more than once, I know. But for me, it was a bond as close as the bonds of blood. Even though sometimes when I woke to share his thoughts, his first articulated sentences in weeks. I remember he said: Even at your best, Inge, yours was not a mind that encouraged intimacy.

   Yes.

*

86

What are the intimacies of betrayal? Dependence? Hatred? Animal terror. And a sexuality that breaks some private taboo. These things exist like a raw pain in the gut. It is not a pain you grow out of. The wound remains unhealed.

– You left me lonely, he sighed: I've been a lonely man.

And I remembered those nights in Vienna and Paris. Alone, alert, and damned into my own insomnia. Waiting for him to return. And closed my eyes. Again. Listening for dogs.

Once again I heard his old offer of compromise: Why not accept a decent arrangement? And my reply?

– I will never condone something which would break my spirit.

But on other days he said: My own love, the whole relationship with that other girl was nothing but a dream; a lovely dream, certainly, but one that vanished under my eye. Or your own clear vision.

I remembered Hilde's own clear eyes.

It was then I realized, for the first time, that whatever poor Hans did, it had to wound someone.

During the night, I began to hear Hans' voice mumbling in my ear again. Some dream has unlocked his tongue, I sensed; but when I woke, finding our arms around one another and his lips against my forehead, I saw he had been lying awake for a long time, and that his eyes were alert.

A stone weight fell from me, as I listened.

– We need somewhere to stay. Food. Friends, and patience, Inge, he said.

And looking into his face he seemed as serene now as he had looked so close to madness in the last months. It made me obedient and attentive. His manhood had been restored him.

If you ask me why, I can only say that it is as if some human beings, who function timidly and awkwardly in the circumstances of ordinary life, work peculiarly well when the whole world is under the same stress. As the whole of

France fell into chaos, so Hans seemed to find again a God-given decisiveness. And is it so astonishing? Who better to have at one's side, when the machines fail, and the ordinary expectations of daily life with them, than someone who has never learnt to manipulate or depend on either? The man in the dream becomes a hero.

So it was. Gratefully, I put my affairs in his hands.

– The Germans may be as far south as the Pyrenees now, he murmured.

Such was indeed the rumour.

– But when there is Armistice who knows? We shall gain nothing by rushing like lemmings into the hands of the first new supporter of Pétain who wishes to claim us as his due.

Pétain had not yet taken office, so I listened without altogether understanding.

– The first thing is to discover where we are. And then, to look for a big town.

– Not a village?

– What should we do in a village? How could we conceal ourselves? What function could we perform that would not make us instantly obvious? Besides, in every country the peasantry are the last bastion of suspicion. And since you have learnt only as much French as you needed to move round a laboratory, lie here, my love, quietly, while I make some local inquiries.

– Who will you look for? I whispered.

– An unpatriotic school master, he smiled.

And so it was we pushed no further towards the Pyrenees in June, and were able when the Armistice terms were decided, to make our way by train through unoccupied France to Marseilles.

But, by 23 August, we had new enemies who knew more than I guessed. The Communists had been taught to collaborate with their former enemies. I was more shocked than Hans, whose instincts were also pacifist.

88

– In the ordinary way, it would be the most sensible tactic, he said, in a measured tone which at the same time declared our terrible separation from those who were around us.

We were separate because we were Jews and because we were foreigners.

– The resistance to the Germans will only come later. When the French discover what it is to be under a German heel.

He decided Marseilles was our best chance. Around the 'Vieux Port', where there were enough whores and criminals to pay for the police not to bother anyone. Hans took my gold ring, and a necklace, which he had brought himself (I had put it aside as a gift that carried too many memories) and he went off to deal with the pawnbroker himself. He brought us back more money than I had hoped.

I can see on your face that you wonder why I talk of days *more* painful than hiding in fear, and on the run. Well, I only tell you my feelings. With Hans at my side I felt as if my centre of balance had been restored to me. Such is the insanity of a love like mine. There were other terrors – yes, *we* knew of them. What were rumours in Marseilles, were realities for us. Leon Blum might expect to settle quietly in the South of France; but we knew what happened to those deported to the East. For the ordinary Frenchman, after the mad rush South was over, it was not at all clear that joining the Free French under de Gaulle was the obvious moral response. Aside from physical danger, emigration meant facing criminal charges, and could easily be seen as a shameful attempt at escape. And, the British made it almost impossible for many to support them, when they bombed the French fleet at Mers-El-Kebir.

All this we easily understood. Who could understand a complexity of loyalties more clearly than we could? Nevertheless, the passivity of the Vichy regime, which Pétain was to claim as a shield to keep France from

89

becoming a ruin like Poland, was already an obvious lie. If, in Marseilles we saw no Germans, there was nevertheless little guile in the French support for Vichy. Not then.

And this, even though the Germans had sealed off the whole of the southern zone, not only physically, but even to the post. And Laval was known to have plans, quite independent of anything the Germans might demand, to clean up, as he liked to put it. We talked of all this every night in the cafés and brothels under the eye of querulous pimps. We had no doubt that ultimately we would have to bolt for it. If Hitler was a friend of Vichy, then we were on enemy territory. As if to prove as much, our landlord suddenly decided to double our rent.

It was September. I was the one he asked; and I replied weakly that I could not give him my answer until my husband returned. Hans said we had no choice. He had been trying, without much success to find a vehicle that would take us as far as the Spanish frontier. But we could not afford to leave at all if our last reserves were drained away. I remember I began to cry: I shall never see my son again. I shall never see Frederick again.

At length he said: We cannot buy a car. We shall have to borrow one or steal one. Trust me.

Just for a moment an old pang of suspicion and pain touched me. It must have touched him as well, for he put a hand to my face, and said: Poor Inge, I have destroyed you. Forgive me. It was never my intention. Believe that.

I believed him altogether.

He fixed it somehow. We never discussed how.

And then it was a question of waiting for the car.

It must be what damnation is like, such waiting. People deal with it in different ways. I sleep. I have an insatiable hunger, it seems, to hide in blackness. The pain comes, though, with the first moment of waking. Into knowledge. No, you experience the pain *first*. Then the knowledge crystallizes around the pain and deepens it.

And fear? It dries your mouth. Have you felt that kind of fear? That destroys saliva, freezes the blood in your wrists, and squeezes the muscle of the blood's entry to the heart.

Hans lay awake instead, and let his thoughts ramble round and about irrelevant pieces of the past. He kept the light on, with an open book in his hand. A poor light, naturally; so the print could hardly be made out. And he muttered at me old thoughts squashed together into each night, and become a single, interminable stream.

You ask what kind of thoughts? So many. So muddled. So different. A mix of resentment, and self-hatred. He would tell me: You try too hard to be rational. The world we live in does not fit your model.

And I would turn into my sleep conceding wanly, it is possible. Why should I be ashamed of working as a scientist? And then my words would annoy him.

– Possible. Possible. Can't you ever offer some comment? Don't you have any opinion of your own?

And I would plead weariness, endless and hopeless fatigue.

And all the time I tried to close myself away from them, his words still had the power to bite into my brain like acid. Of course I wanted the change in him; the new direction and purpose. As if his strength could cure all the uncertainties inside me that went deeper than our desperate situation. Sometimes I had to defend my whole way of life as something worthwhile to pass on.

– The greatness of the past? he would tease me and provoke me to tears.

– This rubbishy age, I once dared to reply: You realize this age is going to look shit to the people after us? They aren't going to envy us living in this age, I can tell you.

– So when was it good? he could always counter.

– Writers scrabbling after fame. Where are the fine minds of this age? The decent human endeavour? I demanded him

91

to recognize it as science. But I knew he believed none of it. I envied him his new certainty.

Sometimes he seemed to speak out of the Vienna we had left and lost.

– Lonely. I feel lonely. I should have married someone who would share my world. Why weren't *you* lonely, living as we did? You never even *wanted* a life with people and fun. *Did* you? You wouldn't even feel deprived in prison. Isn't it peace you wanted? To get on with whatever you do? Isn't *that* your real life? What *is* real, I might have said. But you see, I didn't want to argue. I was afraid to break the tenuous link between us.

– *Praise*, that's what you live on, I once risked saying.

And he laughed, as he admitted some truth in it. And what did I need? Friendship, I thought. And love. *Your* love.

– And where do my *needs* come in? he wondered.

What horror, I thought. To be sipped at. Like a child suckling a mother. No. More like a vampire. Just to think the word made me feel bloodless, drained, fearful.

And sometimes it was inexplicably different. I would wake up happily, listening to a voice that was sweet and loving.

– My lovely. You rescued me, I see it all now. How kind you always were. I see the whole past differently.

Until I thought: I'm dreaming this.

– Thank you, I whispered all the same.

– Sleep, my lovely, he crooned.

The words went on spilling out. Good words. I didn't sleep, but lay there drawing them in like balm. And when at last I admitted so much to myself I let myself turn towards him.

When his voice whispered in my ears without bitterness, I remembered how he had once been a joyful spirit, wanting to share everything he took pleasure in; and how he's always liked so many things. The sea. Wild animals. The countryside. Everything he did with the same energy. Shopping. Frying sprats, outside a tent. Cooking chestnuts in the ashes of a country fire. Pulling the burning skins off with his strong hands.

Yes, he'd been tender once, I loved him for that. If he wasn't always tender now; if I remembered so much bitterness that had grown between us, that was something we had to share the guilt for. We were like a machine that had worked badly; faults didn't come into it, I thought. The question was only whether it had all been inevitable. Whether the change had been avoidable by either of us.

We set out from Marseilles by car, on 25 September, and passed through villages built of pale stone, rising from valleys rich with olive trees. Travelling by night at first. We were in a landscape charred by fires; and under the moonlight, the earth looked white and thirsty. We could already see what Hans called the sacred mountain of Canigou, a pyramid rising above the other mountains. It looked like stone. At one place, where we stopped for Hans to piss, it was a desert of pale grey stone everywhere, as if some volcanic eruption had shaped the place. When Hans came back to the car he showed me a piece of agate embedded in basalt. And he gave it to me. I still have it. I don't know if it is exactly out of superstition.

I confess I was hopeful. Spain was still neutral. There were many rumours. Franco, for all he had taken Hitler's support, had left his frontier open to France. I remember being told before we left Paris in a hushed whisper that Franco himself had a Jewish grandparent. But my fatigue was too grave to speak of anything. Hans, in contrast, was insomniac, and spent the night chattering away to the driver.

I remember Hans asked me: Do you believe in miracles now?

– I'll tell you what, I said; I think there can't have been

enough magic to go round, like everything else. And it has been used up. Now all the wise men find their little spells won't work anymore. They have to use bigger and bigger magic even to get rid of a wart, let alone anything major. So now we're all on our own.

– Physicist, he teased me gently.

The road through the Pyrenees was not only unfamiliar, it was much more circuitous than we had expected. Our car was not up to it. We had to travel the last miles on foot; and in my case, since I suffered from vertigo, on my hands and knees.

Hans was in much better shape than I was physically. He carried all our effects slung about his chest with a rope, and was still able to hold out a hand, when I needed to drag myself upwards.

The last few miles took twelve hours. I cannot remember a single word we exchanged. Now that we were on the move, Hans appeared to have lost all fear; but I was shaking with my own cowardice; I drew strength only from him. At one point, what looked like a short cut brought us up to a face of rock which seemed insurmountable. I was ready to give in, with exhaustion, and sat down in the path. But Hans had been an Alpine walker and climber in the old days; and the sheer face of the crag did not put him off. Unloading his bag, he made his own way up by handholds I could scarcely make out with my myopic vision. I was afraid for him, but as he reached the top, he waved back to cheer me.

Then he asked me to throw up the bags. I had to throw them twice before they went high enough. Then, patiently, he undid the straps, and the rope; and made them into something which I could hold on to as I made myself follow his directions blindly.

– There, he called: Over a bit! There!

I obeyed him with my eyes shut, sick to my stomach. But when I reached the top of that crag, I saw the path leading down to Port Bou.

Our papers were by no means in perfect order; we were officially without nationality. But most of those who set out for the border in a similar condition had been allowed to pass across it. It was said to be a decision left to individual frontier guards.

We arrived in Port Bou by the evening, to be told that the border had been closed the day before. Our particular frontier guard had no love for Jews, and enjoyed applying his duty strictly. Every passport was looked at carefully at the police station under his command. It was up to him to grant entry stamps.

Ahead of us were four women, begging and pleading without success. The man looked self-important, and impatient; not very likely to accept a bribe, even if we had enough money left to do so effectively. All of us were escorted to the local hotel. That was where we first heard that Walter Benjamin occupied a room in more or less the same conditions.

Hans was all for going up there and then to greet him. He had not seen him since his Paris days. Some premonitory dread, rather than any word of mine, kept him lingering in our own room, however. I thought I had seen him downstairs a little earlier; and perhaps I had.

We were all supposed to be under guard; but I do not think it was fear for himself that prevented Hans from going boldly to knock on Walter's door. It was more a kind of moral delicacy.

The next morning at seven the news of Benjamin's death filled the hotel. It was premature; though certainly Benjamin *was* dying. The rumours multiplied. It was apoplexy. It was this or that. It was any kind of thing that the tongue could give word to. But Hans and I knew at once he had *chosen* to die. He had always been prepared to do so. It was certain that he had no thought of involving anyone else; but, in fact, his action produced a shiver of horror in the whole village, and there was no question of any inquiry being made into our papers for the next twenty-four hours. Indeed, the matter of our entry into Spain had now fallen out of the hands of the border guard into those of the local Mayor, Judge and Priest.

The whisper that Walter Benjamin had taken his own life passed among those of us held in the hotel with consternation. Hans tried to reassure them again and again that Walter had often thought of death; that it was something he had prepared for, that he had struggled too long against poverty and hunger, and could not face the failure of his own energy.

But they could not help reading more into his choice. It spelled out the bleakness of our own chances. The Europe to which we might be forcibly returned rang with the cries of the damned. We began to exchange stories of tormented friends who would gladly have died to be spared the torture cells even now being prepared for us.

For the first time in my life, I reflected how easy it was to die; how much easier, at least, than to suffer great pain. Or worse, forced to watch damage inflicted on the body of someone you loved. I am not a brave woman. As we watched Benjamin's corpse being removed, under blankets, by the police, I was hypnotised by the logic of his decision. Hans, too, seemed to pale at the physical evidence of peace that the silent body offered beneath its covers.

It was in that pause, that Hans, whose resolution had never failed him along the road, began to have doubts about the wisdom not only of entering Spain but also of our further plan to go to Australia.

Of course, if we could have found any means to secure visas to America that *would* have been infinitely more cheering a prospect. Neither of us knew anyone in Australia, and whenever we looked at the continent on a map, it was so far from Europe that it was like taking a long farewell from everyone we loved. It seemed equally far from our son Frederick, who had moved to the East Coast.

– Don't think of it as permanent, I pleaded with him: After the war we can return.

– Who knows if we shall live to see the end?

– We shall not live even to see its first stages, unless we take what chance has given us.

I found my energy restored as his diminished. He had often remarked upon that phenomenon; and thought it denoted something sick in our relationship. As if I preferred him low and weak.

He said as much then, and a few other things there is no need to repeat now. I brushed them aside.

It was true that a few other inmates of the hotel had already decided to be returned to a detention camp at Figueras.

And we had so little money. How could he look at the open door of our prison and even consider returning into it? I reminded him what had happened to one of my uncles who had failed to leave Vienna in time. The Germans had tortured him with cigarette butts; pulled out his finger nails; then threw him outdoors in the snow without clothes so that he froze into the ground and died like a man of snow. Worse deaths had been reported.

– Not in France, he said cunningly.

– Not yet, I argued.

– And who is to say we will even reach Australia? Who is to say that Franco will not make a new arrangement with Hitler? They are allies, after all. France was at least at the beginning of the war *against* Germany. How could I wildly consider committing our lives to a government actually put in power by German armed strength?

– What is really worrying you? I asked.

It was not that his arguments failed to convince me. I was as much affected by Walter Benjamin's death as he had been. But it seemed to me that not to cross was part of the same temptation. I was not altogether free of it myself. I put this to him, and he shrugged.

97

– You saw the hatred in the Customs Official, he said: Suppose that is the true face of Spain?

– We don't know that, I said. The hysteria was mounting in my voice.

– Arendt is still in Marseilles.

It was true.

– I don't hear of her running to Spain.

– All this we knew before we set off, I cried.

– I am not sure we were wise to expose ourself to so much attention, he argued.

There on the frontier, at Port Bou itself, we had one of the longest and least hopeful arguments of our life together.

What was he truly afraid of? Was it the thought of exile? The silence that seemed to emanate from the red desert of a continent where we knew no names? I don't know.

– Go on ahead, he said.

I refused.

– There you are, he said.

– I will not leave you now, I said, my voice rising to a shout: How can you even think I would do so?

Inge paused in her narration. She looked at the face of her grandson, and its questioning.

– And that is not what happened. What happened is more difficult to explain than the simplicities of desertion.

Inge took a full glass of brandy before continuing to tell her story.

You must try and understand. In so many ways our disastrous trek across Europe had cost me more than it had cost Hans. A writer – and perhaps particularly a poet – needs only paper and ink. Some writers can memorize their own works, and hold them in their head, or give them to other friends to carry in their memory. A scientist is another matter altogether. To work on the run, in hiding, out of touch with current thought, and above all without a bench and equipment, in my case expensive equipment, is impossible. I am not a mathematical physicist like so many of my generation. Of course mathematics is a tool; but I needed others too. Expensive tools. These I would find in Australia. I was sure of that.

But Hans was leaving behind, not only the world of his language (there would probably be a few German speakers in any country) but also his whole tradition, the stream in which his thoughts came together. Our interests were not the same. Was that part of his hesitation?

I didn't think so. I remembered his resolution in Marseilles; and his courage in the Pyrenees. Whatever held him back was something that he had not admitted to me.

I was a little light-headed myself, we had hardly eaten anything for the last two days. I felt dizzy and off-balance, as though my legs were almost floating as I walked. Looking at Hans I guessed he must be feeling similarly weak.

– Please. Wait here, I begged, knowing that he was capable of wandering off. Being lost. So that I would be forced to cross alone. My heart banged as I wondered what I *would* do if he disappeared. But I had absolutely no idea how I would find anything to eat. We had little enough money, and the only security I had were our boat tickets to Australia from Lisbon.

I came out into sunlight, which was unexpectedly fierce, so that my dizziness increased to the point where I was on the edge of hallucination. As I stared at faces in the street, they all reminded me of people I knew well, one from Vienna, another from Paris, another from Berlin. And yet, there they were in black peasant dress, and I knew as I came up to each, the resemblance would disappear.

And then I saw the back view of someone I remembered from Vienna as part of our old salon: a back view, not only familiar, but dressed in the shabby clothes appropriate to our situation. An old suit, once well-cut, and now shiny.

– Uncle Fritz! I called out.

And the figure turned, and was not an illusion. He had never been an uncle I had particularly liked; but to find a member of my own family in such a desperate situation put all such memories out of my mind. And I prayed he too would forget his own disapproval of me.

We threw ourselves into one another's arms. And I have to confess that the childhood memories of his snuff and peppermint that still, inexplicably, clung to his coat almost brought tears to my eyes.

– Will you have a coffee with me? he asked simply.

I nodded.

– Do they have a café in this god-forsaken hole?

– Inside. In these parts they get out of the sun. And of course, it is not a café in our sense, poor child. But yes, there is a village bar. Perhaps you would prefer a cognac?

– I have no money, I confessed abruptly. It suddenly occurred to me that his enthusiasm, like mine, might arise from his own need.

– I have a little, he reassured me: Where is your husband?

– In the hotel. He is not well.

He seemed surprised to hear we were together.

– Rumour had it that you went your separate ways long ago. Didn't he follow his mistress to Moscow?

– Do not let's speak of that, I begged him.

Inside the bar, the darkness blinded me for a moment; and then I saw all around us alien, seamed, dark-skinned villagers. Some were drinking at barstools; others taking food at the uncovered tables.

– Are you hungry? my uncle asked, as he followed my gaze.

– Very. But I am worried about Hans.

I bit my lips. What worried me, though I could hardly say as much to a man already reading my face with pity, was that Hans might not after all be still in his room. If I stayed long enough to eat the food that was being offered me, I might miss the chance to keep him with me.

My uncle shook his head, in a commiseration that I felt was insulting.

– Don't be sorry for me, I said hotly: Hans has usually been a good husband. I don't recall your own marriage, but I can hardly believe you have lived blamelessly. For me all that counts is our closeness *now*. And without him, we should never have reached Port Bou.

– Inge. Inge, he sighed: You carried him all your life like a stone.

– That's not true, I said angrily.

– A poet. What kind of work is that?

– Let's not argue, I said, suddenly enfeebled.

And I let him buy me a bowl of soup. But all the time I sat there my legs ached to be moving. To be running back to the hotel. To be checking up on him, I suppose. What other way was there of putting it? My uncle had activated old fears with the true ones. What if? I found my brain thinking. What if this strange hesitation of his *is* in some way connected to his old love? What if some message has been smuggled to him? Out of my sight. I can't be vigilant every moment. Perhaps even now while I try my utmost to help him, he is off to some prearranged meeting place?

– If such a thing had ever happened to me I would never forgive it, said my uncle, spooning food into his own mouth and watching me closely.

I felt my stomach clench, hungry as I was, against the good soup in front of me. All my hunger had gone. It was as much as I could do to pretend to be eating, still less allow the food to enter my mouth. I was faint and sick. It was as if, with his words, an old poison had entered my blood stream.

– I should never trust any such person again, my Uncle concluded.

– Trust? I tried to smile: That's a big word, Uncle. For a few moments out of one another's sight.

101

– Eat your soup, he advised me.

He was like a devil, noticing my weakness. There had always been something sadistic in him, I remembered. A Prussian uncle. What was he doing in Port Bou?

I asked as much.

He gave a melancholy smile.

– Tainted, like the rest of you. As it turned out.

My hands began to tremble, and I could feel moisture in my palms and beginning to form at my hairline.

– You don't look well, he said.

– Listen, I said thickly: What can I take back to the hotel? A few slices of salami perhaps, and a hunk of bread?

– You are agitated, he said.

– Yes. These times agitate us all, I said.

– Your crossing is arranged?

I did not reply to that, and he waved a waiter towards us. He could buy me the salami and bread I had asked for. But all the time he eyed me quizzically, as if he guessed my panic, and its cause, and felt contempt for anyone who could behave so submissively.

– I have never understood why people praise the love between men and women, he remarked as the package was put into my hands.

The strong garlic wafted to my nose, but did not touch me to hunger. On the contrary, it increased my panicky perspiration so that I had to ask my uncle for a handkerchief to dab my face and the palms of my hands.

– You worry too much, he commented.

– The heat, I tried to explain.

But really, I could hardly believe I had not imagined him, this Uncle from my past. In his presence I felt like a child again, suspected of all kinds of heresies because of my interest in science. I had to get out of his presence. I was in an agony to be at Hans' side.

– I have no money for any of this, I therefore explained abruptly.

– My pleasure, he bowed.

When I got back to the hotel I asked three times, in broken French, whether M. Wendler was still in his room. I could get no sense out of the man who had control of the keys. With something like terror, I then observed that the key to our room had gone. What could that mean? Was there a pass key? It will give you some idea of my state of unreasoning terror if I tell you that it was only as I put my hand in my pocket to find a pen that I realized that I had taken the key out with me.

A feeling of intense, if temporary sensation of relief flooded my veins.

Hans was in his room, but I could see at once that my anxiety was not altogether unfounded. Something had happened, something had happened. He too was afraid; and his face was wet with fear. I sat at his bed, and mopped at his forehead with my Uncle's handkerchief which I had carelessly taken from him.

– What is it? Has someone called? Have there been any messages?

He shook his head helplessly, as if he had no reply to any of my questions.

– K–k–k– he began.

And my blood froze.

He had never been affected with so severe a stammer in my presence alone. I could not make out what the word was he was trying to say.

– Can't? Captain? I guessed.

He shook his head again, and motioned for me to find him a pen and paper.

When I did so, he wrote in sprawling letters very clearly.

– KURT.

At first the name meant nothing to me. Then I remembered he had been a young student who had attended Hans' classes in Vienna.

A wave of superstition flooded me, as I suddenly

103

remembered his connection with Hilde.

But surely Kurt was in Moscow, or had been a year ago?

– Do you mean you have *seen* him? I asked.

He nodded.

– It's impossible, what would he be doing in Port Bou?

With horror, I wondered if he had come only to look for Hans.

– This heat, this town, it breeds phantoms of our past, I said.

How could I make him explain? He put the pen and paper aside as if he had no more to say.

Mutely, I offered him the sandwich. He did not seem to be affected with my own anorexic revulsion. On the contrary, he wolfed it down eagerly and gratefully.

Meanwhile, as I wracked my brains for ways, if not to persuade, then to kidnap him into leaving this accursed village I felt his head.

– You are running a temperature I declared. I will bring you some Vichy water and you can take a pill for it. I had in mind to give him two of my sleeping tablets. It occurred to me that with a little ingenuity, I could arrange a wheelchair and take him forcibly across the border as if he were unconscious.

– No, he said.

It was the first clear word he had uttered. Surely he could not imagine I would try to poison him?

I left the room with the door open, and hurried downstairs. I was afraid of the tap water, as all our generation were, no doubt correctly. All the while I waited for him to return I thought to myself: he always distrusted Kurt; Kurt destroyed him; surely he cannot have forgotten how Kurt behaved? And underneath all that was the fear: what if he is an emissary? If he comes from Hilde, how will he not respond as if his sanity has been restored to him, will he not recover from this terrible tranced condition?

What is he planning, what?

When I returned with my fizzy water, and my pills, the room was empty. Empty.

Can you not imagine how I scoured the village. Where could he be, unless some car had been waiting for him, how far could he have gone, and why?

I had one moment's hope when I thought he might have gone to the cemetery, to pay homage to his friend Walter Benjamin in his grave. The cemetery faces a small bay high over the sea. It is laid out in terraces, carved in stone, as if into the mountains themselves. It was as fantastic a place as any of the events and the people who had pursued us to its reaches. But there was no sign of Hans there. No message for me at the police station. No memory in anyone's mind of him leaving his room. Or of walking along a street. Or of getting into the car.

What to do?

You see, I could not leave without him. It was a terrible trap. That was something I could hardly forgive him for, that he knew I would be locked in the trap of that loyalty, that it might cost me my life, and yet he had left without a word.

You might say it was unlike him. Because in his own way he was a good and loyal man. And, thinking that, I stayed on, waiting and longing without hope. When I forced myself out, into the streets, I must have seen the half-remembered figure of Kurt many times; imagined him under a hundred disguises. Each one I approached, with tentative recognition, returned my desperate, searching gaze with a smile that showed the bad teeth of the very poor. Nowhere did I see anyone who looked like Hans.

Most of the time I sat in my hotel room, weeping. Sometimes it is impossible not to weep. The dignity we try to preserve is of little moment beside the greater blows of life. I have never met anyone who has been sustained by it; even in the camps, those who had most self-respect were often the first to collapse. I had collapsed easily before; but this was

105

worse than any pain I had known before. A nameless, plum-shaped pain that stuck in my throat.

Not the worst pain, though. You weep first, without understanding; and sometimes it is premonitory of worse than you expect.

The police brought a body to my room. They said it was Hans.

The clothes were his, certainly. But the face was shattered. Only his hands were unmistakable. His warm, soft hands. Loving hands. To my knowledge Hans had no gun. I understood nothing. And the police had no further information. He had been found in the main street; the very street I had run up and down in my agony of wondering what had become of him. No one had heard a shot or seen the accident.

If it was Kurt who had been deputed by some unimaginable agency to have him killed, then why? I felt only the pain. It is not a pain from which I have ever recovered. Though, as you see, I continue to live.

Sometimes I wake in the night, wondering was it really Hans' body I was shown? Could he be still alive in Europe? Wandering. Lost. And thinking I had abandoned him? It is all nonsense, of course. And yet, men like him managed, somehow, to survive German occupation.

Kurt was picked up a few days after Hans was buried. And then he was interned as a foreigner. Nothing worse, since at the time Russians, as allies of the Germans, were not harassed severely. Communism was another matter. But in those days many people escaped from French camps. Englishmen returned home with their wives, I understand. German nationals, who had acquired other passports by marriage, found it equally easy. I remember in Lisbon everyone who came through for several days was, by repute, Egyptian.

Kurt made no attempt to escape. He simply sat around and scribbled all day long. Mostly letters, I understand. He must have become altogether mad. He wrote many letters to his mother in Vienna; and she was already dead, poor soul. Dead, and known to her son to be so. They might have offered some clue. About *why*.

Or even if? Perhaps I had invented a link between Kurt's presence and Hans' death. Even now I am bewildered what to think.

Perhaps I was most bewildered because I learnt to see Hans as he saw himself. The sickness of his own self-hatred infected me. That hidden sickness was less easy to recognize than a mysterious stammer that came and went.

My blindness was something to do with the weight I gave our two disciplines. As I saw it, there was something altogether nobler in the activity of science. And so I suppose I felt entitled to a measure of approval, which I failed to accord him. I was not so far away from my uncle as I should like to have been. I thought of myself as a good scientist; regarded with more interest than I deserved, perhaps, because I was a woman in a field where men were accustomed to strive alone.

What friend was it suggested that *envy* lay behind Kurt's actions? Sexual jealousy I might have considered myself. Perhaps that was what Hans had in mind when he first discovered himself alone with his killer. But Kurt was not more than casually interested in Hilde. He enjoyed an easy success with women.

But what could Kurt envy in Hans? What else, but his gift. For language, the written language, and the poetry of his youth.

I don't understand even now. I feel as if all my life I have been part of an unequal duel, one in which I cried out in terror long before being beaten. I have always been defeated, not in one duel but in many.

In the massacres around us, one man's death counts little with God. What is important must be living out your own

107

life, not someone else's. My own failure weighs all the more heavily upon me.

For this failure to understand I am in need, for ever, of Hans' pardon, and can never win it now he is dead.

– And so, my beautiful grandson, we should drink a toast to Hans' spirit. Did you know, this evening ends the Jewish Day of Atonement? Let us drink. To the forgiveness of all our infidelities!

Part Six

HANS WENDLER'S
POEMS IN EXILE

1

After Europe, Dido, all winter
the days rushed through me
as if I were dead, the
brown sea pouring into the cities
at night, the rain-smell of fish,

and when you ask for my story, how
we came to be blown along your
dock-streets, pocked and scuffed,
I see only my mother laced in silk,
myopic, her small feet picking over rubble.

How to make you imagine
our squares and streets, the glass
like falls of water, the gold-leaf
in the opera houses. There were
summer birds golden as weeds,

the scent of coffee and halva
rising from marble tables,
and on dark afternoons
the trams grinding on wet rails
round the corners of plaster palaces

such a babble of Empire
now extinguished, we can
never go home, Dido,
only ghosts remain
to know that we exist.

2

Unrepentant, treacherous, lecherous
　　we loved beauty, in the tenderness
of violins, or the gentle voice of a girl,
　　but we built over the stink of our dead,
our rivers ran yellow with the forgotten,
　　Dido: the cruel cannot be blessed.

The endless sunshine, frangipani, gulls calling:
　　How can you ease my pain or give me rest?
I had so little strength, had to believe
　　my own voice would return
and win me power,
　　no village kingdom satisfies that hunger.
In any case, the cruel cannot be blessed.

Things come too late to save.
　　On the last boat, we'll sing
old prayers, and some will dream of quiet,
　　but the sea will have most of us.
I am not prepared for white soot, cold ash,
　　or the red sands of Australia. Forget me,
Dido: The cruel cannot be blessed.

3

Last night, my sad Creusa, quietly
　　crept into my dream. As if
dry leaves could speak, she whispered,
　　but I could not catch her words,
Dido, and I was afraid

of what had wakened her.
　　She was a loyal wife, in times
when nothing was forbidden
　　no pleasure thought too gross:
and contrition as poor-spirited as cowardice.

Shall I spread that disease
   over the known world in a single colour?
Dido, I swear it was Venus' weather in the cave
   the day our mouths first opened to each other,
sweetness in our veins, was innocent.

Monsters and blood I dream of now,
   and a long voyage, lost,
although the wind has filled our sails.
   I must not falter in my mission,
Dido, at whatever cost.

BALTHAZAR

by the same author

★

JUSTINE (*a novel*)
MOUNTOLIVE
CLEA
THE BLACK BOOK
CEFALU (Editions Poetry London)

★

BITTER LEMONS
REFLECTIONS ON A MARINE VENUS
PROSPERO'S CELL
ESPRIT DE CORPS
STIFF UPPER LIP

★

(*poetry*)
SELECTED POEMS
THE TREE OF IDLENESS
ON SEEMING TO PRESUME
A PRIVATE COUNTRY
SAPPHO: A PLAY IN VERSE

★

(*essays*)
KEY TO MODERN POETRY (Peter Nevill)

★

(*for the young*)
WHITE EAGLES OVER SERBIA

BALTHAZAR

a novel

by

LAWRENCE
DURRELL

FABER AND FABER
24 Russell Square
London

First published in April mcmlviii
by Faber and Faber Limited
24 Russell Square London W.C.1
Second impression April mcmlviii
Printed in Great Britain by
Latimer Trend & Co Ltd Plymouth

NOTE

The characters and situations in this novel, the second of a group—a sibling, not a sequel to JUSTINE—*are entirely imaginary, as is the personality of the narrator. Nor could the city be less unreal.*

Modern literature offers us no Unities, so I have turned to science and am trying to complete a four-decker novel whose form is based on the relativity proposition.

Three sides of space and one of time constitute the soup-mix recipe of a continuum. The four novels follow this pattern.

The three first parts, however, are to be deployed spatially (hence the use of "sibling" not "sequel") and are not linked in a serial form. They interlap, interweave, in a purely spatial relation. Time is stayed. The fourth part alone will represent time and be a true sequel.

The subject-object relation is so important to relativity that I have tried to turn the novel through both subjective and objective modes. The third part, MOUNTOLIVE, *is a straight naturalistic novel in which the narrator of* JUSTINE *and* BALTHAZAR *becomes an object, i.e. a character.*

This is not Proustian or Joycean method—for they illustrate Bergsonian "Duration" in my opinion, not "Space-Time".

The central topic of the book is an investigation of modern love.

These considerations sound perhaps somewhat immodest or even pompous. But it would be worth trying an experiment to see if we cannot discover a morphological form one might appropriately call "classical" —for our time. Even if the result proved to be a "science-fiction" in the true sense.

L.D.
Ascona, 1957

The mirror sees the man as beautiful, the mirror loves the man; another mirror sees the man as frightful and hates him; and it is always the same being who produces the impressions.

Justine
(D. A. F. de Sade)

Yes, we insist upon those details, you veil them with a decency which removes all their edge of horror; there remains only what is useful to who-ever wishes to become familiar with man; you have no conception how helpful these tableaux are to the development of the human spirit; perhaps we are still so benighted with respect to this branch of learning only because of the stupid restraint of those who wish to write upon such matters. Inhabited by absurd fears, they only discuss the puerilities with which every fool is familiar and dare not, by turning a bold hand to the human heart, offer its gigantic idiosyncrasies to our view.

Justine
(D. A. F. de Sade)

To

MY MOTHER

these memorials of an unforgotten city

PART I

I

Landscape-tones: brown to bronze, steep skyline, low cloud, pearl ground with shadowed oyster and violet reflections. The lion-dust of desert: prophets' tombs turned to zinc and copper at sunset on the ancient lake. Its huge sand-faults like watermarks from the air; green and citron giving to gunmetal, to a single plum-dark sail, moist, palpitant: sticky-winged nymph. Taposiris is dead among its tumbling columns and seamarks, vanished the Harpoon Men . . . Mareotis under a sky of hot lilac.

> *summer: buff sand, hot marble sky.*
> *autumn: swollen bruise-greys.*
> *winter: freezing snow, cool sand.*
>> *clear sky panels, glittering with mica.*
>> *washed delta greens.*
>> *magnificent starscapes.*

And spring? Ah! there is no spring in the Delta, no sense of refreshment and renewal in things. One is plunged out of winter into: wax effigy of a summer too hot to breathe. But here, at least, in Alexandria, the sea-breaths save us from the tideless weight of summer nothingness, creeping over the bar among the warships, to flutter the striped awnings of the cafés upon the Grande Corniche. I would never have . . .

o o o o o

The city, half-imagined (yet wholly real), begins and ends in us, roots lodged in our memory. Why must I return to it night after night, writing here by the fire of carob-wood while the Aegean wind clutches at this island house, clutching and releasing it, bending back the cypresses like bows? Have I not said enough about Alexandria? Am I to be reinfected once more by the dream of it and the memory of its inhabitants? Dreams I had thought safely locked up on paper, confided to the strong-rooms of memory! You will think I am indulging myself. It is not so. A single chance factor has altered everything, has turned me back upon my tracks. A memory which catches sight of itself in a mirror.

o   o   o   o   o

Justine, Melissa, Clea. . . . There were so few of us really— you would have thought them easily disposed of in a single book, would you not? So would I, so *did* I. Dispersed now by time and circumstance, the circuit broken forever. . . .

I had set myself the task of trying to recover them in words, reinstate them in memory, allot to each his and her position in my time. Selfishly. And with that writing complete, I felt that I had turned a key upon the doll's house of our actions. Indeed, I saw my lovers and friends no longer as living people but as coloured transfers of the mind; inhabiting my papers now, no longer the city, like tapestry figures. It was difficult to concede to them any more common reality than to the words I had used about them. What has recalled me to myself?

But in order to go on, it is necessary to go back: not that anything I wrote about them is untrue, far from it. Yet when I wrote, the full facts were not at my disposal. The picture I drew was a provisional one—like the picture of a lost civilisation deduced from a few fragmented vases, an inscribed tablet, an amulet, some human bones, a gold smiling death-mask.

o   o   o   o   o

"We live" writes Pursewarden somewhere, "lives based upon selected fictions. Our view of reality is conditioned by our position in space and time—not by our personalities as we like to think. Thus every interpretation of reality is based upon

14

a unique position. Two paces east or west and the whole picture is changed." Something of this order. . . .

And as for human characters, whether real or invented, there are no such animals. Each psyche is really an ant-hill of opposing predispositions. Personality as something with fixed attributes is an illusion—but a necessary illusion *if we are to love!*

As for the something that remains constant . . . the shy kiss of Melissa is predictable, for example (amateurish as an early form of printing), or the frowns of Justine, which cast a shadow over those blazing dark eyes—orbits of the Sphinx at noon. "In the end," says Pursewarden, "everything will be found to be true of everybody. Saint and Villain are co-sharers." He is right.

I am making every attempt to be matter of fact. . . .

o o o o o

In the last letter which reached me from Balthazar he wrote: "I think of you often and not without a certain grim humour. You have retired to your island, with, as you think, all the data about us and our lives. No doubt you are bringing us to judgment on paper in the manner of writers. I wish I could see the result. It must fall very far short of *truth*: I mean such truths as I could tell you about us all—even perhaps about yourself. Or the truths Clea could tell you (she is in Paris and has stopped writing to me altogether). I picture you, wise one, poring over *Moeurs*, the diaries of Justine, Nessim, etc., imagining that the truth is to be found in them. Wrong! Wrong! A diary is the last place to go if you wish to seek the truth about a person. Nobody dares to make the final confession to themselves on paper: or at least, not about love. Do you know whom Justine really loved? You believed it was yourself, did you not? Confess!"

My only answer was to send him the huge bundle of paper which had grown up so stiffly under my slow pen and to which

I had loosely given her name as a title—though *Cahiers* would have done just as well. Six months passed after this—a blessed silence indeed, for it suggested that my critic had been satisfied, silenced.

I cannot say that I forgot the city, but I let the memory of it sleep. Yet of course, it was always there, as it always will be, hanging in the mind like the mirage which travellers so often see. Pursewarden has described the phenomenon in the following words:

"We were still two or three clear hours' steaming distance before land could possibly come into sight when suddenly my companion shouted and pointed at the horizon. We saw, inverted in the sky, a full-scale mirage of the city, luminous and trembling, as if painted on dusty silk: yet in the nicest detail. From memory I could clearly make out its features, Ras El Tin Palace, the Nebi Daniel Mosque and so forth. The whole representation was as breath-taking as a masterpiece painted in fresh dew. It hung there in the sky for a considerable time, perhaps twenty-five minutes, before melting slowly into the horizon mist. An hour later, the *real* city appeared, swelling from a smudge to the size of its mirage."

o   o   o   o   o

The two or three winters we have spent in this island have been lonely ones—dour and windswept winters and hot summers. Luckily, the child is too young to feel as I do the need for books, for conversation. She is happy and active.

Now in the spring come the long calms, the tideless, scentless days of premonition. The sea tames itself and becomes attentive. Soon the cicadas will bring in their crackling music, background to the shepherd's dry flute among the rocks. The scrambling tortoise and the lizard are our only companions.

I should explain that our only regular visitant from the outside world is the Smyrna packet which once a week crosses the headland to the south, always at the same hour, at the same speed, just after dusk. In winter, the high seas and winds make it invisible, but now—I sit and wait for it. You hear at first only the faint drumming of engines. Then the creature slides round the cape, cutting its line of silk froth in the sea, brightly lit up in the moth-soft darkness of the Aegean night—condensed, but without outlines, like a cloud of fireflies moving. It travels fast, and disappears all too soon round the next headland, leaving behind it perhaps only the half-uttered fragment of a popular song, or the skin of a tangerine which I will find next day, washed up on the long pebbled beach where I bathe with the child.

The little arbour of oleanders under the planes—this is my writing-room. After the child has gone to bed, I sit here at the old sea-stained table, waiting for the visitant, unwilling to light the paraffin lamp before it has passed. It is the only day of the week I know by name here—Thursday. It sounds silly, but in an island so empty of variety, I look forward to the weekly visit like a child to a school treat. I know the boat brings letters for which I shall have to wait perhaps twenty-four hours. But I never see the little ship vanish without regret. And when it has passed, I light the lamp with a sigh and return to my papers. I write so slowly, with such pain. Pursewarden once, speaking about writing, told me that the pain that accompanied composition was entirely due, in artists, to the fear of madness; "force it a bit and tell yourself that you don't give a damn if you *do* go mad, and you'll find it comes quicker, you'll break the barrier." (I don't know how true this all is. But the money he left me in his will has served me well, and I still have a few pounds between me and the devils of debt and work.)

I describe this weekly diversion in some detail because it was into this picture that Balthazar intruded one June evening with a suddenness that surprised me—I was going to write "deafened"—there is no one to talk to here—but "surprised me". This evening something like a miracle happened. The little steamer, instead of disappearing as usual, turned abruptly through an arc of 150 degrees and entered the lagoon, there to lie in a furry cocoon of its own light: and to drop into the centre of the golden puddle it had created the long slow anchor-chain whose symbol itself is like a search for truth. It was a moving sight to one who, like myself, had been landlocked in spirit as all writers are—indeed, become like a ship in a bottle, sailing nowhere—and I watched as an Indian must perhaps have watched the first white man's craft touch the shores of the New World.

The darkness, the silence, were broken now by the uneven lap-lap of oars; and then, after an age, by the chink of city-shod feet upon shingle. A hoarse voice gave a direction. Then silence. As I lit the lamp to set the wick in trim and so deliver myself from the spell of this departure from the norm, the grave dark face of my friend, like some goat-like apparition from the Underworld, materialised among the thick branches of myrtle. We drew a breath and stood, smiling at each other in the yellow light: the dark Assyrian ringlets, the beard of Pan. "No —I am real!" said Balthazar with a laugh and we embraced furiously. Balthazar!

The Mediterranean is an absurdly small sea; the length and greatness of its history makes us dream it larger than it is. Alexandria indeed—the true no less than the imagined—lay only some hundreds of sea-miles to the south.

"I am on my way to Smyrna," said Balthazar, "from where I was going to post you this." He laid upon that scarred old table the immense bundle of manuscript I had sent him— papers now seared and starred by a massive interlinear of sentences, paragraphs and question-marks. Seating himself opposite with his Mephistophelean air, he said in a lower, more hesitant tone:

18

"I have debated in myself very long about telling you some of the things I have put down here. At times it seemed a folly and an impertinence. After all, your concern—was it with *us* as *real* people or as 'characters'? I didn't know. I still don't. These pages may lose me your friendship without adding anything to the sum of your knowledge. You have been painting the city, touch by touch, upon a curved surface—was your object poetry or fact? If the latter, then there are things which you have a right to know."

He still had not explained his amazing appearance before me, so anxious was he about the central meaning of the visitation. He did so now, noticing my bewilderment at the cloud of fireflies in the normally deserted bay. He smiled.

"The ship is delayed for a few hours with engine trouble. It is one of Nessim's. The captain is Hasim Kohly, an old friend: perhaps you remember him? No. Well, I guessed from your description roughly where you must be living; but to be landed on your doorstep like this, I confess!" His laughter was wonderful to hear once more.

But I hardly listened, for his words had plunged me into a ferment, a desire to study his interlinear, to revise—not my book (that has never been of the slightest importance to me for it will never even be published), but my view of the city and its inhabitants. For my own personal Alexandria had become, in all this loneliness, as dear as a philosophy of introspection, almost a monomania. I was so filled with emotion I did not know what to say to him. "Stay with us, Balthazar—" I said, "stay awhile. . . ."

"We leave in two hours" he said, and patting the papers before him: "This may give you visions and fevers" he added doubtfully.

"Good—" I said, "I ask for nothing better."

"We are all still real people," he said, "whatever *you* try and do to us—those of us who are still alive. Melissa, Pursewarden

—they can't answer back because they are dead. At least, so one thinks."

"So one thinks. The best retorts always come from beyond the grave."

We sat and began to talk about the past, rather stiffly to be sure. He had already dined on board and there was nothing I could offer him beyond a glass of the good island wine which he sipped slowly. Later he asked to see Melissa's child, and I led him back through the clustering oleanders to a place from which we could both look into the great firelit room where she lay looking beautiful and grave, asleep there with her thumb in her mouth. Balthazar's dark cruel eye softened as he watched her, lightly breathing. "One day," he said in a low voice, "Nessim will want to see her. Quite soon, mark. He has begun to talk about her, be curious. With old age coming on, he will feel he needs her support, mark my words." And he quoted in Greek: "First the young, like vines, climb up the dull supports of their elders who feel their fingers on them, soft and tender; then the old climb down the lovely supporting bodies of the young into their proper deaths." I said nothing. It was the room itself which was breathing now—not our bodies.

"You have been lonely here" said Balthazar.

"But splendidly, desirably lonely."

"Yes, I envy you. But truthfully."

And then his eye caught the unfinished portrait of Justine which Clea in another life had given me.

"That portrait" he said, "which was interrupted by a kiss. How good to see that again—how good!" He smiled. "It is like hearing a loved and familiar statement in music which leads one towards an emotion always recapturable, never-failing." I did not say anything. I did not dare.

He turned to me. "And Clea?" he said at last, in the voice of someone interrogating an echo. I said: "I have heard nothing from her for perhaps two years, perhaps more. Time doesn't count here. I expect she has married, has gone away to another country, has children, a reputation as a painter . . . everything one would wish her."

He looked at me curiously and shook his head. "No" he said; but that was all.

It was long after midnight when the seamen called him from the dark olive groves. I walked to the beach with him, sad to see him leave so soon. A rowboat waited at the water's edge with a sailor standing to his oars in it. He said something in Arabic.

The spring sea was enticingly warm after a day's sunshine and as Balthazar entered the boat the whim seized me to swim out with him to the vessel which lay not two hundred yards away from the shore. This I did and hovered to watch him climb the rail, and to watch the boat drawn up. "Don't get caught in the screw" he called, and "Go back before the engines start"—"I will"—"But wait—before you go—" He ducked back into a stateroom to reappear and drop something into the water beside me. It fell with a soft splash. "A rose from Alexandria," he said, "from the city which has everything but happiness to offer its lovers." He chuckled. "Give it to the child."

"Balthazar, good-bye!"

"Write to me—if you dare!"

Caught like a spider between the cross mesh of lights, and turning towards those yellow pools which still lay between the dark shore and myself, I waved and he waved back.

I put the precious rose between my teeth and dog-paddled back to my clothes on the pebble beach, talking to myself.

And there, lying upon the table in the yellow lamplight, lay the great interlinear to *Justine*—as I have called it. It was cross-hatched, crabbed, starred with questions and answers in different-coloured inks, in typescript. It seemed to me then to be somehow symbolic of the very reality we had shared—a palimpsest upon which each of us had left his or her individual traces, layer by layer.

Must I now learn to see it all with new eyes, to accustom myself to the truths which Balthazar has added? It is impossible to describe with what emotion I read his words—sometimes so detailed and sometimes so briefly curt—as for example in the list he had headed "Some Fallacies and Misapprehensions" where he said coldly: "Number 4. That Justine 'loved' you. She 'loved', if anyone, Pursewarden. 'What does that mean'? She was forced to use you as a decoy in order to protect him from the jealousy of Nessim whom she had married. Pursewarden himself did not care for her at all—supreme logic of love!"

In my mind's eye the city rose once more against the flat mirror of the green lake and the broken loins of sandstone which marked the desert's edge. The politics of love, the intrigues of desire, good and evil, virtue and caprice, love and murder, moved obscurely in the dark corners of Alexandria's streets and squares, brothels and drawing-rooms—moved like a great congress of eels in the slime of plot and counter-plot.

It was almost dawn before I surrendered the fascinating mound of paper with its comments upon my own real (inner) life and like a drunkard stumbled to my bed, my head aching, echoing with the city, the only city left where every extreme of race and habit can meet and marry, where inner destinies intersect. I could hear the dry voice of my friend repeating as I fell asleep: "How much do you *care* to know . . . how much more do you *care* to know?"—"I must know *everything* in order to be at last delivered from the city," I replied in my dream.

o   o   o   o   o   o

"When you pluck a flower, the branch springs back into place. This is not true of the heart's affections" is what Clea once said to Balthazar.

o   o   o   o   o

And so, slowly, reluctantly, I have been driven back to my starting-point, like a man who at the end of a tremendous journey is told that he has been sleepwalking. "Truth," said Balthazar to me once, blowing his nose in an old tennis sock, "Truth is what most contradicts itself in time."

And Pursewarden on another occasion, but not less memorably: "If things were always what they seemed, how impoverished would be the imagination of man!"

How will I ever deliver myself from this whore among cities –sea, desert, minaret, sand, sea?

No. I must set it all down in cold black and white, until such time as the memory and impulse of it is spent. I know that the key I am trying to turn is in myself.

II

Le cénacle Capodistria used to call us in those days when we gathered for an early morning shave in the Ptolemaic parlour of Mnemjian, with its mirrors and palms, its bead curtains and the delicious mimicry of clear warm water and white linen: a laying out and anointing of corpses. The violet-eyed hunchback himself officiated, for we were valued customers all (dead Pharaohs at the natron baths, guts and brains to be removed, renovated and replaced). He himself, the barber, was often unshaven having just hurried down from the hospital after shaving a corpse. Briefly we met here in the padded chairs, in the mirrors, before separating to go about our various tasks—Da Capo to see his brokers, Pombal to totter to the French consulate (mouth full of charred moths, hangover, sensation of having walked about all night on his eyeballs), I to teach, Scobie to the Police Bureau, and so on. . . .

I have somewhere a faded flashlight photograph of this morning ritual, taken by poor John Keats, the Global Agency correspondent. It is strange to look at it now. The smell of the gravecloth is on it. It is a speaking likeness of an Alexandrian spring morning: quiet rubbing of coffee pestles, curdled crying of fat pigeons. I recognize my friends by the very sounds they make: Capodistria's characteristic *"Quatsch"* and *"Pouagh"* at some political remark, followed by that dry cachinnation—the retching of a metal stomach; Scobie's tobacco cough *"Teauch, Teuch"*: Pombal's soft *"Tiens"*, like someone striking a triangle. *"Tiens"*.

And in one corner there I am, in my shabby raincoat—the perfected image of a schoolteacher. In the other corner sits poor little Toto de Brunel. Keats's photograph traps him as he is raising a ringed finger to his temple—the fatal temple.

Toto! He is an *original*, a *numéro*. His withered witch's features and small boy's brown eyes, widow's peak, queer *art nouveau* smile. He was the darling of old society women too proud to pay for gigolos. *"Toto, mon chou, c'est toi!"* (Madame Umbada), *"Comme il est charmant ce Toto!"* (Athena Trasha). He lives on these dry crusts of approbation, an old woman's man, with the dimples sinking daily deeper into the wrinkled skin of an ageless face, quite happy, I suppose. Yes.

"Toto—comment vas-tu?"—*"Si heureux de vous voir, Madame Martinengo!"*

He was what Pombal scornfully called "a Gentleman of the Second Declension". His smile dug one's grave, his kindness was anaesthetic. Though his fortune was small, his excesses trivial, yet he was right in the social swim. There was, I suppose, nothing to be done with him for he was a woman: yet had he been born one he would long since have cried himself into a decline. Lacking charm, his pederasty gave him a kind of illicit importance. *"Homme serviable, homme gracieux"* (Count Banubula, General Cervoni—what more does one want?).

Though without humour, he found one day that he could split sides. He spoke indifferent English and French, but whenever at loss for a word he would put in one whose meaning he did not know and the grotesque substitution was often delightful. This became his standard mannerism. In it, he almost reached poetry—as when he said "Some flies have come off my typewriter" or "The car is trepanned to-day" or "I ran so fast I got dandruff". He could do this in three languages. It excused him from learning them. He spoke a Toto-tongue of his own.

Invisible behind the lens itself that morning stood Keats— the world's sort of Good Fellow, empty of ill intentions. He smelt lightly of perspiration. *C'est le métier qui exige.* Once he

25

had wanted to be a writer but took the wrong turning, and now his profession had so trained him to stay on the superficies of real life (acts and facts about acts) that he had developed the typical journalist's neurosis (they drink to still it): namely that Something has happened, or is about to happen, in the next street, and that they will not know about it until it is too late to "send". This haunting fear of missing a fragment of reality which one knows in advance will be trivial, even meaningless, had given our friend the conventional tic one sees in children who want to go to the lavatory—shifting about in a chair, crossing and uncrossing of legs. After a few moments of conversation he would nervously rise and say "I've just forgotten something—I won't be a minute." In the street he would expel his breath in a swish of relief. He never went far but simply walked around the block to still the unease. Everything always seemed normal enough, to be sure. He would wonder whether to phone Mahmoud Pacha about the defence estimates or wait till to-morrow. . . . He had a pocketful of peanuts which he cracked in his teeth and spat out, feeling restless, unnerved, he did not know why. After a walk he would come trotting back into the café, or barber's shop, beaming shyly, apologetically: an "Agency Man"—our best-integrated modern type. There was nothing wrong with John except the level on which he had chosen to live his life—but you could say the same about his famous namesake, could you not?

I owe this faded photograph to him. (Much later he is to be killed in the desert, in full possession of his imbecility.) The mania to perpetuate, to record, to photograph everything! I suppose this must come from the feeling that you don't enjoy anything fully, indeed are taking the bloom off it with every breath you draw. His "files" were enormous, bulging with signed menus, bands off memorial cigars, postage stamps, picture postcards. . . . Later this proved useful, for somehow he had captured some of Pursewarden's *obiter dicta*.

Farther to the east sits good old big-bellied Pombal, under each eye a veritable diplomatic bag. Now here is someone on whom one can really lavish a bit of affection. His only pre-occupation is with losing his job or being *impuissant*: the national worry of every Frenchman since Jean-Jacques. We quarrel a good deal, though amicably, for we share his little flat which is always full of unconsidered trifles and trifles more considered: *les femmes*. But he is a good friend, a tender-hearted man, and really loves women. When I have insomnia or am ill: *"Dis donc, tu vas bien?"* Roughly, in the manner of a *bon copain*. *"Ecoute— tu veux une aspirine?"* or else *"Ou bien—j'ai une jaune amie dans ma chambre si tu veux. . . ."* (Not a misprint: Pombal called all *poules* *"jaunes femmes"*.) *"Hein? Elle n'est pas mal—et c'est tout payé, mon cher. Mais ce matin, moi je me sens un tout petit peu anti-féministe—j'en ai marre, hein!"* Satiety fell upon him at such times. *"Je deviens de plus en plus anthropophage"* he would say, rolling that comical eye. Also, his job worried him; his reputa-tion was pretty bad, people were beginning to talk, especially after what he calls *"l'affaire Sveva"*; and yesterday the Consul General walked in on him while he was cleaning his shoes on the Chancery curtains. . . . *"Monsieur Pombal! Je suis obligé de vous faire quelques observations sur votre comportement officiel!"* Ouf! A reproof of the first grade. . . .

It explains why Pombal now sits heavily in the photograph, debating all this with a downcast expression. Lately we have become rather estranged because of Melissa. He is angry that I have fallen in love with her, for she is only a dancer in a night-club, and as such unworthy of serious attention. There is also a question of snobbery, for she is virtually living at the flat now and he feels this to be demeaning: perhaps even diplomatically unwise.

"Love" says Toto, "is a liquid fossil"—a felicitous epigram in all conscience. Now to fall in love with a banker's wife, that would be forgivable, though ridiculous. . . . Or would it? In

Alexandria, it is only intrigue *per se* which is wholeheartedly admired; but to fall in love renders one ridiculous in society. (Pombal is a provincial at heart.) I think of the tremendous repose and dignity of Melissa in death, the slender body bandaged and swaddled as if after some consuming and irreparable accident. Well.

And Justine? On the day this picture was taken, Clea's painting was interrupted by a kiss, as Balthazar says. How am I to make this comprehensible when I can only visualise these scenes with such difficulty? I must, it seems, try to see a new Justine, a new Pursewarden, a new Clea. . . . I mean that I must try and strip the opaque membrane which stands between me and the reality of their actions—and which I suppose is composed of my own limitations of vision and temperament. My envy of Pursewarden, my passion for Justine, my pity for Melissa. Distorting mirrors, all of them. . . . The way is through fact. I must record what more I know and attempt to render it comprehensible or plausible to myself, if necessary, by an act of the imagination. Or can facts be left to themselves? Can you say "he fell in love" or "she fell in love" without trying to divine its meaning, to set it in a context of plausibilities? "That bitch" Pombal said once of Justine. *"Elle a l'air d'être bien chambrée!"* And of Melissa *"Une pauvre petite poule quelconque. . . ."* He was right, perhaps, yet the true meaning of them resides elsewhere. Here, I hope, on this scribbled paper which I have woven, spider-like, from my inner life.

And Scobie? Well, he at least has the comprehensibility of a diagram—plain as a national anthem. He looks particularly pleased this morning for he has recently achieved apotheosis. After fourteen years as a Bimbashi in the Egyptian Police, in what he calls "the evening of his life" he has just been appointed to . . . I hardly dare to write the words for I can see his shudder of secrecy, can see his glass eye rolling portentously round in its socket . . . the Secret Service. He is not alive any more, thank God, to read the words and tremble. Yes, the Ancient Mariner, the secret pirate of Tatwig Street, the man himself. How much the city misses him. (His use of the word "uncanny"!)

Elsewhere I have recounted how I answered a mysterious summons to find myself in a room of splendid proportions with my erstwhile pirate friend facing me across a desk, whistling through his ill-fitting dentures. I think his new assignment was as much a puzzle to him as it was to me, his only confidant. It is true of course that he had been long in Egypt and knew Arabic well; but his career had been comparatively obscure. What could an intelligence agency hope to get out of him? More than this—what did he hope to get out of me? I had already explained in detail that the little circle which met every month to hear Balthazar expound the principles of the Cabala had no connection with espionage; it was simply a group of hermetic students drawn by their interest in the matter of the lectures. Alexandria is a city of sects—and the shallowest inquiry would have revealed to him the existence of other groups akin to the one concerned with the hermetic philosophy which Balthazar addressed: Steinerites, Christian Scientists, Ouspenskyists, Adventists. . . . What was it that riveted attention particularly on Nessim, Justine, Balthazar, Capodistria, etc? I could not tell, nor could he tell me.

"They're up to something" he repeated weakly. "Cairo says so." Apparently, he did not even know who his own masters were. His work was invisibly dictated by a scrambler telephone, as far as I could understand. But whatever "Cairo" was it paid him well: and if he had money to throw about on nonsensical investigations who was I to prevent him throwing it to me? I thought that my first few reports on Balthazar's Cabal would successfully damp all interest in it—but no. They wanted more and again more.

And this very morning, the old sailor in the photograph was

celebrating his new post and the increase of salary it carried by having a haircut in the upper town, at the most expensive of shops—Mnemjian's.

I must not forget that this photograph also records a "Secret Rendezvous"; no wonder Scobie looks distraught. For he is surrounded by the very spies into whose activities it is necessary to inquire—not to mention a French diplomat who is widely rumoured to be head of the French *Deuxième*. . . .

Normally Scobie would have found this too expensive an establishment to patronise, living as he did upon a tiny nautical pension and his exiguous Police salary. But now he is a great man.

He did not dare even to wink at me in the mirror as the hunchback, tactful as a diplomat, elaborated a full-scale haircut out of mere air—for Scobie's glittering dome was very lightly fringed by the kind of fluff one sees on a duckling's bottom, and he had of late years sacrificed the torpedo beard of a wintry sparseness.

"I must say," he is about to say throatily (in the presence of so many suspicious people we "spies" must speak "normally"), "I must say, old man, you get a spiffing treatment here, Mnemjian really does understand." Clearing his throat, "The whole art." His voice became portentous in the presence of technical terms. "It's all a question of Graduation—I had a close friend who told me, a barber in Bond Street. You simply got to graduate." Mnemjian thanked him in his pinched ventriloquist's voice. "Not at all" said the old man largely. "I know the wrinkles." *Now* he could wink at me. I winked back. We both looked away.

Released, he stood up, his bones creaking, and set his piratical jaw in a look of full-blooded health. He examined his reflection in the mirror with complacence. "Yes," he said, giving a short authoritative nod, "it'll do."

"Electric friction for scalp, sir?"

Scobie shook his head masterfully as he placed his red flowerpot *tarbush* on his skull. "It brings me out in goose pimples" he said, and then with a smirk, "I'll nourish what's left with *arak*." Mnemjian saluted this stroke of wit with a little gesture. We were free.

But he was really not elated at all. He drooped as we walked slowly down Chérif Pacha together towards the Grande Corniche. He struck moodily at his knee with the horsehair fly-swatter, puffing moodily at his much-mended briar. Thought. All he said with sudden petulance was "I can't stand that Toto fellow. He's an open nancy-boy. In my time we would have. . . ." He grumbled away into his skin for a long time and then petered into silence again.

"What is it, Scobie?" I said.

"I'm troubled" he admitted. "Really troubled."

When he was in the upper town his walk and general bearing had an artificial swagger—it suggested a White Man at large, brooding upon problems peculiar to White Men—their Burden as they call it. To judge by Scobie, it hung heavy. His least gesture had a resounding artificiality, tapping his knee, sucking his lip, falling into brooding attitudes before shop windows. He gazed at the people around him as if from stilts. These gestures reminded me in a feeble way of the heroes of domestic English fiction who stand before a Tudor fireplace, impressively whacking their riding-boots with a bull's pizzle.

By the time we had reached the outskirts of the Arab quarter, however, he had all but shed these mannerisms. He relaxed, tipped his *tarbush* up to mop his brow, and gazed around him with the affection of long familiarity. Here he belonged by adoption, here he was truly at home. He would defiantly take a drink from the leaden spout sticking out of a wall near the Goharri mosque (a public drinking fountain) though the White Man in him must have been aware that the water was far from safe to drink. He would pick a stick of sugar-cane off a stall as he passed, to gnaw it in the open street: or a sweet locust-bean. Here, everywhere, the cries of the open street greeted him and he responded radiantly.

"*Y'alla, effendi, Skob*"

"*Naharak said, ya Skob*"

"*Allah salimak.*"

He would sigh and say "Dear people"; and "How I love the place—you have no idea!" dodging a liquid-eyed camel as it humped down the narrow street threatening to knock us down with its bulging sumpters of *bercim*, the wild clover which is used as fodder.

"May your prosperity increase"

"By your leave, my mother"

"May your day be blessed"

"Favour me, O Sheik."

Scobie walked here with the ease of a man who has come into his own estate, slowly, sumptuously, like an Arab.

To-day we sat together for a while in the shade of the ancient mosque listening to the clicking of the palms and the hooting of sea-going liners in the invisible basin below.

"I've just seen a directive" said Scobie at last, in a sad withered little voice, "about what they call a Peddyrast. It's rather shaken me, old man. I don't mind admitting it—I didn't know the word. I had to look it up. At all costs, it says, we must exclude them. They are dangerous to the security of the net." I gave a laugh and for a moment the old man showed signs of wanting to respond with a weak giggle, but his depression overtook the impulse, to leave it buried, a small hollowness in those cherry-red cheeks. He puffed furiously at his pipe. "Peddyrast" he repeated with scorn, and groped for his matchbox.

"I don't think they quite understand at Home" he said sadly. "Now the Egyptians, they don't give a damn about a man if he has Tendencies—provided he's the Soul of Honour, like me." He meant it. "But now, old man, if I am to work for the . . . You Know What . . . I ought to tell them—what do you say?"

"Don't be a fool, Scobie."

"Well, I don't know" he said sadly, "I want to be honest with them. It isn't that I cause any harm. I suppose one shouldn't have Tendencies—any more than warts or a big nose. But what can I do?"

"Surely at your age very little?"

"Below the belt" said the pirate with a flash of his old form. "Dirty. Cruel. Narky." He looked archly at me round his pipe and suddenly cheered up. He began one of those delightful rambling monologues—another chapter in the saga he had composed around his oldest friend, the by now mythical Toby Mannering. "Toby was once Driven Medical by his excesses— I think I told you. No? Well, he was. Driven Medical." He was obviously quoting and with relish. "Lord how he used to go it as a young man. Stretched the limit in beating the bounds. Finally he found himself under the Doctor, had to wear an Appliance." His voice rose by nearly an octave. "He went about in a leopard-skin muff when he had shore leave until the Merchant Navy rose in a body. He was put away for six months. Into a Home. They said 'You'll have to have Traction'— whatever that is. You could hear him scream all over Tewkes-bury, so Toby says. They say they cure you but they don't. They didn't him at any rate. After a bit, they sent him back. Couldn't do anything with him. He was afflicted with Dumb Insolence, they said. Poor Toby!"

He had fallen effortlessly asleep now, leaning back against the wall of the Mosque. ("A cat-nap," he used to say, "but always woken by the ninth wave." For how much longer, I wondered?) After a moment the ninth wave brought him back through the surf of his dreams to the beach. He gave a start and sat up. "What was I saying? Yes, about Toby. His father was

C   33

an M.P. Very High Placed. Rich man's son. Toby tried to go into the Church first. Said he felt The Call. I think it was just the costume, myself—he was a great amateur theatrical, was Toby. Then he lost his faith and slipped up and had a tragedy. Got run in. He said the Devil prompted him. "See he doesn't do it again" says the Beak. "Not on Tooting Common, anyway." They wanted to put him in chokey—they said he had a rare disease—cornucopia I think they called it. But luckily his father went to the Prime Minister and had the whole thing hushed up. It was lucky, old man, that at that time the whole Cabinet had Tendencies too. It was uncanny. The Prime Minister, even the Archbishop of Canterbury. They sympathised with poor Toby. It was lucky for him. After that, he got his master's ticket and put to sea."

Scobie was asleep once more; only to wake again after a few seconds with a histrionic start. "It was old Toby" he went on, without a pause, though now crossing himself devoutly and gulping, "who put me on to the Faith. One night when we were on watch together on the *Meredith* (fine old ship) he says to me: 'Scurvy, there's something you should know. Ever heard of the Virgin Mary?' I had of course, vaguely. I didn't know what her duties were, so to speak. . . ."

Once more he fell asleep and this time there issued from between his lips a small croaking snore. I carefully took his pipe from between his fingers and lit myself a cigarette. This appearance and disappearance into the simulacrum of death was somehow touching. These little visits paid to an eternity which he would soon be inhabiting, complete with the comfortable forms of Toby and Budgie, and a Virgin Mary with specified duties. . . . And to be obsessed by such problems at an age when, as far as I could judge, there was little beyond verbal boasting to make him a nuisance. (I was wrong—Scobie was indomitable.)

After a while he woke again from this deeper sleep, shook

himself and rose, knuckling his eyes. We made our way together to the sordid purlieus of the town where he lived, in
Tatwig Street, in a couple of tumbledown rooms. "And yet"
he said once more, carrying his chain of thought perfectly, "it's
all very well for you to say I shouldn't tell them. But I wonder."
(Here he paused to inhale the draught of cooking Arab bread
from the doorway of a shop and the old man exclaimed "It
smells like mother's lap!") His ambling walk kept pace with
his deliberations. "You see the Egyptians are marvellous, old
man. Kindly. They know me well. From some points of view,
they might look like felons, old man, but felons in a state of
grace, that's what I always say. They make allowances for each
other. Why, Nimrod Pascha himself said to me the other day
'Peddyrasty is one thing—*hashish* quite another.' He's serious,
you see. Now I never smoke *hashish* when I'm on duty—that
would be bad. Of course, from another point of view, the
British couldn't do anything to a man with an O.B.E. like me.
But if the Gyppos once thought they were—well, critical about
me—old man, I might lose both jobs, and both salaries. That's
what troubles me."

We mounted the fly-blown staircase with its ragged rat-
holes. "It smells a bit," he agreed, "but you get quite used to
it. It's the mice. No, I'm not going to move. I've lived in this
quarter ten years now—ten years. Everybody knows me and
likes me. And besides, old Abdul is only round the corner."

He chuckled and stopped for breath on the first landing,
taking off his flowerpot the better to mop his brow. Then he
hung downwards, sagging as he always did when he was thinking seriously as if the very weight of the thought itself bore
down upon him. He sighed. "The thing" he said slowly, and
with the air of a man who wishes at all costs to be explicit, to
formulate an idea as clearly as lies within his power, "the
thing is about Tendencies—you only realize it when you're not
a hot-blooded young sprig any more." He sighed again. "It's

the lack of *tenderness*, old man. It all depends on cunning some-how, you get lonely. Now Abdul is a true friend." He chuckled and cheered up once more. "I call him the Bul Bul Emir. I set him up in his business, just out of friendly affection. Bought him everything: his shop, his little wife. Never laid a finger on him nor ever could, because I love the man. I'm glad I did now, because though I'm getting on, I still have a true friend. I pop in every day to see them. It's uncanny how happy it makes me. I really do enjoy their happiness, old man. They are like son and daughter to me, the poor perishing coons. I can't hardly bear to hear them quarrel. It makes me anxious about their kids. I think Abdul is jealous of her, and not without cause, mark you. She looks flirty to me. But then, sex is so powerful in this heat—a spoonful goes a long way as we used to say about rum in the Merchant Navy. You lie and dream about it like ice-cream, sex, not rum. And these Moslem girls—old boy—they circumcise them. It's cruel. Really cruel. It only makes them harp on the subject. I tried to get her to learn knitting or crewel-work, but she's so stupid she didn't under-stand. They made a joke of it. Not that I mind. I was only trying to help. Two hundred pounds it took me to set Abdul up—all my savings. But he's doing well now—yes, very well."

The monologue had had the effect of allowing him to muster his energies for the final assault. We addressed the last ten stairs at a comfortable pace and Scobie unlocked the door of his rooms. Originally he had only been able to rent one—but with his new salary he had rented the whole shabby floor.

The largest was the old Arab room which served as a bedroom and reception-room in one. It was furnished by an uncomfort-able looking truckle bed and an old-fashioned cake-stand. A few joss-sticks, a Police calendar, and Clea's as yet unfinished portrait of the pirate stood upon the crumbling mantelpiece. Scobie switched on a single dusty electric light bulb—a recent innovation of which he was extremely proud ("Paraffin gets in the food")—and looked round him with unaffected pleasure. Then he tiptoed to the far corner. In the gloom I had at first overlooked the room's other occupant: a brilliant green Amazonian parrot in a brass cage. It was at present shrouded in a dark cloth, and this the old man now removed with a faintly defensive air.

"I was telling you about Toby," he said, "because last week he came through Alex on the Yokohama run. I got this from him—he had to sell—the damn bird caused such a riot. It's a brilliant conversationalist, aren't you Ron, eh? Crisp as a fart, aren't you?" The parrot gave a low whistle and ducked. "That's the boy" said Scobie with approval and turning to me added "I got Ron for a very keen price, yes, a very keen price. Shall I tell you why?"

Suddenly, inexplicably, he doubled up with laughter, nearly joining nose to knee and whizzing soundlessly like a small human top, to emerge at last with an equally soundless slap on his own thigh—a sudden paroxysm. "You'd never imagine the row Ron caused" he said. "Toby brought the bird ashore. He knew it could talk, but not Arabic. By God. We were sitting at a café yarning (I haven't seen Toby for five whole years) when Ron suddenly started. In Arabic. You know, he recited the Kalima, a very sacred, not to mention holy text from the Koran. The Kalima. And at every other word, he gives a fart, didn't you Ron?" The parrot agreed with another whistle. "It's so sacred, the Kalima," explained Scobie gravely, "that the next thing was a raging crowd round us. It was lucky I knew what was going on. I knew that if a non-Moslem was caught reciting this particular text he was liable to Instant Circumcision!" His eye flashed. "It was a pretty poor outlook for Toby to be circumcised like that while one was taking shore leave and I was worried. (I'm circumcised already.) However, my presence of mind didn't desert me. He wanted to punch a few heads, but I restrained him. I was in Police uniform you see, and that made it easier. I made a little speech to the crowd saying that I was going to take the infidel and his perishing bird into chokey to hand them over to the Parquet. That satisfied them. But there was no way of silencing Ron, even under his little veil, was there Ron? The little bastard recited the Kalima all the way back here. We had to run for it. My word, what an experience!"

He was changing out of his Police rig as he talked, placing his *tarbush* on the rusty iron nail above his bed, above the crucifix in the little alcove where a stone jar of drinking-water also stood. He put on a frayed old blazer with tin buttons, and still mopping his head went on: "I must say—it was wonderful to see old Toby again after so long. He had to sell the bird, of course, after such a riot. Didn't dare go through the dock area again with it. But now I'm doubtful, for I daren't take it out of the room hardly for fear of what more it knows." He sighed. "Another good thing" he went on, "was the recipe Toby brought for Mock Whisky—ever heard of it? Nor had I. Better than Scotch and dirt cheap, old man. From now on I'm going to brew all my own drinks, thanks to Toby. Here. Look at this." He indicated a grubby bottle full of some fiery-looking liquid. "It's home-made beer," he said, "and jolly good too. I made three, but the other two exploded. I'm going to call it Plaza beer."

"Why?" I asked. "Are you going to sell it?"

"Good Lord, no!" said Scobie. "Just for home use." He rubbed his stomach reflectively and licked his lips. "Try a glass" he said.

"No thanks."

The old man now consulted a huge watch and pursed his lips. "In a little while I must say an Ave Maria. I'll have to push you out, old man. But just let's have a look and see how the Mock Whisky is getting on for a moment, shall we?"

I was most curious to see how he was conducting these new

experiments and willingly followed him out on to the landing again and into the shabby alcove which now housed a gaunt galvanised iron bath which he must have bought specially for these illicit purposes. It stood under a grimy closet window, and the shelves around it were crowded with the impedimenta of the new trade—a dozen empty beer bottles, two broken, and the huge chamberpot which Scobie always called "the Heirloom"; not to mention a tattered beach umbrella and a pair of goloshes. "What part do these play?" I could not help asking, indicating the latter. "Do you tread the grapes or potatoes in them?"

Scobie took on an old-maidish, squinting-down-the-nose expression which always meant that levity on the topic under discussion was out of place. He listened keenly for a moment, as if to sounds of fermentation. Then he got down on one shaky knee and regarded the contents of the bath with a doubtful but intense eye. His glass eye gave him a more than mechanical expression as it stared into the rather tired-looking mixture with which the bath was brimming. He sniffed dispassionately and tutted once before rising again with creaking joints. "It doesn't look as good as I hoped" he admitted. "But give it time, it has to be given time." He tried some on his finger and rolled his glass eye. "It seems to have gone a bit turpid" he admitted. "As if someone had peed in it." As Abdul and himself shared the only key to this illicit still I was able to look innocent.

"Do you want to try it?" he asked doubtfully.

"Thank you, Scobie—no."

"Ah well," he said philosophically, "maybe the copper sulphate wasn't fresh. I had to order the rhubarb from Blighty. Forty pounds. *That* looked pretty tired when it got here, I don't mind telling you. But I know the proportions are right because I went into it all thoroughly with young Toby before he left. It needs time, that's what it needs."

And made buoyant once more by the hope, he led the way

back into the bedroom, whistling under his breath a few staves of the famous song which he only sang aloud when he was drunk on brandy. It went something like this:

> *"I want*
> *Someone to match my fancy*
> *I want*
> *Someone to match my style*
> *I've been good for an awful long while*
> *Now I'll take her in my arms*
> *Tum ti Tum Tum ti charms. . . ."*

Somewhere here the melody fell down a cliff and was lost to sight, though Scobie hummed out the stave and beat time with his finger.

He was sitting down on the bed now and staring at his shabby shoes. "Are you going to the party Nessim's giving for Mountolive to-night?"—"I suppose so" I said. He sniffed loudly. "I'm not invited. At the Yacht Club, isn't it?"

"Yes."

"He is Sir David now, isn't he? I saw it in the paper last week. Young to be a lord, isn't he? I was in charge of the Police Guard of Honour when he arrived. They all played out of tune but he didn't notice anything, thank God!"

"Not so young."

"And to be Minister?"

"I suppose he's in his late forties?"

Abruptly, without apparent premeditation (though he closed his eyes fast as if to shut the subject away out of sight forever) Scobie lay back on the bed, hands behind his head, and said:

"Before you go, there's a small confession I'd like to make to you, old man. Right?"

I sat down on the uncomfortable chair and nodded. "Right" he said emphatically and drew a breath. "Well then: sometimes at the full moon, *I'm Took*. I come under *An Influence*."

This was on the face of it a somewhat puzzling departure from accepted form, for the old man looked quite disturbed by his own revelation. He gobbled for a moment and then went on in a small humbled voice devoid of his customary swagger. "I don't know what comes over me." I did not quite understand all this. "Do you mean you walk in your sleep or what?" He shook his head and gulped again. "Do you turn into a were-wolf, Scobie?" Once more he shook his head like a child upon the point of tears. "I slip on female duds and my Dolly Varden" he said, and opened his eyes fully to stare pathetically at me.

"You *what?*" I said.

To my intense surprise he rose now and walked stiffly to a cupboard which he unlocked. Inside, hanging up, moth-eaten and unbrushed, was a suit of female clothes of ancient cut, and on a nail beside it a greasy old cloche hat which I took to be the so-called "Dolly Varden". A pair of antediluvian court shoes with very high heels and long pointed toes completed this staggering outfit. He did not know how quite to respond to the laugh which I was now compelled to utter. He gave a weak giggle. "It's silly, isn't it?" he said, still hovering somewhere on the edge of tears despite his smiling face, and still by his tone inviting sympathy in misfortune. "I don't know what comes over me. And yet, you know, it's always the old thrill. . . ."

A sudden and characteristic change of mood came over him at the words: his disharmony, his discomfiture gave place to a new jauntiness. His look became arch now, not wistful, and crossing to the mirror before my astonished eyes, he placed the hat upon his bald head. In a second he replaced his own image with that of a little old tart, button-eyed and razor-nosed—a tart of the Waterloo Bridge epoch, a veritable Tuppeny Up-right. Laughter and astonishment packed themselves into a huge parcel inside me, neither finding expression. "For God's sake!" I said at last. "You don't go around like that, do you, Scobie?"

"Only" said Scobie, sitting helplessly down on the bed again and relapsing into a gloom which gave his funny little face an even more comical expression (he still wore the Dolly Varden), "only when the Influence comes over me. When I'm not fully Answerable, old man."

He sat there looking crushed. I gave a low whistle of surprise which the parrot immediately copied. This was indeed serious. I understood now why the deliberations which had consumed him all morning had been so full of heart-searching. Obviously if one went around in a rig like that in the Arab quarter. . . . He must have been following my train of thought, for he said "It's only sometimes when the Fleet's in." Then he went on with a touch of self-righteousness: "Of course, if there was ever any trouble, I'd say I was in disguise. I am a policeman when you come to think of it. After all, even Lawrence of Arabia wore a nightshirt, didn't he?" I nodded. "But not a Dolly Varden" I said. "You must admit, Scobie, it's most original . . ." and here the laughter overtook me.

Scobie watched me laugh, still sitting on the bed in that fantastic headpiece. "Take it off!" I implored. He looked serious and preoccupied now, but made no motion. "Now you know all" he said. "The best and the worst in the old skipper. Now what I was going to——"

At this moment there came a knock at the landing door. With surprising presence of mind Scobie leaped spryly into the cupboard, locking himself noisily in. I went to the door. On the landing stood a servant with a pitcher full of some liquid which he said was for the Effendi Skob. I took it from him and got rid of him, before returning to the room and shouting to the old man who emerged once more—now completely himself, bareheaded and blazered.

"That was a near shave" he breathed. "What was it?" I

indicated the pitcher. "Oh, that—it's for the Mock Whisky. Every three hours."

"Well," I said at last, still struggling with these new and indigestible revelations of temperament, "I must be going." I was still hovering explosively between amazement and laughter at the thought of Scobie's second life at full moon—how had he managed to avoid a scandal all these years?—when he said: "Just a minute old man. I only told you all this because I want you to do me a favour." His false eye rolled around earnestly now under the pressure of thought. He sagged again. "A thing like that could do me Untold Harm," he said, "Untold Harm, old man."

"I should think it could."

"Old man," said Scobie, "I want you to confiscate my duds. It's the only way of controlling the Influence."

"Confiscate them?"

"Take them away. Lock them up. It'll save me, old man. I know it will. The whim is too strong for me otherwise, when it comes."

"All right" I said.

"God bless you, son."

Together we wrapped his full-moon regalia in some newspapers and tied the bundle up with string. His relief was tempered with doubt. "You won't lose them?" he said anxiously.

"Give them to me" I said firmly and he handed me the parcel meekly. As I went down the stairs he called after me to express relief and gratitude, adding the words: "I'll say a little prayer for you, son." I walked back slowly through the dock-area with the parcel under my arm, wondering whether I would ever dare to confide this wonderful story to someone worth sharing it with.

The warships turned in their inky reflections—the forest of masts and rigging in the Commercial Port swayed softly among the mirror-images of the water: somewhere a ship's radio was blaring out the latest jazz-hit to reach Alexandria:

> *Old Tiresias*
> *No-one half so breezy as,*
> *Half so free and easy as*
> *Old Tiresias.*

o   o   o   o   o

III

The sinking sun which had emptied the harbour roads of all but the black silhouettes of the foreign warships had nevertheless left a flickering greyness—the play of light without colour or resonance upon the surface of a sea still dappled with sails. Dinghies racing for home moved about the floor of the inner harbour, scuttling in and out among the ships like mice among the great boots of primitive cottagers. The sprouting tier of guns on the *Jean Bart* moved slowly—tilted—and then settled back into brooding stillness, aimed at the rosy heart of the city whose highest minarets still gleamed gold in the last rays of the sunset. The flocks of spiring pigeons glittered like confetti as they turned their wings to the light. (Fine writing!)

But the great panels of the brass-framed windows in the Yacht Club blazed like diamonds, throwing a brilliant light upon the snowy tables with their food, setting fire to the glasses and jewellery and eyes in a last uneasy conflagration before the heavy curtains would be drawn and the faces which had gathered to greet Mountolive took on the warm pallors of candlelight.

The triumphs of polity, the resources of tact, the warmth, the patience. . . . Profligacy and sentimentality . . . killing love by taking things easy . . . sleeping out a chagrin. . . . This was Alexandria, the unconsciously poetical mother-city exemplified in the names and faces which made up her history. Listen.

Tony Umbada, Baldassaro Trivizani, Claude Amaril, Paul Capodistria, Dmitri Randidi, Onouphrios Papas, Count Banubula, Jacques de Guéry, Athena Trasha, Djamboulat Bey, Delphine de Francueil, General Cervoni, Ahmed Hassan

Pacha, Pozzo di Borgo, Pierre Balbz, Gaston Phipps, Haddad Fahmy Amin, Mehmet Adm, Wilmot Pierrefeu, Toto de Brunel, Colonel Neguib, Dante Borromeo, Benedict Dangeau, Pia dei Tolomei, Gilda Ambron. . . . The poetry and history of commerce, the rhyme-schemes of the Levant which had swallowed Venice and Genoa. (Names which the passer-by may one day read upon the tombs in the cemetery.)

The conversation rose in a steamy cloud to envelop Mount-olive whose personal triumph it was and who stood talking to Nessim, his host, with the gentle-mannered expression on his face which, like a lens, betrayed all the stylised diffidence of his perfect breeding. The two men indeed were much alike; only Nessim's darkness was smooth, cleanly surfaced, and his eyes and hands restless. Despite a difference of age they were well matched—even to the tastes they shared, which the years had done nothing to diminish though they had hardly corre-sponded directly all the time Mountolive had been away from Egypt. It had always been to Leila that he wrote, not to her sons. Nevertheless, once he had returned, they were much together and found they had as much to discuss as ever in the past. You would hear the sharp pang of their tennis racquets every spring afternoon on the Legation court at an hour when everyone normally slept. They rode in the desert together or sat for hours side by side, studying the stars, at the telescope which Justine had had installed in the Summer Palace. They painted and shot in company. Indeed, since Mountolive's return they had become once more almost inseparables. To-night the soft light touched them both with an equal distinc-tion, yet softly enough to disguise the white hairs at Mountolive's temples and the crow's-feet around those thought-ful arbitrator's eyes. By candlelight the two men seemed exactly of an age if indeed not of the same family.

A thousand faces whose reverberating expressions I do not understand ("We are all racing under sealed handicaps" says a

46

character in Pursewarden's book), and out of them all there is one only I am burning to see, the black stern face of Justine. I must learn to see even myself in a new context, after reading those cold cruel words of Balthazar. How does a man look when he is "in love"? (The words in English should be uttered in a low bleating tone.) *Peccavi!* Imbecile! There I stand in my only decent suit, whose kneecaps are bagged and shiny with age, gazing fondly and short-sightedly around me for a glimpse of the woman who. . . . What does it matter? I do not need a Keats to photograph me. I do not suppose I am uglier than anyone else or less pleasant; and certainly my vanity is of a very general order—for how have I never stopped to ask myself for a second why Justine should turn aside to bestow her favours on me?

What could I give her that she could not get elsewhere? Does she want my bookish talk and amateurish love-making— she with the whole bargain-basement of male Alexandria in her grasp? "A decoy!" I find this very wounding to understand, to swallow, yet it has all the authority of curt fact. Moreover, it explains several things which have been for me up to now inexplicable—such as the legacy Pursewarden left me. It was his guilt, I think, for what he knew Justine was doing to Melissa: in "loving" me. While she, for her part, was simply protecting him against the possible power of Nessim (how gentle and calm he looks in the candlelight). He once said with a small sigh: "Nothing is easier to arrange in our city than a death or a disappearance."

A thousand conversations, seeking out for each other like the tap-roots of trees for moisture—the hidden meaning of lives disguised in brilliant smiles, in hands pressed upon the eyes, in malice, in fevers and contents. (Justine now breakfasted silently surrounded by tall black footmen, and dined by candlelight in brilliant company. She had started from nothing —from the open street—and was now married to the city's handsomest banker. How had all this come about? You would never be able to tell by watching that dark, graceful form with its untamed glances, the smile of the magnificent white teeth. . . .) Yet one trite conversation can contain the germ of a whole life. Balthazar, for example, meeting Clea against a red brocade curtain, holding a glass of Pernod, could say: "Clea, I have something to tell you"; taking in as he spoke the warm gold of her hair and a skin honeyed almost to the tone of burnt sugar by sea-bathing in the warm spring sunshine. "What?" Her candid eyes were as blue as corn-flowers and set in her head like precision-made objects of beauty—the life-work of a jeweller. "Speak, my dear." Black head of hair (he dyed it), lowered voice set in its customary sardonic croak, Balthazar said: "Your father came to see me. He is worried about an illicit relationship you are supposed to have formed with another woman. Wait—don't speak, and don't look hurt." For Clea looked now as if he were pressing upon a bruise, the sad grave mouth set in a childish expression, imploring no further penetration. "He says you are an innocent, a goose, and that Alexandria does not permit innocent people to. . . ."

"Please, Balthazar."

"I would not have spoken had I not been impressed by his genuine anguish—not about scandal: who cares for gossip? But he was worried lest you should be hurt."

In a small compressed voice, like some packaged thought squeezed to a hundredth of its size by machinery, Clea said: "I have not been alone with Justine for a year. Do you understand? It ended when the painting ended. If you wish us to be friends you will never refer to this subject again" smiling a little tremulously, for in the same breath Justine came sailing down upon them, smiling warmly, radiantly. (It is quite possible to love those whom you most wound.) She passed, turning in the candlelight of the room like some great sea-bird, and came at last to where I was standing. "I cannot come to-night" she whispered. "Nessim wants me to stay at home." I can feel still the uncomprehending weight of my disappointment at the words. "You must" I muttered. Should I have known that not ten minutes before she had said to Nessim, knowing he hated bridge: "Darling, can I go and play bridge with the Cervonis—do you need the car?" It must have been one of those rare evenings when Pursewarden consented to meet her out in the desert—meetings to which she went unerringly, like a sleep-walker. Why? *Why?*

Balthazar at this moment is saying: "Your father said: 'I cannot bear to watch it, and I do not know what to do. It is like watching a small child skipping near a powerful piece of unprotected machinery.'" Tears came into Clea's eyes and slowly vanished again as she sipped her drink. "It is over" she said, turning her back upon the subject and upon Balthazar in one and the same motion. She turned her sullen mouth now to the discussion of meaningless matters with Count Banubula, who bowed and swung as gallantly as Scobie's green parrot ducking on its perch. She was pleased to see that her beauty had a direct, clearly discernible effect upon him, like a shower of golden arrows. Presently, Justine herself passed again, and in passing caught Clea's wrist. "How is it?" said Clea, in the manner of one who asks after a sick child. Justine gave the shadow of a grimace and whispered dramatically: "Oh, Clea—it is very bad. What a terrible mistake. Nessim is wonderful—I should never have done it. *I am followed everywhere.*" They stared at each other sympathetically for a long moment. It was their first encounter for months. (That afternoon, Pursewarden had written: "A few hasty and not entirely unloving words from my sickbed about this evening." He was not in bed but sitting at a café on the sea-front, smiling as he wrote.) Messages spoken and unspoken, crossing and interlacing, carrying the currents of our lives, the fears, dissimulations, the griefs. Justine was speaking now about her marriage which still exhibited to the outer world a clearness of shape and context—the plaster cast of a perfection which I myself had envied when first I met them both. "The marriage of true minds" I thought; but where is the "magnificent two-headed animal" to be found? When she first became aware of the terrible jealousy of Nessim, the jealousy of the spiritually impotent man, she had been appalled and terrified. She had fallen by mistake into a trap. (All this, like the fever-chart of a stricken patient, Clea watched, purely out of friendship with no desire to renew the love she felt for this dispersed unself-comprehending Jewess.)

Justine put the matter to herself another way, a much more primitive way, by thinking: up to now she had always judged her men by their smell! This was the first time ever that she had neglected to consult the sense. And Nessim had the odourless purity of the desert airs, the desert in summer, unconfiding and dry. Pure. How she hated purity! Afterwards? Yes, she was revolted by the little gold cross which nestled in the hair on his chest. He was a Copt—a Christian. This is the way women work in the privacy of their own minds. Yet out of shame at such thoughts she became doubly passionate and attentive to her husband, though even between kisses, in the depths of her mind, she longed only for the calm and peace of widowhood! Am I imagining this? I do not think so.

How had all this come about? To understand it is necessary to work backwards, through the great Interlinear which Balthazar has constructed around my manuscript, towards that point in time where the portrait which Clea was painting was interrupted by a kiss. It is strange to look at it now, the portrait, standing unfinished on the old-fashioned mantelpiece of the island house. "An idea had just come into her mind, but had not yet reached the lips." And then, softly, her lips fell where the painter's wet brush should have fallen. Kisses and brush-strokes—I should be writing of poor Melissa!

How distasteful all this subject-matter is—what Pursewarden has called "the insipid kiss of familiars"; and how innocent! The black gloves she wore in the portrait left a small open space when they were buttoned up—the shape of a heart. And that innocent, ridiculous kiss only spoke admiration and pity for the things Justine was telling her about the loss of her child—the daughter which had been stolen from her while it was playing on the river-bank. "Her wrists, her small wrists. If you could have seen how beautiful and tame she was, a squirrel." In the hoarseness of the tone, in the sad eyes and the down-pointed mouth with a comma in each cheek. And holding out a hand with finger and thumb joined to describe the circuit of those small wrists. Clea took and kissed the heart in the black glove. She was really kissing the child, the mother. Out of this terrible sympathy her innocence projected the consuming shape of a sterile love. But I am going too fast. Moreover, how am I to make comprehensible scenes which I myself see only with such difficulty—these two women, the blonde and the bronze in a darkening studio at Saint Saba, among the rags and the paintpots and the warm gallery of portraits which lined the walls, Balthazar, Da Capo, even Nessim himself, Clea's dearest friend? It is hard to compose them in a stable colour so that the outlines are not blurred.

Justine at this time . . . coming from nowhere, she had done one trick regarded as clever by the provincials of Alexandria. She had married Arnauti, a foreigner, only to earn the contempt of society by letting him in the end divorce and abandon her. Of the fate of the child, few people knew or cared. She was not "in society" as the saying goes. . . . Poverty forced her to do a little modelling at so many piastres an hour for the art-students of the Atelier. Clea, who knew her only by hearsay, passed through the long gallery one day when she was posing, and struck by the dark Alexandrian beauty of her face, engaged her for a portrait. That was how those long conversations grew up in the silences of the painter; for Clea liked her subjects to talk freely, provided they stayed still. It gave a submarine life to their features, and filled their looks with unconscious interpretations of thought—the true beauty in otherwise dead flesh.

Clea's generous innocence—it needed something like that to see the emptiness in which Justine lived with her particular sorrows—factual illustrations merely of a mind at odds with itself: for we create our own misfortunes and they bear our own fingerprints. The gesture itself was simply a clumsy attempt to appropriate the mystery of true experience, true suffering—as by touching a holy man the supplicant hopes for a transference of the grace he lacks. The kiss did not for a moment expect itself to be answered by another—to copy itself like the reflections of a moth in a looking-glass. That would have been too expensive a gesture had it been premeditated. So it proved! Clea's own body simply struggled to disengage itself from the wrappings of its innocence as a baby or a statue struggles for life under the fingers or forceps of its author. Her bankruptcy was one of extreme youth, Justine's ageless; her innocence was as defenceless as memory itself. Seeking and admiring only the composure of Justine's sorrow she found herself left with all the bitter lye of an uninvited love.

She was "white of heart", in the expressive Arabic phrase, and painting the darkness of Justine's head and shoulders she suddenly felt as if, stroke by stroke, the brush itself had begun to imitate caresses she had neither foreseen nor even thought to permit. As she listened to that strong deep voice recounting these misfortunes, so desirable in that they belonged to the active living world of experience, she caught her breath between her teeth, trying now to think only of the unconscious signs of good breeding in her subject: hands still in the lap, voice low, the reserve which delineates true power. Yet even she, from her inexperience, could do little but pity Justine when she said things like "I am not much good, you know. I can only inflict sadness, Arnauti used to say. He brought me to my senses and taught me that nothing matters except pleasure —which is the opposite of happiness, its tragic part, I expect." Clea was touched by this because it seemed clear to her that Justine had never really experienced pleasure—one has to be generous for that. Egotism is a fortress in which the *conscience de soi-même*, like a corrosive, eats away everything. True pleasure is in giving, surely.

"As for Arnauti, he nearly drove me mad with his inquisitions. What I lost as a wife I gained as a patient—his interest in what he called 'my case' outweighed any love he might have had for me. And then losing the child made me hate him where before I had only seen a rather sensitive and kindly man. You have probably read his book *Moeurs*. Much of it is invented— mostly to satisfy his own vanity and get his own back on me for the way I wounded his pride in refusing to be 'cured'—so-called. You can't put a soul into splints. If you say to a Frenchman 'I can't make love to you unless I imagine a palm-tree,' he will go out and cut down the nearest palm-tree."

Clea was too noble to love otherwise than passionately; and yet at the same time quite capable of loving someone to whom she spoke only once a year. The deep still river of her heart hoarded its images, ever reflecting them in the racing current, letting them sink deeper into memory than most of us can. Real innocence can do nothing that is trivial, and when it is allied to generosity of heart, the combination makes it the most vulnerable of qualities under heaven.

In this sudden self-consuming experience, comparable in its tension and ardour to those ridiculous passions which school-girls have so often for their mistresses—yet touched in by the fierce mature lines of nature (the demonic line-drawings of an expert love which Justine could always oppose as a response to those who faced her)—she felt really the growing-pains of old age: her flesh and spirit quailing before demands which it knows it cannot meet, which will tear it to rags. Inside herself she had the first stirrings of a sensation new to her: the sensation of a yolk inside her separating from the egg. These are the strange ways in which people grow up.

Poor dear, she was to go through the same ridiculous contortions as the rest of us—feeling her body like a bed of quicklime clumsily slaked to burn away the corpse of the criminal it covered. The world of secret meetings, of impulses that brand one like an iron, of doubts—this suddenly descended upon her. So great was her confusion of mind that she would sit and stare at the metamorphosed Justine and try to remember what she really looked like on the other side of the transforming membrane, the cataract with which Aphrodite seals up the sick eyes of lovers, the thick, opaque form of a sacred sightlessness.

She would be in a fever all day until the appointed moment when her model met her. At four she stood before the closed door of the studio, seeing clearly through it to the corner where Justine already sat, turning over the pages of a *Vogue* and smoking as she waited, legs crossed. The idea crossed her mind. "I pray to God she has not come, is ill, has gone away. How eagerly I would welcome indifference!" Surprised too, for these disgusts came from precisely the same quarters as the desire to hear once more that hoarse noble voice—they too arose only from the expectation of seeing her beloved once more. These polarities of feeling bewildered and frightened her by their suddenness.

Then sometimes she wished to go away simply in order to belong more fully to her familiar! Poor fool, she was not spared anything in the long catalogue of self-deceptions which constitute a love affair. She tried to fall back on other pleasures, to find that none existed. She knew that the heart wearies of monotony, that habit and despair are the bedfellows of love, and she waited patiently, as a very old woman might, for the flesh to outgrow its promptings, to deliver itself from an attachment which she now recognised was not of her seeking. Waited in vain. Each day she plunged deeper. Yet all this, at any rate, performed one valuable service for her, proving that relationships like these did not answer the needs of her nature. Just as a man knows inside himself from the first hour that he has married the wrong woman but that there is nothing to be done about it. She knew she was a woman at last and belonged to men—and this gave her misery a fugitive relief.

But the distortions of reality were deeply interesting to someone who recognised that for the artist in herself some confusions of sensibility were valuable. "Walking towards the studio she would suddenly feel herself becoming breathlessly insubstantial, as if she were a figure painted on canvas. Her breathing became painful. Then after a moment she was overtaken by a feeling of happiness and well-being so intense that she seemed to have become weightless. Only the weight of her shoes, it seemed, held her to the ground. At any moment she might fly off the earth's surface, breaking through the membrane of gravity, unable to stop. This feeling was so piercing that she had to stop and hold on to the nearest wall and then to walk along it bent double like someone on the deck of a liner in a hurricane. This was itself succeeded by other disagreeable sensations—as of a hot clamp round her skull, pressing it, of the beating of wings in her ears. Half-dreaming in bed, suddenly horns rammed downward into her brain, impaling her mind; in a brazen red glare she saw the bloodshot eyes of the mithraic animal. It was a cool night with soft pockets of chemical light in the Arab town. The Ginks were abroad with their long oiled plaits and tinselled clothes; the faces of black angels; the men-women of the suburbs." (I copy these words from the diary of a female mental patient who came under Balthazar's professional care—a nervous breakdown due to "love"—requited or unrequited who can say? Does it matter?

The aetiology of love and madness are identical except in degree, and this passage could serve not only for Clea but indeed for all of us.

But it was not only of the past that Justine spoke but of a present which was weighing upon her full of decisions which must be taken. In a sense, everything that Clea felt was at this time meaningless to her. As a prostitute may be unaware that her client is a poet who will immortalize her in a sonnet she will never read, so Justine in pursuing these deeper sexual pleasures was unaware that they would mark Clea for years: enfeeble her in her power of giving undivided love—what she was most designed to give by temperament. Her youth, you see. And yet the wretched creature meant no harm. She was simply a victim of that Oriental desire to please, to make this golden friend of hers free of treasures which her own experience had gathered and which, in sum, were as yet meaningless to her. She gave everything, knowing the value of nothing, a true *parvenue* of the soul. To love (from any quarter) she could respond, but only with the worn felicities of friendship. Her body really meant nothing to her. It was a dupe. Her modesty was supreme. This sort of giving is really shocking because it is as simple as an Arab, without precociousness, unrefined as a drinking habit among peasants. It was born long before the idea of love was formed in the fragmented psyche of European man—the knowledge (or invention) of which was to make him the most vulnerable of creatures in the scale of being, subject to hungers which could only be killed by satiety, but never satisfied; which nourished a literature of affectation whose subject-matter would otherwise have belonged to religion—its true sphere of operation. How does one say these things?

Nor, in another scale of reference, is it of the slightest importance—that a woman disoriented by the vagaries of her feelings, tormented, inundated by frightening aspects of her own unrecognised selves, should like a soldier afraid of death,

56

throw herself into the heart of the *mêlée* to wound those whom truly she most loved and most admired—Clea, myself, lastly Nessim. Some people are born to bring good and evil in greater measure than the rest of us—the unconscious carriers of diseases they cannot cure. I think perhaps we must study them, for it is possible that they promote creation in the very degree of the apparent corruption and confusion they spread or seek. I dare not say even now that she was stupid or unfeeling; only that she could not recognise what passed within herself ("the camera obscura of the heart"), could not put a precise frame around the frightening image of her own meaninglessness in the world of ordinary action. The sort of abyss which seemed to lie around her was composed of one quality—a failure of value, a failure to attach meaning which kills joy—which is itself only the internal morality of a soul which has discovered the royal road to happiness, whose nakedness does not shame itself. It is easy for me to criticise now that I see a little further into the truth of her predicament and my own. She must, I know, have been bitterly ashamed of the trick she was playing on me and the danger into which she put me. Once at the Café El Bab where we were sitting over an *arak*, talking, she burst into tears and kissed my hands, saying: "You are a good man, really a good man. And I am so sorry." For what? For her tears? I had been speaking about Goethe. Fool! Imbecile! I thought I had perhaps moved her by the sensibility with which I expressed myself. I gave her presents. So had Clea, so did Clea now: and the strange thing was that for the first time her taste in choosing objects of *vertu* deserted this most gifted and sensitive of painters. Ear-rings and brooches of a commonness which was truly Alexandrian! I am at a loss to understand this phenomenon, unless to love is to become besotted. . . .

But then I don't know; I am reminded of Balthazar's dry marginal comment on the matter. "One is apt" he writes, "to take a high moral tone about these things—but in fact, who will criticise himself for reaching up to pluck an apple lying ripe upon a sun-warmed wall? Most women of Justine's temperament and background would not have the courage to imitate her even if they were free to do so. Is it more or less expensive to the spirit to endure dreams and Petit Mal so that the physician will always find a hot forehead and a guilty air? I don't know. It is hard to isolate a moral quality in the free act. And then again, all love-making to one less instructed than oneself has the added delicious thrill which comes from the consciousness of perverting, of pulling them down into the mud from which passions rise—together with poems and theories of God. It is wiser perhaps not to make a judgment."

But outside all this, in the sphere of daily life, there were problems about which Justine herself needed reassurance. "I am astonished and a little horrified that Nessim whom I hardly know, has asked to marry me. Am I to laugh, dearest Clea, or be ashamed, or both?" Clea in her innocence was delighted at the news for Nessim was her dearest friend and the thought of him bringing his dignity and gentleness to bear on the very real unhappiness of Justine's life seemed suddenly illuminating —a solution to everything. When one invites rescue by the mess one creates around oneself, what better than that a knight should be riding by? Justine put her hands over her eyes and said with difficulty "For a moment my heart leapt up and I was about to shout 'yes'; ah, Clea my dear, you will guess why. I need his riches to trace the child—really, somewhere in the length and breadth of Egypt it must be, suffering terribly, alone, perhaps ill-treated." She began to cry and then stopped abruptly, angrily. "In order to safeguard us both from what would be a disaster I said to Nessim 'I could never love a man like you: I could never give you an instant's happiness. Thank you and good-bye.' "

"But are you sure?"

"To use a man for his fortune, by God I'll never."

"Justine, what do you want?"

"First the child. Then to escape from the eyes of the world into some quiet corner where I can possess myself. There are whole parts of my character I do not understand. I need time. To-day again Nessim has written to me. What can he want? He knows all about me."

The thought crossed Clea's mind: "The most dangerous thing in the world is a love founded on pity." But she dismissed it and allowed herself to see once more the image of this gentle, wise, undissimulating man breasting the torrent of Justine's misfortunes and damming them up. Am I unjust in crediting her with another desire which such a solution would satisfy? (Namely, to be rid of Justine, free from the demands she made upon her heart and mind. She had stopped painting altogether.) The kindness of Nessim—the tall dark figure which drifted unresponsively around the corridors of society—needed some such task; how could a knight of the order born acquit himself if there were no castles and no desponding maidens weaving in them? Their preoccupations matched in everything—save the demand for love.

"But the money is nothing" she said; and here indeed she was speaking of what she knew to be precisely true of Nessim. He himself did not really care about the immense fortune which was his. But here one should add that he had already made a gesture which had touched and overwhelmed Justine. They met more than once, formally, like business partners, in the lounge of the Cecil Hotel to discuss the matter of this marriage with the detachment of Alexandrian brokers planning a cotton merger. This is the way of the city. We are mental people, and worldly, and have always made a clear distinction between the passional life and the life of the family. These distinctions are part of the whole complex of Mediterranean life, ancient and touchingly prosaic.

"And lest an inequality of fortune should make your decision

59

difficult," said Nessim, flushing and lowering his head, "I propose to make you a birthday present which will enable you to think of yourself as a wholly independent person—simply as a woman, Justine. This hateful stuff which creeps into everyone's thoughts in the city, poisoning everything! Let us be free of it before deciding anything." He passed across the table a slim green cheque with the words "Three Thousand Pounds" written on it. She stared at it for a long time with surprise but did not touch it. "It has not offended you" he said hastily, at last, stammering in his anxiety. "No" she said. "It is like everything you do. Only what can I do about not loving you?"

"You must, of course, never try to."

"Then what sort of life could we make?"

Nessim looked at her with hot shy eyes and then lowered his glance to the table, as if under a cruel rebuke. "Tell me" she said after a silence. "Please tell me. I cannot use your fortune and your position and give you nothing in exchange, Nessim."

"If you would care to try," he said gently, "we need not delude each other. Life isn't very long. One owes it to oneself to try and find a means to happiness."

"Is it that you want to sleep with me?" asked Justine suddenly: disgusted yet touched beyond measure by his tone. "You may. Yes. O! I would do anything for you, Nessim—anything."

But he flinched and said: "I am speaking about an understanding in which friendship and knowledge can take the place of love until and if it comes as I hope. Of course I shall sleep with you—myself a lover, and you a friend. Who knows? In a year perhaps. All Alexandrian marriages are business ventures after all. My God, Justine, what a fool you are. Can't you see that we might possibly need each other without ever fully realising it? It's worth trying. Everything may stand in the way. But I can't get over the thought that in the whole city the woman I most *need* is you. There are any number a man may want, but to want is not to need. I may want others—you I need! I do not dare to say the same for you. How cruel life is, and how absurd." Nobody had said anything like that to her before—had offered her a partnership as coolly designed, as wholly pure in intention. It must be admired from this point of view. "You are not the sort of man to stake everything on a single throw at *rouge et noir*" she said slowly. "Our bankers who are so brilliant with money are notoriously weak in the head when it comes to women." She put her hand upon his wrist. "You should have your doctor examine you, my dear. To take on a woman who has said that she can never love you—what sort of temerity is that? Ah, no!"

He did not say anything at all, recognising that her words were really not addressed to him: they were part of a long internal argument with herself. How beautiful her disaffected face looked—chloroformed by its own simplicity: she simply could not believe that someone might value her for herself—if she had a self. He was indeed, he thought, like a gambler putting everything on the turn of a wheel. She was standing now upon the very edge of a decision, like a sleepwalker on a cliff: should she awake before she jumped, or let the dream continue? Being a woman, she still felt it necessary to pose conditions; to withdraw herself further into secrecy as this man encroached upon it with his steady beguiling gentleness. "Nessim," she said, "wake up." And she shook him gently.

"I am awake" he said quietly.

Outside in the square with its palms nibbled by the sea-wind, a light rain was falling. It was the tenth Zu-el-Higga, the first day of Courban Bairam, and fragments of the great procession were assembling in their coloured robes, holding the great silk banners and censers, insignia of the religion they honoured, and chanting passages from the litany: litany of the forgotten Nubian race which every year makes its great resurrection at the Mosque of Nebi Daniel. The crowd was brilliant, spotted with primary colours. The air rippled with tambourines, while here and there in the lags of silence which fell over the shouts and chanting, there came the sudden jabbering of the long drums as their hide was slowly stiffened at the hissing braziers. Horses moaned and the gonfalons bellied like sails in the rain-starred afternoon. A cart filled with the prostitutes of the Arab town in coloured robes went by with shrill screams and shouts, and the singing of painted young men to the gnash of cymbals and scribbling of mandolines: the whole as gorgeous as a tropical animal.

"Nessim" she said foolishly. "On one sole condition—that we sleep together absolutely to-night." His features drew tight against his skull and he set his teeth tightly as he said angrily: 'You should have some intelligence to go with your lack of breeding—where is it?"

"I'm sorry" seeing how deeply and suddenly she had annoyed him. "I felt in need of reassurance." He had become quite pale.

"I proposed something so different" he said, replacing the cheque in his wallet. "I am rather staggered by your lack of understanding. Of course we can sleep together if you wish to make it a condition. Let us take a room at the hotel here, now, this minute." He looked really splendid when he was wounded like this, and suddenly there stirred inside her the realisation that his quietness was not weakness, and that an uncommon sort of sensibility underlay these confusing thoughts and deliberate words, perhaps not altogether good, either. "What could we prove to each other" he went on more gently, "by it or by its opposite: never making love?" She saw now how hopelessly out of context her words had been. "I'm bitterly ashamed of my vulgarity." She said this without really meaning the words, as a concession to his world as much as to himself—a world which dealt in the refinements of manners she was as yet too coarse to enjoy, which could afford to cultivate emotions *posées* by taste. A world which could only be knocked off its feet when you were skin to skin with it, so to speak! No, she did not mean the words, for vulgar as the idea sounded, she knew that she was right by the terms of her intuition since the thing she proposed is really, for women, the vital touchstone to a man's being; the knowledge, not of his qualities which can be analysed or inferred, but of the very flavour of his personality. Nothing except the act of physical love tells us this truth about one another. She bitterly regretted his unwisdom in denying her a concrete chance to see for herself what underlay his beauty and persuasion. Yet how could one insist?

"Good," he said, "for our marriage will be a delicate affair, and very much a question of manners, until——"

"I'm sorry," she said, "I really did not know how to treat honourably with you and avoid disappointing you."

He kissed her lightly on the mouth as he stood up. "I must go first and get the permission of my mother, and tell my brother. I am terribly happy, even though now I am furious with you."

They went out to the car together and Justine suddenly felt very weak, as if she had been carried far out of her depth and abandoned in mid-ocean. "I don't know what more to say."

"Nothing. You must start living" he said as the car began to draw away, and she felt as if she had received a smack across the mouth. She went into the nearest coffee-shop and ordered a cup of hot chocolate which she drank with trembling hands. Then she combed her hair and made up her face. She knew her beauty was only an advertisement and kept it fresh with disdain. No, somewhere she was truly a woman.

Nessim took the lift up to his office, and sitting down at his desk wrote upon a card the following words: "My dearest Clea, Justine has agreed to marry me. I could never do this if I thought it would qualify or interfere in any way with either her love for you or mine. . . ."

Then, appalled by the thought that whatever he might write to Clea might sound mawkish, he tore the note up and folded his arms. After a long moment of thought he picked up the polished telephone and dialled Capodistria's number. "Da Capo" he said quietly. "You remember my plans for marrying Justine? All is well." He replaced the receiver slowly, as if it weighed a ton, and sat staring at his own reflection in the polished desk.

o   o   o   o   o

IV

It was now, having achieved the major task of persuasion, that his self-assurance fled and left him face to face with a sensation entirely new to him, namely an acute shyness, an acute unwillingness to face his mother directly, to confront her with his intentions. He himself was puzzled by it, for they had always been close together, their confidences linked by an affection too deep to need the interpretation of words. If he had ever been shy or awkward it was with his awkward brother, never with her. And now? It was not as if he even feared her disfavour—he knew she would fall in with his wishes as soon as they were spoken. What then inhibited him? He could not tell. Yet he flushed as he thought of her now, and passed the whole of that morning in restless automatic acts, picking up a novel only to lay it down, mixing a drink only to abandon it, starting to sketch and then abruptly dropping the charcoal to walk out into the garden of the great house, ill at ease. He had telephoned his office to say that he was indisposed and then, as always when he had told a lie, began to suffer in truth with an attack of indigestion.

Then he started to ask for the number of the old country house where Leila and Narouz lived, but changed his mind and asked the operator instead for the number of his garage. The car would be back, they told him, cleaned and greased by noon. He lay down and covered his face with his hands. Then he rang up Selim, his secretary, and told him to telephone to his brother and say that he was coming to Karm Abu Girg for the week-end. Heavens! what could be more normal? "You go on like a chambermaid who has got engaged" he told himself hotly. Then for a moment he thought of taking someone with him to ease the strain of the meeting—Justine? Impossible. He picked up a novel of Pursewarden's and came upon the phrase: "Love is like trench warfare—you cannot see the enemy, but you know he is there and that it is wiser to keep your head down."

The doorbell rang. Selim brought him some letters to sign and then went silently upstairs to pack his bag and briefcase. There were papers he must take for Narouz to see—papers about the lift machinery needed to drain and reclaim the desert which fringed the plantations. Business matters were a welcome drug.

The Hosnani fortunes were deployed in two directions, separated into two spheres of responsibility, and each brother had his own. Nessim controlled the banking house and its ancillaries all over the Mediterranean, while Narouz lived the life of a Coptic squire, never stirring from Karm Abu Girg where the Hosnani lands marched with the fringe of the desert, gradually eating into it, expropriating it year by year, spreading their squares of cultivation—carob and melon and corn—and pumping out the salt which poisoned it.

"The car is here" said the hawk-faced secretary as he returned. "Am I to drive you sir?" Nessim shook his head and dismissed him quietly, before crossing the garden once more, chin in hand. He paused by the lily pond to study the fish—those expensive toys of the ancient Japanese Emperors, survivals from an age of luxury, which he had imported at such cost, only to find them gradually dying off of some unknown illness —homesickness, perhaps? Pursewarden spent hours watching them. He said that they helped him to think about art!

The great silver car stood at the door with the ignition key in the dashboard. He got in thoughtfully and drove slowly across the town, examining its parks and squares and buildings with a serene eye, but deliberately dawdling, irresolutely, emptying his mind by an act of will every time the

66

thought of his destination came upon him. When he reached the sea he turned at last down the shining Corniche in the sunlight to watch the smooth sea and cloudless air for a moment, the car almost at a standstill. Then suddenly he changed gear and began to travel along the sea-shore at a more resolute pace. He was going home.

Soon he turned inland, leaving the town with its palms crackling in the spring wind and turning towards the barren network of faults and dried-out lake-beds where the metalled road gave place to the brown earth tracks along embankments lined with black swamps and fringed by barbed reeds and a cross-hatching of sweet-corn plantations. The dust came up between his wheels and filled the air of the saloon, coating every-thing in a fine-grained pollen. The windscreen became gradually snowed-up and he switched on the wipers to keep it clear.

Following little winding lanes which he knew by heart he came, after more than an hour, to the edge of a spit flanked by bluer water and left the car in the shadow of a tumbledown house, the remains perhaps of some ancient customs-shed built in the days when river traffic plied between Damietta and the Gulf: now drying up day by day, withering and cracking under the brazen Egyptian sky, forgotten by its keepers.

He locked the car carefully and followed a narrow path across a holding of poverty-stricken beanrows and dusty melons, fringed with ragged and noisy Indian corn, to come out upon a landing-stage where an aged ferryman awaited him in a ramshackle boat. At once he saw the horses waiting upon the other side, and the foreshortened figure of Narouz beside them. He threw up an excited arm in an awkward gesture of pleasure as he saw Nessim. Nessim stepped into the boat with beating heart.

"Narouz!" The two brothers, so unlike in physique and looks, embraced with feeling which was qualified in Nessim by the silent agony of a shyness new to him.

The younger brother, shorter and more squarely built than Nessim, wore a blue French peasant's blouse open at the throat and with the sleeves rolled back, exposing arms and hands of great power covered by curly dark hair. An old Italian cartridge bandolier hung down upon his haunches. The ends of his baggy Turkish trousers with an old-fashioned drawstring, were stuffed into crumpled old jackboots of soft leather. He ducked, excitedly, awkwardly, into his brother's arms and out again, like a boxer from a clinch. But when he raised his head to look at him, you saw at once what it was that had ruled Narouz' life like a dark star. His upper lip was split literally from the spur of the nose—as if by some terrific punch: it was a hare-lip which had not been caught up and basted in time. It exposed the ends of a white tooth and ended in two little pink tongues of flesh in the centre of his upper lip which were always wet. His dark hair grew down low and curly, like a heifer's, on to his brow. His eyes were splendid: of a blueness and innocence that made them almost like Clea's: indeed his whole ugliness took splendour from them. He had grown a ragged and uneven moustache over his upper lip, as someone will train ivy over an ugly wall—but the scar showed through wherever the hair was thin: and his short, unsatisfactory beard too was a poor disguise: looked simply as if he had remained unshaven for a week. It had no shape of its own and confused the outlines of his taurine neck and high cheekbones. He had a curious hissing shy laugh which he always pointed downward into the ground to hide his lip. The whole sum of his movements was ungainly—arms and legs somewhat curved and hairy as a spider—but they gave off a sensation of overwhelming strength held rigidly under control. His voice was deep and thrilling and held something of the magic of a woman's contralto.

Whenever possible they tried to have servants or friends with them when they met—to temper their shyness; and so to-day Narouz had brought Ali, his factor, with the horses to meet the ferry. The old servant with the cropped ears took a pinch of dust from the ground before Nessim's feet and pressed it to his forehead before extending his hand for a handshake, and then diffidently partook of the embrace Nessim offered him—as someone he had loved from his childhood onwards. Narouz was charmed by his brother's easy, comradely but feeling gesture—and he laughed downwards into the ground with pleasure.

"And Leila?" said Nessim, in a low voice, raising his fingers to his temple for a moment as he did so.

"Is well" said Narouz in the tone that springs from a freshly rosined bow. "This past two months. Praise God."

Their mother sometimes went through periods of mental instability lasting for weeks, always to recover again. It was a quiet surrender of the real world that surprised no-one any longer, for she herself now knew when such an attack was coming on and would make preparations for it. At such times, she spent all day in the little hut at the end of the rose-garden, reading and writing, mostly the long letters which Mountolive read with such tenderness in Japan or Finland or Peru. With only the cobra for company, she waited until the influence of the *afreet* or spirit was spent. This habit had lasted for many years now, since the death of their father and her illness, and neither son took any account of these departures from the normal life of the great house. "Leila is well in her mind" said Narouz again in that thrilling voice. "So happy too that Mountolive is back. She looks years younger."

"I understand."

The two brothers now mounted their horses and started slowly along the network of embankments and causeways which led them over the lake with its panels of cultivation. Nessim always loved this ride for it evoked his real childhood—so much richer in variety and beauty than those few years spent in the house at Aboukir where Leila had moved for a while after their father's death. "All your new lift pumps should be here next month" he shouted, and Narouz chuckled with pleasure; but with another part of his mind he allowed the soft black earthworks of the river with its precarious tracks separating the squares of cultivated soil to lead him steadily back to the remembered treasures of his childhood here. For this was really Egypt—a Copt's Egypt—while the white city, as if in some dusty spectrum, was filled with the troubling and alien images of lands foreign to it—the intimations of Greece, Syria, Tunis.

It was a fine day and shallow draught boats were coursing among the beanfields towards the river tributaries, with their long curved spines of mast, lateen rigs bent like bows in the freshets. Somewhere a boatman sang and kept time on a finger-drum, his voice mixing with the sighing of *sakkias* and the distant village bangings of wheelwrights and carpenters manufacturing disc-wheels for wagons or the shallow-bladed ploughs which worked the alluvial riverside holdings.

Brilliant kingfishers hunted the shallows like thunderbolts, their wings slurring, while here and there the small brown owls, having forgotten the night habits of their kind, flew between the banks, or nestled together in songless couples among the trees.

The fields had begun to spread away on either side of the little cavalcade now, green and scented with their rich crops of *bercim* and beanrows, though the road still obstinately followed along the banks of the river so that their reflections rode with them. Here and there were hamlets whose houses of unbaked mud wore flat roofs made brilliant now by stacks of Indian corn which yellowed them. They passed an occasional line of camels moving down towards a ferry, or a herd of great black *gamoose*—Egyptian buffalo—dipping their shiny noses in the rich ooze and filth of some backwater, flicking the flies from their papery skins with lead tails. Their great curved horns belonged to forgotten frescoes.

It was strange now how slowly life moved here, he reflected with pleasure as he moved towards the Hosnani property—women churning butter in goatskins suspended from bamboo tripods or walking in single file down to the river with their pots. Men in robes of blue cotton at the waterwheels, singing, matrons swathed from crown to ankle in the light dusty black robes which custom demanded, blue-beaded against the evil eye. And then all the primeval courtesies of the road exchanged between passers-by to which Narouz responded in his plangent voice, sounding as if it belonged to the language as much as to the place. "*Naharak Said!*" he cried cheerfully, or "*Said Embarak!*" as the wayfarers smiled and greeted them. "May your day be blessed" thought Nessim in remembered translation as he smiled and nodded, overcome at the splendour of these old-fashioned greetings one never heard except in the Arab quarter of the city; "may to-day be as blessed as yesterday."

He turned and said "Narouz" and his brother rode up beside him tenderly, saying "Have you seen my whip?" Laughing downwards again, his tooth showing through the rent in his lip. He carried a splendid hippopotamus-hide whip, loosely coiled at his saddle-bow. "I found the perfect one—after three years. Sheik Bedawi sent it down from Assuan. Do you know?" He turned those brilliant blue eyes upwards for a moment to stare into the dark eyes of his brother with intense joy. "It is better than a pistol, at any rate a ·99" he said, thrilled as a child. "I've been practising hard with it—do you want to see?"

Without waiting for an answer he tucked his head down and rode forward at a trot to where some dozen chickens were scratching at the bare ground near a herdsman's cot. A frightened rooster running faster than the others took off under his horse's hooves: Nessim reined back to watch. Narouz' arm shot up, the long lash uncurled slowly on the air and then went rigid with a sudden dull welt of sound, a sullen thwack, and laughing, the rider dismounted to pick up the mutilated creature, still warm and palpitating, its wings half-severed from its body, its head smashed. He brought it back to Nessim in triumph, wiping his hand casually on his baggy trousers. "What do you think?" Nessim gripped and admired the great whip while his brother threw the dead fowl to his factor, still laughing himself, and so slowly remounted. They rode side by side now, as if the spell upon their communication were broken, and Nessim talked of the new machinery which had been ordered and heard of Narouz' battle against drought and sand-drift. In such neutral subjects they could lose themselves and become natural. United most closely by such topics, they were like two blind people in love who can only express themselves through touch: the subject of their lands.

The holdings became richer now, planted out with tamarisk and carob, though here and there they passed the remains of properties abandoned by owners too poor or too lazy to contend with the deserts, which encircled the fertile strip on three sides. Old houses, fallen now into desuetude, abandoned and overgrown, stared out across the water with unframed windows and shattered doors. Their gates, half-smothered in bougain-villaea, opened rustily into gardens of wild and unkempt beauty where marble fountains and rotted statuary still testified to a glory since departed. On either side of them one could glimpse the well-wooded lands which formed the edge, the outer perimeter of the family estates—palm, acacia and syca-more which still offered the precarious purchase to life which without shade and water perished, reverted to the desert. Indeed, one was conscious of the desert here although one could not see it—melodramatically tasteless as a communion wafer.

Here an old island with a ruined palace; there tortuous paths and channels of running water where the slim bird-forms of river-craft moved about their task of loading *tibbin* (corn); they were nearing the village now. A bridge rose high upon mud-banks, crowned by a magnificent grove of palms, with a row of coloured boats waiting for the boom to lift. Here on the rise one glimpsed for a moment the blue magnetic haze of a desert horizon lying beyond this hoarded strip of plenty, of green plantations and water.

Round a corner they came upon a knot of villagers waiting for them who set up cries of "What honour to the village!" and "You bring blessings!" walking beside them as they rode smiling onwards. Some advanced on them, the notables, catching a hand to kiss, and some even kissing Nessim's stirrup-irons. So they passed through the village against its patch of emerald water and dominated by the graceful fig-shaped minaret, and the cluster of dazzling beehive domes which distinguished the Coptic church of their forefathers. From here, the road turned back again across the fields to the great house within its weather-stained outer walls, ruined and crumbling with damp in many places, and in others covered by such *graffiti* as the superstitious leave to charm the *afreet*—black talismanic handprints, or the legend *"B'ism'illah ma'sha'llah"* (may God avert evil). It was for these pious villagers that its tenants had raised on the corners of the wall tiny wooden windmills in the shape of men with revolving arms, to scare the *afreet* away. This was the manor-house of Karm Abu Girg which belonged to them.

Emin, the chief steward, was waiting at the outer gate with the usual gruff greetings which custom demanded, surrounded by a group of shy boys to hold the horses and help their riders dismount.

The great folding doors of the courtyard with their pistol bolts and inscribed panels were set back so that they could walk directly into the courtyard against which the house itself was built, tilted upon two levels—the ceremonial first floor looking down sideways along the vaulted arches below—a courtyard with its granaries and reception-rooms, storehouses and stables. Nessim did not cross the threshold before examining once more the faded but still visible cartoons which decorated the wall at the right-hand side of it—and which depicted in a series of almost hieroglyphic signs the sacred journey he had made to bathe in the Jordan: a horse, a motor-car, a ship, an aeroplane, all crudely represented. He muttered a pious text, and the little group of servants smiled with satisfaction, understanding by this that his long residence in the city had not made him forget country ways. He never forgot to do this. It was like a man showing his passport. And Narouz too was grateful for the tact such a gesture showed—which not only endeared his brother to the dependants of the house, but also strengthened his own position with them as the ruling master of it.

On the other side of the lintel, a similar set of pictures showed that he also, the younger brother, had made the pious pilgrimage which is incumbent upon every Copt of religious principles.

The main gateway was flanked on each side by a pigeon-tower—those clumsy columns built of earthen pitchers pasted together anyhow with mud-cement: which are characteristic of country houses in Egypt and which supplied the choicest dish for the country squire's table. A cloud of its inhabitants fluttered and crooned all day over the barrel-vaulted court. Here all was activity: the negro night-watchman, the *ghaffirs*, factors, stewards came forth one by one to salute the eldest brother, the heir. He was given a bowl of wine and a nosegay of flowers while Narouz stood by proudly smiling.

Then they went at ceremonial pace through the gallery with its windows of many-coloured glass which for a brief moment transformed them into harlequins, and then out into the rose garden with its ragged and unkempt arbour and winding paths towards the little summer-house where Leila sat reading, unveiled. Narouz called her name once to warn her as they neared the house, adding "Guess who has come!" The woman quickly replaced her veil and turned her wise dark eyes towards the sunlit door saying: "The boy did not bring the milk again. I wish you would tell him, Narouz. His mind is salt. The snake must be fed regularly or it becomes ill-tempered." And then the voice, swerving like a bird in mid-air, foundered and fell to a rich melodious near-sob on the name "Nessim". And this she repeated twice as they embraced with such trembling tenderness that Narouz laughed, swallowing, and tasted both the joy of his brother's love for Leila and his own bitterness in realising that he, Nessim, was her favourite—the beautiful son. He was not jealous of Nessim; only heartsick at the melody in his mother's voice—the tone she had never used in speaking to him. It had always been so.

"I will speak to the boy" he said, and looked about him for signs of the snake. Egyptians regard the snake as too lucky a visitant to a house to kill and so tempt ill-luck, and Leila's long self-communing in the little summer-house would not have been complete without this indolent cobra which had learned to drink milk from a saucer like a cat.

Still holding hands they sat down together and Nessim started to speak of political matters with those dark, clever, youthful eyes looking steadily into his. From time to time, Leila nodded vigorously, with a determined air, while the younger son watched them both hungrily, with a heavy admiration at the concise way Nessim abbreviated and expressed his ideas—the fruit of a long public life. Narouz felt these abstract words fall dully upon his ear, fraught with meanings he only half-guessed, and though he knew that they concerned him as much as anyone, they seemed to him to belong to some rarer world inhabited by sophists or mathematicians—creatures

75

who would forge and give utterance to the vague longings and incoherent desires he felt forming inside him whenever Egypt was mentioned or the family estates. He sucked the knuckle of his forefinger, and sat beside them, listening, looking first at his mother and then back to Nessim.

"And now Mountolive is back," concluded Nessim, "and for the first time what we are trying to do will be understood. Leila—he will help us, if it is possible. He understands."

The name of Mountolive struck two ways. The woman lowered her eyes to her own white hands which lay before her upon a half-finished letter—eyes so brilliantly made up with kohl and antimony that to discern tears in them would have been difficult. Yet there were none. They sparkled only with affection. Was she thinking of those long letters which she had so faithfully written during the whole period of their separation? But Narouz felt a sudden stirring of jealousy in his brain at the mention of the name, under which, interred as if under a tombstone, he had hidden memories of a different epoch—of the young secretary of the High Commission whom his mother had—(mentally he never used the word "loved" but left a blank space in his thoughts where it should stand); moreover of the sick husband in the wheelchair who had watched so uncomplainingly. Narouz' soul vibrated with his father's passion when Mountolive's name, like a note of music, was struck. He swallowed and stirred uneasily now as he watched his mother tremblingly fold a letter and slide it into an envelope. "Can we trust him?" she asked Nessim. She would have struck him over the mouth if he had answered "No." She simply wanted to hear him pronounce the name again. Her question was a prompting, nothing more. He kissed her hand, and Narouz greedily admired his courtier's smiling air as he replied "If we cannot trust Mountolive, who can we trust?"

As a girl, Leila had been both beautiful and rich. The daughter of a blue-stocking, convent-bred and very much in society, she had been among the first Coptic women to abandon the veil and to start to take up the study of medicine against her parents' will. But an early marriage to a man very much older than herself had put an end to these excursions into the world of scope where her abilities might have given her a foothold. The temper of Egyptian life too was hostile to the freedom of women, and she had resigned a career in favour of a husband she very much admired and the uneventful round of country life. Yet somehow, under it all, the fire had burned on. She had kept friends and interests, had visited Europe every few years, had subscribed to periodicals in four languages. Her mind had been formed by solitude, enriched by books which she could only discuss in letters to friends in remote places, could only read in the privacy of the *harim*. Then came the advent of Mountolive and the death of her husband. She stood free and breathing upon the brink of a new world with no charge upon her but two growing sons. For a year she had hesitated between Paris and London as a capital of residence, and while she hesitated, all was lost. Her beauty, of which until then she had taken no particular account, as is the way with the beautiful, had been suddenly ravaged by a confluent smallpox which melted down those lovely features and left her only the magnificent eyes of an Egyptian sibyl. The black hideous veil which so long had seemed to her a symbol of servitude became now a refuge in which she could hide the ruins of a beauty which had been considered outstanding in her youth. She had not the heart now to parade this new melted face through the capitals of Europe, to brave the silent condolences of friends who might remember her as she had once been. Turned back upon her tracks so summarily, she had decided to stay on and end her life in the family estates in such seclusion as might be permitted to her. Her only outlet now would be in letter-writing and in reading—her only care the bringing up of her children. All the unsteadiness of her passions was canalized into this narrow field. A whole world of relations had to be mastered and she turned her resolution to it like a man. Ill-health, loneliness, boredom—she faced them one by one and overcame them—living here in retirement like a dethroned Empress, feeding her snake and writing her interminable letters which were full of the liveliness and sparkle of a life which now the veil masked and which could escape only through those youthful dark eyes.

She was now never seen in society and had become something of a legend amongst those who remembered her in the past, and who indeed had once nicknamed her the "dark swallow". Now she sat all day at a rough deal table, writing in that tall thoughtful handwriting, dipping her quill into a golden inkpot. Her letters had become her very life, and in the writing of them she had begun to suffer from that curious sense of distorted reality which writers have when they are dealing with real people; in the long years of writing to Mountolive, for example, she had so to speak re-invented him so successfully that he existed for her now not so much as a real human being but as a character out of her own imagination. She had even almost forgotten what he looked like, what to expect of his physical presence, and when his telegram came to say that he expected to be in Egypt again within a few months, she felt at first nothing but irritation that he should intrude, bodily as it were, upon the picture projected by her imagination. "I shall not see him" she muttered at first, angrily; and only then did she start to tremble and cover her ravaged face with her hands.

"Mountolive wants to see you" said Nessim, at last, as the conversation veered round in his direction again. "When may I bring him? The Legation is moving up to summer quarters soon, so he will be in Alexandria all the time."

"He must wait until I am ready" she said, once more feeling the anger stir in her at the intrusion of this beloved figment.

"After all these years." And then she asked with a pathetic lustful eagerness, "Is he old now—is he grey? Is his leg all right? Can he walk? That ski-ing fall in Austria. . . ."

To all this Narouz listened with cocked head and sullen heavy heart: he could follow the feeling in her voice as one follows a line of music.

"He is younger than ever," said Nessim, "hasn't aged by a day": and to his surprise she took his hand, and putting it to her cheek she said brokenly "Oh—you are horrible, horrible, both of you. Go. Leave me alone now. I have letters to write."

She permitted no mirrors in the *harim* since the illness which had deprived her of her self-esteem; but privately in a gold-backed pocket-mirror, she touched and pencilled her eyes in secret—her remaining treasure—practising different make-ups on them, practising different glances and matching them to different remarks—trying to give what was left of her looks a vocabulary as large as her lively mind. She was like a man struck suddenly blind learning to spell, with the only member left him, his hands.

Now the two men walked back into the old house, with its cool but dusty rooms whose walls were hung with ancient carpets and embroidered mats, and crowded with gigantic carcasses of furniture long since outmoded—a sort of Ottoman Buhl such as one sees in the old houses of Egypt. Nessim's heartstrings were tugged by the memory of its ugliness, its old-fashioned Second Empire pieces and its jealously guarded routines. The steward, according to custom, had stopped all the clocks. This, in the language of Narouz, said "Your stay with us is so brief, let us not be reminded of the flight of the hours. God made eternity. Let us escape from the despotism of time altogether." These ancient and hereditary politenesses filled Nessim with emotion. Even the primitive sanitary arrangements—there were no bathrooms—seemed to him

79

somehow in keeping with the character of things, though he loved hot water. Narouz himself slept naked winter and summer. He washed in the courtyard—a servant threw water over him from a pitcher. Indoors, he usually wore an old blue cloak and Turkish slippers. He smoked tobacco too in a narguileh the length of a musket.

While the elder brother unpacked his clothes, Narouz sat on the end of the bed studying the papers which filled the brief-case, musing with a quiet intentness, for they related to the machinery with the help of which he proposed to keep up and extend his attack on the dead sand. In the back of his mind he could see an army of trees and shrubs marching steadily forward into the emptiness—carob and olive, vine and jujube, pistachio, peach and apricot, spreading around them the green colours of quickness in those tenantless areas of dust choked with sea-salt. He looked almost lustfully upon the pictures of equipment in the shiny brochures Nessim had brought him, lovingly touching them with his finger, hearing in his imagination the suck and swell of sweet water through pumps gradually expressing the dead salts from the ground and quickening it to nourish the sipping roots of his trees. Gebel Maryut, Abusir—his mind winged away like a swallow across the dunes into the Nitrian desert itself—mentally conquering it.

"The desert" said Narouz. "By the way, will you ride out with me to the tents of Abu Kar to-morrow? I have been promised an Arab and I want to break it myself. It would make a pleasant excursion." Nessim was at once delighted at the prospect. "Yes" he said. "But early," said Narouz, "and we can pass the olive plantation for you to see what progress we're making. Will you? Please do!" He squeezed his arm. "Since we started with the Tunisian *chimlali* we haven't had a single casualty. Oh, Nessim! I wish you stayed here. Your place is here."

Nessim as always was beginning to wish the same. That night they dined in the old-fashioned way—so different from

80

the impertinent luxury of Alexandrian forms—each taking his napkin from the table and proceeding to the yard for the elaborate handwashing ceremony which preceded a meal in the country. Two servants poured for them as they stood side by side, washing their fingers with yellow soap, and rinsed them off with orange-water. Then to the table where their only cutlery was a wooden spoon each for dealing with soup—otherwise they broke the flat thin cakes of the country to dip into the dishes of cooked meats. Leila had always dined alone in the women's quarters, and retired to bed early so that the two brothers were left alone to their repast. They ate in leisurely fashion, with long pauses between the courses, and Narouz acted host, placing choice morsels upon Nessim's plate and breaking up the fowl and the turkey with his strong fingers the better to serve his guest. At last, when sweetmeats and fruit had been served, they returned once more to where the waiting servants stood and washed their hands again.

In the interval, the table had been cleared of dishes and set back to make room for the old-fashioned divans to pass through the room and out on to the balcony. Smoking materials had been set out—the long-barrelled narguilehs with Narouz' favourite tobacco and a silver dish of sweets. Here they sat together for a while in silence to drink their coffee. Nessim had kicked off his slippers and drawn his legs up under him: he sat with his chin in his hand wondering how he could impart his news, the marriage which nibbled at the edge of his mind: and whether he should be frank about his motives in choosing for a wife a woman who was of a different faith from his own. The night was hot and still, and the scent of magnolia blossom came up to the balcony in little drifts and eddies of air which made the candles flutter and dance; he was gnawed by irresolution.

In such a mood every promise of distraction offered relief, and he was pleased when Narouz suggested that the village singer should be called to play for them, a custom which they had so often enjoyed as youths. There is nothing more appropriate to the heavy silence of the Egyptian night than the childish poignance of the *kemengeh's* note. Narouz clapped his hands and despatched a message and presently the old man came from the servant's quarters where he dined each night on the charity of the house, walking with the slow and submissive step of extreme old age and approaching blindness. The sounding-board of his small viol was made from half a coconut. Narouz sprang up and settled him upon a cushion at the end of the balcony. There came footsteps in the courtyard and a familiar voice, that of the old schoolmaster Mohammed Shebab who climbed the stairs, smiling and wrinkled, to clasp Narouz' hand. He had the bright hairy face of a monkey and wore, as usual, an immaculate dark suit with a rose in his button-hole. He was something of a dandy and an epicure and these visits to the great house were his only distraction, living as he did for the greater part of the year buried in the depths of the delta; he had brought the old treasured *narguileh* mouthpiece which he had owned for a quarter of a century. He was delighted to hear some music and listened with emotion to the wild *quasidas* that the old man sang—songs of the Arab canon full of the wild heart-sickness of the desert. The old voice, crumpled here and there like a fragile leaf, rose and fell upon the night; tracing the quavering melodic line of the songs as if it were following the ancient highways of half-obliterated thoughts and feelings. The little viol scribbled its complaints upon the text reaching back into their childhood. And now suddenly the singer burst into the passionate pilgrim song which expresses so marvellously the Moslem's longing for Mecca and his adoration of the Prophet—and the melody fluttered inside the brothers' hearts, imprisoned like a bird with beating wings. Narouz, though a Copt, was repeating "All-*ah*, All-*ah*!" in a rapture of praise.

82

"Enough, enough" cried Nessim at last. "If we are to be up early, we should sleep early, don't you think?"

Narouz sprang up too, and still acting the host, called for lights and water and walked before him to the guest-room. Here he waited until Nessim had washed and undressed and climbed into the creaking old-fashioned bed before bidding him good night. As he stood in the doorway, Nessim said impulsively: "Narouz—I've something to tell you." And then, overcome once more with shyness, added: "But it will keep until to-morrow. We shall be alone, shan't we?" Narouz nodded and smiled. "The desert is such torture for them that I always send them back at the fringe, the servants."

"Yes." Nessim well knew that Egyptians believe the desert to be an emptiness populated entirely by the spirits of demons and other grotesque visitants from Eblis, the Moslem Satan.

Nessim slept and awoke to find his brother, fully dressed, standing beside his bed with coffee and cigarettes. "It's time" he said. "I suppose in Alexandria you sleep late. . . ."

"No," said Nessim, "strangely enough I am usually at my office by eight."

"Eight! O! my poor brother" said Narouz mockingly, and helped him to dress. The horses were waiting and together they rode out upon a dawn with a thick bluish mist rising from the lake. Crisp air, inclining to frost—but already the sun was beginning to soak into the upper air and dry up the dew upon the minaret of the mosque.

Narouz led now, down winding ways, along the tortuous bridle paths, and across embankments, quite unerringly, for the whole land existed in his mind like the most detailed map by a master cartographer. He carried it always in his head like a battle-plan, knowing the age of every tree, the poundage of every well's water, the drift of sand to an inch. He was possessed by it.

Slowly they made a circuit of the great plantation, soberly assessing progress and discussing plans for the next offensive when the new machinery should be installed. And then, presently when they had come to a lonely spot by the river, screened on all sides by reeds, Narouz said "Wait a second ..." and dismounted, taking as he did so the old leather game-bag from his shoulders. "Something to hide" he said, smiling downwards shyly. Nessim watched him idly as he turned the bag over to tip its contents into the dank waters of the river. But he was not prepared to see a shrunken human head, lips drawn back over yellow teeth, eyes squinting inwards upon each other, roll out of the bag and sink slowly out of sight into the green depths beneath. "What the devil's that?" he asked, and Narouz gave his little hissing titter at the ground and replied: "Abdel-Kader—head of." He knelt down and started washing the bag out in the water, moving it vigorously to and fro, and then with a gesture turned it inside out as one might turn a sleeve and returned to his horse. Nessim was thinking deeply. "So you had to do it at last," he said, "I was afraid you might."

Narouz turned his brilliant eyes upon his brother for a moment and said seriously: "More troubles with Bedouin labour could have cost us a thousand trees next year. It was too much of a risk to take. Besides, he was going to poison me."

He said no more and they rode on in silence until they reached the thinning edges of cultivation—the front line so to speak where the battle was actually being joined at present—a long ragged territory like the edges of a wound. Along the whole length of it infiltration from the arable land on the one side and the desert drainage on the other, both charged with the rotten salts, had poisoned the ground and made it the image of desolation.

Here only giant reeds and bulrushes grew or an occasional thorn bush. No fish could live in the brackish water. Birds shunned it. It lay in the stagnant belt of its own foul air, weird, obsessive and utterly silent—the point at which the desert and the sown met in a death-embrace. They rode now among towering rushes whose stems were bleached and salt-encrusted, glittering in the sun. The horses gasped and scrambled through the dead water which splashed upon them, crystallizing into spots of salt wherever it fell; pools of slime were covered with a crust of salt through which their plunging hooves broke, releasing horrible odours from the black mud beneath and sudden swarms of small stinging flies and mosquitoes. But Narouz looked about him with interest even here, his eyes alight, for he had already mentally planted this waste with carobs and green shrubs—conquered it. But they both held their breath and did not speak as they traversed this last mephitic barrier and the long patches of wrinkled mummy-like soil to which it gave place. Then at last they were on the edge of the desert and they paused in shadow while Narouz. fished in his clothes for the little stick of blue billiard-marker's chalk. They rubbed a little chalk under each of their eyelids with a finger against the glare—as they had always done, even as children; and each tied a cloth around his head in Bedouin fashion.

And then: the first pure draughts of desert air, and the nakedness of space, pure as a theorem, stretching away into the sky drenched in all its own silence and majesty, untenanted except by such figures as the imagination of man has invented to people landscapes which are inimical to his passions and whose purity flays the mind.

Narouz gave a shout and the horses, suddenly awoken and filled with a sense of new freedom and space around them, started their peculiar tearing plunging gallop across the dunes, manes and tassels tossing, saddles creaking. They raced like this for many minutes, Nessim giggling with excitement and joy. It was so long since he had ridden at this wild gallop.

But they held it, completing a slow arc eastwards across scrubby land where wild flowers bloomed and butterflies tippled amongst the waste of dunes and the dingy tenacious specimens of plant-life. Their hooves rattled across shingle floors, through stone valleys with great sandstone needles and chines of rosy shale filling in the known horizons. Nessim was busy with his memories of those youthful nights camped out here under a sky hoary with stars, in a booming tent (whose frosted guy-ropes glittered like brilliants) pitched under Vega, the whole desert spread around them like an empty room. How did one come to forget the greatest of one's experiences? It was all lying there like a piano that one could play but which one had somehow forgotten to touch for years. He was irradiated by the visions of his inner eye and followed Narouz blindly. He saw them in all that immensity—two spots like pigeons flying in an empty sky.

They halted for a short rest in the shadow of a great rock— a purple oasis of darkness—panting and happy. "If we put up a desert wolf" said Narouz, "I'll run it down with my *kurbash*," and he caressed the great whip lovingly, running it through his fingers.

When they set off again, Narouz started a slow tacking path, questing about for the ancient caravan route—the *masrab* which would take them to the Quasur el Atash (Castles of the Thirsty) where the Sheik's men were due to meet them before noon. Once Nessim too had known these highways by heart—the smugglers' roads which had been used for centuries by the caravans which plied between Algiers and Mecca—the "bountiful highways" which steered the fortunes of men through the wilderness of the desert, taking spices and stuffs from one part of Africa to another or affording to the pious their only means of reaching the Holy City. He was suddenly jealous of his brother's familiarity with the desert they had once equally owned. He copied him eagerly.

Presently Narouz gave a hoarse shout and pointed and in a little while they came upon the *masrab*—a highway of camel-tracks, deeply worn in some places into solid rock, but running in a wavy series, parallel from horizon to horizon. And here once more the younger brother set the pace. His blue shirt was now stained violet at the armpits. "Nearly there" he cried, and out of the trembling pearly edges of the sky there swam slowly a high cluster of reddish basalt blocks, carved into the vague semblance (like a face in the fire) of a sphinx tortured by thirst; and there, gibbering in the dark shade of a rock, the little party waited to conduct them to the Sheik's tents—four tall lean men, made of brown paper, whose voices cracked at the edges of meaning with thirst, and whose laughter was like fury unleashed. To them they rode—into the embrace of arms like dry sticks and the thorny clicking of an unfamiliar Arabic in which Narouz did all the talking and explaining.

Nessim waited, feeling suddenly like a European, city-bred, a visitor: for the little party carried with them all the feeling of the tight inbred Arab world—its formal courtesies and feuds —its primitiveness. He surprised himself by seeking in his own mind the memory of a painting by Bonnard or a poem by Blake—as a thirsty man might grope at a spring for water. In such a way might a traveller present himself to some rude clan of Scotsmen, admiring their bunioned feet and coarse hairy legs, but grateful too that the sum of European culture was not expressed by their life-hating, unpleasure-loving strength. Here he suddenly lost his brother, parted company with him, for Narouz had plunged into the life of these Arabian herdsmen with the same intensity as he plunged into the life of his land, his trees. The great corded muscles in his hairy body were tense with pride, for he, a city-bred Alexandrian—almost a despised *Nasrany*—could out-shoot, out-talk and out-gallop any of them. On him whose mettle they knew they kept a speculative aboriginal eye; the gentle Nessim they had seen in many guises before, his well-kept hands betrayed a city gentleman. But they were polite.

A knowledge of forms only was necessary now, not insight, for these delightful desert folk were automata; thinking of Mountolive Nessim smiled suddenly and wondered where the British had found the substance of their myths about the desert Arab? The fierce banality of their lives was so narrow, so regulated. If they stirred one at all it was as the bagpipe can, without expressing anything above the level of the primitive. He watched his brother handle them, simply from a knowledge of their forms of behaviour as a showman handles dancing fleas. Poor souls! He felt the power and resource of his city-bred intelligence stir in him.

They all rode now in a compact group to the Sheik's tents, down long ribbed inclines of sand, through mirages of pastures which only the rain clouds imagined, until they came there, to the little circle of tents, manhood's skies of hide, invented by men whose childish memories were so fearful they had had perforce to invent a narrower heaven in which to contain the germ of the race; in this little cone of hide the first child was born, the first privacy of the human kiss invented. . . . Nessim wished bitterly that he could paint as well as Clea. Absurd thoughts, and out of place.

But the Sheik's tents were extensive, covering nearly two thousand square feet with a tent-cloth woven of goat-hair in broad stitches of black, green, maroon and white. Long tassels hung down from the seams, playing in the wind.

The Sheik and his sons, like a gallery of playing cards, awaited them with the conventional greetings to which Narouz at least knew every response. The Sheik himself conducted them to a tent saying "This house is your house; do as you please. We are your servants." And behind him pressed the water-carriers to bathe their hands and feet and faces—the latter now somewhat dry and blistered by the journey. They rested for at least an hour, for the heat of the day was at full, in that brown darkness. Narouz lay snoring upon the cushions with arms and legs outspread while Nessim dozed fitfully, awakening from time to time to watch him—the effortless progress of sleep which physical surrender to action always brings. He brooded upon his brother's ugliness—the magnificent set of white teeth showing through the pink rent in his upper lip. From time to time, too, as they rested, the headmen of the tribe called noiselessly, taking off their shoes at the entrance of the tent, to enter and kiss Nessim's hand. Each uttered the single word of welcome "*Mahubbah*" in a whisper.

It was late in the afternoon when Narouz woke and calling for water doused his body down, asking at the same time for a change of clothes which were at once brought to him by the Sheik's eldest son. He strode out into the heat of the sand saying: "Now for the colt. It may take a couple of hours? You won't mind? We'll be back a bit late, eh?" Cushions had been set for them in the shade and here Nessim was glad to recline and watch his brother moving quickly across the dazzle of sand towards a group of colts which had been driven up for him to examine.

They played gracefully and innocently, the tossing of their heads and manes seeming to him "like the surf of the June sea" as the proverb has it. Narouz stopped keenly as he neared them, watching. Then he shouted something and a man raced out to him with a bridle and bit. "The white one" he cried hoarsely and the Sheik's sons shouted a response which Nessim did not catch. Narouz turned again, and softly with a queer ducking discretion, slipped in among the young creatures and almost before one could think was astride a white colt after having bridled it with a single almost invisible gesture.

The mythical creature stood quite still, its eye wide and lustrous as if fully to comprehend this tremendous new intelligence of a rider upon its back, then a slow shudder rippled through its flesh—the tides of the panic which always greets such a collision of human and animal worlds. Horse and rider stood as if posing for a statue, buried in thought.

Now the animal suddenly gave a low whistling cry of fear, shook itself and completed a dozen curious arching jumps, stiffly as a mechanical toy, coming down savagely on its forelegs each time with the downthrust. This did not dislodge Narouz who only leaned forward and growled something in its ear that drove it frantic for it now set off at a ragged plunging tossing canter, turning and curvetting and ducking. They made a slow irregular circle round the tents until at last they came back to where the crowd of Arabs stood at the doorway of the main tent, watching silently. And now the poor creature, as if aware that some great portion of its real life—its childhood perhaps —was irrevocably over, gave another low whistling groan and broke suddenly into the long tireless flying gallop of its breed, aimed like a shooting-star to pierce the very sky, and whirled away across the dunes with its rider secured to it by the powerful scissors of his legs—firm as a figure held by ringbolts —diminishing rapidly in size until both were lost to sight. A great cry of approval went up from the tents and Nessim accepted, besides the curd cheese and coffee, the compliments which were his brother's due.

Two hours later Narouz brought her back, glistening with sweat, dejected, staggering, with only enough fight in her to blow dejectedly and stamp, conquered. But he himself was deliriously exhausted, dazed as if he had ridden through an oven, while his bloodshot eyes and drawn twitching face testified to the severity of the fight. The endearments he uttered to the horse came from between parched and cracked lips. But he was happy underneath it all—indeed radiant—as he croaked for water and begged leave of half an hour's rest before they should set out once more on the homeward journey. Nothing could finally tire that powerful body—not even the orgasm he had experienced in long savage battle. But closing his eyes now as he felt the water pouring over his head, he saw again the dark bleeding sun which shimmered behind their lids, image of fatigue, and felt the desert glare parching and cracking the water on his very skin. His mind was a jumble of sharp stabbing colours and apprehensions—as if the whole sensory apparatus had melted in the heat like a colour-box, fusing thought and wish and desire. He was light-headed with joy and felt as unsubstantial as a rainbow. Yet in less than half an hour he was ready for the journey back.

They set off with a different escort this time across the inclining rays of sunlight which threw their rose and purple shadows into the sockets of the dunes. They made good time to the Quasur el Atash. Narouz had made arrangements for the white colt to be delivered him later in the week by the Chief's sons, and he rode at ease now, occasionally singing a stave or two of a song. Darkness fell as they reached the Castles of the Thirsty and having said good-bye to their hosts set off once more across the desert.

They rode slowly at ease, watching the brindled waning moon come up on a silence broken only by the sudden stammer of their horses' hooves on shingle beds, or the far-away ululations of jackals, and now, quite suddenly, Nessim found the barrier lifted and was able to say: "Narouz, I am going to be married. I want you to tell Leila for me. I don't know why but I feel shy about it."

For a minute Narouz felt himself turned to ice—a figure in a coat of mail; he seemed to sway in his saddle as with a delight so forced and hollow that it made his voice snap off short he crabbed out the words: "To Clea, Nessim? To Clea?" feeling the blood come rushing back to his ticking nerves when his brother shook his head and stared curiously at him. "No. Why? To Arnauti's ex-wife" replied Nessim with a controlled, a classical precision of utterance. They rode on with creaking saddles and Narouz, who was now grinning to himself with relief, cried "I am so happy, Nessim! At last! You will be happy and have children."

But here Nessim's mortal shyness overcame him again and he told Narouz all that he had learned about Justine and about the loss of her child, adding: "She does not love me now, and does not pretend to: but who knows? If I can get her child back and give her some peace of mind and security, anything is possible." He added after a moment "Don't you think?" not because he wished for an opinion on the matter but simply to bridge the silence which poured in between them like a drifting dune. "As for the child, it is difficult. The Parquet have investigated as best they could—and what little evidence they have points to *Magzub* (the Inspired One); there was a festival in the town that evening and he was there. He has been several times accused of kidnapping children but the case has always been dropped for lack of evidence." Narouz pricked up his ears and bristled like a wolf. "You mean the hypnotist?" Nessim said thoughtfully: "I have sent to offer him a large sum of money— very large indeed—for what I want to know. Do you see?" Narouz shook his head doubtfully and picked at his short beard. "He is the one who is mad" he said. "He used to come to Saint Damiana every year. But strange-mad. *Zein-el-Abdin.* He is holy too."

"That is the one" said Nessim; and as if struck by an after-thought Narouz reined both horses and embraced him, utter-ing the conventional congratulations in the family tongue. Nessim smiled and said: "You will tell Leila? Please, my brother."

"Of course."

"After I have gone?"

"Of course."

With the release of this tension and Narouz' ready com-pliance Nessim suddenly felt a load lifted from his mind. And correspondingly he suddenly felt very tired and on the point of sleep. They travelled briskly but without haste and it was towards midnight when they came once more within sight of the desert's edge. Here the horses put up a startled hare and Narouz made an attempt to ride it down with his whip but he missed it in the half-darkness.

"It is very good news" he cried on returning to Nessim's side, as if the little gallop across the moonlit dunes had given him all the time and detachment he needed to come to a considered opinion. "Will you bring her to us next week—to Leila? I think I must have met her but cannot remember. Very dark? 'A firefly's light in darkness for such eyes' as the song goes?" He laughed his downward laugh.

Nessim yawned sleepily. "Ach! my bones ache. That is what I get for living in Alexandria. Narouz, before I fall asleep there was one other thing I meant to ask you. I have not seen Pursewarden. The meetings?"

Narouz drew a hissing inward breath and turned his bright eyes to his brother, saying "Yes. Very well. The next one is to be at the *mulid* of Saint Damiana, in the desert." He flexed the great muscles of his shoulders. "The whole ten families are coming—can you believe it?"

"You will be careful" said his brother, "to see that everything is done privately and there are no leaks."

"Of course!" he cried.

"I mean" said Nessim, "that in the early stages this should not have a political character. It must grow slowly with the understanding of the matter. Eh? I do not think, for example, it is necessary for you to actually speak to them, but rather to discuss. We can't risk. You see, it is not only the British."

Narouz jaunted a leg impatiently and picked his teeth. He thought of Mountolive and sighed.

"It is also the French—and they are at cross-purposes. If we are to use them both. . . ."

93

"I know, I know" said Narouz impatiently. Nessim looked at him keenly. "Attend," he said sharply, "for much depends on your understanding just how far we can go at this stage."

His reproof crushed Narouz. He flushed and joined his hands together as he looked at his brother. "I do" he said in a low hoarse voice. Nessim at once felt ashamed of himself and took his arm. He went on in his low confiding tone.

"You see, there are mysterious leaks from time to time. Old Cohen, for example, the furrier who died last month. He was working for the French in Syria. On his return, the Egyptians knew all about his mission. How? Nobody knows. Among our friends we certainly have enemies—in Alexandria itself. Do you see?"

"I see."

The next morning it was time for Nessim to return and the two brothers rode out across the fields at a leisurely pace to the point of rendezvous at the ferry. "Why do you never come into the town?" said Nessim. "Come with me to-day. There's a ball at the Randidis'. You'd enjoy it as a change." Narouz as always wore a hang-dog expression when anyone suggested an excursion into the city. "I shall come at Carnival" he said slowly, looking at the ground, and his brother laughed and touched his arm. "I knew you'd say that! Always, once a year at Carnival. I wonder why!"

But he knew; Narouz' mortal shyness about his hare-lip had driven him into a seclusion almost as unbroken as that of his mother. Only the black domino of the carnival balls permitted him to disguise the face he had come to loathe so much that he could no longer bear to see it even in a shaving-mirror. At the carnival ball he felt free. And yet there was another and indeed unexpected reason—a passion for Clea which had lasted for years now; for a Clea to whom he had never spoken, and indeed only twice seen when she came down with Nessim to ride on the estate. This was a secret which could not have been dragged out of him under torture, but to every carnival dance he came and drifted about in the crowd hoping vaguely that he might by accident meet this young woman whose name he had never uttered aloud to anyone until that day.

(He never knew that Clea loathed the carnival season and spent the time quietly drawing and reading in her studio.)

They parted now with a warm embrace and Nessim's car scribbled its pennants of dust across the warm air of the fields, eager to regain the coast road once more. A battleship in the basin was firing a twenty-one gun salute, in honour perhaps of some Egyptian dignitary, and the explosions appeared to make the clouds of pearl which always overhung the harbour in spring, tremble and change colour. The sea was high to-day, and four fishing-boats tacked furiously towards the town harbour with their catch. Nessim stopped only once, to buy himself a carnation for his buttonhole from the flower-vendor on the corner of Saad Zaghloul. Then he went to his office, pausing to have his shoe-shine on the way up. The city had never seemed more beautiful to him. Sitting at his desk he thought of Leila and then of Justine. What would his mother have to say about his decision?

Narouz walked out to the summer-house that morning to discharge his mission; but first he picked a mass of blooms from the red and yellow roses with which to refill the two great vases which stood on either side of his father's portrait. His mother was asleep at her desk but the noise he made lifting the latch woke her at once. The snake hissed drowsily and then lowered its head to the ground once more.

"Bless you, Narouz" she said as she saw the flowers and rose at once to empty her vases. As they started to trim and arrange the new blooms, Narouz broke the news of his brother's marriage. His mother stood quite still for a long time, undisturbed but serious as if she were consulting her own inmost thoughts and emotions. At last she said, more to herself than anyone,

"Why not?" repeating the phrase once or twice as if testing its pitch.

Then she bit her thumb and turning to her younger son said "But if she is an adventuress, after his money, I won't have it. I shall take steps to have her done away with. He needs my permission anyhow."

Narouz found this overwhelmingly funny and gave an appreciative laugh. She took his hairy arm between her fingers. "I will" she said.

"Please."

"I swear it."

He laughed now until he showed the pink roof of his mouth. But she remained abstracted, still listening to an inner monologue. Absently she patted his arm as he laughed and whispered "Hush"; and then after a long pause she said, as if surprised by her own thoughts, "The strange thing is, I mean it."

"And you can't count on me, eh?" he said, still laughing but with the germ of seriousness in his words. "You can't trust me to watch over my own brother's honour." He was still swollen up toad-like by the laughter, though his expression had now become serious. "My God," she thought, "how ugly he is." And her fingers went to the black veil, pressing through it to the rough cicatrices in her own complexion, touching them fiercely as if to smooth them out.

"My good Narouz" she said, almost tearfully, and ran her fingers through his hair; the wonderful poetry of the Arabic stirred and soothed him in one. "My honeycomb, my dove, my good Narouz. Tell him yes, with my embrace. Tell him yes."

He stood still, trembling like a colt, and drinking in the music of her voice and the rare caresses of that warm and capable hand.

"But tell him he must bring her here to us."

"I will."

96

"Tell him to-day."

And he walked with his queer jerky sawing stride to the telephone in the old house. His mother sat at her dusty table and repeated twice in a low puzzled tone; "Why should Nessim choose a Jewess?"

V

So much have I reconstructed from the labyrinth of notes which Balthazar has left me. "To imagine is not necessarily to invent," he says elsewhere, "nor dares one make a claim for omniscience in interpreting people's actions. One assumes that they have grown out of their feelings as leaves grow out of a branch. But can one work backwards, deducing the one from the other? Perhaps a writer could if he were sufficiently brave to cement these apparent gaps in our actions with interpretations of his own to bind them together? What was going on in Nessim's mind? This is really a question for you to put to yourself.

"Or in Justine's for that matter? One really doesn't know; all I can say is that their esteem for each other grew in inverse ratio to their regard—for there never by common consent was any love between them as I have shown you. Perhaps it is as well. But in all the long discussions I had with them separately, I could not find the key to a relationship which failed signally —one could see it daily sinking as land sinks, as the level of a lake might sink, and not know why. The surface colouring was brilliantly executed and so perfect as to deceive most observers like yourself, for example. Nor do I share Leila's view—who never liked Justine. I sat beside her at the presentation which Narouz organised at the great *mulid* of Abu Girg which falls towards Easter every year. Justine had by then renounced Judaism to become a Copt in obedience to Nessim's wish, and as he could only marry her privately since she had already once been married, Narouz had to be content with a party which would present her to the great house and its dependants whose lives he was always anxious to cement into the family pattern.

"For four days then a huge encampment of tents and marquees grew up around the house—carpets and chandeliers and brilliant decorations. Alexandria was stripped bare of hothouse flowers and not less of its great social figures who made the somewhat mocking journey down to Abu Girg (nothing excites so much mocking amusement in the city as a fashionable wedding) to pay their respects and congratulate Leila. Local mudirs and sheiks, peasants innumerable, dignitaries from near and far had flocked in to be entertained—while the Bedouin, whose tribal grounds fringed the estate, gave magnificent displays of horsemanship, galloping round and round the house firing their guns—for all the world as if Justine were a young bride—a virgin. Imagine the smiles of Athena Trasha, of the Cervonis! And old Abu Kar himself rode up the steps of the house on his white Arab and into the very reception-rooms with a bowl of flowers. . . .

"As for Leila, she never for one moment took those clever eyes off Justine. She followed her with care like someone studying a historical figure. 'Is she not lovely?' I asked as I followed her glance and she turned a quick bird-like glance in my direction before turning back to the subject of her absorbed study. 'We are old friends, Balthazar, and I can talk to you. I was telling myself that she looked something like I did once, and that she is an adventuress; like a small dark snake coiled up at the centre of Nessim's life.' I protested in a formal manner at this; she stared into my eyes for a long moment and then gave a slow chuckle. I was surprised by what she said next. 'Yes, she is just like me—merciless in the pursuit of pleasure and yet arid—all her milk has turned into power-love. Yet she is also like me in that she is tender and kindly and a real man's woman. I hate her because she is like me, do you understand? And I fear her because she can read my mind.' She began to laugh. 'My darling,' she called out to Justine, 'come over here and sit by me.' And she thrust upon her the one sort of confectionery she herself most loathed—crystallized violets—which I saw Justine accept with reserve—for she loathed them too. And so the two of them sat there, the veiled sphinx and the unveiled, eating sugar violets which neither could bear. I was delighted to be able to see women at their most primitive like this. Nor can I tell you very much about the validity of such judgments. We all make them about each other.

"The curious thing was, that despite this antipathy between the two women—the antipathy of affinity, you might say—there sprang up side by side with it a strange sympathy, a sense of identification with each other. For example when Leila at last dared to meet Mountolive it was done secretly and arranged by Justine. It was Justine who brought them together, both masked, during the carnival ball. Or so I heard.

"As for Nessim, I would, at the risk of over-simplification, say something like this: he was so innocent that he had not realised that you cannot live with a woman without in some degree falling in love with her—that possession is nine points of the jealousy! He was dismayed and terrified by the extent of his own jealousy for Justine and was honestly trying to practise something new for him—indifference. True or false? I don't know.

"And then, turning the coin round, I would say that what irked Justine herself unexpectedly was to find that the contract of wife undertaken so rationally, and at the level of a financial bargain, was somehow more binding than a wedding-ring. One does not, as a woman (if passion seems to sanction it) think twice about being unfaithful to a husband; but to be unfaithful to Nessim seemed like stealing money from the till. What would you say?"

My own feeling (*pace* Balthazar) is that Justine became slowly aware of something hidden in the character of this solitary endearing long-suffering man; namely a jealousy all the more terrible and indeed dangerous for never allowing itself any outlet. Sometimes . . . but here I am in danger of revealing confidences which Justine made to me during the period of the so-called love affair which so much wounded me and in which, as I learn now, she was only using me as a cover for other activities. I have described the progress of it all elsewhere; but if I were now to reveal all she told me of Nessim in her own words I should be in danger, primo, of setting down material perhaps distasteful to the reader and indeed unfair to Nessim himself. Secundo: I am not sure any more of its relative truth since it might have been part of the whole grand design of deception! In my own mind even those feelings ("important lessons learned" etc.) are all coloured by the central doubt which the Interlinear has raised in my mind. "Truth is what most contradicts itself. . ."! What a farce it all is!

But what he says of the jealousy of Nessim is true, however, for I lived for a while in its shadow, and there is no doubt about the effect it had on Justine. Almost from the beginning she had found herself followed, kept under surveillance, and very naturally this gave her a feeling of uncertainty: uncertainty made terrible by the fact that Nessim never openly spoke of it. It rested, an invisible weight of suspicion dogging and dis-colouring her commonest remarks, the most innocent of after-dinner walks. He would sit between the tall candles gently smiling at her while a whole silent inquisition unrolled reverberating in his mind.

The simplest and most sincere actions—a visit to a public library, a shopping list, a message on a place-card—became baffling to the eye of a jealousy founded in emotional impo-tence. Nessim was torn to rags by her demands; she was torn to rags by the doubts she saw reflected in his eyes—by the very tenderness with which he put a wrap around her shoulders. It felt as if he were slipping a noose over her neck. In a queer sort of way this relationship echoed the psycho-analytic relationship described in *Moeurs* by her first husband—where Justine became for them all a Case rather than a person, chased almost out of her right mind by the tiresome inquisitions of those who never know when to leave ill alone. Yes, she had fallen into a trap, there is no doubt. The thought echoed in her mind like mad laughter. I hear it echo still.

So they went on side by side, like runners perfectly matched, offering to Alexandria what seemed the perfect pattern of a relationship all envied and none could copy. Nessim the indulgent, the uxorious, Justine the lovely and contented wife.

"In his own way," notes Balthazar, "I suppose he was only hunting for the truth. Isn't this becoming rather a ridiculous remark? We should drop it by common consent! It is after all such an odd business. Shall I give you yet another example from another quarter? Your account of Capodistria's death on the lake is the version which we all of us accepted at the time as likely to be true: in our own minds, of course.

"But in the Police depositions, everyone concerned mentioned one particular thing—namely that when they raised his body from the lake in which it was floating, with the black patch beside it in the water, his false teeth fell into the boat with a clatter, and startled them all. Now listen to this: three months later I was having dinner with Pierre Balbz who was his dentist. He assured me that Da Capo had an almost perfect set of teeth and certainly no false teeth which could possibly have fallen out. Who, then, was it? I don't know. And if Da Capo simply disappeared and arranged for some decoy to take his place, he had every reason: leaving behind him debts of over two million. Do you see what I mean?

"Fact is unstable by its very nature. Narouz once said to me that he loved the desert because there 'the wind blew out one's footsteps like candle-flames'. So it seems to me does reality. How then can we hunt for the truth?"

○   ○   ○   ○   ○

Pombal was hovering between diplomatic tact and the low cunning of a provincial public prosecutor; the conflicting emotions played upon his fat face as he sat in his gout-chair with his fingers joined. He had the air of a man in complete agreement with himself. "They say" he said, watching me keenly, "that you are now in the British *Deuxième*. Eh? Don't tell me, I know you can't speak. Nor can I if you ask me about myself. You *think* you know that I am in the French—but I deny the whole thing most strenuously. What I am asking is whether I should have you living in the flat. It seems somehow . . . how do you say? . . . Box and Cox. No? I mean, why don't we sell each other ideas, eh? I know you won't. Neither will I. Our sense of humour . . . I mean only *if* we are in the . . . ahem. But of course, you deny it and I deny it. So we are not. But you are not too proud to share my women, eh? *Autre chose.* Have a drink, eh? The gin bottle is over there. I hid it from Hamid. Of course, I know that something is going on. I don't despair of finding out. Something . . . I wish I knew . . . Mountolive, eh?"

"What have you done to your face?" I say to change the subject. He has recently started to grow a moustache. He holds on to it defensively as if my question constituted a threat to shave it off forcibly. "My moustache, ah that! Well, recently I have had so many reproofs about work, not attending to it, that I analysed myself deeply, *au fond.* Do you know how many man-hours I am losing through women? You will never guess. I thought a moustache (isn't it hideous?) would put them off a bit, but no. It is just the same. It is a tribute, dear boy, not to my charm but to the low standards here. They seem to love me because there is nothing better. They love a well-hung diplomat —how do you say *faisandé*? Why do you laugh? You are losing a lot of woman-hours too. But then you have the British Government behind you—the pound, eh? That girl was here again to-day. *Mon Dieu,* so thin and so uncared for! I offered her some lunch but she would not stay. And the mess in your room! She takes hashish, doesn't she? Well, when I go to Syria on leave you can have the whole place. Provided you respect my firescreen—isn't it good as for art, *hein*?"

He has had an immense and vivid firescreen made for the flat which bears the legend "LEGERETE, FATALITE, MATERNITE" in poker-work.

"Ah well," he continues, "so much for art in Alexandria. But as for that Justine, that is a better barbarian for you no? I bet she—eh? Don't tell. Why are you not happier about it? You Englishmen, always gloomy and full of politics. *Pas de remords, mon cher*. Two women in tandem—who would want better? And one Left-Handed—as Da Capo calls Lesbians. You know Justine's reputation? Well, for my part, I am renouncing the whole——"

So Pombal flows in great good humour over the shallow river bed of his experience and standing on the balcony I watch the sky darkening over the harbour and hear the sullen hooting of ships' sirens, emphasising our loneliness here, our isolation from the warm Gulf Stream of European feelings and ideas. All the currents slide away towards Mecca or to the incomprehensible desert and the only foothold in this side of the Mediterranean is the city we have come to inhabit and hate, to infect with our own self-contempts.

And then I see Melissa walk down the street and my heart contracts with pity and joy as I turn to open the flat door.

o   o   o   o   o

These quiet bemused island days are a fitting commentary to the thoughts and feelings of one walking alone on deserted beaches, or doing the simple duties of a household which lacks a mother. But I carry now the great Interlinear in my hand wherever I go, whether cooking or teaching the child to swim, or cutting wood for the fireplace. But these fictions all live on as a projection of the white city itself whose pearly skies are broken in spring only by the white stalks of the minarets and the flocks of pigeons turning in clouds of silver and amethyst; whose veridian and black marble harbour-water reflects the snouts of foreign men-of-war turning through their slow arcs, depicting the prevailing wind; or swallowing their own inky reflections, touching and overlapping like the very tongues and sects and races over which they keep their uneasy patrol: symbolising the western consciousness whose power is exemplified in steel—those sullen preaching guns against the yellow metal of the lake and the town which breaks open at sunset like a rose.

o   o   o   o   o

PART II

VI

"**P**ursewarden!" writes Balthazar.

"I won't say that you have been less than just to him—only that he does not seem to resurrect on paper into a recognisable image of the man I knew. He seems to be a sort of enigma to you. (It is not enough, perhaps, to respect a man's genius—one must love him a little, no?) It may have been the envy you speak of which blinded you to his qualities, but somehow I doubt it; it seems to me to be very hard to envy someone who was so single-minded and moreover such a simpleton in so many ways, as to make him a real original (for example: money terrified him). I admit that I regarded him as a great man and I knew him well—even though I have never, to this day, read a single book of his, not even the last trilogy which made such a noise in the world, though I pretend to have done so in company. I have dipped here and there. I feel I don't need to read more.

"I put down a few notes upon him here then, not to contradict you, wise one, but simply to let you compare two dissimilar images. But if you are wrong about him, you are not less wrong than Pombal who always credited him with an *humeur noire* so dear to the French heart. But there was no spleen in the man and his apparent world-weariness was not feigned; while his cruelties of tongue were due to his complete simplicity and a not always delightful sense of mischief. Pombal never recovered I think from being nicknamed '*Le Prépuce Barbu*'; and if you will forgive me neither did you from Pursewarden's criticism of your own novels. Remember? 'These books have a curious and rather forbidding streak of cruelty—a lack of humanity which puzzled me at first. But it is simply the way a sentimentalist would disguise his weakness. Cruelty here is the obverse of sentimentality. He wounds because he is afraid of going all squashy.' Of course, you are right in saying that he was contemptuous of your love of Melissa—and the nickname he gave you must have wounded also, suiting as it did your initials (Lineaments of Gratified Desire). 'There goes old Lineaments in his dirty mackintosh.' A poor joke, I know. But all this is not very real.

"I am turning out a drawer full of old mementoes and notes to-day in order to think about him a bit on paper; it is a holiday and the clinic is closed. It is risky work, I know, but perhaps I can answer a question which you must have put to yourself when you read the opening pages of the Interlinear: 'How could Pursewarden and Justine. . . ?' I know.

"He had been to Alexandria before twice, before he met us all, and had once spent a whole winter at Mazarita working on a book: but this time he came back to do a course of lectures at the Atelier, and as Nessim and I and Clea were on the committee, he could not avoid the side of Alexandrian life which most delighted and depressed him. In a letter to Mountolive:

' "My dear David,

' "I see you are named in to-day's papers as the new Plenipot. I wish I had known you were coming. I might have stayed instead of giving ground and being upon the point of departure myself. Damn! But frankly Egypt is an unenviable post at present with the break-up of the High Commission. Terrible dog-fights between fragments of the old agencies and no one to arbitrate. You will have headache-size decisions to make if you indeed are coming—I suppose early spring? I am as usual in disfavour for neglect of duty and trenchant opinions about the way things should be. I have nothing really to lose. And your Chancery is full of queer fish. Errol, a Labour peer, that strangest of all animals, aflame with zeal and ignorance, and Donkin who has grown a beard and turned Moslem. . . . But I won't frighten you too much. My contract is hinged for April, my views most unwelcome here, so that I foresee a move. Frankly I would not mind. But it would be fun to welcome you to this policy cockshy where everything is upside down. But if the work side is horrid, you will still have Alexandria as it was and ever will be; a Babylon of Buhl. Nessim, Narouz and their invisible and eccentric mum . . . I could tell you a deal about them, but not on paper. If I get sacked I'll try and reach you through the Bag Room. When do you leave Russia? Post-card please. I must have a talk to you before you set off, as there is quite a lot going on under the surface here to which I am privy, and about which your blissful Chancery knows nothing.

" 'Yours,

" 'L.P.'

"Physical features, as best I remember them. He was fair, a good average height and strongly built though not stout. Brown hair and moustache—very small this. Extremely well-kept hands. A good smile though when not smiling his face wore a somewhat quizzical almost impertinent air. His eyes were hazel and the best feature of him—they looked into other eyes, into other ideas, with a real candour, rather a terrifying sort of lucidity. He was somewhat untidy in dress but always spotlessly clean of person and abhorred dirty nails and collars. Yes, but his clothes were sometimes stained with spots of the red ink in which he wrote. There!

"Really, I think his sense of humour had separated him from the world, into a privacy of his own, or else he had discovered for himself the uselessness of having opinions and in consequence made a habit of usually saying the opposite of what he thought in a joking way. He was an ironist, hence he appeared often to violate good sense: hence too his equivocal air, the apparent frivolity with which he addressed himself to large subjects. This sort of serious clowning leaves footmarks in conversation of a peculiar kind. His little sayings stayed like the pawmarks of a cat in a pat of butter. To stupidities he would respond only with the word '*kwatz*'.

"He believed, I think, that success was inherent in greatness. His own lack of success (he made very little money from his work and it all went to his wife and two children who lived in England) was inclined to make him doubt his powers. Perhaps he should have been born an American? I don't know.

"I remember going down to the dock to meet his boat with the panting Keats—who proposed to interview him. We were late and only caught up with him as he was filling in an immigration form. Against the column marked 'religion' he had written '*Protestant—purely in the sense that I protest.*'

"We took him ashore for a drink so that Keats could interview him at leisure. The poor boy was absolutely nonplussed. Pursewarden had a particular smile for the Press. I still have the picture Keats took that morning. The sort of smile which might have hardened on the face of a dead baby. Later I got to know this smile and learned that it meant he was about to commit an outrage on accepted good sense with an irony. He was trying to amuse no-one but himself, mind you. Keats panted and puffed, looked 'sincere' and probed, but all in vain. Later I asked him for a carbon copy of his interview which he typed out and gave me with his puzzled air, explaining that there was no 'news' in the man. Pursewarden had said things like 'It is the duty of every patriot to hate his country creatively' and 'England cries out for brothels'; this last somewhat shocked poor Keats who asked him if he felt that 'unbridled licence' would be a good thing in England. Did Pursewarden want to undermine religion?

"I can see as I write the wicked air with which my friend replied in shocked tones: 'Good Lord, no! I would simply like to put an end to the cruelty to children which is such a distressing feature of English life—as well as the slavish devotion to pets which borders on the obscene.' Keats must have gulped his way through all this, dotting and dashing in his shorthand book with rolling eye, while Pursewarden studied the further horizon. But if the journalist found this sort of exchange enigmatic, he was doubly puzzled by some of the answers to his political questions. For example, when he asked Pursewarden what he thought of the Conference of the Arab Committee which was due to start in Cairo that day, he replied: 'When the English feel they are in the wrong, their only recourse is to cant.' 'Am I to understand that you are criticising British policy?' 'Of course not. Our statesmanship is impeccable.' Keats fanned himself all the harder and abandoned politics forthwith. In answer to the question 'Are you planning to write a novel while you are here?' Pursewarden said: 'If I am denied every other means of self-gratification.'

"Later Keats, poor fellow, still fanning that pink brow, said 'He's a thorny bastard isn't he?' But the odd thing was that he wasn't at all. Where can a man who really thinks take refuge in the so-called real world without defending himself against stupidity by the constant exercise of equivocation? Tell me that. Particularly a poet. He once said: 'Poets are not really serious about ideas or people. They regard them much as a Pasha regards the members of an extensive *harim*. They are pretty, yes. They are for use. But there is no question of them being true or false, or having souls. In this way the poet preserves his freshness of vision, and finds everything miraculous. And this is what Napoleon meant when he described poetry as a *science creuse*. He was quite right from his own point of view.'

"This robust mind was far from splenetic though its judgments were harsh. I have seen him so moved in describing Joyce's encroaching blindness and D. H. Lawrence's illness that his hand shook and he turned pale. He showed me once a letter from the latter in which Lawrence had written: '*In you I feel a sort of profanity—almost a hate for the tender growing quick in things, the dark Gods. . . .'* He chuckled. He deeply loved Lawrence but had no hesitation in replying on a post-card: *'My dear DHL. This side idolatry—I am simply trying not to copy your habit of building a Taj Mahal around anything as simple as a good f——k.'*

"He said to Pombal once: *'On fait l'amour pour mieux refouler et pour décourager les autres.'* And added: 'I worry a great deal about my golf handicap.' It always took Pombal a few moments to work out these non-sequiturs. *'Quel malin, ce type-là!'* he would mutter under his breath. Then and only then would Pursewarden permit himself a chuckle—having scored his personal victory. They were a splendid pair and used to drink together a great deal.

"Pombal was terribly affected by his death—really overcome, he retired to bed for a fortnight. Could not speak of him without tears coming into his eyes; this used to infuriate Pombal himself. 'I never knew how much I loved the blasted man' he would say. . . . I hear Pursewarden's wicked chuckle in all this. No, you are wrong about him. His favourite adjective was 'uffish'! or so he told me.

"His public lectures were disappointing, as you may remember. Afterwards, I discovered why. He read them out of a book. They were someone else's lectures! But once when I took him up to the Jewish school and asked him to talk to the children of the literary group, he was delightful. He began by showing them some card tricks and then congratulated the winner of the Literary Prize, making him read the prize essay aloud. Then he asked the children to write down three things in their notebooks which might help them some day if they didn't forget them. Here they are:

1. Each of our five senses contains an art.
2. In questions of art great secrecy must be observed.
3. The artist must catch every scrap of wind.

"Then he produced from his mackintosh pocket a huge packet of sweets upon which they all fell, he no less, and completed the most successful literary hour ever held at the school.

"He had some babyish habits, picked his nose, and enjoyed taking his shoes off under the table in a restaurant. I remember hundreds of meetings which were made easy and fruitful by his naturalness and humour but he spared no-one and made enemies. He wrote once to his beloved DHL: '*Maître, Maître, watch your step. No-one can go on being a rebel too long without turning into an autocrat.*'

"When he wished to discuss a bad work of art he would say in tones of warm approbation 'Most effective.' This was a feint. He was not interested enough in art to want to argue about it with others ('dogs snuffing over a bitch too small to mount') so he said 'Most effective.' Once when he was drunk he added: 'The effective in art is what rapes the emotion of your audience without nourishing its values.'

"Do you see? Do you see?

"All this was brought to bear on Justine like a great charge of swan-shot, scattering her senses and bringing her for the first time something she had despaired of ever encountering: namely laughter. Imagine what one touch of ridicule can do to a Higher Emotion! 'As for Justine,' said Pursewarden to me when he was drunk once, 'I regard her as a tiresome old sexual turnstile through which presumably we must all pass—a somewhat vulpine Alexandrian Venus. By God, what a woman she would be if she were really natural and felt no guilt! Her behaviour would commend her to the Pantheon—but one cannot send her up there with a mere recommendation from the Rabbinate—a bundle of Old Testament ravings. What would old Zeus say?' He saw my reproachful glance at these cruelties and said, somewhat shamefacedly, 'I'm sorry, Balthazar. I simply dare not take her seriously. One day I will tell you why.'

"Justine herself wished very much to take him seriously but he absolutely refused to command sympathy or share the solitude from which he drew so much of his composure and self-possession.

"Justine herself, you know, could not bear to be alone.

"He was due, I remember, to lecture in Cairo to several societies affiliated to our own Arts Society, and Nessim, who was busy, asked Justine to take him down by car. That was how they came to find themselves together on a journey which threw up a sort of ludicrous shadow-image of a love-relationship, like a clever magic-lantern picture of a landscape, created by, strangely—not Justine at all—but a worse mischief-maker—the novelist himself. 'It was Punch and Judy, all right!' said Pursewarden ruefully afterwards.

"He was at that time deeply immersed in the novel he was writing, and as always he found that his ordinary life, in a distorted sort of way, was beginning to follow the curvature of his book. He explained this by saying that any concentration of the will displaces life (Archimedes' bath-water) and gives it bias in motion. Reality, he believed, was always trying to copy the imagination of man, from which it derived. You will see from this that he was a serious fellow underneath much of his clowning and had quite comprehensive beliefs and ideas. But also, he had been drinking rather heavily that day as he always did when he was working. Between books he never touched a drop. Riding beside her in the great car, someone beautiful, dark and painted with great eyes like the prow of some Aegean ship, he had the sensation that his book was being rapidly passed underneath his life, as if under a sheet of paper containing the iron filings of temporal events, as a magnet is in that commonplace experiment one does at school: and somehow setting up a copying magnetic field.

"He never flirted, mind you; and if he started to approach Justine it was simply to try out a few speeches and attitudes, to verify certain conclusions he had reached in the book before actually sending it to the printer, so to speak! Afterwards, of course, he bitterly repented of this piece of self-indulgence. He was at that moment trying to escape from the absurd dictates of narrative form in prose: 'He said' 'She said' 'He cocked an eye, shot a cuff, lifted a lazy head, etc.' Was it possible, had he succeeded in 'realising' character without the help of such props? He was asking himself this as he sat there in the sand. ('Her eyelashes brushed his cheek.' *Merde alors!* Had he written that?) Justine's thick black eyelashes were like . . . what? So it was that his kisses were really warm and wholehearted in an absent-minded way because they were in no way meant for her. (One of the great paradoxes of love. Concentration on the love-object and possession are the poisons.) And he discovered to her the fact that she was ridiculous, with a series of disarming and touching pleasantries at which she found herself laughing with a relief that seemed almost sinful. As for her: it was not only that his skin and hair were fresh and that his love-making was full of a lazy, unblushing enterprise; he was wholly himself in a curious way. It aroused in her an unfamiliar passionate curiosity. And then, the things he said! 'Of course I've read *Moeurs* and had you pointed out a hundred times as the tragic central character. It's all right, written by a born *lettré*, of course, and smells fashionably of armpits and *eau de javel*. But surely you are making yourself a little self-important about it all? You have the impertinence to foist yourself on us as a problem—perhaps because you have nothing else to offer? It is foolish. Or perhaps it is that the Jew loves punishment and always comes back for more?' And suddenly, but completely, to take her firmly by the nape of the neck and force her down into the hot sand before she could find time to measure the extent of the insult or form a response in her mind. And then, while he was still kissing, to say something so ludicrous that the laughter and tears in her mind became one and the same sort of things, a mixture of qualities hard to endure.

" 'For God's sake!' she said, having decided to behave as if outraged. He had been too quick for her. He had surprised her while she was half-asleep in her mind, so to speak.

" 'Didn't you want to make love? My mistake!'

"She looked at him, a little disarmed by the mock-repentance of his expression. 'No, of course not. Yes.' Something inside her repeated 'Yes, yes.' An attachment without fingerprints—something as easy as sailing a boat or diving into deep water: 'Fool!' she cried, and to her own surprise started laughing. A conquest by impudence? I don't know. I am only putting down my own views.

"She explained this to herself later by saying that for him sex was the nearest thing to laughter—quite free of particularity, neither sacred nor profane. Pursewarden himself has written that he thought it comic and sinister and divine in one. But she could not grasp and define the thing as she wished, for when she said to him 'You are hopelessly promiscuous, like I am' he was really angry, really outraged. 'Imbecile,' he replied, 'you have the soul of a clerk. For those who love poetry there is no such thing as *vers libre*.' She did not understand this.

" 'O stop behaving like a pious old sin-cushion into which we all have to stick the rusty pins of our admiration' he snapped. In his diary he added drily: 'Moths are attracted by the flame of personality. So are vampires. Artists should take note and beware.' And in the mirror he cursed himself roundly for this lapse, a self-indulgence which had brought him what most bored him—an intimate relationship. But in the sleeping face he too saw the childish inhabitant of Justine, the 'calcimine imprint of a fern in chalk'. He saw now how she must have looked on the first night of love—hair torn and trailing over the pillow like a ruffled black dove, fingers like tendrils, warm mouth inhaling the airs of sleep; warm as a figure of pastry fresh from the oven. 'Oh damn!' he cried aloud.

"Then in bed with her in a hotel crowded with Alexandrian acquaintances who might easily observe their rashness and carry their gossip back to the city they had left together that morning, he swore again. Pursewarden had much to hide, you know. He was not all he seemed. And at this time he did not dare to prejudice his relations with Nessim. The Bloody woman! I hear his voice.

"'Ecoute. . . .'

"'Rien—silence.'

"'Mais chéri, nous sommes seuls.' She was still sleepy. Cast an eye to a bolted door. She felt a momentary disgust at this bourgeois fear of his; afraid of intruders, spies, a husband?

"'Qu'est-ce que c'est?'

"'Je m'écoute moi-même.' Yellow eyes without a trace of discernible divinity in them; he was like a slender rock-god, with ruffled moustache. Past lives? 'Le coeur qui bat.' Derisively he quoted a popular song.

"'Tu n'es pas une femme pour moi—pas dans mon genre.'

"This made her feel like a whipped dog specially as a moment ago he had been kissing her, breaking her down into successive images of pain and pleasure with an importunity which belonged, she now knew, only to his passion and not to himself.

"'What do you want?' she said, and struck him across the face to feel at once the stinging retort on her own cheek—like spray dashing over her. And now he began to fool again until she could not prevent herself from laughing. All this is there in the third volume—the passage with the prostitute is based on these incidents. I came upon it in my dipping.

"This weird translation of feelings into gestures which belied words and words which belied gestures, confused and disoriented her. She needed someone to tell her whether to laugh or to cry.

"As for Pursewarden, he believed with Rilke that no woman adds anything to the sum of Woman, and from satiety he had now taken refuge in the plenty of the imagination—the true field of merit for the artist. This is perhaps what made him seem to her somehow cold and unfeeling. 'Somewhere inside you there is a nasty little Anglican clergyman' she told him and he considered the remark gravely on its merits. 'Perhaps' he said, and added after a pause 'But your humourlessness has made you an enemy of pleasure. *The* enemy. You have a premeditated approach to experience. I am a truer pagan.' And he began to laugh. Great honesty can be crueller than anything else.

"He was sick, I think too, of all the 'mud thrown up by the wheels of life'—so he writes. He had done his best to scrape off as much as he could, to tidy himself up. Was he now to be saddled with the inquisitions and ardours of a Justine—the marshy end of a personality which in a funny sort of way he had himself transcended? 'By God, no!' he told himself. Can you see what a fool he was?

"His life had been a various and full one, and he had held a number of contract posts for some political branch of the Foreign Office, largely, I gather, connected with cultural relations. This work had taken him to several countries and he spoke at least three languages well. He was married and had two children although he was separated from his wife—and indeed never spoke about her without stammering—though I gather they corresponded affectionately and he was always most scrupulous in sending her money. What else? Yes, his real name was Percy and he was somewhat sensitive about it because of the alliteration, I suppose; hence his choice of Ludwig as a signature to his books. He was always delighted when his reviewers took him to be of German extraction.

"I think what frightened and delighted Justine about him most, however, was his somewhat contemptuous repudiation of Arnauti and his book *Moeurs*. Mind you, this too was overdone—he actually admired the book very much. But he used it as a stick to belabour Justine, describing her ex-husband as a 'tiresome psychoanalytical turnkey with a belt full of rusty complexes'. I must say, this delighted her. You see, here was someone who set no store by jargon and refused to regard her as a Case. Of course Pursewarden, the silly fool, was simply trying to get rid of her and this was not a very good way. Yet as a doctor I can testify to the therapeutic effects of insults in cases where medicine is at a loss to make any headway! Indeed, had Justine succeeded in making herself really interesting to him, she might have learned a lot of valuable lessons. Odd, isn't it? He really *was* the right man for her in a sort of way; but then as you must know, it is a law of love that the so-called 'right' person always comes too soon or too late. As for Pursewarden, he withdrew his favours so abruptly that there was hardly time for her to measure the full force of his personality.

"But at the time of which I am writing he was busy insulting her in his somewhat precise idiosyncratic English or French (he had a few pet neologisms which he used with pleasure—one was the noun 'bogue' which he had coined from 'bogus'; *c'est de la grande bogue ca* or 'what bloody bogue')—he insulted her, if one can use the expression, simply to discourage her. I must say I can hardly repress a laugh when I think of it: you could as easily discourage Justine as an equinox, and she was not disposed to abandon this experiment before she had learned as much as possible about herself from it. Predatory Judaic characteristic! Pursewarden was like Doctor Foster in the nursery rhyme.

"For her, his easy detachment gave him freshness of heart. Justine had never had anyone who *didn't* want or who could do without her before! All kinds of new resonances sprang out of making love to such a person. (Am I inventing this? No. I knew them both well and discussed each with the other.) Then, he could make her laugh—quite the most dangerous thing to do to a woman for they prize laughter most after passion. Fatal! No, he was not wrong when he told himself in the mirror: 'Ludwig, thou art an imbecile.'

"Worse, the mockery of his cruelty hurt her, and after making love, say, made her think something like this: 'What he does is simple as a domestic impulse become habit—cleaning his shoes on a mat.' Then unexpectedly would come some terrible mocking phrase like 'We are all looking for someone lovely to be unfaithful to—did you think you were original?' Or else 'The human race! If you can't do the trick with the one you've got, why—shut your eyes and imagine the one you can't get. Who knows? It's perfectly legal and secret. It's the marriage of true minds!' He was standing at the washbasin cleaning his teeth in white wine. She could have murdered him for looking so gay and self-possessed.

"Coming back from Cairo they had several rows. 'As for your so-called illness—have you ever thought it might be just due to an inflamed self-pity?' She became so furious that she nearly drove the car off the road into a tree. 'Miserable Anglo-Saxon!' she cried, on the point of tears—'Bully!'

"And he thought to himself: 'Great Heavens! Here we are quarrelling like a couple of newly-weds. Soon we shall marry and live in filthy compatibility, feasting on each other's blackheads. Ugh! Dreadful isogamy of the Perfect Match. Perce, you gone and done it again.' I can reconstruct this because he always spoke to himself in cockney when he was drunk as well as when he was alone.

"'If you try to hit me,' he said happily, 'we shall have a crash.' And he thought of a bitter little short story into which he might insert her. 'What we need to establish for sex in art' he muttered, 'is a revulsion coefficient.' She was still angry. 'What are you muttering about?'—'Praying.'

"For her, the moiety which remained after love-making then was not disgust or despair as it usually was, but laughter; and though furious with him she nevertheless found herself smiling at some absurdity of his even as she realised with a pang that he could never be achieved, attained as a man, nor would he even become a friend, except on his own terms. He offered an uncompanionate, compassionless ardour which in a funny sort of way made his kisses thrilling. They were as healthy as the bite of a hungry child into a cooking-apple. And regretting this, with another part of her mind (there was an honest woman somewhere deep down) she found herself hoping he would never abandon this entrenched position, or retreat from it. Like all women, Justine hated anyone she could be certain of; and you must remember she had never had anyone as yet whom she could wholly admire—though that may sound strange to you. Here at last was someone she could not punish by her infidelities—an intolerable but delightful novelty. Women are very stupid as well as very profound.

"As for Justine, she was surprised by the new emotions he seemed capable of provoking. Quite simple things—for example she found her love extending itself to inanimate objects concerned with him, like his old meerschaum pipe with the much basted stem. Or his old hat, so battered and weather-stained—it hung behind the door like a water-colour of the man himself. She found herself cherishing objects he had touched or thrown aside. It seemed to her an infuriating sort of mental captivity to find herself stroking one of his old note-books as if she were caressing his body, or tracing with her finger the words he had written on the shaving-mirror with his brush (from Stendhal): 'You must boldly face a little anatomy if you want to discover an unknown principle' and 'Great souls require nourishment.'

"Once, when she discovered an Arab prostitute in his bed (while he himself was shaving in the other room and whistling an air from Donizetti) she was surprised to find that she was not jealous but curious. She sat on the bed and pinning the arms of the unfortunate girl to the pillow set about questioning her closely about what she had felt while making love to him. Of course, this scared the prostitute very much. 'I am not

123

angry,' Justine repeated to the wailing creature, 'I am puzzled. Tell me what I ask of you.'

"Pursewarden had to come in and release his visitant and they all three sat on the bed together, Justine feeding her with crystallized fruit to calm her fears.

"Shall I go on? This analysis may give you pain—but if you are a real writer you will want to follow things to their conclusion, no? All this shows you how hard it was for Melissa. . . .

"If he succeeded in infuriating her it was because he could feel concern about her without any real affection. He did not always clown, or stay beyond her reach; that is what I mean by his honesty. He gave intellectual value for money—in fact he told her the real secret which lay hidden under the enigma of his behaviour. You will find it in one of his books. I know this because Clea quoted it to me as his most profound statement on human relationships. He said to her one night: 'You see, Justine, I believe that Gods are men and men Gods; they intrude on each other's lives, trying to express themselves through each other—hence such apparent confusion in our human states of mind, our intimations of powers within or beyond us. . . . And then (listen) I think that very few people realise that sex is a psychic and not a physical act. The clumsy coupling of human beings is simply a biological paraphrase of this truth—a primitive method of introducing minds to each other, engaging them. But most people are stuck in the physical aspect, unaware of the poetic *rapport* which it so clumsily tries to teach. That is why all your dull repetitions of the same mistake are simply like a boring great multiplication table, and will remain so until you get your head out of the paper bag and start to think responsibly.'

"It is impossible to describe the effect these words had on her: they threw her life and actions into relief in an entirely new way. She saw him all of a sudden in a new light, as a man whom one could 'really love'. Alas, he had already withdrawn his favours. . . .

"When he next went to Cairo he elected to go alone and, made restless by his absence, she made the mistake of writing him a long passionate letter in which she clumsily tried to thank him for a friendship of whose real value to her he was *completely unaware*—that is true of all love again. He regarded this simply as another attempt to intrude upon him and sent her a telegram. (They corresponded through me. I have it still.)

'First nobody can own an artist so be warned. Second what good is a faithful body when the mind is by its very nature unfaithful? Third stop whining like an Arab, you know better. Fourth neurosis is no excuse. Health must be won and earned by a battle. Lastly it is honourable if you can't win to hang yourself.'

"Once she happened upon him when he was very drunk at the Café Al Aktar; I gather that you and I had just left. You remember the evening? He had been rather insulting. It was the evening when I tried to show you how the nine-point proposition of the Cabal worked. I did not know then that you would type it all out and send it to the Secret Service! What a marvellous jest! But I love to feel events overlapping each other, crawling over one another like wet crabs in a basket. No sooner had we left than Justine entered. It was she who helped him back to his hotel and pushed him safely on to his bed. 'Oh, you are the most despairing man!' she cried at that recumbent figure, at which he raised his arms and responded 'I know it, I know it! I am just a refugee from the long slow toothache of English life. It is terrible to love life so much you can hardly breathe!' And he began to laugh—a laughter which was overtaken by nausea. She left him being sick in the washbasin.

"The next morning she went round early with some French reviews in one of which there was an article about his work. He was wearing nothing but a pyjama jacket and a pair of spectacles. On his mirror he had written with a wet shaving-stick, some words from Tolstoy: 'I do not cease to reflect upon art and upon every form of temptation which obscures the spirit.'

"He took the books from her without a word and made as if to shut the door in her face. 'No,' she said, 'I'm coming in.' He cleared his throat and said: 'This is for the last time. I'm sick of being visited as one might visit the grave of a dead kitten.' But she took him by the arms and he said, more gently: 'A definite and complete stop, see?' He had been having some interviews in Cairo.

"She sat down on the end of the bed and lit a cigarette, considering him, as one might a specimen. 'I am curious, after all your talk about self-possession and responsibility, to see just how Anglo-Saxon you are—unable to finish anything you start. Why do you look furtive?' This was a splendid line of attack. He smiled. 'I'm going to work to-day.'

" 'Then I'll come to-morrow.'

" 'I shall have 'flu.'

" 'The day after.'

" 'I shall be going to the Zoo.'

" 'I shall come too.'

"Pursewarden was now extremely rude; she knew she had scored a victory and was delighted. She listened to his honeyed insults as she tapped the carpet with her foot. 'Very well,' she said at last, 'we shall see.' (I am afraid you will have to make room in this for the essential comedy of human relations. You give it so little place.) The next day he put her out of his hotel-room by the neck, like a pet cat. The following day he woke and found the great car parked once more outside the hotel. 'Merde' he cried and just to spite her dressed and went to the Zoo. She followed him. He spent the morning looking at the monkeys with the greatest attention. She was not blind to the insult. She followed him to a bench where he sat, eating the peanuts which he had originally bought to feed the monkeys. She always looked splendid when she was angry, with her nostrils quivering, and clad in that spotless sharkskin suit with a flower at her lapel.

" 'Pursewarden' she said, sitting down.

" 'You won't believe me,' he said, 'you bloody tiresome obsessive society figure. From now on you are going to leave me alone. Your money won't help you.'

"It is a measure of his stupidity that he could use such language. She was delighted at making him so alarmed. You, of course, know how determined she is. But there was a reason—and underneath the insults she detected a genuine concern—something that did not bear at all on their relationship such as it was. Something else. What?

"You have already noted that she was an unerring mind-reader; and sitting beside him, watching his face, she said like someone reading a badly-written manuscript—'Nessim. Something to do with Nessim. You are afraid . . . not of him.' And then in a flash the intuitive contact was made and she blurted out: 'There is something regarding Nessim which you cannot afford to compromise: I understand.' And she heaved a great sigh. 'O Fool, why did you not tell me? Am I to forfeit your friendship because of this? Of course not. I don't care whether you want to sleep with me or not. But you—that is different. Thank God I've discovered what it was.'

"He was too astonished to say anything. This mind-reading performance surprised him more than anything about her. He simply stared at her and said nothing, for a long time. 'O, I am glad' she went on, 'for that is so easily arranged. And it will not prevent us from meeting. We need never sleep together again if you don't wish it. But at least I shall be able to see you.' Another category of the 'love-beast', one which I am unable to define. She would have gone through fire for him by now.

"The silences of Nessim had already assumed huge proportions in her mind. They stretched away on every side like the desert itself—unnerving her. And since her own conscience was by its nature and even without reason, a guilty one, she had already begun to build up a defensive circle of friends whose harmless presences might obviate suspicion of her—the little court of homosexuals like Toto and Amar, whose activities and predispositions were sufficiently well-known to everybody to offer no cause for heart-burnings. She moved now like some sulky planet in the social life of the town, accepting the attentions of these neuters purely as a defence. In this way a general will utilize the features of a town he wishes to defend by building up ring within ring of earthworks. She did not know, for example, that the silences of Nessim betokened only despair and not suspense—for he never broke them.

"In your manuscripts, you hardly mention the question of the child—I told you once before that I thought Arnauti neglected that aspect of affairs in *Moeurs* because it seemed to him melodramatic. 'To the childless all things are without resonance' says Pursewarden somewhere. But now the question of the child had become as important to Nessim as to Justine herself—it was his sole means of enlisting the love he desired from her—or so he thought. He fell upon the central problem like a fury, thinking that this would be the one means of penetrating the affective armour of his beautiful tacit wife; the wife he had married and hung up in a cobwebbed corner of his life, by the wrists, like a marionette on strings! Thank God I have never 'loved', wise one, and never will! Thank God!

"Pursewarden writes somewhere (again from Clea): 'English has two great forgotten words, namely "helpmeet" which is much greater than "lover" and "loving-kindness" which is so much greater than "love" or even "passion".'

"Now Justine one day overheard part of a telephone conversation which led her to believe that Nessim had either located the missing child or knew something about it which he did not

128

wish to reveal to her. As she passed through the hall he was putting down the telephone after having said: 'Well then, I count on your discretion. She must never know.' Never know what? Who was the 'she'? One can be forgiven for jumping to conclusions. As he did not speak of the conversation for several days she taxed him with it. He now made the fatal mistake of saying that it had never taken place, that she had misheard a conversation with his secretary. Had he said that it related to something quite different, he would have been all right, but to accuse her of not hearing the words which had been ringing in her ears for several days like an alarm bell, this was fatal.

"At one blow she lost confidence in him and began to imagine all sorts of things. Why should he wish to keep from her any knowledge he might have gained about her child? After all, his original promise had been to do what he could to discover its fate. Was it then too horrible to speak of? Surely Nessim would tell her anything if indeed he knew anything? Why should he hold back a hypothetical knowledge of its fate? She simply could not guess but inside herself she felt that in some way the information was being held as a hostage is held —against something—what? Good behaviour?

"But Nessim, who had destroyed by this last clumsiness the last vestiges of regard she had for him, was grappling with a new set of factors. He himself had set great store by the recovery of the child as a means to the recovery of Justine herself; he simply did not dare to tell her—or indeed himself, so painful was it—that one day, after he had exhausted all his resources in an attempt to find out the truth, Narouz telephoned to say: 'I saw the Magzub by chance last night and forced the truth out of him. The child is dead.'

"This now rose between them like a great wall of China, shutting them off from any further contact, and making her afraid that he might even intend her harm. And this is where you come in.''

Yes, this alas is where I come in again, for it was approximately now that Justine must have come to my lecture on Cavafy and thence carried me off to meet the gentle Nessim; simple "as an axe falling"—cleaving my life in two! It is inexpressibly bitter to-day to realise that she was putting me to a considered purpose of her own, the monster, trailing me before Nessim as a bullfighter trails a cloak, and simply to screen her meetings with a man with whom she herself did not even wish to sleep! But I have already described it all, so painfully, and in such great detail—trying to omit no flavour or crumb which would give the picture the coherence I felt it should possess. And yet, even now I can hardly bring myself to feel regret for the strange ennobling relationship into which she plunged me—presumably herself feeling nothing of its power—and from which I myself was to learn so much. Yes, truly it enriched me, but only to destroy Melissa. We must look these things in the face. I wonder why only *now* I have been told all this? My friends must all have known all along. Yet nobody breathed a word. But of course, the truth is that nobody ever does breathe a word, nobody interferes, nobody whispers while the acrobat is on the tight-rope; they just sit and watch the spectacle, waiting only to be wise after the event. But then, from another point of view, how would I, blindly and passionately in love with Justine, have received such unwelcome truths at the time? Would they have deflected me from my purpose? I doubt it.

I suppose that in all this Justine had surrendered to me only one of the many selves she possessed and inhabited—to this timid and scholarly lover with chalk on his sleeve!

Where must one look for justifications? Only I think to the facts themselves; for they might enable me to see now a little further into the central truth of this enigma called "love". I see the image of it receding and curling away from me in an infinite series like the waves of the sea; or, colder than a dead moon, rising up over the dreams and illusions I fabricated from it—but like the real moon, always keeping one side of the truth hidden from me, the nether side of a beautiful dead star. My "love" for her, Melissa's "love" for me, Nessim's "love" for her, her "love" for Pursewarden—there should be a whole vocabulary of adjectives with which to qualify the noun—for no two contained the same properties; yet all contained the one indefinable quality, one common unknown in treachery. Each of us, like the moon, had a dark side—could turn the lying face of "unlove" towards the person who most loved and needed us. And just as Justine used my love, so Nessim used Melissa's. . . . One upon the back of the other, crawling about "like crabs in a basket".

It is strange that there is not a biology of this monster which lives always among the odd numbers, though by all the romances we have built around it it should inhabit the evens: the perfect numbers the hermetics use to describe marriage!

"What protects animals, enables them to continue living? A certain attribute of organic matter. As soon as one finds life one finds it, it is inherent in life. Like most natural phenomena it is polarized—there is always a negative and a positive pole. The negative pole is pain, the positive pole sex. . . . In the ape and man we find the first animals, excluding tame animals, in which sex can be roused without an external stimulus. . . . The result is that the greatest of all natural laws, periodicity, is lost in the human race. The periodic organic condition which should rouse the sexual sense has become an absolutely useless, degenerate, pathological manifestation."* (Pursewarden brooding over the monkey-house at the Zoo! Capodistria in his tremendous library of pornographic books, superbly bound! Balthazar at his occultism! Nessim facing rows and rows of figures and percentages!)

And Melissa? Of course, she was ill, indeed seriously ill, so that in a sense it is melodramatic in me to say that I killed her, or that Justine killed her. Nevertheless, nobody can measure the weight of the pain and neglect which I directly caused her. I remember now one day that Amaril came to see me, sentimental as a great dog. Balthazar had sent Melissa to him for X-rays and treatment.

Amaril was an original man in his way and a bit of a dandy withal. The silver duelling-pistols, the engraved visiting-cards in their superb case, clothes cut in all the elegance of the latest fashions. His house was full of candles and he wrote for preference on black paper with white ink. For him the most splendid thing in the world was to possess a fashionable woman, a prize greyhound, or a pair of invincible fighting-cocks. But he was an agreeable man and not without sensibility as a doctor, despite these romantic foibles.

His devotion to women was the most obvious thing about him; he dressed for them. Yet it was accompanied by a delicacy, almost a pudicity, in his dealings with them—at least in a city where a woman was, as provender, regarded as something like a plateful of mutton; a city where women cry out to be abused.

But he idealized them, built up romances in his mind about them, dreamed always of a complete love, a perfect understanding with one of the tribe. Yet all this was in vain. Ruefully he would explain to Pombal or to myself: "I cannot understand it. Before my love has a chance to crystallize, it turns into a deep, a devouring *friendship*. These devotions are not for you womanisers, you wouldn't understand. But once this happens, passion flies out of the window. Friendship consumes us, paralyses us. Another sort of love begins. What is it? I don't know. A tenderness, a *tendresse*, something melting. *Fondante.*" Tears come into his eyes. "I am really a woman's man and women love me. But—" shaking his handsome head and blowing the smoke from his cigarette upwards to the ceiling he adds smiling, but without self-pity, "I alone among men can say that while all women love me no one woman ever has. Not properly. I am as innocent of love (not sexual love, of course) as a virgin. Poor Amaril!"

It is all true. It was his very devotion to women which dictated his choice in medicine—gynaecology. And women gravitate to him as flowers do to the sunlight. He teaches them what to wear and how to walk; chooses their scents for them, dictates the colour of their lipsticks. Moreover, there is not a woman in Alexandria who is not proud to be seen out on his arm; there is not one who *if asked* (but he never asks) would not be glad to betray her husband or her lover for him. And yet . . . and yet. . . . A connecting thread has been broken somewhere, a link snapped. Such desires as he knows, the stifling summer desires of the body in the city of sensuality, are stifled among shop-girls, among his inferiors. Clea used to say "One feels a special sort of fate in store for Amaril. Dear Amaril!"

Yes. Yes. But what? What sort of fate lies in store for such a romantic—such a devoted, loving, patient student of women? These are the questions I ask myself as I see him, elegantly gloved and hatted, driving with Balthazar to the hospital for an operation. . . .

He described to me Melissa's condition adding only: "It would help her very much if she could be loved a bit." A remark which filled me with shame. It was that very night that I had borrowed the money from Justine to send her to a clinic in Palestine much against her own will.

We walked together to the flat after having spent a few minutes in the public gardens discussing her case. The palms looked brilliant in the moonlight and the sea glittered under the spring winds. It seemed so out of place—serious illness—in this scheme of things. Amaril took my arms as we climbed the stairs and squeezed them gently. "Life is hard" he said. And when we entered the bedroom once more to find her lying there in a trance with her pallid little face turned to the ceiling

133

and the *hashish* pipe beside her on the table, he added, taking up his hat: "It is always . . . don't think I blame you . . . no, I envy you Justine . . . yet it is always *in extremis* that we doctors make the last desperate prescription for a woman patient—when all the resources of science have failed. Then we say 'If only she could be loved!' " He sighed and shook his handsome head.

There are always a hundred ways of justifying oneself but the sophistries of paper logic cannot alter the fact that after reading these passages in the Interlinear, the memory of those days haunts me afresh, torments me with guilts which I might never have been aware of before! I walk now beside the child which Melissa had by Nessim during that brief love-affair (was it "love" again, or was he trying to use her to find out all he could about his wife? Perhaps one day I shall discover): I walk beside the child I say on these deserted beaches like a criminal, going over and over these fragments of the white city's life with regrets too deep even to alter the tone of voice in which I talk to her. Where does one hunt for the key to such a pattern?

But it is clear that I was not alone in feeling such guilt: Pursewarden himself must have been feeling guilty—how else can I explain the money he left me in his will with the express request that it should be spent with Melissa? That at least is one problem solved.

Clea too, I know, felt the guilt of the wound we were all of us causing Melissa—though she felt it, so to speak, on behalf of Justine. She took it, so to speak, upon herself—appalled at the mischief which her lover was causing to us both for so little cause. It was she who now became Melissa's friend, champion and counsellor and who remained her closest confidante until she died. The selfless and innocent Clea, another fool! It does not pay to be honest in love! She said of Melissa: "It is terrible to depend so utterly on powers that do not wish you well. To see someone always in your thoughts, like a stain upon reality. . . ." I think she was also thinking, perhaps, of Justine, up there in the big house among the tall candles and the oil-paintings by forgotten masters.

Melissa also said to her of me: "With his departure *every-thing in nature* disappeared." This was when she was dying. But nobody has the right to occupy such a place in another's life, nobody! You can see now upon what raw material I work in these long and passionate self-communings over a winter sea. "She loved you" said Clea again, "because of your weakness— —this is what she found endearing in you. Had you been strong you would have frightened away so timid a love." And then lastly, before I bang the pages of the manuscript shut with anger and resentment against Balthazar, one last remark of Clea's which burns like a hot iron: "Melissa said: 'You have been my friend, Clea, and I want you to love him after I am gone. Do it with him, will you, and think of me? Never mind all this beastly love business. Cannot a friend make love on another's behalf? I ask you to sleep with him as I would ask the Panaghia to come down and bless him while he sleeps—like in the old ikons.' " How purely Melissa, how Greek!

On Sundays we would walk down together to visit Scobie, I remember; Melissa in her bright cotton frock and straw hat, smiling and eager at the thought of a full holiday from the dusty cabaret. Along the Grande Corniche with the waves dancing and winking across the bar, and the old horse-drawn cabs with their black jarveys in red flowerpots driving their dilapidated and creaking "taxis-of-love"; and as we walked past they would call "Love-taxi sir, madam. Only ten piastres an hour. I know a quiet place. . . ." And Melissa would giggle and turn away as we walked to watch the minarets glisten like pearls upon the morning light and the bright children's kites take the harbour wind.

Scobie usually spent Sundays in bed, and in winter nearly

always contrived to have a cold. He would lie between the coarse linen sheets after having made Abdul give him what he called "a cinnamon rub" (I never discovered what this was); with some formality, too, he would have a brick heated and placed at his feet to keep them warm. He had a small knitted cap on his head. As he read very little, he carried, like an ancient tribe, all his literature in his head and would, when alone, recite to himself for hours. He had quite an extensive repertoire of ballads which he thundered out with great energy, marking the beat with his hand. "The Arab's Farewell to his Steed" brought real tears to his good eye, as did "The harp that once through Tara's Halls"; while among the lesser-known pieces was an astonishing poem the metre of which by its galloping quality virtually enabled him to throw himself out of bed and half-way across the room if recited at full gale force. I once made him write it out for me in order to study its construction closely:

"By O'Neil close beleaguered, the spirits might droop
Of the Saxon three hundred shut up in their coop
Till Bagnal drew forth his Toledo and swore
On the sword of a soldier to succour Portmore.

His veteran troops in the foreign wars tried,
Their features how bronzed and how haughty their stride,
Step't steadily on; Ah! 'twas thrilling to see
That thunder-cloud brooding o'er Beal-an-atha-Buidh!

Land of Owen Aboo! and the Irish rushed on.
The foe fired one volley—their gunners are gone.
Before the bare bosoms the steel coats have fled,
Or despite casque and corslet, lie dying or dead.

And the Irish got clothing, coin, colours, great store,
Arms, forage, and provender—plunder go *leor*.

They munched the white manchets, they champed the brown
chine,
Fuliluah! for that day how the natives did dine!"

Disappointingly, he could tell me nothing about it; it had
lain there in his memory for half a century like a valuable
piece of old silver which is only brought out on ceremonial
occasions and put on view. Among the few other such treasures
which I recognised was the passage (which he always declaimed
with ardour) which ends:

> "*Come the four corners of the world in arms,*
> *We'll shock 'em.*
> *Trust Joshua Scobie to shock 'em!*"

Melissa was devoted to him and found him extraordinarily
quaint in his sayings and mannerisms. He for his part was fond
of her—I think chiefly because she always gave him his full
rank and title—Bimbashi Scobie—which pleased him and made
him feel of consequence to her as a "high official".

But I remember one day when we found him almost in tears.
I thought perhaps he had moved himself by a recital of one of
his more powerful poems ("We Are Seven" was another
favourite); but no. "I've had a quarrel with Abdul—for the
first time" he admitted with a ludicrous blink. "You know
what, old man, he wants to take up circumcision."

It was not hard to understand: to become a barber-surgeon
rather than a mere cutter and shaver was a normal enough step
for someone like Abdul to want to take; it was like getting
one's Ph.D. But of course, I knew too Scobie's aversion to circumcision. "He's gone and bought a filthy great pot of leeches"
the old man went on indignantly. "*Leeches!* Started opening
veins, he has. I said to him I said 'If you think, my boy, that I
set you up in business so as you could spend your time
hyphenating young children for a piastre a time you're wrong,'

I said to him I said." He paused for breath, obviously deeply affected by this development. "But Skipper," I protested, "It seems very natural for him to want to become a barber-surgeon. After all, circumcision is practised everywhere, even in England now." Ritual circumcision was such a common part of the Egyptian scene that I could not understand why he should be so obviously upset by the thought. He pouted, tucked his head down, and ground his false teeth noisily. "No', he said obstinately. "I won't have it." Then he suddenly looked up and said "D'you know what? He's actually going to study under Mahmoud Enayet Allah—that old butcher!"

I could not understand his concern; at every festival or *mulid* the circumcision booth was a regular part of the festivities. Huge coloured pictures, heavily beflagged with the national colours, depicting barber-surgeons with pen-knives at work upon wretched youths spread out in dentists' chairs were a normal if bizarre feature of the side-shows. The doyen of the guild was Mahmoud himself, a large oval man, with a long oiled moustache, always dressed in full fig and apart from his red tarbush conveying the vague impression of some French country practitioner on French leave. He always made a resounding speech in classical Arabic offering circumcision free to the faithful who were too poor to meet the cost of it. Then, when a few candidates were forthcoming, pushed forward by eager parents, his two negro clowns with painted faces and grotesque clothes used to gambol out to amuse and distract the boys, inveigling them by this means into the fatal chair where they were, in Scobie's picturesque phrase, "hyphenated", their screams being drowned by the noise of the crowd, almost before they knew what was happening.

I could not see what was amiss in Abdul's wanting to learn all he could from this don, so to speak, of hyphenation. Then I suddenly understood as Scobie said "It's not the boy—they can do him for all I care. It's the girl, old man. I can't bear to think of that little creature being mutilated. I'm an Englishman, old man, you'll understand my feelings. I WON'T HAVE IT." Exhausted by the force of his own voice, he sank back upon his pillow and went on "And what's more, I told Abdul so in no uncertain terms. 'Lay a finger on the girl,' I said, 'and I'll get you run in—see if I don't.' But of course, it's heartbreaking, old man, 'cause they've been such friends, and the poor coon doesn't understand. He thinks I'm mad!" He sighed heavily twice. "Their friendship was the best I ever had with anyone except Budgie, and I'm not exaggerating, old man. It really was. And now they're puzzled. They don't understand an Englishman's feelings. And I hate using the Influence of My Position." I wondered what this exactly meant. He went on. "Only last month we ran Abdel Latif in and got him closed down, with six months in chokey for unclean razors. He was spreading syphilis old man. I had to do it, even though he was a friend. My duty. I warned him countless times to dip his razor. No, he wouldn't do it. They've got a very poor sense of disinfection here old man. You know, they use styptic—shaving styptic for the circumcisions. It's considered more modern than the old mixture of black gunpowder and lemon-juice. Ugh! No sense of disinfection. I don't know how they don't all die of things, really I don't. But they were quite scared when we ran Abdel Latif in and Abdul has taken it to heart. I could see him watching me while I was telling him off. Measuring my words, like."

But the influence of company always cheered the old man up and banished his phantoms, and it was not long before he was talking in his splendid discursive vein about the life history of Toby Mannering. "It was he who put me on to Holy Writ, old man, and I was looking at The Book yesterday when I found a lot about circumcision in it. You know? The Amalekites used to collect foreskins like we collect stamps. Funny isn't it?" He gave a sudden snort of a chuckle like a bull-frog.

"I must say they were ones! I suppose they had dealers, assorted packets, a regular trade, eh? Paid more for perforations!" He made a straight face for Melissa who came into the room at this moment. "Ah well" he said, still shaking visibly at his own jest. "I must write to Budgie to-night and tell him all the news." Budgie was his oldest friend. "Lives in Horsham, old man, makes earth-closets. He's collected a regular packet from them, has old Budgie. He's an FRZS, I don't quite know what it means, but he has it on his notepaper. Charles Donahue Budgeon FRZS. I write to him every week. Punctual. Always have done, always will do. Staunch, that's me. Never give up a friend."

It was to Budgie, I think, the unfinished letter which was found in his rooms after his death and which read as follows:

"Dear old pal, The whole world seems to have turned against me since I last wrote. I should have"

Scobie and Melissa! In the golden light of those Sundays they live on, bright still with the colours that memory gives to those who enrich our lives by tears or by laughter—unaware themselves that they have given us anything. The really horrible thing is that the compulsive passion which Justine lit in me was quite as valuable as it would have been had it been "real"; Melissa's gift was no less an enigma—what could she have offered me, in truth, this pale waif of the Alexandrian littoral? Was Clea enriched or beggared by her relations with Justine? Enriched—immeasurably enriched, I should say. Are we then nourished only by fictions, by lies? I recall the words Balthazar wrote down somewhere in his tall grammarian's handwriting: "We live by selected fictions," and also: "Everything is true of everybody. . . ." Were these words of Pursewarden's quarried from his own experience of men and women, or simply from a careful observation of us, our behaviours and their result? I don't know. A passage comes to mind from a novel in which Pursewarden speaks about the role of the artist in life. He says something like this: "Aware of every discord, of every calamity in the nature of man himself, he can do nothing to warn his friends, to point, to cry out in time and to try to save them. It would be useless. For they are the deliberate factors of their own unhappiness. All the artist can say as an imperative is: 'Reflect and weep.' "

Was it consciousness of tragedy irremediable contained—not in the external world which we all blame—but in ourselves, in the human condition, which finally dictated his unexpected suicide in that musty hotel-room? I like to think it was, but perhaps I am in danger of putting too much emphasis on the artist at the expense of the man. Balthazar writes: "Of all things his suicide has remained for me an extraordinary and quite inexplicable freak. Whatever stresses and strains he may have been subjected to I cannot quite bring myself to believe it. But then I suppose we live in the shallows of one another's personalities and cannot really see into the depths beneath. Yet I should have said this was surprisingly out of character. You see, he was really at rest about his work which most torments the artists, I suppose, and really had begun to regard it as 'divinely unimportant'—a characteristic phrase. I know this for certain because he once wrote me out on the back of an envelope an answer to the question 'What is the object of writing?' His answer was this: 'The object of writing is to grow a personality which in the end enables man to transcend art.'

"He had odd ideas about the constitution of the psyche. For example, he said 'I regard it as completely unsubstantial as a rainbow—it only coheres into identifiable states and attributes when attention is focused on it. The truest form of right attention is of course love. Thus "people" are as much of an illusion to the mystic as "matter" to the physicist when he is regarding it as a form of energy.'

"He never failed to speak most slightingly of my own

interests in the occult, and indeed in the work of the Cabal whose meetings you attended yourself. He said of this 'Truth is a matter of direct apprehension—you can't climb a ladder of mental concepts to it.'

"I can't get away from the feeling that he was at his most serious when he was most impudent. I heard him maintaining to Keats that the best lines of English poetry ever written were by Coventry Patmore. They were:

> *The truth is great and will prevail*
> *When none care whether it prevail or not.*

"And then, having said this, he added: 'And their true beauty resides in the fact that Patmore when he wrote them did not know what he meant. *Sich lassen!*' You can imagine how this would annoy Keats. He also quoted with approval a mysterious phrase of Stendhal, namely: 'The smile appears on the skin outside.'

"Are we to assume from all this the existence of a serious person underneath the banter? I leave the question to you—your concern is a direct one.

"At the time when we knew him he was reading hardly anything but science. This for some reason annoyed Justine who took him to task for wasting his time in these studies. He defended himself by saying that the Relativity proposition was directly responsible for abstract painting, atonal music, and formless (or at any rate cyclic forms in) literature. Once it was grasped they were understood too. He added: 'In the Space and Time marriage we have the greatest Boy meets Girl story of the age. To our great-grandchildren this will be as poetical a union as the ancient Greek marriage of Cupid and Psyche seems to us. You see, Cupid and Psyche were facts to the Greeks, not concepts. Analogical as against analytical thinking! But the true poetry of the age and its most fruitful poem is the mystery which begins and ends with an *n*.'

" 'Are you serious about all this?'

" 'Not a bit.'

"Justine protested: 'The beast is up to all sorts of tricks, even in his books.' She was thinking of the famous page with the asterisk in the first volume which refers one to a page in the text which is mysteriously blank. Many people take this for a printer's error. But Pursewarden himself assured me that it was deliberate. 'I refer the reader to a blank page in order to throw him back upon his own resources—which is where every reader ultimately belongs.'

"You speak about the plausibility of our actions—and this does us an injustice, for we are all living people and have the right as such to take refuge in the suspended judgment of God if not the reader. So, while I think of it, let me tell you the story of Justine's laughter! You will admit that you yourself never heard it, not once, I mean in a way that was not mordant, not wounded. But Pursewarden did—at the tombs in Saqarra! By moonlight, two days after *Sham el Nessim*. They were there among a large party of sightseers, a crowd under cover of which they had managed to talk a little, like the conspirators they were: already at this time Pursewarden had put an end to her private visitations to his hotel-room. So it gave them a forbidden pleasure, this exchange of a few hoarded secret words; and at last this evening they came by chance to be alone, standing together in one of those overbearing and overwhelming mementoes to a specialised sense of death: the tombs.

"Justine had laddered her stockings and filled her shoes with sand. She was emptying them, he was lighting matches and gazing about him, and sniffing. She whispered she had been terribly worried of late by a new suspicion that Nessim had discovered something about her lost child which he would not tell her. Pursewarden was absently listening when suddenly he snapped his fingers which he had burnt on a match and said: 'Listen, Justine—you know what? I re-read *Moeurs* again last week for fun and I had an idea; I mean if all the song and dance about Freud and your so-called childhood rape and so on are true—are they? I don't know. You could easily make it all up. But since you knew who the man in the wretched eyepiece was and refused to reveal his name to the wretched army of amateur psychologists headed by Arnauti, you must have had a good reason for it. What was it? It puzzles me. I won't tell anyone, I promise. Or is it all a lie?' She shook her head, 'No.'

"They walked out in a clear milk-white moonlight while Justine thought quietly. Then she said slowly: 'It wasn't just shyness or an unwillingness to be cured as they called it—as he called it in the book. The thing was, he was a friend of ours, of yours, of all of us.' Pursewarden looked at her curiously. 'The man in the black patch?' he said. She nodded. They lit cigarettes and sat down on the sand to wait for the others. Feeling that everything she confided in him was absolutely secure she said quietly: 'Da Capo.' There was a long silence. 'Well, stap me! The old Porn himself!' (He had coined this nickname from the word 'pornographer'.) And then very quietly and tentatively, Pursewarden went on: 'I suddenly had the idea of re-reading all that stuff, you know, that if I had been in your shoes and the whole damn thing wasn't just a lie to make yourself more interesting to the psychopomps—I'd . . . well, I'd bloody well try and sleep with him again and try to lay the image that way. The idea suddenly came to me.'

"This betrays, of course, his total ignorance of psychology. Indeed, it was a fatal step to suggest. But here, to his own surprise, she began to laugh—the first effortless, musical laugh he had ever heard her give. 'I did,' she said, now laughing almost too much for speech, 'I did. You'll never guess what an effort it cost me, hanging about in the dark road outside his house, trying to pluck up courage to ring the bell. Yes, it occurred to me too. I was desperate. What would he say? We had been friends for years—with never of course a reference to this event. He had never referred to *Moeurs* and, you know, I don't believe he has read it ever. Perhaps he preferred, I always thought, to disregard the whole thing—to bury it tactfully.'

"Laughter again overtook her, shaking her body so much that Pursewarden took her arm anxiously, not to let her interrupt the recital. She borrowed his handkerchief to mop her eyes and continued: 'I went in at last. He was there in his famous library! I was shaking like a leaf. You see, I didn't know what note to strike, something dramatic, something pathetic? It was like going to the dentist. Really, it was funny, Pursewarden. I said at last "Dear Da Capo, old friend, you have been my demon for so long that I have come to ask you to exorcise me once and for all. To take away the memory of a horrible childhood event. You must sleep with me!" You should have seen Da Capo's face. He was terribly thrown off guard and stammered: "*Mais voyons, Justine, je suis un ami de Nessim!*" and so on. He gave me a whisky and offered me an aspirin—sure that I had gone out of my mind. "Sit down" he said putting out a chair for me with shaking hands and sitting nervously down opposite me with a comical air of alarm—like a small boy accused of stealing apples.' Her side was hurting and she pressed her hand to it, laughing with such merriment that it infected him and involuntarily he began to laugh too. 'Poor Da Capo,' she said, 'he was so terribly shocked and alarmed to be told he had raped me when I was a street arab, a child. I have never seen a man more taken aback. He had completely forgotten, it is clear, and completely denied the whole thing from start to finish. In fact, he was outraged and began to protest. I wish you could have seen his face! Do you know what slipped out in the course of his self-justifications? A marvellous phrase *"Il y a quinze ans que je n'ai pas fait ça!"* ' She threw herself now face downward on to Pursewarden's lap and stayed a moment, still shaking with laughter; and then she raised her head once more to wipe her eyes. She said 'I finished my whisky at last and left, much to his relief; as I was at the door he called after me "Remember you are both dining with me on Wednesday. Eight for eight-fifteen, white tie," as he had done these past few years. I went back home in a daze and drank half a bottle of gin. And you know, I had a strange thought that night in bed —perhaps you will find it shockingly out of place; a thought about Da Capo forgetting so completely an act which had cost me so many years of anxiety and indeed mental illness and had made me harm so many people. I said to myself "This is perhaps the very way God himself forgets the wrongs he does to us in abandoning us to the mercies of the world." ' She threw back her smiling head and stood up.

"She saw now that Pursewarden was looking at her with tears of admiration in his eyes. Suddenly he embraced her warmly, kissing her more passionately perhaps than he had ever done. When she was telling me all this, with a pride unusual in her, she added: 'And you know, Balthazar, that was better than any lover's kiss, it was a real reward, an accolade. I saw then that if things had been different I had it in me to make him love me—perhaps for the very defects in my character which are so obvious to everyone.'

"Then the rest of the party came chattering up among the tombs and . . . I don't know what. I suppose they all drove back to the Nile and ended up at a night-club. What the devil am I doing scribbling all these facts down for you? Lunacy! You will only hate me for telling you things you would prefer not to know as a man and prefer perhaps to ignore as an artist. . . . These obstinate little dispossessed facts, the changelings of our human existence which one can insert like a key into a lock— or a knife into an oyster: will there be a pearl inside? Who can say? But somewhere they must exist in their own right, these grains of a truth which *just slipped out*. Truth is not what is uttered in full consciousness. It is always what 'just slips out' —the typing error which gives the whole show away. Do you understand me, wise one? But I have not done. I shall never have the courage to give you these papers, I can see. I shall finish the story for myself alone.

"So from all this you will be able to measure the despair of Justine when that wretched fellow Pursewarden went and killed himself. In the act of being annoyed with him I find myself smiling, so little do I believe in his death as yet. She found this act as completely mysterious, as completely unforeseen as I myself did; but she poor creature had organised her whole careful deception around the idea of his living on! There was nobody except myself in whom to confide now; and you whom, if she did not love, God knows she did not hate, were in great danger. It was too late to do anything except make plans to go away. She was left with the 'decoy'! Does one learn anything from these bitter truths? Throw all this paper into the sea, my dear boy, and read no more of the Interlinear. But I forget. I am not going to let you see it, am I? I shall leave you content with the fabrications of an art which 'reworks reality to show its significant side'. What significant side could she turn, for example, to Nessim who at that time had become a prey to those very preoccupations which made him appear to everyone —himself included—mentally unstable? Of his more serious preoccupations at this time I could write a fair amount, for I have in the interval learned a good deal about his affairs and his political concerns. They will explain his sudden change-over into a great entertainer—the crowded house which you describe so well, the banquets and balls. But here . . . the question of censorship troubles me, for if I were to send you this and if you were, as you might, to throw this whole disreputable jumble of paper into the water, the sea might float it back to Alexandria perhaps directly into the arms of the Police. Better not. I will tell you only what seems politic. Perhaps later on I shall tell you the rest.

"Pursewarden's face in death reminded me very much of

147

Melissa's; they both had the air of just having enjoyed a satisfying private joke and of having fallen off to sleep before the smile had fully faded from the corners of the mouth. Some time before he had said to Justine: 'I am ashamed of one thing only: because I have disregarded the first imperative of the artist, namely, create and starve. I have never starved, you know. Kept afloat doing little jobs of one sort or another: caused as much harm as you and more.'

"That night, Nessim was already there in the hotel-room sitting with the body when I arrived, looking extraordinarily composed and calm but as if deafened by an explosion. He had been telephoning to Mountolive in the summer residence on the hill. Perhaps the impact of reality had dazed him? He was at this time going through that period of horrible dreams of which he had a transcript made, some of which you reproduce in your MS. They are strangely like echoes of Leila's dreams of fifteen years ago—she had a bad period after her husband died and I attended her at Nessim's request. Here again in judging him you trust too much to what your subjects say about themselves—the accounts they give of their own actions and their meaning. You would never make a good doctor. Patients have to be found out—for they *always* lie. Not that they can help it, it is part of the defence-mechanism of the illness—just as your MS. betrays the defence-mechanism of the dream which does not wish to be invaded by reality! Perhaps I am wrong? I do not wish to judge anyone unjustly or intrude upon your private territory. Will all these notes of mine cost me your friendship? I hope not, but I fear it.

"What was I saying? Yes, Pursewarden's face in death! It had the same old air of impudent contrivance. One felt he was play-acting—indeed, I still do, so alive does he seem to me.

"It was Justine first who alerted me. Nessim sent her to me with the car and a note which I did not let her read. It was clear that Nessim had either learned of the intention or the fact before any of us—I suspect a telephone call by Pursewarden himself. At any rate, my familiarity with suicide cases—I have handled any number for Nimrod's night-patrol—made me cautious. Suspecting perhaps barbiturates or some other slow compound, I took the precaution of carrying my little stomach-pump with me among my antidotes. I confess that I thought with pleasure of my friend's expression when he woke up in hospital. But it seems I misjudged both his pride and his thoroughness for he was thoroughly and conclusively dead when we arrived.

"Justine raced ahead of me up the staircases of the gaunt hotel which he had loved so much (indeed, he had christened it Mount Vulture Hotel—I presume from the swarm of whores who fluttered about in the street outside it, like vultures.)

"Nessim had locked himself into the room—we had to knock and he let us in with a certain annoyance, or so it seemed to me. The place was in the greatest disorder you can imagine. Drawers turned out, clothes and manuscripts and paintings everywhere; Pursewarden was lying on the bed in the corner with his nose pointing aloofly at the ceiling. I paused to unpack my big-intestine kit—method is everything in moments of stress—while Justine went unerringly across to the bottle of gin on the corner by the bed and took a long swig. I knew that this might contain the poison but said nothing—at such times there is little to say. The minute you get hysterical you have to take this kind of chance. I simply unpacked and unwound my aged stomach-pump which has saved more useless lives (lives impossible to live, shed like ill-fitting garments) than any such other instrument in Alexandria. Slowly, as befits a third-rate doctor, I unwound it, and with method, which is all a third-rate doctor has left to face the world with. . . .

"Meanwhile Justine turned to the bed and leaning down said audibly: 'Pursewarden, wake up.' Then she put her palms to the top of her head and let out a long pure wail like an Arab woman—a sound abruptly shut off, confiscated by the night in that hot airless little room. Then she began to urinate in little squirts all over the carpet. I caught her and pushed her into the bathroom. It gave me the respite I needed to have a go at his heart. It was silent as the Great Pyramid. I felt angry about it, because it was clear he had resorted to some beastly cyanide preparation—favoured, by the way, by your famous Secret Service. I was so exasperated that I clipped him over the ear—a blow he had long merited!

"All this time I had been aware that Nessim was suddenly active, but now I recovered, so to speak, and could turn my attention to him. He was turning out drawers and desks and cupboards like a maniac, examining manuscripts and papers, tossing things aside and picking things up with a complete lack of his usual phlegm. 'What the hell are you doing?' I said angrily, to which he replied 'There must be nothing for the Egyptian Police to find.' And then he stopped as if he had said too much. Every mirror bore a soap-inscription. Nessim had partly obliterated one. I could only make out the letters OHEN . . .
. . . ASTINE . . . .

"It was not long before there came the familiar knocking at the door and the faces and tumult inseparable from such scenes everywhere in the world. Men with notebooks, and journalists, and priests—Father Paul of all people turned up. At this, I half-expected the corpse to rise up and throw something . . . but no; Pursewarden remained with his nose cocked to the ceiling, in his amused privacy.

"We stumbled out together, the three of us, and drove back to the studio where the great failed paintings soothed us, and where whisky gave us new courage to continue living. Justine said not a word. Not a mortal word."

o   o   o   o   o

VII

I turn now to another part of the Interlinear, the passage which Balthazar marked: "So Narouz decided to *act*," underlining the last word twice. Shall I reconstruct it—the scene I see so clearly, and which his few crabbed words in green ink have detonated in my imagination? Yes, it will enable me to dream for a moment about an unfrequented quarter of Alexandria which I loved.

The city, inhabited by these memories of mine, moves not only backwards into our history, studded by the great names which mark every station of recorded time, but also back and forth in the living present, so to speak—among its contemporary faiths and races; the hundred little spheres which religion or lore creates and which cohere softly together like cells to form the great sprawling jellyfish which is Alexandria to-day. Joined in this fortuitous way by the city's own act of will, isolated on a slate promontory over the sea, backed only by the moonstone mirror of Mareotis, the salt lake, and its further forevers of ragged desert (now dusted softly by the spring winds into satin dunes, patternless and beautiful as cloudscapes), the communities still live and communicate—Turks with Jews, Arabs and Copts and Syrians with Armenians and Italians and Greeks. The shudders of monetary transactions ripple through them like wind in a wheatfield; ceremonies, marriages and pacts join and divide them. Even the place-names on the old tram-routes with their sandy grooves of rail echo the unforgotten names of their founders—and the names of the dead captains who first landed here, from Alexander to Amr; founders of this anarchy of flesh and **fever,** of money-love and mysticism. Where else on earth will you find such a mixture?

And when night falls and the white city lights up the thousand candelabra of its parks and buildings, tunes in to the soft unearthly drum-music of Morocco or Caucasus, it looks like some great crystal liner asleep there, anchored to the horn of Africa—her diamond and fire-opal reflections twisting downwards like polished bars into the oily harbour among the battleships.

At dusk it can become like a mauve jungle, anomalous, stained with colours as if from a shattered prism; and rising into the pearly sky of the sunset falter up the steeples and minarets like stalks of giant fennel in a swamp rising up over the long pale lines of the sea-shore and the barbaric cafés where the negroes dance to the pop and drub of a finger-drum or to the mincing of clarinets.

"There are only as many realities as you care to imagine" writes Pursewarden.

Narouz always shunned Alexandria while he loved it passionately, with an exile's love; his hare-lip had made him timid to visit the centre, to encounter those he might know. He always hovered about its outskirts, not daring to go directly into the great lighted heart of it where his brother lived a life of devoted enterprise and *mondanité*. He came into it always humbly, on horseback, dressed as he was always dressed, to fulfil the transactions which concerned the property. It took a great effort to persuade him to put on a suit and visit it by car, though when absolutely necessary he had been known to do this also, but reluctantly. For the most part he preferred to do his work through Nessim; and of course the telephone guarded him from many such unwelcome journeys. Yet when his brother rang up one day and said that his agents had been unable to make the Magzub tell them what he knew about Justine's child, Narouz felt suddenly elated—as if fired by the consciousness that this task had now devolved on him. "Nessim," he said, "what is the month? Yes, *Misra*. Quite soon there will come the feast of *Sitna Mariam*, eh? I shall see if he is there and try to make him tell us something." Nessim pondered this offer for so long that Narouz thought the line had been cut and cried sharply "Hallo—hallo!" Nessim answered at once. "Yes, yes. I am here. I am just thinking: you will be careful, won't you?" Narouz chuckled hoarsely and promised that he would. But he was always stirred by the thought that perhaps he might be able to help his brother. Curiously, he thought not at all about Justine herself, or what such information might mean to her; she was simply an acquisition of Nessim's whom he liked, admired, loved deeply, indeed automatically, because of Nessim. It was his duty to do whatever was necessary to help Nessim help her. No more. No less.

So it was that with soft stride, the awkward jaunty step (rising and falling on his toes, swinging his arms), he walked across the brown dusk-beshadowed *meidan* outside the main railway station of Alexandria on the second day of *Sitna Mariam*. He had stabled his horse in the yard of a friend, a carpenter, not far from the place where the festivities of the saint were held. It was a hot rank summer night.

With the dusk that vast and threadbare expanse of empty ground always turned first gold and then brown—to brown cracked cardboard—and then lastly to violet as the lights began to prick the on-coming darkness, as the backcloth of the European city itself began to light up window by window, street by street, until the whole looked like a cobweb in which the frost has set a million glittering brilliants.

Camels somewhere snorted and gnarred, and the music and odour of human beings came across the night towards him, rich with the memories of the fairs he had visited with his parents as a child. In his red tarbush and work-stained clothes he knew

153

he would not be singled out by the crowd as one different from themselves. It was characteristic too that, though the festival of *Sitna Mariam* celebrated a Christian Coptic saint, it was attended and enjoyed by all, not least the Moslem inhabitants of the town, for Alexandria is after all still Egypt: all the colours run together.

A whole encampment of booths, theatres, brothels and shops —a complete township—had sprung up in the darkness, fitfully lit by oil and paraffin stoves, by pressure lamps and braziers, by candle-light and strings of dazzling coloured electric bulbs. He walked lightly into the press of human beings, his nostrils drinking in the scent of aromatic foods and sweetmeats, of stale jasmine and sweat, and his ears the hum of voices which provided a background to those common sounds which always followed the great processions through the town, lingering on the way at every church for a recital of sacred texts, and coming gradually to the site of the festival.

To him all this scattered novelty—the riches of bear-dancers and acrobats, the fire-swallowers blowing six-foot plumes of flame from up-cast mouths—the dancers in rags and particoloured caps—everything that to the stranger would have been a delight was so to him only because it was utterly commonplace—so much a belonging part of his own life. Like the small child he once was he walked in the brilliance of the light, stopping here and there with smiling eyes to stare at some familiar feature of the fair. A conjurer dressed in tinsel drew from his sleeve endless many-coloured handkerchiefs, and from his mouth twenty small live chicks, crying all the time in the voice of the seabird: *"Galli-Galli-Galli-Galli Houp!"*; Manouli the monkey in a paper hat brilliantly rode round and round his stall on the back of a goat. Towering on either side of the thoroughfare rose the great booths with their sugar figurines brilliant with tinsel, depicting the loves and adventures of the creatures inhabiting the folk-lore of the Delta—

154

heroes like Abu Zeid and Antar, lovers like Yunis and Aziza. He walked slowly, with an unpremeditated carelessness, stopping for a while to hear the storytellers, or to buy a lucky talisman from the famous blind preacher Hussein who stood like an oak tree, magnificent in the elf-light, reciting the ninety-nine holy names.

From the outer perimeter of darkness came the crisp click of sportsmen at singlestick, dimly sounding against the hoarse rumble of the approaching procession with its sudden bursts of wild music—kettle-drums and timbrels like volleys of musketry—and the long belly-thrilling rolls of the camel-drums which drowned and refreshed the quavering deep-throated flute-music. "They are coming. They are coming." A confused shouting rose and the children darted here and there like mice among the stalls. From the throat of a narrow alley, spilled like a widening circle of fire upon the darkness, burst a long tilting gallery of human beings headed by the leaping acrobats and dwarfs of Alexandria, and followed at a dancing measure by the long grotesque cavalcade of gonfalons, rising and falling in a tide of mystical light, treading the peristaltic measures of the wild music—nibbled out everywhere by the tattling flutes and the pang of drums or the long shivering orgasm of tambourines struck by the dervishes in their habits as they moved towards the site of the festival. "All-*ah* All-*ah*" burst from every throat.

Narouz took a stick of sugar-cane from a stall and nibbled it as he watched the wave moving forward to engulf him. Here came the Rifiya dervishes, who could in their trances walk upon embers or drink molten glass or eat live scorpions—or dance the turning measure of the universe out, until reality ran down like an overwound spring and they fell gasping to the earth, dazed like birds. The banners and torches, the great openwork braziers full of burning wood, the great paper lanterns inscribed with texts, they made staggering loops and patterns of light upon the darkness of the Alexandrian night, rising and falling, and now the pitches were swollen with spectators, worrying at the procession like mastiffs, screaming and pulling; and still the flood poured on with its own wild music (perhaps the very music that the dying Antony in Cavafy's poem heard) until it engulfed the darkness of the great *meidan*, spreading around it the fitful contours of robes and faces and objects without context but whose colours sprang up and darkened the edges of the sky with colour. Human beings were setting fire to each other.

Somewhere in that black hinterland of smashed and tumbled masonry, of abandoned and disembowelled houses, was a small garden with a tomb in it marking the site which was the sum and meaning of this riot. And here, before a glimmering taper would be read a Christian prayer for a Christian saint, while all around rode the dark press and flood of Alexandria. The dozen faiths and religions shared a celebration which time had sanctified, which was made common to all and dedicated to a season and a landscape, completely obliterating its canon referents in lore and code. To a religious country all religions were one and while the faithful uttered prayers, for a chosen saint, the populace enjoyed the fair which had grown up around the celebration, a rocking carnival of light and music.

And through it all (sudden reminders of the city itself and the full-grown wants and powers of a great *entrepôt*) came the whistles of steam-engines from the dark goods-yards or a sniff of sound from the siren of a liner, negotiating the tortuous fairways of the harbour as it set off for India. The night accommodated them all—a prostitute singing in the harsh chipped accents of the land to the gulp and spank of a finger-drum, the cries of children on the swings and sweating round-abouts and goose-nests, the cock-shies and snake-charmers, the freaks (Zubeida the bearded woman and the calf with five legs), the great canvas theatre outside which the muscle-dancers stood, naked except for loin-cloths, to advertise their skill, and motionless, save for the incredible rippling of their bodies—the flickering and toiling of pectoral, abdominal and dorsal muscles, deceptive as summer lightning.

Narouz was rapt and looked about him with the air of a drunkard, revelling in it all, letting his footsteps follow the haphazard meanderings of this township of light. At the end of one long gallery, having laughingly shaken off the grasp of a dozen girls who plied their raucous trade in painted canvas booths among the stalls, he came to the brilliantly lighted circumcision booths of which the largest and most colourful was that of Abdul's master, Mahmoud Enayet Allah, splendid with lurid cartoons of the ceremony, painted and framed, and from whose lintel hung a great glass jar cloying with leeches. The doyen himself was there to-night, haranguing the crowd and promising free circumcision to any of the faithful too poor to pay the ordinary fee. His great voice rolled out and boomed, while his two assistants stood at attention behind the ancient brass-bound shoe-black's chair with their razors at the alert. Inside the booth, two elderly men in dark suits sipped coffee with the air of philologists at a congress.

Business was slack. "Come along, come along, be purified, ye faithful" boomed the old man, his thumbs behind the lapels of his ancient frock-coat, the sweat pouring down his face under his red tarbush. A little to one side, rapt in the performance of his trade sat a cousin of Mahmoud, tattooing the breast of a magnificent-looking male prostitute whose oiled curls hung down his back and whose eyes and lips were heavily painted. A glass panel of great brilliance hung beside him, painted with a selection of designs from which his clients could choose—purely geometric for Moslems, or Texts, or the record of a vow, or simply beloved names. Touch by touch he filled in the pores of his subject's skin, like a master of needle-craft, smiling from time to time as if at a private joke, building up his *pointilliste* picture while the old *doyen* roared and boomed from the step above him "Come along, come along, ye faithful!"

Narouz bent to the tattooist and said in a hoarse voice: "Is the Magzub here to-night?" and the man raised his startled eye and paused. "Yes," he said, "I think. By the tombs."

Narouz thanked him and turned back once more to the crowded booths, picking his way haphazardly among the narrow thoroughfares until he reached the outskirts of the light. Somewhere ahead of him in the darkness lay a small cluster of abandoned shrines shadowed by leaning palms, and here the gaunt and terrible figure of the famous religious maniac stood, shooting out the thunderbolts of a hypnotic personality on to a fearful but fascinated crowd.

Even Narouz shuddered as he gazed upon that ravaged face, the eyes of which had been painted with crayon so that they looked glaring, inhuman, like the eyes of a monster in a cartoon. The holy man hurled oaths and imprecations at the circle of listeners, his fingers curling and uncurling into claws as he worked upon them, dancing this way and that like a bear at bay, turning and twirling, advancing and retreating upon the crowd with grunts and roars and screams until it trembled before him, fascinated by his powers. He had "come already into his hour", as the Arabs say, and the power of the spirit had filled him.

The holy man stood in an island of the fallen bodies of those he had hypnotized, some crawling about like scorpions, some screaming or bleating like goats, some braying. From time to time he would leap upon one of them uttering hideous screams and ride him across the ring, thrashing at his buttocks like a maniac, and then suddenly turning, with the foam bursting from between his teeth, he would dart into the crowd and pick upon some unfortunate victim, shouting: "Are you mocking me?" and catching him by his nose or an ear or an arm, drag him with superhuman force into the ring where with a sudden quick pass of his talons he would "kill his light" and hurl him down among the victims already crawling about in the sand at his feet, to utter shrill cries for mercy which were snuffed out by the braying and hooting of those already under his spell. One felt the power of his personality shooting out into the tense crowd like sparks from an anvil.

Narouz sat down on a tombstone to watch, in the darkness outside the circle. "Fiends, unclean ones" shrieked the Magzub, thrusting forward his talons so that the circle gave before each onslaught. "You and You and You and You" his voice rising to a terrible roar. He feared and respected no-one when he was "in his hour".

A respectable-looking sheik with the green turban which proclaimed him to be of the seed of the Prophet was walking across the outskirts of the crowd when the Magzub caught sight of him and with flying robes burst through the crowd to the old man's side, shouting: "He is impure." The old sheik turned upon his accuser with angry eyes and started to expostulate, but the fanatic thrust his face close to him and sank those terrible eyes into him. The old sheik suddenly went dull, his head wobbled on his neck and with a shout the Magzub had him down on all fours, grunting like a boar, and dragged him by the turban to hurl him among the others. "Enough" cried the crowd, outraged at this indifference to a man of holiness, but the Magzub twisted round and with flickering fingers rushed back towards the crowd, shrieking: "Who cries 'enough', who cries 'enough'?"

And now, obedient to the commands of this terrible nightmare-mystic, the old sheik rose to his feet and began to perform a lonely little ceremonial dance, crying in thin bird-like tones: "Allah. Allah!" as he trod a shaky measure round the circle of bodies, his voice suddenly breaking into the choking cries of a dying animal "Desist," called the crowd, "desist, O Magzub."

And the hypnotist made a few blunt passes and thrust the old sheik out of the ring, heaping horrible curses upon him.

The old man staggered and recovered himself. He was wide awake now and seemed little the worse for his experience. Narouz came to his side as he was readjusting his turban and dusting his robes. He saluted him and asked him the name of the Magzub, but the old sheik did not know. "But he is a very good man, a holy man" he said. "He was once alone in the desert for years." He walked serenely off into the night and Narouz went back to his tombstone to meditate on the beauty of his surroundings and to wait until he might approach the Magzub whose animal shrieks still sounded upon the night, piercing the blank hubbub of the fair and the drone of the holy men from some nearby shrine. He had as yet not decided how best to deal with the strange personage of the darkness. He waited upon the event, meditating.

It was late when the Magzub ended his performance, releasing the imprisoned menagerie about his feet and driving the crowd away by smacking his hands together—for all the world as if they were geese. He stood for a while shouting imprecations after them and then turned abruptly back among the tombs. "I must be careful" thought Narouz, who intended using force upon him, "not to get within his eyes." He had only a small dagger which he now loosened in its sheath. He began to follow, slowly and purposefully.

The holy man walked slowly, as if bowed down by the weight of preoccupations too many to number and almost too heavy for a mortal to bear. He still groaned and sobbed under his breath, and once he fell to his knees and crawled along the ground for a few paces, muttering. Narouz watched all this with head on one side, like a gun-dog, waiting. Together they skirted the ragged confines of the festival in the half-darkness of the hot night, and at last the Magzub came to a long broken wall of earth-bricks which had once demarcated gardens now abandoned and houses now derelict. The noise of the fair had diminished to a hum, but a steam-engine still pealed from somewhere near at hand. They walked now in a peninsula of darkness, unable to gauge relative distances, like wanderers in an unknown desert. But the Magzub had become more erect now, and walked more quickly, with the eagerness of a fox that is near its earth. He turned at last into a great deserted yard, slipping through a hole in the mud-brick wall. Narouz was afraid he might lose trace of him among these shattered fragments of dwellings and dust-blown tombs. He came around a corner full upon him—the figure of a man now swollen by darkness into a mirage of a man, twelve foot high. "O Magzub," he called softly, "give praise to God," and all of a sudden his apprehension gave place, as it always did when there was violence to be done, to a savage exultation as he stepped forward into the radius of this holy man's power, loosening the dagger and half-drawing it from the sheath.

The fanatic stepped back once and then twice; and suddenly they were in a shaft of light which, leaking across the well of darkness from some distant street-lamp, set them both alive, giving to each other only a lighted head like a medallion. Dimly Narouz saw the man's arms raised in doubt, perhaps in fear, like a diver, and resting upon some rotten wooden beam which in some forgotten era must have been driven into the supporting wall of a byre as a foundation for a course of the soft earth-brick. Then the Magzub turned half sideways to join his hands, perhaps in prayer, and with precise and deft calculation Narouz performed two almost simultaneous acts. With his right hand he drove his dagger into the wood, pinning the Magzub's arms to it through the long sleeves of his coarse gown; with his left he seized the beard of the man, as one might seize a cobra above its hood to prevent it striking. Lastly, instinctively, he thrust his face forward, spreading his split lip to the full, and hissing (for deformity also confers magical powers in the East) in almost the form of an obscene kiss, as he whispered: "O beloved of the Prophet."

They stood like this for a long moment, like effigies of a forgotten action entombed in clay or bronze, and the silence of the night about them took up its palpitating proportions once more. The Magzub breathed heavily, almost plaintively, but he said nothing; but now staring into those terrible eyes, which he had seen that evening burning like live coals, Narouz could discern no more power. Under the cartoon image of the crayon, they were blank and lustreless, and their centres were void of meaning, hollow, dead. It was as if he had pinned a man already dead to this corner of the wall in this abandoned yard. A man about to fall into his arms and breathe his last.

The knowledge that he had nothing to fear, now that the Magzub was "not in his hour", flooded into Narouz' mind on waves of sadness—apologetic sadness: for he knew he could measure the divinity of the man, the religious power from which he took refuge in madness. Tears came into his eyes and he released the saint's beard, but only to rub the matted hair of his head with his hand and whisper in a voice full of loving tears "Ah, beloved of the Prophet! Ah! Wise one and beloved" —as if he were caressing an animal—as if the Magzub now had transformed himself into some beloved hunting-dog. Narouz ruffled his ears and hair, repeating the words in the low magical voice he always used with his favourite animals. The magician's eye rolled, focused and became bleary, like that of a child suddenly overcome with self-pity. A single sob broke from his very heart. He sank to a kneeling position on the dry earth with both hands still crucified to the wall. Narouz bowed and fell with him, comforting him with hoarse inarticulate sounds. Nor was this feigned. He was in a passion of reverence for one who he knew had sought the final truths of religion beneath the mask of madness.

But one side of his mind was still busy with the main

problem, so that he now said, not in the tender voice of a hunter wheedling a favourite, but in the tone of a man who carries a dagger: "Now you will tell me what I wish to know, will you not?" The head of the magician still lolled wearily, and he turned his eyes upwards into his skull with what seemed to be a fatigue which almost resembled death. "Speak" he said hoarsely; and quickly Narouz leaped up to reclaim his dagger, and then, kneeling beside him with one hand still laid about his neck, told him what he wanted to know.

"They will not believe me" moaned the man. "And I have seen it by my own scope. Twice I have told them. I did not touch the child." And then with a sudden flashing return in voice and glance to his own lost power, he cried: "Shall I show you too? Do you wish to see?"—but sank back again. "Yes," cried Narouz, who trembled now from the shock of the encounter, "yes." It was as if an electric current were passing in his legs, making them tremble. "Show me."

The Magzub began to breathe heavily, letting his head fall back on his bosom after every breath. His eyes were closed. It was like watching an engine charge itself, from the air. Then he opened his eyes and said, "Look into the ground."

Kneeling upon that dry baked earth he made a circle in the dust with his index finger, and then smoothed out the sand with the palm of his hand. "Here where the light is" he whispered, touching the dust slowly, purposefully; and then "look with your eye into the breast of the earth" indicating with his finger a certain spot. "Here."

Narouz knelt down awkwardly and obeyed. "I see nothing" he said quietly after a moment. The Magzub blew his breath out slowly in a series of long sighs. "*Think* to see in the ground" he insisted. Narouz allowed his eyes to enter the earth and his mind to pour through them into the spot under the magician's finger. All was still. "I conceive" he admitted at last. Now suddenly, clearly, he saw a corner of the great lake with its interlinking network of canals and the old palm-shaded house of faded bricks where once Arnauti and Justine had lived—where indeed he had started *Moeurs* and where the child. . . . "I see her" he said at last. "Ah" said the Magzub. "Look well."

Narouz felt as if he were subtly drugged by the haze rising from the water of the canals. "Playing by the river" he went on. "She has fallen"; he could hear the breathing of his mentor becoming deeper. "She has fallen" intoned the Magzub. Narouz went on: "No-one is near her. She is alone. She is dressed in blue with a butterfly brooch." There was a long silence; then the magician groaned softly before saying in a thick, almost gurgling tone: "You have seen—to the very place. Mighty is God. In Him is my scope." And he took a pinch of dust and rubbed it upon his forehead as the vision faded.

Narouz, deeply impressed by these powers, kissed and embraced the Magzub, never for one moment doubting the validity of the information he had been granted in the vision. He rose to his feet and shook himself like a dog. They greeted one another now in low whispers and parted. He left the magician sitting there, as if exhausted, upon the ground, and turned his steps once more towards the fair-lights. His body was still shaking with the reaction as if afflicted by pins and needles—or as if an electric current were discharging through his loins and thighs. He had, he realised, been very much afraid. He yawned and shivered as he walked and struck his arms against his legs for warmth—as if to restore a sluggish circulation.

In order to reach the carpenter's yard where his horse was stabled, he had to traverse the eastern corner of the festival ground, where despite the lateness of the hour there was a good deal of hubbub around the swings, and the lights still blazed. It was the time when the prostitutes came into their own, the black, bronze and citron women, impenitent seekers for the money-flesh of men; flesh of every colour, ivory or gold or black. Sudanese with mauve gums and tongues as blue as chows'. Waxen Egyptians. Circassians golden-haired and blue of eye. Earth-blue negresses, pungent as wood-smoke. Every variety of the name of flesh, old flesh quailing upon aged bones, or the unquenched flesh of boys and women on limbs infirm with desires that could be represented in effigy but not be slaked except in mime—for they were desires engendered in the forests of the mind, belonging not to themselves but to remote ancestors speaking through them. Lust belongs to the egg and its seat is below the level of psyche.

The hot blank Alexandrian night burned as brightly as a cresset, reaching up through the bare soles of the black feet to incorrigible hearts and minds. In all this frenzy and loveliness Narouz felt himself borne along, buoyant as a lily floating on a river, yet burrowing deeply into the silence of his own mind as he went to where the archetypes of these marvellous images waited for him.

It was now that he saw, idly, a short scene enacted before his eyes—a scene whose meaning he did not grasp, and which indeed concerned someone he had never met and would never meet: except in the pages of this writing—Scobie.

Somewhere in the direction of the circumcision booths a riot had started. The frail canvas and paper walls with their lurid iconography trembled and shook, voices snarled and screamed and hobnailed boots thundered upon the impermanent flooring of duck-boards; and then, bursting through those paper walls into the white light, holding a child wrapped in a blanket, staggered an old man dressed in the uniform of an Egyptian Police Officer, his frail putteed shanks quavering under him as he ran. Behind him streamed a crowd of Arabs yelling and growling like savage but cowardly dogs. This whole company burst in a desperate sortie right across Narouz' tracks. The old man in uniform was shouting in a frail voice, but what he shouted was lost in the hubbub; he staggered across the road to an ancient cab and climbed into it. It set off at once at a ragged trot followed by a fusillade of stones and curses. That was all.

As Narouz watched this little scene, his curiosity aroused by it, a voice spoke out of the shadows at his side—a voice whose sweetness and depth could belong to one person only: Clea. He was stabbed to the quick—drawing his breath sharply, painfully, and joining his hands in a sudden gesture of childish humility at the sound. The voice was the voice of the woman he loved but it came from a hideous form, seated in half-shadow—the grease-folded body of a Moslem woman who sat unveiled before her paper hut on a three-legged stool. As she spoke, she was eating a sesame cake with the air of some huge caterpillar nibbling a lettuce—and at the same time speaking in the veritable accents of Clea!

Narouz went to her side at once, saying in a low wheedling voice: "Oh my mother, speak to me"; and once more he heard those perfectly orchestrated tones murmuring endearments and humble blandishments to draw him towards the little torture-chamber. (Petesouchos the crocodile goddess, no less.)

Blind now to everything but the cadences of the voice he followed her like an addict, standing inside the darkened room with eyes closed, his hands upon her great quivering breasts —as if to drink up the music of these slowly falling words of love in one long wholesome draught. Then he sought her mouth feverishly, as if he would suck the very image of Clea from her breath—from that sesame-laden breath. He trembled with excitement—the perilous feeling of one about to desecrate a sacred place by some irresistible obscenity whose meaning flickered like lightning in the mind with a horrible beauty of its own. (Aphrodite permits every conjugation of the mind and sense in love.)

He loosened his clothing and pressed this great doll of flesh slowly down upon the dirty bed, coaxing from her body with

166

his powerful hands the imagined responses he might have coaxed perhaps from another and better-loved form. "Speak, my mother," he whispered hoarsely, "speak while I do it. Speak." Expressing from this great white caterpillar-form one rare and marvellous image, rare perhaps as an Emperor moth, the beauty of Clea. Oh but how horrible and beautiful to lie there at last, squeezed out like an old paint-tube among the weeping ruins of intestate desires: himself, his own inner man, thrown finally back into the isolation of a personal dream, transitory as childhood, and not less heartbreaking: Clea!

But he was interrupted, yes; for now as I read these scenes in the Interlinear, my memory revives something which it had forgotten; memories of a dirty booth with a man and woman lying together in a bed and myself looking down at them, half-drunk, waiting my turn. I have described the whole scene in another place—only then I took the man to be Mnemjian. I now believe it was Narouz. "They lay there like the victims of some terrible accident, clumsily engaged, as if in some incoherent experimental fashion they were the first partners in the history of the human race to think out this peculiar means of communication."

And this woman, with her "black spokes of toiling hair", that lay in Narouz' arms—would Clea or Justine recognise themselves in a mother-image of themselves woven out of moneyed flesh? Narouz was drinking Clea thirstily out of this old body hired for pleasure, just as I myself wished only to drink Justine. Once again "the austere, mindless primeval face of Aphrodite!"

Yes, but thirst *can* be quenched like this, by inviting a succubus to one's bed; and Narouz later wandered about in the darkness, incoherent as a madman, swollen with a relief he could barely stand. He felt like singing. Indeed, if one cannot say that he had completely forgotten Clea at this moment, one can at least assert that the act had delivered him from her image. He was wholly purged of her—and indeed would have had at this moment even the courage to *hate* her. Such is the polarity of love. "True" love.

He went back slowly, by winding ways, to his carpenter friend and claimed his horse, after first rousing the family to reassure them that it was not a thief who was making a noise in the stable at this hour.

Then he rode back to his lands, the happiest young man alive, and reached the manor as the first streaks of dawn were in the sky. As no-one was about he wrapped himself in a cloak and rested on the balcony until the sun should wake him up. He wanted to tell his brother the news.

But Nessim listened quietly and seriously to his whole story the next morning, wondering that the human heart makes no sound when the blood drains out of it drop by drop—for he thought he saw in this piece of information a vital check to the growth of the confidence he wished to foster in his wife. "I do not suppose" said Narouz, "that after so long we could find the body but I'll go over with Faraj and some grapnels and see —there can be no harm in trying. Shall I?" Nessim's shoulders had contracted. His brother paused for a moment and then went on in the same level tone: "Now I did not know anything before about how the child was dressed. But I will describe what I saw in the ground. She had a blue frock with a brooch in the shape of a butterfly." Nessim said, almost impatiently: "Yes. Perfectly true. It was the description Justine gave to the Parquet. I remember the description. So, well, Narouz . . . what can I say? It is true. I want to thank you. But as for the dragging—it has been done at least a dozen times by the Parquet. Yes, without result. There is a cut there in the canal and a runaway with a strong undercurrent."

"I see" said Narouz, cast down.

"It is difficult to know." But Nessim's voice sharpened its

edge as he added: "But one thing, promise me. She must never know the truth from your lips. Promise."

"I promise you that" said his brother as Nessim turned aside from the hall telephone and came face to face with his wife. Her face was pale and her great eyes searched his with suspense and curiosity. "I must go now" said Nessim hurriedly and put down the receiver as he turned to face her and take her hands in his. In memory, I always see them like this, staring at each other with clasped hands, so near together, so far apart. The telephone is a modern symbol for communications which never take place.

o   o   o   o   o

VIII

"I told you of Scobie's death (so wrote Balthazar) but I did not tell you in detail the manner of it. I myself did not know him very well but I knew of your affection for him. It was not a very pleasant business and I was concerned in it entirely by accident—indeed, only because Nimrod, who runs the Secretariat, and was Scobie's chief at three removes happened to be dining with me on that particular evening.

"You remember Nimrod? Well, we had recently been competing for the favours of a charming young Athenian actor known by the delightful name of Socrates Pittakakis, and as any serious rivalry might have caused a bad feeling between us which neither could afford on the official level (I am in some sense a consultant to his department) we had sensibly decided to bury our jealousy and frankly share the youth—as all good Alexandrians should. We were therefore dining *à trois* at the *Auberge Bleue* with the young man between us like the filling in a meat sandwich. I must admit that I had a slight advantage over Nimrod whose Greek is poor, but in general the spirit of reason and measure reigned. The actor, who drank champagne in stout all evening—he was recovering he explained from a wasting malady by this method—in the last analysis refused to have anything to do with either of us, and indeed turned out to be passionately in love with a heavily moustached Armenian girl in my clinic. So all this effort was wasted—I must say Nimrod was particularly bitter as he had had to pay for this grotesque dinner. Well, as I say, here we all were when the great man was called away to the telephone.

"He came back after a while, looking somewhat grave, and

said: 'It was from the Police Station by the docks. Apparently an old man has been kicked to death by the ratings of H.M.S. *Milton*. I have reason to believe that it might be one of the eccentrics of Q branch—there is an old Bimbashi employed there. . . .' He stood irresolutely on one leg. 'At any rate,' he went on, 'I must go down and make sure. You never know. Apparently' he lowered his voice and drew me to one side in confidence, 'he was dressed in woman's clothes. There may be a scandal.'

"Poor Nimrod! I could see that while his duty pressed him hard, he was most reluctant that I should be left alone with the actor. He hovered and pondered heavily. At last, however, my finer nature came to my rescue just when I had given up hope. I too rose. Undying sportsmanship! 'I had better come with you' said I. The poor man broke into troubled smiles and thanked me warmly for the gesture. We left the young man eating fish (this time for brain fag) and hurried to the car park where Nimrod's official car was waiting for him. It did not take us very long to race along the Corniche and turn down into the echoing darkness of the dock-area with its cobbled alleys and the flickering gas light along the wharves which makes it seem so like a corner of Marseilles circa 1850. I have always hated the place with its smells of sea-damp and urinals and sesame.

"The police post was a red circular building like a Victorian post office consisting of a small charge-room and two dark sweating dungeons, airless and terrible in that summer night. It was packed with jabbering and sweating policemen all showing the startled whites of their eyes like horses in the gloom. Upon a stone bench in one of the cells lay the frail and ancient figure of an old woman with a skirt dragged up above the waist to reveal thin legs clad in green socks held by suspenders and black naval boots. The electric light had failed and a wavering candle on the sill above the body dripped wax on to one withered old hand, now beginning to settle with the approach of the rigor into a histrionic gesture—as of someone warding off a stage blow. It was your friend Scobie.

"He had been battered to death in ugly enough fashion. A lot of broken crockery inside that old skin. As I examined him a phone started to nag somewhere. Keats had got wind of something: was trying to locate the scene of the incident. It could only be a matter of time before his battered old Citroen drew up outside. Obviously a grave scandal might well be the upshot and fear lent wings to Nimrod's imagination. 'He must be got out of these clothes' he hissed and started beating out right and left with his cane, driving the policemen out into the corridor and clearing the cell. 'Right' I said, and while Nimrod stood with sweating averted face, I got the body out of its clothes as best I could. Not pleasant, but at last the old reprobate lay there 'naked as a psalm' as they say in Greek. That was stage one. We mopped our faces. The little cell was like an oven.

" 'He must' said Nimrod hysterically, 'be somehow got back into uniform. Before Keats comes poking around here. I tell you what, let's go to his digs and get it. I know where he lives.' So we locked the old man into his cell: his smashed glass eye gave him a reproachful, mournful look—as if he had been subjected to an amateur taxidermist's art. Anyway, we jumped into the car and raced across the docks to Tatwig Street while Nimrod examined the contents of the natty little leatherette handbag with which the old man had equipped himself before setting out on his adventure. In it he found a few coins, a small missal, a master's ticket, and a packet of those old-fashioned rice-papers (one hardly ever sees them now) resembling a roll of cigarette paper. That was all. 'The bloody old fool' Nimrod kept saying as we went. 'The bloody old fool.'

"We were surprised to find that all was chaos in the old

man's lodgings, for in some mysterious way the neighbourhood had already got to hear of his death. At least, so I presumed. All the doors of his rooms had been burst open and cupboards rifled. In a sort of lavatory there was a bathtub full of some brew which smelt like *arak* and the local people had apparently been helping themselves freely, for there were prints from countless wet feet on the stairs and wet hands on the walls. The landing was awash. In the courtyard, a boab dancing round his stave and singing—a most unusual sight. Indeed, the whole neighbourhood seemed to wear an air of raffish celebration. It was most uncanny. Though most of Scobie's things had been stolen, his uniform was hanging quite safely behind the door and we grabbed it. As we did so, we got a tremendous start for a green parrot in a cage in the corner of the room said in what Nimrod swore was a perfect imitation of Scobie's voice:

> *'Come the four corners of the world in arms,*
> *We'll (hic) shock 'em.'*

"It was clear that the bird was drunk. Its voice sounded so strange in that dismal empty room. (I have not told Clea any of this, for fear that it would upset her, as she too cared for him very much.)

"Well, back to the police post with the uniform, then. We were in luck, for there was no sign of Keats. We locked ourselves into the cell again, gasping at the heat. The body was setting so fast that it seemed impossible to get the tunic on without breaking his arms—which, God knows, were so frail that they would have snapped off like celery, or so it seemed: so I compromised by wrapping it round him. The trousers were easier. Nimrod tried to help me but was overtaken by violent nausea and spent most of the time retching in a corner. He was indeed much moved by the whole thing and kept repeating under his breath 'Poor old bugger'. Anyway, by a smart bit of work, the scandal he feared was averted, and hardly had we brought your Scobie into line with the general proprieties than we heard the unmistakable rumble of the *Globe* car at the door and the voice of Keats in the charge-room.

"I must not forget to add that during the following few days there were two deaths and over twenty cases of acute *arak* poisoning in the area around Tatwig Street so that Scobie may be said to have left his mark on the neighbourhood. We tried to get an analysis of the stuff he was brewing, but the Government analyst gave up after testing several samples. God knows what the old man was up to.

"Nevertheless the funeral was a great success (he was buried with full honours as an officer killed in the execution of his duty) and everyone turned out for it. There was quite a contingent of Arabs from around his home. It is rare to hear Moslem ululations at a Christian graveside, and the R.C. Chaplain, Father Paul, was most put out, fearing perhaps the *afreets* of Eblis conjured up by home-made *arak*—who knows? Also there were the usual splendid inadvertencies, so characteristic of life here (grave too small, grave-diggers strike for more pay in the middle of widening it, Greek consul's carriage runs away with him and deposits him in a bush, etc., etc.) I think I described all this in a letter. It was just what Scobie would have desired—to lie covered with honours while the Police Band blew the Last Post—albeit waveringly and with a strong suggestion of Egyptian quarter-tones—over the grave. And the speeches, the tears! You know how people let themselves go on such occasions. You would have thought he was a saint. I kept remembering the body of the old woman in the police cell!

"Nimrod tells me that once he used to be very popular in his *quartier*, but that latterly he had started to interfere with ritual circumcision among the children and became much hated. You know how the Arabs are. Indeed, that they threatened to poison him more than once. These things preyed upon his mind as one may understand. He had been many years down there and I suppose he had no other life of his own. It happens to so many expatriates, does it not? Anyway, latterly he began to drink and to 'walk in his sleep' as the Armenians say. Everyone tried to make allowances for him and two constables were detailed to look after him on these jaunts. But on the night of his death he gave them all the slip.

" 'Once they start dressing up' says Nimrod (he is really utterly humourless), 'it's the beginning of the end.' And so there it is. Don't mistake my tone for flippancy. Medicine has taught me to look on things with ironic detachment and so conserve the powers of feeling which should by rights be directed towards those we love and which are wasted on those who die. Or so I think.

"What on earth, after all, is one to make of life with its grotesque twists and turns? And how, I wonder, has the artist the temerity to try and impose a pattern upon it which he infects with his own meanings? (This is aimed slightly in your direction) I suppose you would reply that it is the duty of the pilot to make comprehensible the shoals and quicksands, the joys and misfortunes, and so give the rest of us power over them. Yes, but. . . .

"I desist for to-night. Clea took in the old man's parrot; it was she who paid the expenses of his funeral. Her portrait of him still stands I believe upon a shelf in her now untenanted room. As for the parrot, it apparently still spoke in his voice and she said she was frequently startled by the things it came out with. Do you think one's soul could enter the body of a green Amazon parrot to carry the memory of one forward a little way into Time? I would like to think so. But this is old history now."

IX

Whenever Pombal was grievously disturbed about something ("*Mon Dieu!* to-day I am decomposed!" He would say in his quaint English) he would take refuge in a magistral attack of gout in order to remind himself of his Norman ancestry. He kept an old-fashioned high-backed court chair, covered in red velveteen, for such occasions. He would sit with his wadded leg up on a footstool to read the *Mercure* and ponder on the possible reproof and transfer which might follow upon his latest *gaffe* whatever that might happen to be. His whole Chancery, he knew, was against him and considered his conduct (he drank too much and chased women) as prejudicial to the service. In fact, they were jealous because his means, which were not large enough to free him altogether from the burden of working for a living, permitted him nevertheless to live more or less *en prince*—if you could call the smoky little flat we shared princely.

As I climbed the stairs to-day I knew that he was in a decomposed state from the peevish tone in which he spoke. "It is *not* news" he was repeating hysterically. "I forbid you to publish." One-eyed Hamid met me in the hall which smelt of frying, and waved a tender hand in the air. "The Miss has gone," he whispered, indicating Melissa's departure, "back six o'clock. Mr. Pombal very not good." He pronounced my friend's name as if it contained no vowels: thus: Pmbl.

I found Keats was with him in the sitting-room, his large and perspiring frame stretched awkwardly across the sofa. He was grinning and his hat was on the back of his head. Pombal was perched in his gout-chair, looking mournful and peevish. I recognized the signs not only of a hangover but of yet another committed *gaffe*. What had Keats got hold of now? "Pombal," I said, "what the devil has happened to your car?" He groaned and clutched his dewlaps as if imploring me to leave the whole subject alone; obviously Keats had been teasing him about just that.

The little car in question, so dear to Pombal's heart, now stood outside the front door, badly buckled and smashed. Keats gave a snuffle-gulp. "It was Sveva" he explained, "and I'm not allowed to print it." Pombal moaned and rocked. "He won't tell me the whole story."

Pombal began to get really angry. "Will you please get out?" he said, and Keats, always easily discountenanced before some-one whose name appeared on the diplomatic list, rose and pocketed his notebook, wiping the smile off his face as he did so. "All right, he said, punning feebly, "*Chacun à son* gout, I suppose," and clambered slowly down the stairs. I sat down opposite Pombal and waited for him to calm down.

"Another *gaffe*, my dear boy," he said at last, "the worst yet in the *affaire Sveva*. It was she . . . my poor car . . . you have seen it? Here, feel this bump on my neck. Eh? A bloody rock."

I asked Hamid for some coffee while he recounted his latest mishap with the usual anguished gesticulations. He had been unwise ever to embark on this affair with the fiery Sveva, for now she loved him. "Love!" Pombal groaned and twisted in his chair. "I am so weak about women," he admitted, "and she was so easy. God, it was like having something put on one's plate which one hadn't ordered—or which someone else had and which had been sent to one's table by mistake; she came into my life like a *bifteck à point*, like a stuffed eggplant. . . . What was I to do?

"And then yesterday I thought: 'Taking everything into account, her age, the state of her teeth, and so on, illness might very well intervene and cause me expense.' Besides, I don't *want* a mistress in *perpetuum mobile*. So I decided to take her out to a quiet spot on the lake and say good-bye. She went mad. In a flash she was on the bank of the river where she found a huge pile of rocks. Before I knew what to say *Piff Paff Pang Bong.*" His gestures were eloquent. "The air was full of rocks. Windscreen, headlights, everything . . . I was lying beside the clutch screaming. Feel this lump on my neck. She had gone mad. When all the glass was gone, she picked up a huge boulder and began to stove the car in screaming the word '*Amour. Amour*' to punctuate each bang like a maniac. I never want to hear the word again. Radiator gone, all the wings twisted. You have seen? You would never believe a girl could do such a thing. Then what? Then I'll tell you what. *She threw herself into the river.* Figure to yourself my feelings. She can't swim, nor can I. The *scandal* if she died! I threw myself in after her. We held each other and screamed like a pair of cats making love. The water I swallowed! Some policemen came and pulled us out. Long *procès-verbal*, etc. I simply dare not ring the Chancery this morning. Life isn't worth living."

He was on the point of tears. "This is my third scandal this month" he said. "And to-morrow is carnival. Do you know what? After long thought I have evolved an idea." He smiled a wintry smile. "I shall make sure about the carnival—even if I do drink too much and get in a scrape as I usually do. I shall go in an impenetrable disguise. Yes." He rinsed his fingers and repeated "An impenetrable disguise." Then he considered me for a moment as if trying to decide whether to trust me or not. His scrutiny seemed to satify him for he turned abruptly towards the cupboard and said: "If I show you, you'll keep my secret, eh? We are friends after all. Fetch me the hat from the top shelf in there. You will get a laugh."

Inside the cupboard I found an immense, old-fashioned picture-hat of the 1912 variety, trimmed with a bunch of faded osprey feathers and secured by a thick hatpin with a large blue stone head. "This?" I said incredulously, and he chuckled

178

complacently as he nodded. "Who will ever recognise me in this? Give it here. . . ."

He looked so funny with it on that I was forced to sit down and laugh. He reminded me of Scobie in his own absurd Dolly Varden. Pombal looked . . . it is quite indescribable what this ridiculous creation did to his fat face. He began to laugh too as he said "Wonderful, no? My bloody colleagues will never know who the drunk woman was. And if the Consul General isn't in domino I shall . . . make advances to him. I shall drive him out of his mind with passionate kisses. The swine!" His face set in a grimace of hate looked even more ludicrous. As with Scobie, I was forced to plead: "Take it off, for God's sake!"

He did so and sat grinning at me, consumed by the brilliance of his plan. At least, he thought, such indiscretions as he might commit would not be attributable to him. "I have a whole costume" he added proudly. "So look out for me, will you? You are going, aren't you? I hear that there are two full-scale balls going so we shall weave about from one to the other, eh? Good. I am a bit relieved, aren't you?"

But it was this fatal hat of Pombal's which led directly to Toto de Brunel's mysterious death next evening at the Cervonis'— the death which Justine believed her husband had reserved for her and which I. . . . But I must follow the Interlinear back upon my tracks.

"The question of the watch-key" writes Balthazar, "—the one you helped me hunt for among the crevices of the Grande Corniche on that winter day—turned out oddly. As you know, my timepiece stopped and I had to order another little gold ankh to be made for it. But in the interval the key was returned under strange circumstances. One day Justine came into the clinic and, kissing me warmly, produced it from her handbag. 'Do you recognise this?' she asked me smiling, and then went on apologetically 'I am so sorry for your concern, my dear

Balthazar. It is the first time in my life that I have been forced to turn pickpocket. You see, there is a wall-safe in the house to which I was determined to gain access. At first glance the keys seemed similar and I wanted to see whether your watch-key fitted the lock. I had intended to return it next morning before you had time to worry, but I found that someone had removed it from my dressing-table. You won't repeat this. I thought that perhaps Nessim himself had caught sight of it, and had suspected my motive, and had therefore confiscated it in order to try it in the lock of his safe himself. Fortunately (or unfortunately) it does not fit, and I could not open the little safe. But, nor could I make a fuss about the thing for fear that he had not in fact seen it; I did not want to draw his attention to its existence and its similarity to his own. I asked Fatma discreetly and went through my jewel-cases. No luck. Then two days later Nessim himself produced it and said he had found it in his stud-box; he recognised its similarity to his own but did not mention the safe. He simply asked me to give it back to you, which I herewith do, with genuine apologies for the delay.'

"I was of course annoyed, and told her so. 'And anyway, why should you wish to poke about in Nessim's private safe?' I said. 'It seems to me unlike your normal behaviour, and I must say I feel a good deal of contempt for you after the way Nessim has treated you.' She hung her head and said 'I only hoped to discover something about the child—something which I think he is hiding from me.' ''

∘ ∘ ∘ ∘ ∘

PART III

X

"I suppose (writes Balthazar) that if you wished somehow to incorporate all I am telling you into your own Justine manuscript now, you would find yourself with a curious sort of book—the story would be told, so to speak, in layers. Unwittingly I may have supplied you with a form, something out of the way! Not unlike Pursewarden's idea of a series of novels with 'sliding panels' as he called them. Or else, perhaps, like some medieval palimpsest where different sorts of truth are thrown down one upon the other, the one obliterating or perhaps supplementing another. Industrious monks scraping away an elegy to make room for a verse of Holy Writ!

"I don't suppose such a analogy would be a bad one to apply to the reality of Alexandria, a city at once sacred and profane; between Theocritus, Plotinus, and the Septuagint one moves on intermediate levels which are those of race as much as anything—like saying Copt, Greek and Jew or Moslem, Turk and Armenian. . . . Am I wrong? These are the slow accretions of time itself on place. Just as life on the individual face lays down, wash by successive wash, the wrinkles of experiences in which laughter and tears are utterly indistinguishable. Worm-casts of experience on the sands of life. . . ."

So writes my friend, and he is right; for the Interlinear now raises for me much more than the problem of objective "truth to life", or if you like "to fiction". It raises, as life itself does —whether one makes or takes it—the harder-grained question of form. How then am I to manipulate this mass of crystallized data in order to work out the meaning of it and so give a coherent picture of this impossible city of love and obscenity?

I wish I knew. I wish I knew. So much has been revealed to me by all this that I feel myself to be, as it were, standing upon the threshold of a new book—a new Alexandria. The old evocative outlines which I drew, intertwining them with the names of the city's exemplars—Cavafy, Alexander, Cleopatra and the rest—were subjective ones. I had made the image my own jealous personal property, and it was true yet only within the limitations of a truth only partially perceived. Now, in the light of all these new treasures—for truth, though merciless as love, must always be a treasure—what should I do? Extend the frontiers of original truth, filling in with the rubble of this new knowledge the foundations upon which to build a new Alexandria? Or should the dispositions remain the same, the characters remain the same—and is it only truth *itself* which has changed in contradiction?

All this spring on my lonely island I have been weighed down by this grotesque information, which has so altered my feelings about things—oddly enough even about things past. Can emotions be retrospective, retroactive?

So much I wrote was based upon Justine's fears of Nessim—genuine fears, genuinely expressed. I have seen with my own eyes that cold speechless jealousy upon his face—and seen the fear written on hers. Yet now Balthazar says that Nessim would never have done her harm. What am I to believe?

We dined so often together, the four of us; and there I sat speechless and drunk upon the memory of her actual kisses, believing (only because she told me so) that the presence of the fourth—Pursewarden—would lull Nessim's jealous brain and offer us the safety of chaperonage! Yet if now I am to believe Balthazar, it was I who was the decoy. (Do I remember, or only imagine, a special small smile which from time to time would appear at the corner of Pursewarden's lips, perhaps cynical or perhaps comminatory?) I thought then that I was sheltering behind the presence of the writer while he was in fact sheltering

184

behind mine! I am prevented from fully believing this by . . . what? The quality of a kiss from the lips of one who could murmur, like a being submitting its body to the rack, the words "I love you." Of course, of course. I am an expert in love—every man believes himself to be one: but particularly the Englishman. So I am to believe in the kiss rather than in the statements of my friend? Impossible, for Balthazar does not lie. . . .

Is love by its very nature a blindness? Of course, I know I averted my face from the thought that Justine might be unfaithful to me while I possessed her—who does not? It would have been too painful a truth to accept, although in my heart of hearts I knew full well, that she could never be faithful to me for ever. If I ever dared to whisper the thought to myself I hastily added, like every husband, every lover, "But of course, whatever she does, I am the one she truly loves!" The sophistries which console—the lies which keep love going!

Not that she herself ever gave me direct reason to doubt. I do however remember an occasion on which the faintest breath of suspicion roused itself against Pursewarden, only to be immediately stilled. He walked out of the studio one day towards us with some lipstick on his mouth. But almost immediately I caught sight of the cigarette in his hand—he had obviously picked up a cigarette which Justine had left burning in an ashtray (a common habit with her) for the end of it was red. In matters of love everything is easy to explain.

The wicked Interlinear, freighted with these doubts, presses like a blunt thumb, here and here, always in bruised places. I have begun to copy it whole—the whole of it—slowly and painfully; not only to understand more clearly wherein it differs from my own version of reality, but also to catch a glimpse of it as a separate entity—as a manuscript existing in its own right, as the determined view of another eye upon events which I interpreted in my own way, because that was the way in which I lived them—or they lived me. Did I really miss so much that was going on around me—the connotation of smiles, of chance words and gestures, messages scribbled with a finger in wine spilt upon a table-top, addresses written in the corner of newspapers and folded over? Must I now re-work my own experiences in order to come to the heart of the truth? "Truth has no heart" writes Pursewarden. "Truth is a woman. That is why it is enigmatic. Of women, the most we can say, not being Frenchmen, is that they are burrowing animals."

According to Balthazar, I have misread the order of Justine's fears in so far as they concerned Nessim. The incident of the car I have recorded elsewhere; how she was racing towards Cairo one night to meet Pursewarden when the lights of the great moth-coloured Rolls went out. Blinded by darkness she lost control of it and it swarmed off the road, bouncing from dune to dune and throwing up spouts of sand like the spray thrown up by the death-agonies of a whale. Then "whistling like an arrow" it buried itself to the windscreens in a dune and lay trembling and murmuring. Fortunately, she was not hurt and had the presence of mind to switch off the engine. But how had the accident come about? In telling me of it she said that when the car was examined the wiring was found to have been filed down—by whom?

This was, as far as I know, the first time that her fears con-cerning Nessim, and a possible attempt on her own life, became articulate. She had spoken of his jealousy before, yes; but not of anything like this, not of anything so concrete—so truly Alexandrian. My own alarm may well be imagined.

Yet now Balthazar in his notes says that some ten days before this incident, she had seen Selim from the studio window walk across the lawn towards the car, and there believing him-self unobserved, lift the bonnet to take out from under it one of the little wax rollers which she thought she recognised as part of the equipment belonging to the dictaphone which Nessim often used in the office. He had wrapped the object in a cloth and carried it indoors. She sat at the window for a long time, musing and smoking before acting. Then she took the car out on to the desert road to a lonely place the better to examine it. Under the bonnet she found a small apparatus which she did not recognise but which seemed to her to be possibly a recording machine. Presumably a wire lead connected it to a small microphone buried somewhere among the coloured coils of the dashboard wiring, but she could not trace it. With her nail file, however, she cut the wire at several points while leaving the whole contrivance in place and apparently in working order. It was now, according to Balthazar, that she must by accident have disturbed or half-severed one of the leads to the car's headlights. At least, this is what she told him, though she gave me no such explanation. If I am to believe him, all this time, while she went on and on about the heedless folly of our public behaviour and the risks we were taking, she was really drawing me on—trailing me before the eyes of Nessim like a cape before a bull!

But this was only at first; later, says my friend, came something which really made her feel that some action against her was contemplated by her husband: namely the murder of Toto de Brunel during the carnival ball at the Cervonis'. Why have I never mentioned this? It is true that I was even there at the time, and yet somehow the whole incident though it belonged to the atmosphere of the moment escaped me in the press of other matters. Alexandria had many such unsolved mysteries at that time. And while I knew the interpretation Justine put upon it I did not myself believe it at the time. Nevertheless, it is strange that I should not have mentioned it, even in passing. Of course, the true explanation of the matter was only given to me months later: almost when I myself was on the point of leaving Alexandria for ever as I thought, with the child of Melissa—Nessim's child by her. Clea one night told me the truth with her own lips!

The carnival in Alexandria is a purely social affair—having no calendar relationship to the other religious festivals of the city. I suppose it must have been instituted by the three or four great Catholic families in the place—perhaps vicariously they enjoyed through it a sense of identity with the other side of the Mediterranean, with Venice and Athens. Nevertheless, there is to-day no rich family which does not keep a cupboard full of velvet dominoes against the three days of folly—be it Copt, Moslem or Jewish. After New Year's Eve it is perhaps the greatest Christian celebration of the year—for the ruling spirit of the three days and nights is—utter anonymity: the anonymity conferred by the grim black velvet domino which shrouds identity and sex, prevents one distinguishing between man and woman, wife and lover, friend and enemy.

The maddest aberrations of the city now come boldly forward under the protection of the invisible lords of Misrule who preside at this season. No sooner has darkness fallen than the maskers begin to appear in the streets—first in ones and twos then in small companies, often with musical instruments or drums, laughing and singing their way to some great house or to some night-club where already the frosty air is bathed in the nigger warmth of jazz—the cloying grunting intercourse of saxophones and drums. Everywhere they spring up in the pale moonlight, cowled like monks. The disguise gives them all a gloomy fanatical uniformity of outline which startles the white-robed Egyptians and fills them with alarm—the thrill of a fear which spices the wild laughter pouring out of the houses, carried by the light offshore winds towards the cafés on the sea-front; a gaiety which by its very shrillness seems to tremble always upon the edge of madness.

Slowly the bluish spring moon climbs the houses, sliding up the minarets into the clicking palm-trees, and with it the city seems to uncurl like some hibernating animal dug out of its winter earth, to stretch and begin to drink in the music of the three-day festival.

The jazz pouring up from the cellars displaces the tranquil winter air in the parks and thoroughfares, mingling as it reaches the sealine with the drumming perhaps of a liner's screws in the deepwater reaches of the estuary. Or you may hear and see for a brief moment the rip and slither of fireworks against a sky which for a moment curls up at the edges and blushes, like a sheet of burning carbon paper: wild laughter which mixes with the hoarse mooing of an old ship outside the harbour bar—like a cow locked outside a gate.

"The lover fears the carnival" says the proverb. And with the emergence of these black-robed creatures of the night everywhere, all is subtly altered. The whole temperature of life in the city alters, grows warm with the subtle intimations of spring. *Carni vale*—the flesh's farewell to the year, unwinding its mummy wrappings of sex, identity and name, and stepping forward naked into futurity of the dream.

All the great houses have thrown open their doors upon fabulous interiors warm with a firelight which bristles upon china and marble, brass and copper, and upon the blackleaded faces of the servants as they go about their duties. And down every street now, glittering in the moonlit gloaming, lounge the great limousines of the brokers and gamblers, like liners in dock, the patient and impressive symbols of a wealth which is powerless to bring true leisure or peace of mind for it demands everything of the human soul. They lie webbed in a winter light, expressing only the silence and power of all machinery which waits for the fall of man, looking on at the maskers as they cross and recross the lighted windows of the great houses, clutching each other like black bears, dancing to the throb of nigger music, the white man's solace.

Snatches of music and laughter must rise to Clea's window

where she sits with a board on her knees, patiently drawing while her little cat sleeps in its basket at her feet. Or perhaps in some sudden lull the chords of a guitar may be plucked to stay and wallow in the darkness of the open street until they are joined by a voice raised in remote song, as if from the bottom of a well. Or screams, cries for help.

But what stamps the carnival with its spirit of pure mischief is the velvet domino—conferring upon its wearers the disguise which each man in his secret heart desires above all. To become anonymous in an anonymous crowd, revealing neither sex nor relationship nor even facial expression—for the mask of this demented friar's habit leaves only two eyes, glowing like the eyes of a Moslem woman or a bear. Nothing else to distinguish one by; the thick folds of the blackness conceal even the contours of the body. Everyone becomes hipless, breastless, faceless. And concealed beneath the carnival habit (like a criminal desire in the heart, a temptation impossible to resist, an impulse which seems preordained) lie the germs of something: of a freedom which man has seldom dared to imagine for himself. One feels free in this disguise to do whatever one likes without prohibition. All the best murders in the city, all the most tragic cases of mistaken identity, are the fruit of the yearly carnival; while most love affairs begin or end during these three days and nights during which we are delivered from the thrall of personality, from the bondage of ourselves. Once inside that velvet cape and hood, and wife loses husband, husband wife, lover the beloved. The air becomes crisp with the saltpetre of feuds and follies, the fury of battles, of agonizing night-long searches, of despairs. You cannot tell whether you are dancing with a man or a woman. The dark tides of Eros, which demand full secrecy if they are to overflow the human soul, burst out during carnival like something long dammed up and raise the forms of strange primeval creatures—the perversions which are, I suppose, the psyche's aliment—in forms which you would think belonged to the Brocken or to Eblís. Now hidden satyr and maenad can rediscover each other and unite. Yes, who can help but love carnival when in it all debts are paid, all crimes expiated or committed, all illicit desires sated—without guilt or premeditation, without the penalties which conscience or society exact?

But I am wrong about one thing—for there is one distinguishing mark by which your friend or enemy may still identify you: hands. Your lover's hands, if you have ever noticed them at all, will lead you to her in the thickest press of maskers. Or by arrangement she may wear, as Justine does, a familiar ring —the ivory intaglio taken from the tomb of a dead Byzanteni youth—worn upon the forefinger of the right hand. But this is all, and it is only just enough. (Pray that you are not as unlucky as Amaril who found the perfect woman during carnival but could not persuade her to raise her hood and stand identified. They talked all night, lying in the grass by the fountain, making love together with their velvet faces touching, their eyes caressing each other. For a whole year now, he has gone about the city trying to find a pair of human hands, like a madman. But hands are so alike! She swore, this woman of his, that she would come back next year to the same place, wearing the same ring with its small yellow stone. And so to-night he will wait trembling for a pair of hands by the lily-pond—hands which will perhaps never appear again in his life. Perhaps she was after all an *afreet* or a vampire—who knows? Yet years later, in another book, in another context, he will happen upon her again, almost by accident, but not here, not in these pages too tangled already by the record of ill-starred loves. . . .)

So then you walk the dark streets, serene as a murderer unidentified, all your traces covered by the black cowl, feeling the fresh wintry airs of the city upon your eyelids. The Egyptians you pass look askance at you, not knowing whether to smile or be afraid at your appearance. They hover in an indeterminate state of mind when carnival comes on—wondering how it should be taken. Passing, you give them a burning stare from the depths of your cowl, glad to see them flinch and avert their faces. Other dominoes like yourself emerge from every corner, some in groups laughing and singing as they walk towards some great house or to neighbouring night-clubs.

Walking like this towards the Cervonis', across the network of streets by the Greek Patriarchate you are reminded of other carnivals, perhaps even in other cities, distinguished by the same wildness and gaiety which is the gift of lost identities. Strange adventures which befell you once. At one corner in the Rue Bartout last year the sound of running feet and cries. A man presents a dagger to your throat, crying, like a wounded animal, "Helen, if you try and run away to-night I swear I'll kill . . ." but the words die as you raise your mask and show your face, and he stammers an apology as he turns away only to burst into sobs and throw himself against an iron railing. Helen has already disappeared, and he will search for her the whole night through!

At a gate into a yard, weirdly lit by the feeble street-lamps, two figures in black are grappling each other, fighting with a tremendous silent fury. They fall, rolling over and over from darkness into light and then back into darkness. Without a word spoken. At the Étoile there is a man hanging from a beam with his neck broken; but when you get close enough you see that it is only a black domino hanging from a nail. How strange that in order to free oneself from guilt by a disguise one should choose the very symbol of the Inquisitor, the cape and hood of the Spanish Inquisition.

But they are not all in domino—for many people are superstitious about the dress and, besides, it can be hot to wear in a crowded room. So you will see many a harlequin and shepherdess, many an Antony and Cleopatra as you walk the streets of the city, many an Alexander. And as you turn into the great iron gates of the Cervonis' house to present your card and climb into the warmth and light and drunkenness within, you will see outlined upon the darkness the feared and beloved shapes and outlines of friends and familiars now distorted into the semblance of clowns and zanies, or clothed in the nothingness of black capes and hoods, infernally joined in a rare and disoriented gaiety.

As if under pressure the laughter squirts up to the ceiling or else, like feathers from a torn quilt, drifts about in clumps in that fevered air. The two string bands, muted by the weight of human voices, labour on in the short staggered rhythms of a maniac jazz—like the steady beating of an airpump. Here on the ballroom floor a million squeakers and trumpets squash and distort the sound while already the dense weight of the coloured paper streamers, hanging upon the shoulders of the dancers, sways like tropical seaweed upon rock-surfaces and trails in ankle-high drifts about the polished floors.

On the night in question, the first night of carnival, there was a dinner-party at the great house. On the long hall sofas the dominoes waited for their tenants while the candlelight still smouldered upon the faces of a Justine and Nessim now framed among the portraits which lined the ugly but imposing dining-room. Faces painted in oils matched by human faces lined by preoccupations and maladies of the soul—all gathered together, made one in the classical brilliance of candlelight. After dinner Justine and Nessim were to go together to the Cervoni ball according to the yearly custom. According to custom too, Narouz at the last moment had excused himself. He would arrive upon the stroke of ten, just in time to claim a domino before the whole party set off, laughing and chattering, for the ball.

As always, he himself had preferred to ride into the city on his horse and to stable it with his friend the carpenter, but as a concession to the event he had struggled into an ancient suit of blue serge and had knotted a tie at his collar. Undress did not matter, since he too would later be wearing a domino. He walked lightly, swiftly across the ill-lit Arab quarter, drinking in the familiar sights and sounds, yet eager for the first sight of the maskers as he reached the end of Rue Fouad and found himself on the confines of the modern town.

At one corner stood a group of shrill-chattering women in domino bent upon mischief. From their language and accent he could detect at once that they were society women, Greeks. These black harpies caught hold of every passer-by to shout jests at him and to pluck at his hood if he were masked. Narouz too had to run the gauntlet: one caught hold of his hand and pretended to tell his fortune; another whispered a proposition in Arabic, setting her hand upon his thigh; the third cackled like a hen and shouted "Your wife has a lover" and other unkindnesses. He could not tell if they recognized him or not.

Narouz flinched, shook himself and burst smiling through their number fending them off good-naturedly and roaring with laughter at the sally about his wife. "Not to-night, my doves" he cried hoarsely in Arabic, thinking suddenly of Clea; and as they showed some disposition to capture him for the evening, he began to run. They chased him a little way, shouting and laughing incoherently down the long dark street, but he easily outdistanced them, and so turned the corner to the great house, still smiling but a little out of breath, and flattered by these attentions which seemed to set the key for the evening's enjoyment. In the silent hall his eye caught the black of dominoes and he put one on before edging open the door of the drawing-room behind which he could hear their voices. It disguised his shabby suit. The cape lay back upon his shoulders.

They were all there by the fire, waiting for him, and he took their cries of welcome greedily and seriously, making his round to kiss Justine on the cheek and to shake hands with the rest in an agony of awkward silence. He put on an artificially sincere expression, looking with distaste into the myopic eyes of Pierre Balbz (he hated him for the goatee and spats) and those of Toto de Brunel (an old lady's lap-dog); but he liked the overblown rose, Athena Trasha, for she used the same scent as his mother; and he was sorry for Drusilla Banubula because she was so clever that she hardly seemed to be a woman at all. With Pursewarden he shared a smile of easy complicity. "Well" he said, expelling his breath at last in relief. His brother handed him a whisky with mild tenderness, which he drank slowly but all in one draught, like a peasant.

"We were waiting for you, Narouz."

"The Hosnani exile" glittered Pierre Balbz ingratiatingly.

"The farmer" cried little Toto.

The conversation which had been interrupted by his sudden appearance closed smoothly over his head once more and he sat down by the fire until they should be ready to leave for the Cervoni house, folding his strong hands one upon the other in a gesture of finality, as if to lock up once and for all his powers. The skin at Nessim's temples appeared to be stretched, he noticed an old sign of anger or strain. The fullness of Justine's dark beauty in her dress (the colour of hare's blood) glowed among the ikons, seeming to enjoy the semi-darkness of the candlelight—to feed upon it and give back the glitter of her barbaric jewellery. Narouz felt full of a marvellous sense of detachment, of unconcern; what these small portents of trouble or stress meant, he did not know. It was only Clea who flawed his self-sufficiency, who darkened the edges of his thought. Each year he hoped that when he arrived at his brother's house he would find she had been included in the party. Yet each year she was not, and in consequence he was forced to drift about all night in the darkness, searching for her as aimlessly as a ghost, not even really hoping to encounter her:

and yet living upon the attenuated wraith of this fond hope as a soldier upon an iron ration.

They had been talking that night of Amaril and his unhappy passion for a pair of anonymous hands and a carnival voice, and Pursewarden was telling one of his famous stories in that crisp uninflected French of his which was just a shade too perfect.

"When I was twenty, I went to Venice for the first time at the invitation of an Italian poet with whom I had been corresponding, Carlo Negroponte. For a middle-class English youth this was a great experience, to live virtually by candlelight in this huge tumbledown palazzo on the Grand Canal with a fleet of gondolas at my disposal—not to mention a huge wardrobe of cloaks lined with silk. Negroponte was generous and spared no effort to entertain a fellow-poet in the best style. He was then about fifty, frail and rather beautiful, like a rare kind of mosquito. He was a prince and a diabolist, and his poetry happily married the influences of Byron and Baudelaire. He went in for cloaks and shoes with buckles and silver walking-sticks and encouraged me to do the same. I felt I was living in a Gothic novel. Never have I written worse poetry.

"That year we went to the carnival together and got separated though we each wore something to distinguish each other by; you know of course that carnival is the one time of the year when vampires walk freely abroad, and those who are wise carry a pig of garlic in their pockets to drive them off—if by chance one were to be encountered. Next morning I went into my host's room and found him lying pale as death in bed, dressed in the white nightshirt with lace cuffs, with a doctor taking his pulse. When the doctor had gone he said: 'I have met the perfect woman, masked; I went home with her and she proved to be a vampire.' Then drawing up his nightshirt he showed me with exhausted pride that his body was covered with great bites, like the marks of a weasel's teeth. He was utterly exhausted but at the same time excited—and frightening to relate, very much in love. 'Until you have experienced it' he said, 'you have no idea what it is like. To have one's blood sucked in darkness by someone one adores.' His voice broke. 'De Sade could not begin to describe it. I did not see her face, but I had the impression she was fair, of a northern fairness; we met in the dark and separated in the dark. I have only the impression of white teeth, and a voice—never have I heard any woman say the things she says. She is the very lover for whom I have been waiting all these years. I am meeting her again to-night by the marble griffin at the Footpads' Bridge. O my friend, be happy for me. The real world has become more and more meaningless to me. Now at last, with this vampire's love, I feel I can live again, feel again, write again!' He spent all that day at his papers, and at nightfall set off, cloaked, in his gondola. It was not my business to say anything. The next day once more I found him, pale and deathly tired. He had a high fever, and again these terrible bites. But he could not speak of his experience without weeping—tears of love and exhaustion. And it was now that he had begun his great poem which begins —you all know it——

'Lips not on lips, but on each other's wounds
Must suck the envenomed bodies of the loved
And through the tideless blood draw nourishment
To feed the love that feeds upon their deaths. . . .'

"The following week I left for Ravenna where I had some studies to make for a book I was writing and where I stayed two months. I heard nothing from my host, but I got a letter from his sister to say that he was ill with a wasting disease which the doctors could not diagnose and that the family was much worried because he insisted on going out at night in his gondola on journeys of which he would not speak but from which he returned utterly exhausted. I did not know what to reply to this.

"From Ravenna, I went down to Greece and it was not until

the following autumn that I returned. I had sent a card to Negroponte saying I hoped to stay with him, but had no reply. As I came down the Grand Canal a funeral was setting off in choppy water, by twilight, with the terrible plumes and emblems of death. I saw that they were coming from the Negroponte Palazzo. I landed and ran to the gates just as the last gondola in the procession was filling up with mourners and priests. I recognised the doctor and joined him in the boat, and as we rowed stiffly across the canal, dashed with spray and blinking at the stabs of lightning, he told me what he knew. Negroponte had died the day before. When they came to lay out the body, they found the bites: perhaps of some tropical insect? The doctor was vague. 'The only such bites I have seen' he said, 'were during the plague of Naples when the rats had been at the bodies. They were so bad we had to dust him down with talcum powder before we could let his sister see the body.' "

Pursewarden took a long sip from his glass and went on wickedly. "The story does not end there; for I should tell you how I tried to avenge him, and went myself at night to the Bridge of the Footpads—where according to the gondolier this woman always waited in the shadow. . . . But it is getting late, and anyway, I haven't made up the rest of the story as yet."

There was a good deal of laughter and Athena gave a well-bred shudder, drawing her shawl across her shoulders. Narouz had been listening open-mouthed, with reeling senses, to this recital: he was spellbound. "But" he stammered, "is all this true?" Fresh laughter greeted his question.

"Of course it's true" said Pursewarden severely, and added: "I have never been in Venice in my life."

And he rose, for it was time for them to be going, and while the impassive black servants waited they put on the velveteen capes and adjusted their masks like the actors they were, comparing their identical reflections as they stood side by side in the two swollen mirrors among the palms. Giggles from Pierre and sallies of wit from Toto de Brunel; and so they stepped laughing into the clear night air, the inquisitors of pleasure and pain, the Alexandrians. . . .

The cars engulfed them while the solicitous domestics and chauffeurs tucked them in, carefully as bales of precious merchandise or spices, tenderly as flowers. "I feel fragile" squeaked Toto at these attentions. "This side up with care, eh? Which side up, I ask myself?" He must have been the only person in the city not to know the answer to his own question.

When they had started, Justine leaned forward in the car and plucked his sleeve. "I want to whisper" she said hoarsely though there was little need for Nessim and Narouz were discussing something in harsh tones (Narouz' voice with the characteristic boyish break in it) and Athena was squibbling to Pierre like a flute. "Toto . . . listen. One great service to-night, if you will. I have put a chalk-mark on your sleeve, here, at the back. Later on in the evening, I want to give you my ring to wear. Shh. I want to disappear for an hour or so on my own. Hush . . . don't giggle." But there were squeaks from the velvet hood. "You will have adventures in my name, dear Toto, while I am gone. Do you agree?"

He threw back his cape to show a delighted face, dancing eyes and that grim little procurer's smile. "Of course" he whispered back, enraptured by the idea and full of admiration. The featureless hood at his side from which the voice of Justine had issued like an oracle glowed with a sort of death's-head beauty of its own, nodding at him in the light from the passing street-lamps. The conversation and laughter around them sealed them in a conspiracy of private silence. "Do you agree?" she said.

"Darling, of course."

The two masked men in the front seats of the car might have been abbots of some medieval monastery, discussing theological niceties. Athena, consumed by her own voice, still babbled away to Pierre. "But of course."

Justine took his arm and turned back the sleeve to show him the chalk-mark she had made. "I count on you" she said, with some of the hoarse imperiousness of her speaking-voice, yet still in a whisper. "Don't let me down!" He took her hand and raised it to his Cupid's lips, kissing the ring from the dead finger of the Byzantine youth as one might kiss the holy picture which had performed a miracle long desired; he was to be turned from a man into a woman. Then he laughed and cried: "And my indiscretions will be on your head. You will spend the rest of your days. . . ."

"Hush."

"What is all this?" cried Athena Trasha, scenting a joke or a scandal worth repetition. "What indiscretions?"

"My own" cried Toto triumphantly into the darkness. "My very own." But Justine lay back in the dark car impassively hooded, and did not speak. "I can't wait to get there" said Athena, and turned back to Pierre. As the car turned into the gate of the Cervoni house, the light caught the intaglio, throwing into relief (colour of burnt milk) a Pan raping a goat, his hands grasping its horns, his head thrown back in ecstasy. "Don't forget" Justine said once more, for the last time, allowing him to maul her hand with gratitude for such a wonderful idea. "Don't forget" allowing her ringed fingers to lie in his, cool and unfeeling as a cow which allows itself to be milked. "Only tell me all the interesting conversations you have, won't you?" He could only mutter "Darling, darling, darling" as he kissed the ring with the ovarian passion of the sexually dispossessed.

Almost at once, like the Gulf Stream breaking up an iceberg with its warm currents, dispersing it, their party disintegrated as it reached the ballroom and merged with the crowd. Abruptly Athena was dragged screaming into the heart of the press by a giant domino who gobbled and roared incomprehensible blasphemies in his hood. Nessim, Narouz, Pierre, they suddenly found themselves turned to ciphers, expelled into a formless world of adventitious meetings, mask to dark mask, like a new form of insect life. Toto's chalk-mark gave him a few fugitive moments of identity as he was borne away like a cork on a stream, and Justine's ring as well (for which I myself was hunting all that evening in vain).

But everything now settled into the mindless chaotic dance-figures of the black jazz supported only by the grinding drums and saxophones, the voices. The spirits of the darkness had taken over, you'd think, disinheriting the daylight hearts and minds of the maskers, plunging them ever deeper into the loneliness of their own irrecoverable identities, setting free the polymorphous desires of the city. The tide washed them up now onto the swampy littorals of their own personalities—symbols of Alexandria, a dead brackish lake surrounded by the silent, unjudging, wide-eyed desert which stretches away into Africa under a dead moon.

Locked in our masks now we prowled about despairingly among the company, hunting from room to room, from floor to lighted floor of the great house, for an identifiable object to direct our love: a rose pinned to a sleeve, a ring, a scarf, a coloured bead. Something, anything, to discover our lovers by. The hoods and masks were like the outward symbols of our own secret minds as we walked about—as single-minded and as dispossessed as the desert fathers hunting for their God. And slowly but with irresistible momentum the great carnival ball gathered pace around us. Here and there, like patches of meaning in an obscure text, one touched upon a familiar identity: a bullfighter drinking whisky in a corridor greeted one in the lisping accents of Tony Umbada, or Pozzo di Borgo unmasked for an instant to identify himself to his trembling wife. Outside in the darkness on the grass by the lily pond sat

Amaril, also trembling and waiting. He did not dare to remain unmasked lest the sight of his face might disgust or disappoint her, should she return this year to the promised assignation. If one falls in love with a mask when one is masked oneself . . . which of you will first have the courage to raise it? Perhaps such lovers would go through life together, remaining masked? (Racing thoughts in Amaril's sentimental brain. . . . Love rejoices in self-torture.)

An expressive washerwoman dressed in a familiar picture-hat and recognisable boots (Pombal, as ever was), had pinned a meagre-looking Roman centurion to a corner of the mantel-piece and was cursing him in a parrot-voice. I caught the word "salaud". The little figure of the Consul General managed to mime his annoyance with choppy gestures and struggles, but it was all in vain, for Pombal held him fast in his great paws. It was fascinating to watch. The centurion's casque fell off, and pushing him to the bandstand Pombal began to beat his behind rhythmically upon the big drum and at the same time to kiss him passionately. He was certainly getting his own back. But as I watched this brief scene, the crowd closed down upon it in a whirl of streamers and confetti and obliterated it. We were packed body to body, cowl to cowl, eye to eye. The music drove us round and round the floor. Still no Justine.

> Old Tiresias
> No one half so breezy as,
> Half so free and easy as
> Old Tiresias.

It must have been about two o'clock that the fire started in one of the chimneys on the first floor, though its results were not serious and it caused more delight than alarm by its appro-priateness. Servants scurried officiously everywhere; I caught a glimpse of Cervoni, running unmasked upstairs, and then a telephone rang. There were pleasing clouds of smoke, suggesting whiffs of brimstone from the bottomless pit. Then within minutes a fire-engine arrived with its siren pealing, and the hall was full of fancy-dress figures of *pompiers* with hatchets and buckets. They were greeted with acclamation as they made their way up to the scene of the fireplace which they virtually demolished with their axes. Others of the tribe had climbed on the roof and were throwing buckets of water down the chimney. This had the effect of filling the first floor with a dense cloud of soot like a London fog. The maskers crowded in shouting with delight, dancing like dervishes. These are the sort of inadvertencies which make a party go. I found myself shouting with them. I suppose I must have been rather drunk by now.

In the great tapestried hall the telephone rang and rang again, needling the uproar. I saw a servant answer it, lay the receiver down, and quest about like a gun-dog until presently he returned with Nessim, smiling and unmasked, who spoke into it quickly and with an air of impatience. Then he too put the receiver down and came to the edge of the dance-floor, staring about him keenly. "Is there anything wrong?" I asked, lifting my own hood as I joined him. He smiled and shook his head. "I can't see Justine anywhere. Clea wants to speak to her. Can you?" Alas! I had been trying to pick up the distinguishing ring all evening without success. We waited, watching the slow rotation of the dancers, keenly as fishermen waiting for a bite. "No" he said and I echoed "No." Pierre Balbz came up and joined us, lifting his cowl, and said "A moment ago I was dancing with her. She went out perhaps."

Nessim returned to the telephone and I heard him say. "She's here somewhere. Yes, quite sure. No. Nothing has happened. Pierre had the last dance with her. Such a crowd. She may be in the garden. Any message? Can I ask her to ring you? Very well. No, it was simply a fire in a chimney. It's out now." He put down the receiver and turned back to us.

"Anyway," he said, "we have a rendezvous in the hall unmasked at three."

And so the great ball rolled on around us, and the firemen who had done their duty now joined the throng of dancers. I caught a glimpse of a large washerwoman being carried, apparently insensible, out into the conservatory by four demons with breasts amid great applause. Pombal had evidently succumbed to his favourite brand of whisky once more. He had lost his hat but had had the forethought to wear under it an immense wig of yellow hair. It is doubtful whether anyone could have recognised him in such a rig.

Punctually at three Justine appeared in the hall from the garden and unmasked herself: Pierre and I had decided not to accept Nessim's offer of a lift home but to stay on and lend our energy to the ball which was beginning to flag now. Little parties were meeting and leaving, cars were being rallied. Nessim kissed her tenderly and said "Where's your ring?" a question which I myself had been burning to put to her though I had not dared. She smiled that innocent and captivating smile as she said: "Toto pinched it from my finger a few minutes ago, during a dance. Where is the little brute? I want it back." We raked the floor for Toto but there was no sign of him and at last Nessim who was tired decided to give him up for lost. But he did not forget to give Justine Clea's message, and I saw my lover go obediently to the telephone and dial her friend's number. She spoke quietly and with an air of mystification for a few moments, and I heard her say: "Of course I'm all right," before bidding Clea a belated good night. Then they stepped down together into the waning moonlight arm in arm, and Pierre and I helped to tuck them into the car. Selim, impassive and hawk-featured, sat at the wheel. "Good night!" cried Justine, and her lips brushed my cheek. She whispered "To-morrow" and the word sang on in my mind like the whistle of a bullet as we turned together back into the lighted house. Nessim's face had been full of a curious impish serenity as of someone resting after a great expenditure of energy.

Someone had heard a ghost murmuring in the conservatory. Much laughter. "No, but I assure you" squealed Athena, "we were sitting on the sofa, Jacques and I, weren't we, Jacques?" A masked figure appeared, blew a squeaker in her face and retired. Something told me it was Toto. I dragged his cowl back and up bobbed the features of Chloe Martinengo. "But I assure you" said Athena, "it moaned a word—something like . . ." she set her face in a grim scowl of concentration and after a pause sang out in a lullaby voice the expiring words "*Justice . . . Justice.*" Everyone laughed heartily and several voices mimicked her: "*Justice*" roared a domino rushing away up the stairs. "*Justice!*"

Alone once more, I found that my irresolution and despondency had turned to physical hunger, and I traversed the dance-floor cautiously in the direction of the supper-room from which I could hear the thirsty snap of champagne corks. The ball itself was still in full swing, and dancers swaying like wet washing in a high wind, the saxophones wailing like a litter of pigs. In an alcove Drusilla Banubula sat with her dress drawn up to her shapely knees, allowing a pair of contrite harlequins to bandage a sprained ankle. She had fallen down or been knocked down it would seem. An African witch-doctor wearing a monocle lay fast asleep on the couch behind her. In the second room a maudlin woman in evening dress was playing jazz on a grand piano and singing to herself while great tears coursed down her cheeks. An old fat man with hairy legs hung over her, dressed as the Venus de Milo. He was crying too. His belly trembled.

The supper-room however was comparatively quiet, and here I found Pursewarden, uncowled and apparently rather tipsy, talking to Mountolive as the latter walked with his curious gliding, limping walk round the table, loading a plate with slices of cold turkey and salad. Pursewarden was inveighing somewhat incoherently against the Cervonis for serving Spumante instead of champagne. "I should watch it," he called out to me, "there's a headache in every mouthful." But he had his glass refilled almost at once, holding it with exaggerated steadiness. Mountolive turned a speculative and gentle eye upon me as I seized a plate, and then greeted me by name with evident relief. "Ah, Darley," he said, "for a moment I thought you were one of my secretaries. They've been following me around all evening. Spoiling my fun. Errol simply refuses to violate protocol and leave before his Chief of Mission; so I had to hide in the garden until they thought I had left, poor dears. As a junior I have so often cursed my Minister for keeping me up on boring evenings that I made a vow never to make my juniors suffer in the same way if I should ever become Head of Mission." His light effortless conversation with its unaffectedness of delivery always made him seem immediately sympathetic, though I realised that his manner was a professional one, the bedside manner of the trained diplomat. He had spent so many years in putting his inferiors at their ease, and in hiding his spirit's condescension, that he had at last achieved an air of utterly professional sincerity which while seeming true to nature could not, in reality, have been less false. It had all the fidelity of great acting. But it was annoying that I should always find myself liking him so much. We circled the table slowly together, talking and filling our plates.

"What did you see in the garden, David?" said Pursewarden in a teasing tone, and the Minister's eye rested speculatively on him for a minute, as if to warn him against saying something which would be indiscreet or out of place. "I saw," said Mountolive smiling and reaching for a glass, "I saw the amorous Amaril by the lake—talking to a woman in a domino. Perhaps his dreams have come true?" Amaril's passion was well-known to everyone. "I do hope so."

"And what *else*?" said Pursewarden in a challenging, rather vulgar tone, as if he shared a private secret with him. "What else, *who* else did you see, David?" He was slightly tipsy and his voice, though friendly, had a bullying note. Mountolive flushed and looked down at his plate.

At this I left them and made my way back, equipped with loaded plate and glass. I felt a certain scorn in my heart for Pursewarden, and a rush of sympathy for Mountolive at the thought of him being put out of countenance. I wanted to be alone, to eat in silence and think about Justine. My cargo of food was nearly upset by three heavily-rouged Graces, all of them men to judge by the deep voices, who were scuffling in the hall. They were attacking each others' private parts with jocular growls, like dogs. I had the sudden idea of going up to the library which would surely be empty at this time. I wondered if the new Cavafy manuscripts would be there, and whether the collection was unlocked. Cervoni was a great collector of books.

On the first floor, a fat man with spindly legs, dressed in the costume of Red Riding Hood, was hammering on a lavatory door; servants were sucking the soot from the carpets of the rooms with Hoovers and talking in undertones. The library was on the floor above. There was a noise in one of the bed-rooms, and from the bathroom below I could hear someone being chromatically sick. I reached the landing and pressed the airtight door with my foot, and it sucked open to admit me. The long room with its gleaming shelves of books was empty save for a Mephistopheles sitting in an armchair by the fire with a book on his knees. He took his spectacles off in order to identify me and I saw that it was Capodistria. He could not have chosen a more suitable costume. It suited his great ravening beak of a nose and those small, keen eyes, set so close together. "Come in" he cried. "I was afraid it might be some-one wanting to make love in which case . . . *toujours la politesse,* I should have felt bound. . . . What are you eating? The fire is lovely. I was just looking up a quotation which has been worrying me all evening."

I joined him and placed my loaded plate as an offering between us to be shared. "I came to see the new Cavafy manuscript" I said.

"All locked up, the manuscripts" he said.

"Well."

The fire crackled brightly and the room was silent and welcoming with its lining of fine books. I took off my cape and sat down after a preliminary quest along the walls, during which Da Capo finished copying something out on to a piece of paper. "Curious thing about Mountolive's father" he said absently. "This huge eight-volume edition of Buddhist texts. Did you know?"

"I had heard" I said vaguely.

"The old man was a judge in India. When he retired he stayed on there, is still there; foremost European scholar on Pali texts. I must say. . . . Mountolive hasn't seen him for nearly twenty years. He dresses like a *saddhu* he says. You English are eccentrics through and through. Why shouldn't the old man work on his texts in Oxford, eh?"

"Climate, perhaps?"

"Perhaps." He agreed. "There. That's what I was hunting for—I knew it was somewhere in the fourth volume." He banged his book shut.

"What is it?"

He held his paper out to the fire and read slowly with an air of puzzled pleasure the quotation he had copied out: "The fruit of the tree of good and evil is itself but flesh; yes, and the apple itself is but an apple of the dust."

"That's not Buddhist, surely" I said.

"No, it's Mountolive père himself, from the introduction."

"I think that. . . ."

But now there came a confused screaming from somewhere

near at hand, and Capodistria sighed. "I don't know why the devil I take part in this damned carnival year after year" he said peevishly, draining his whisky. "It is an unlucky time astrologically. For me, I mean. And every year there are ugly accidents. It makes one uneasy. Two years ago Arnelh was found hanging in the musicians' gallery at the Fontanas' house. Funny eh? Damned inconsiderate if he did it himself. And then Martin Fery fought that duel with Jacomo Forte. . . . It brings out the devil. That is why I am dressed as the devil. I hang about waiting for people to come and sell me their souls. Aha!" He sniffed and rubbed his hands with a parchment sound and gave his little dry cachinnation. And then, standing up and finishing the last slice of turkey, "God, have you seen the time? I must be going home. Beelzebub's bedtime."

"So should I" I said, disappointed that I could not get a look at the handwriting of the old poet. "So should I."

"Can I lift you?" he said, as the sucking door expelled us once more into the trampled musical air of the landing. "Useless to expect to say good-bye to our hosts. Cervoni is probably in bed by now."

We went down slowly chatting into the great hall where the music rolled on in an unbroken stream of syncopated sound. Da Capo had adjusted his mask now and looked like some weird bird-like demon. We stood for a moment watching the dancers, and then yawning he said: "Well, this is where to quote Cavafy the God abandons Antony. Good night. I can't stay awake any longer, though I am afraid the evening will be full of surprises yet. It always is."

Nor was he to be proved wrong. I hovered for a while, watching the dance, and then walked down the stairs into the dark coolness of the night. There were a few limousines and sleepy servants waiting by the gates, but the streets had begun to empty and my own footfalls sounded harsh and exotic as they smacked up from the pavements. At the corner of Fouad there were a couple of European whores leaning dispiritedly against a wall and smoking. They called once hoarsely after me. They wore magnolia blossoms in their hair.

Yawning, I passed the Etoile to see if perhaps Melissa was still working, but the place was empty except for a drunk family which had refused to go home despite the fact that Zoltan had stacked up the chairs and tables around them on the dance-floor. "She went off early" he little man explained. "Band gone. Girls gone. Everyone gone. Only these *canaille* from Assuan. His brother is a policeman; we dare not close." A fat man began to belly-dance with sugary movements of the hips and pelvis and the company began to clap to mark the time. I left and walked past Melissa's shabby lodgings in the vague hope that she might still be awake. I felt I wanted to talk to someone; no, I wanted to borrow a cigarette. That was all. Afterwards would come the desire to sleep with her, to hold that slender cherished body in my arms, inhaling its sour flavours of alcohol and tobacco-smoke, thinking all the time of Justine. But her window was dark; either she was asleep or was not yet home. Zoltan had said that she left with a party of business-men disguised as admirals. "*Des petits commerçants quelconques*" he had added contemptuously, and then turned at once apologetic.

No, it was to be an empty night, with the frail subfusc moonlight glancing along the waves of the outer harbour, the sea licking and relicking the piers, the coastline thinning away in whiteness, glittering away into the greyness like mica. I stood for a while on the Corniche snapping a paper streamer in my fingers, bit by bit, each fragment breaking off with a hard dry finality, like a human relationship. Then I turned sleepily home, repeating in my mind the words of Da Capo: "The evening will be full of surprises."

Indeed, they were already beginning in the house which I had just left, though of course I was not to learn about them until the following day. And yet, surprises though they were, their reception was perfectly in keeping with the city—a city of resignation so deep as almost to be Moslem. For nobody in Alexandria can ever be shocked deeply; among us tragedy exists only to flavour conversation. Death and life are both simply the hazards of a chance which cannot be averted, and merit only smiles and conversations made more animated by the consciousness of their intrusion. No sooner do you tell an Alexandrian a piece of bad news than the words come out of his mouth: "I knew. Something like this was bound to happen. It always does." This, then, is what happened.

In the conservatory of the Cervoni house there were several old-fashioned *chaises-longues* on which a mountain of overcoats and evening-wraps had been piled; as the dancers began to go home there came the usual shedding of dominoes and the hunt for furs and capes. I think it was Pierre who must have made the discovery while hunting in this great tumulus of coats for the velvet smoking-jacket which he had shed earlier in the evening. At any rate, I myself had already left and started to walk home by this time.

Toto de Brunel was discovered, still warm in his velvet domino, with his paws raised like two neat little cutlets, in the attitude of a dog which had rolled over to have its belly scratched. He was buried deep in the drift of coats. One hand had half-tried to move towards the fatal temple but the impulse had been cut off at source before the action was complete, and it had stayed there raised a little higher than the other, as if wielding an invisible baton. The hatpin from Pombal's picture hat had been driven sideways into his head with terrific force, pinning him like a moth into his velvet headpiece. Athena had been making love to Jacques while she was literally lying upon his body—a fact which would under normal circumstances have delighted him thoroughly. But he was dead, *le pauvre Toto*, and what is more he was still wearing the ring of my lover. 'Justice!'

"Of course, something like this happens every year."

"Of course." I was still dazed.

"But Toto—that is rather unexpected, really."

Balthazar rang me up about eleven o'clock the next morning to tell me the whole story. In my stupefied and sleepy condition it sounded not merely improbable, but utterly incomprehensible. "There will be the *procès-verbal*—that's why I'm ringing. Nimrod is making it as easy as he can. One dinner-party witness only—Justine thought perhaps you if you don't mind? Good. Of course. No, I was got out of bed at a quarter to four by the Cervonis. They were in rather a state about it. I went along to . . . do the needful. I'm afraid they can't quite sort it all out as yet. The pin belonged to the hat—yes, your friend Pombal . . . diplomatic immunity, naturally. Nevertheless, he was very drunk too. . . . Of course it is inconceivable that he did it, but you know what the Police are like. Is he up yet?" I had not dared to try and wake him at such an early hour, and I said so. "Well anyway" said Balthazar, "his death has fluttered a lot of dovecotes, not least at the French Legation."

"But he was wearing Justine's ring" I said thickly, and all the premonitions of the last few months gathered in force at my elbow, crowding in upon me. I felt quite ill and feverish and had to lean for a moment against the wall by the telephone. Balthazar's measured tone and cheerful voice sounded to me like an obscenity. There was a long silence. "Yes, I know about the ring," he said, and added with a quiet chuckle "but that too is hard to think of as a possible reason. Toto was also the lover of the jealous Amar, you know. Any number of reasons. . . ."

"Balthazar" I said, and my voice broke.

"I'll ring you if there's anything else. The *procès* is at seven down in Nimrod's office. See you there, eh?"

"Very well."

I put down the phone and burst like a bomb into Pombal's

bedroom. The curtains were still drawn and the bed was in a terrible mess suggesting a recent occupancy, but there was no other sign of him. His boots and various items from the washerwoman's fancy dress lay about the room in various places, enabling me to discern that he had in fact got home the night before. Actually his wig lay on the landing outside the front door: I know this because much later, towards midday, I heard his heavy step climbing the stairs and he entered the flat holding it in his hand.

"I am quite finished" he said briefly, at once. "Finished, *mon ami.*" He looked more plethoric than ever as he made for his gout chair as if anticipating a sudden attack of his special and private malady. "Finished" he repeated, sinking into it with a sigh and distending. I was confused and bewildered, standing there in my pyjamas. Pombal sighed heavily.

"My Chancery has discovered everything" he said grimly setting his jaw. "I first behaved very badly . . . yes . . . the Consul General is having a nervous breakdown to-day. . . ." And then all of a sudden real tears of mixed rage, confusion and hysteria sprang up in his eyes. "Do you know what?" he sneezed. "The *Deuxième* think I went specially to the ball to stick a pin in de Brunel, the best and most trusted agent we have ever had here!"

He burst out sobbing like a donkey now, and in some fantastic way his tears kept turning into laughter; he mopped his streaming eyes and panted as he sobbed and laughed at one and the same time. Then, still blown up by these overmastering paroxysms he rolled out of his chair like a hedgehog on to the carpet and lay there for a while still shaking; and then began to roll slowly to the wainscot where, shaken still with tears and laughter, he began to bang his head rhythmically against the wall, shouting at every bang the pregnant and magnificent word—the *summa* of all despair: "*Merde. Merde. Merde. Merde. Merde.*"

"Pombal," I said weakly, "for God's sake!"

"Go away," he cried from the floor, "I shall never stop unless you go away. Please go away." And so taking pity on him I left the room and ran myself a cold bath in which I lay until I heard him helping himself to bread and butter from the larder. He came to the bathroom door and tapped. "Are you there?" he said. "Yes." "Then forget every word I said" he shouted through the panel. "Please, eh?"

"I have forgotten already."

"Good. Thank you, *mon ami.*"

And I heard his heavy footfalls retreating in the direction of his room. We lay in bed until lunch-time that day, both of us, silent. At one-thirty, Hamid arrived and set out a lunch which neither of us had the appetite to eat. In the middle of it, the telephone rang and I went to answer it. It was Justine. She must have assumed that I had heard about Toto de Brunel for she made no direct mention of the business. "I want" she said, "my dreadful ring back. Balthazar has reclaimed it from the Police. The one Toto took, yes. But apparently someone has to identify and sign for it. At the *procès*. A thousand thanks for offering to go. As you can imagine, Nessim and I . . . it's a question of witnessing only. And then perhaps my darling we could meet and you could give it back to me. Nessim has to fly to Cairo this afternoon on business. Shall we say in the garden of the Aurore at nine? That will give you time. I'll wait in the car. So much want to speak to you. Yes. I must go now. Thank you again. Thank you."

We sat once more to our meal, fellow bondsmen, heavy with a sense of guilt and exhaustion. Hamid waited upon us with solicitude and in complete silence. Did he know what was preoccupying us both? It was impossible to read anything on those gentle pock-marked features, in that squinting single eye.

o   o   o   o   o

214

XI

It was already dark when I dismissed my taxi at Mohammed Ali square and set out to walk to the sub-department of the Prefecture where Nimrod's office was. I was still dazed by the turn events had taken, and weighed down by the dispiriting possibilities they had raised in my mind—the warnings and threatenings of the last few months during which I had lived only for one person—Justine. I burned with impatience to see her again.

The shops were already lit up and the money-changers' counters were crowded with French sailors turning their francs into food and wine, silks, women, boys or opium—every kind of understandable forgetfulness. Nimrod's office was at the back of a grey old-fashioned building set back at an angle to the road. It seemed deserted now, full of empty corridors and open offices. All the clerks had gone off duty at six. My lagging footfalls echoed past the empty porter's lodge and the open doors. It seemed strange to walk about so freely in a Police building unchallenged. At the end of the third long corridor I came to Nimrod's own door and knocked. There were voices inside. His office was a large, indeed rather grandiose room befitting his rank, whose windows gave out on to a bare court-yard where some chickens clucked and picked all day in the dried mud floor. A single tattered palm stood in the middle offering some summer shade.

There was no sign from within the room so I opened the door and stepped in—only to stop short: for the brilliant light and darkness suggested that a cinema-show was taking place. But it was only the huge epidiascope which threw upon the farther wall the blazing and magnified images of the photographs which Nimrod himself was feeding into it one by one from an envelope. Dazzled, I stepped forward and identified Balthazar and Keats in that phosphorescent penumbra around the machine, their profiles magnetically lighted by the powerful bulb.

"Good," said Nimrod, half-turning, and "sit you down," as he abstractedly pushed out a chair for me. Keats smiled at me, full of a mysterious self-satisfaction and excitement. The photographs which they were studying with such care were his own flashlight pictures of the Cervoni ball. At such magnification they looked like grotesque frescoes materialising and vanishing again upon the white wall. "See if you can help on identification" said Nimrod, and I sat down and obediently turned my face to the blaze in which sprawled the silhouettes of a dozen demented monks dancing together. "Not that one" said Keats. The white light of the magnesium had set fire to the outlines of the robed figures.

Blown up to such enormous size the pictures suggested a new art-form, more macabre than anything a Goya could imagine. This was a new iconography—painted in smoke and lightning flashes. Nimrod changed them slowly, dwelling upon each one. "No comment?" he would ask before passing another bloated facsimile of real life before our eyes. "No comment?"

For identification purposes they were quite useless. There were eight in all—each a fearful simulacrum of a death-feast celebrated by satyr-monks in some medieval crypt, each imagined by de Sade! "There's the one with the ring" said Balthazar as the fifth picture came up and hovered before us on the wall. A group of hooded figures, frenziedly swaying with linked arms, wallowed before us, expressionless as cuttlefish, or those other grotesque monsters one sometimes sees lurking in the glooms of aquaria. Their eyes were slits devoid of meaning, their gaiety a travesty of everything human. So this is how Inquisitors behave when they are off duty! Keats sighed in despair. One of the figures had a hand upon another's black-robed arm. The hand bore a just recognisable dash of white to indicate Justine's unlucky ring. Nimrod described it all carefully to himself with the air of a man reading a gauge. "Five maskers . . . somewhere near the buffet, you can see the corner. . . . But the hand. Is it de Brunel's? What do you think?" I stared at it. "I think it must be" I said. "Justine wears the ring on another finger."

Nimrod said "Hah" triumphantly and added "A good point there." Yes, but who were the other figures, snatched thus fortuitously out of nothingness by the flash-bulb? We stared at them and they stared expressionlessly back at us through their velvet slits like snipers.

"No good" said Balthazar at last with a sigh, and Nimrod switched off the humming machine. After an instant's darkness the ordinary electric light came up in the room. His desk was stacked up with typed papers for signature—the *procès-verbal* I had no doubt. On a square of grey silk lay several objects with a direct relationship to our brimming thoughts—the great hatpin with its ugly blue stone head, and the eburnine ring of my lover which I could not see even now without a pang.

"Sign up" said Nimrod, indicating the paper, "when you've read your copy, will you?" He coughed behind his hand and added in a lower tone "And you can take the ring."

Balthazar handed it to me. It felt cold, and it was faintly dusted with fingerprint powder. I cleaned it on my tie and put it in my fob-pocket. "Thank you" I said, and took a seat at the desk to read through the Police formula, while the others lit cigarettes and talked in low voices. Beside the typewritten papers lay another, written in the nervous shallow hand of General Cervoni. It was the invitation list to the carnival ball, still echoing with the majestic poetry of the names which had come to mean so much to me, the names of the Alexandrians. Listen:

Pia dei Tolomei, Benedict Dangeau, Dante Borromeo, Colonel Neguib, Toto de Brunel, Wilmot Pierrefeu, Mehmet Adm, Pozzo di Borgo, Ahmed Hassan Pacha, Delphine de Francueil, Djamboulat Bey, Athena Trasha, Haddad Fahmy Amin, Gaston Phipps, Pierre Balbz, Jacques de Guéry, Count Banubula, Onouphrios Papas, Dmitri Randidi, Paul Capodistria, Claude Amaril, Nessim Hosnani, Tony Umbada, Baldassaro Trivizani, Gilda Ambron. . . .

I murmured the names as I read through the list, mentally adding the word "murderer" after each, simply to see whether it sounded appropriate. Only when I reached the name of Nessim did I pause and raise my eyes to the dark wall—to throw his mental image there and study it as we had studied the pictures. I still saw the expression on his face as I had helped to tuck him into the great car—an expression of curious impish serenity, as of someone resting after a great expenditure of energy.

o   o   o   o   o

PART IV

XII

Despite the season the seafront of the city was gay with light—the long sloping lines of the Grande Corniche curving away to a low horizon; a thousand lighted panels of glass in which, like glorious tropical fish, the inhabitants of the European city sat at glittering tables stocked with glasses of mastic, aniseed or brandy. Watching them (I had eaten little lunch) my hunger overcame me, and as there was some time in hand before my meeting with Justine, I turned into the glittering doors of the Diamond Sutra and ordered a ham sandwich and a glass of whisky. Once again, as always when the drama of external events altered the emotional pattern of things, I began to see the city through new eyes—to examine the shapes and contours made by human beings with the detachment of an entomologist studying a hitherto unknown species of insect. Here it was, the race, each member of it absorbed in the solution of individual preoccupations, loves, hates and fears. A woman counting money on to a glass table, an old man feeding a dog, an Arab in a red flowerpot drawing a curtain.

Aromatic smoke poured from the small sailor taverns along the seafront where the iron spits loaded with a freight of entrails and spices turned monotonously back and forth, or bellied from under the lids of shining copper cauldrons, giving off hot gusts of squid, cuttlefish and pigeon. Here one drank from the blue cans and ate with one's fingers as they do in the Cyclades even to-day.

I picked up a decrepit horse-cab and jogged along by the sighing sea towards the Aurore, drinking in the lighted darkness with regrets and fears so fugitive as to be beyond analysis; but underneath (like a toad under a cool stone, the surface airs of night) I still felt the stirrings of horror at the thought that Justine herself might be endangered by the love which "we bore one another". I turned the thought this way and that in my mind, like a prisoner pressing with all his weight upon doors which denied him an exit from an intolerable bondage, trying to devise an issue from a situation which, it seemed, might as well end in her death as in mine.

The great car was waiting, drawn up off the road in the darkness under the pepper-trees. She opened the door for me silently and I got in, spellbound by my fears.

"Well" she said at last, and giving a little groan which expressed everything, sank into my arms and pressed her warm mouth on mine. "Did you go? Is it over?"

"Yes."

She let in the clutch and the driving wheels spurned the gravel as the car moved out into the pearly nightfall and began to follow the coast road to the outer desert. I studied her harsh Semitic profile in the furry light flung back by the headlights from the common objects of the roadside. It belonged so much to the city which I now saw as a series of symbols stretching away from us on either side—minarets, pigeons, statues, ships, coins, camels and palms; it lived in a heraldic relation to the exhausted landscapes which enclosed it—the loops of the great lake: as proper to the scene as the Sphinx was to the desert.

"My ring" she said. "You brought it?"

"Yes," I polished it once more on my tie and slipped it back once more on to its appropriate finger. Involuntarily I said now: "Justine, what is to become of us?"

She gave me a wild frowning look like a Bedouin woman, and then smiled that warm smile. "Why?"

"Surely you see? We shall have to stop this altogether. I can't bear to think you might be in danger. . . . Or else I should go straight to Nessim and confront him with. . . ." With what? I did not know.

"No," she said softly, "no. You could not do it. You are an Anglo-Saxon . . . you couldn't step outside the law like that, could you? You are not one of us. Besides, you could tell Nessim nothing he does not guess if not actually know. . . . Darling," she laid her warm hand upon mine, "simply wait . . . simply love, above all . . . and we shall see."

It is astonishing now for me to realise, as I record this scene, that she was carrying within her (invisible as the already conceived foetus of a child) Pursewarden's death: that her kisses were, for all I know, falling upon the graven image of my friend—the death-mask of the writer who himself did not love her, indeed regarded her with derision. But such a demon is love that I would not be surprised if in a queer sort of way his death actually enriched our own love-making, filling it with the deceits on which the minds of women feed—the compost of secret pleasures and treacheries which are an inseparable part of every human relation.

Yet what have I to complain of? Even this half-love filled my heart to overflowing. It is she, if anyone, who had cause for complaint. It is very hard to understand these things. Was she already planning her flight from Alexandria then? "The power of woman is such" writes Pursewarden, "that a single kiss can paraphrase the reality of man's life and turn it . . ." but why go on? I was happy sitting beside her, feeling the warmth of her hand as it lay in mine.

The blue night was hoary with stars and the attentive desert stretched away on either side with its grotesque amphitheatres —like the empty rooms in some great cloud-mansion. The moon was late and wan to-night, the air still, the dunes wind-carved. "What are you thinking?" said my lover.

What was I thinking? Of a passage in Proclus which says that Orpheus ruled over the silver race, meaning those who led a "silver" life; on Balthazar's mantelpiece presumably among the pipe-cleaners and the Indian wood-carving of monkeys which neither saw, spoke nor heard evil, under a magic pentacle from Pythagoras. What was I thinking? The foetus in its waxen wallet, the locust squatting in the horn of the wheat, an Arab quoting a proverb which reverberated in the mind. "The memory of man is as old as misfortune." The quails from the burst cage spread upon the ground softly like honey, having no idea of escape. In the Scent Bazaar the flavour of Persian lilac.

"Fourteen thousand years ago" I said aloud, "Vega in Lyra was the Pole Star. Look at her where she burns."

The beloved head turned with its frowning deep-set eyes and once more I see the long boats drawing in to the Pharos, the tides running, the minarets a-glitter with dew; noise of the blind Hodja crying in the voice of a mole assaulted by sunlight; a shuffle-pad of a camel-train clumping to a festival carrying dark lanterns. An Arab woman makes my bed, beating the pillows till they fluff out like white of egg under a whisk; a passage in Pursewarden's book which reads: "They looked at each other, aware that there was neither youth nor strength enough between them to prevent their separation." When Melissa was pregnant by Nessim Amaril could not perform the abortion Nessim so much desired because of her illness and her weak heart. "She may die anyway" he said, and Nessim nodded curtly and took up his overcoat. But she did not die then, she bore the child. . . .

Justine is quoting something in Greek which I do not recognise:

> Sand, dog-roses and white rocks
> Of Alexandria, the mariner's sea-marks,
> Some sprawling dunes falling and pouring
> Sand into water, water into sand,
> Never into the wine of exile
> Which stains the air it is poured through;

> *Or a voice which stains the mind,*
> *Singing in Arabic: "A ship without a sail*
> *Is a woman without breasts." Only that. Only that.*

We walked hand in hand across the soft sand-dunes, laboriously as insects, until we teached Taposiris with its tumble of shattered columns and capitals among the ancient weather-eroded sea-marks. ("Reliques of sensation" says Coleridge, "may exist for an indefinite time in a latent state in the very same order in which they were impressed.") Yes, but the order of the imagination is not that of memory. A faint wind blew off the sea from the Grecian archipelago. The sea was smooth as a human cheek. Only at the edges it stirred and sighed. Those warm kisses remain there, amputated from before and after, existing in their own right like the frail transparencies of ferns or roses pressed between the covers of old books—unique and unfading as the memories of the city they exemplified and evoked: a plume of music from a forgotten carnival-guitar echoing on in the dark streets of Alexandria for as long as silence lasts. . . .

I see all of us not as men and women any longer, identities swollen with their acts of forgetfulness, follies, and deceits—but as beings unconsciously made part of place, buried to the waist among the ruins of a single city, steeped in its values; like those creatures of whom Empedocles wrote "Solitary limbs wandered, seeking for union with one another," or in another place, "So it is that sweet lays hold of sweet, bitter rushes to bitter, acid comes to acid, warm couples with warm." All members of a city whose actions lay just outside the scope of the plotting or conniving spirit: Alexandrians.

Justine, lying back against a fallen column at Taposiris, dark head upon the darkness of the sighing water, one curl lifted by the sea-winds, saying: "In the whole of English only one phrase means something to me, the words: 'Time Immemorial'."

Seen across the transforming screens of memory, how remote that forgotten evening seems. There was so much as yet left for us all to live through until we reached the occasion of the great duckshoot which so abruptly, concisely, precipitated the final change—and the disappearance of Justine herself. But all this belongs to another Alexandria—one which I created in my mind and which the great Interlinear of Balthazar has, if not destroyed, changed out of all recognition.

"To intercalate realities" writes Balthazar, "is the only way to be faithful to Time, for at every moment in Time the possibilities are endless in their multiplicity. Life consists in the act of choice. The perpetual reservation of judgment and the perpetual choosing."

From the vantage-point of this island I can see it all in its doubleness, in the intercalation of fact and fancy, with new eyes; and re-reading, re-working reality in the light of all I now know, I am surprised to find that my feelings themselves have changed, have grown, have deepened even. Perhaps then the destruction of my private Alexandria was necessary ("the artifact of a true work of art never shows a plane surface"); perhaps buried in all this there lies the germ and substance of a truth —time's usufruct—which, if I can accommodate it, will carry me a little further in what is really a search for my proper self. We shall see.

o o o o o

XIII

"Clea and her old father, whom she worships. White-haired, erect, with a sort of haunted pity in his eyes for the young unmarried goddess he has fathered. Once a year, however, on New Year's eve, they dance at the Cecil, stately, urbanely. He waltzes like a clockwork man." Somewhere I once wrote down these words. They bring to mind another scene, another sequence of events.

The old scholar comes to sit at my table. He has a particular weakness for me, I do not know why, but he always talks to me with humorous modesty as we sit and watch his beautiful daughter move around the room in the arms of an admirer, so graceful and so composed. "There is so much of the schoolgirl still about her—or the artist. To-night her cape had some wine on it so she put a mackintosh over her ball gown and ate the toffees which she found in the pockets. I don't know what her mother would say if she were alive." We drank quietly and watched the coloured lights flickering among the dancers. He said "I feel like an old procurer. Always looking out for someone to marry her. . . . Her happiness seems so important, somehow . . . I am going the right way about to spoil it I know, by meddling . . . yet I can't leave it alone . . . I've scraped a dowry together over the years. . . . The money burns my pocket. . . . When I see a nice Englishman like you my instinct is to say: 'For God's sake take her and look after her.' . . . It has been a bitter pleasure bringing her up without a mother. Eh? No fool like an old fool." And he walks stiffly away to the bar, smiling.

Presently that evening Clea herself came and sat beside me in the alcove, fanning herself and smiling. "Quarter of an hour to midnight. Poor Cinderella. I must get my father home before the clock strikes or he'll lose his beauty-sleep!"

We spoke then of Amar whose trial for the murder of de Brunel had ended that afternoon with his acquittal due to lack of direct evidence.

"I know," said Clea softly. "And I'm glad. It has saved me from a *crise de conscience*. I would not have known what to do if he had been convicted. You see, I know he didn't do it. Why? Because, my dear, I know who did and why. . . ." She narrowed those splendid eyes and went on. "A story of Alexandria—shall I tell you? But only if you keep it a secret. Would you promise me? Bury it with the old year—all our misfortunes and follies. You must have had a surfeit of them by now, must you not? All right. Listen. On the night of the carnival I lay in bed thinking about a picture—the big one of Justine. It was all wrong and I didn't know where. But I suspected the hands— those dark and shapely hands. I had got their position quite faithfully, but, well, something in the composition didn't go; it had started to trouble me at this time—months after the thing was finished. I can't think why. Suddenly I said to myself 'Those hands want thinking about,' and I had the thing lugged back to my room from the studio where I stood it against a wall. Well, to no effect, really; I'd spent the whole evening smoking over it, and sketching the hands in different positions from memory. Somehow I thought it might be that beastly Byzantine ring which she wears. Anyway, all my thinking was of no avail so about midnight I turned in, and lay smoking in bed with my cat asleep on my feet.

"From time to time a small group of people passed outside in the street, singing or laughing, but gradually the town was draining itself of life, for it was getting late.

"Suddenly in the middle of the silence I heard feet running at full speed. I have never heard anyone run so fast, so lightly. Only danger or terror or distress could make someone put on such a mad burst of speed, I thought, as I listened. Down Rue Fouad came the footsteps at the same breakneck pace and turned the corner into St. Saba, getting louder all the time. They crossed over, paused, and then crossed back to my side of the street. Then came a wild pealing at my bell.

"I sat up in some surprise and switched on the light to look at the clock. Who could it be at such a time? While I was still sitting there irresolutely, it came again: a long double peal. Well! The electric switch on the front door is shut off at midnight so there was no help for it but to go down and see who it was. I put on a dressing-gown and slipping my little pistol into the pocket I went down to see. There was a shadow on the glass of the front door which was too thick to challenge anyone through, so I had to open it. I stood back a bit. 'Who's there?'

"There was a man standing there, hanging in the corner of the door like a bat. He was breathing heavily for I saw his breast rising and falling, but he made no sound. He wore a domino, but the headpiece was turned back so that I could see his face in the light of the street-lamp. I was of course rather frightened for a moment. He looked as if he were about to faint. It took me about ten seconds before I could put a name to the ugly face with its cruel great hare-lip. Then relief flooded me and my feet got pins and needles. Do you know who it was? His hair was matted with sweat and in that queer light his eyes looked enormous—blue and childish. I realized that it was that strange brother of Nessim's—the one nobody ever sees. Narouz Hosnani. Even this was rather a feat of memory: I only remembered him vaguely from the time when Nessim took me riding on the Hosnani lands. You can imagine my concern to see him like this, unexpectedly, in the middle of the night.

"I did not know what to say, and he for his part was trying to articulate something, but the words would not come. It seemed he had two sentences jammed together in the front of his mind, like cartridges in the muzzle of a gun, and neither would give place to the other. He leaned inwards upon me with a ghastly incoherence, his hands hanging down almost below his knees which gave him an ape-like silhouette, and croaked something at me. You mustn't laugh. It was horrifying. Then he drew a great breath and forced his muscles to obey him and said in a small marionette's voice: 'I have come to tell you that I love you because I have killed Justine.' For a moment I almost suspected a joke. 'What?' I stammered. He repeated in an even smaller voice, a whisper, but mechanically as a child repeating a lesson: 'I have come to tell you that I love you because I have killed Justine.' Then in a deep voice he added 'O Clea, if you but knew the agony of it.' And he gave a sob and fell on his knees in the hall, holding the edge of my dressing-gown, his head bowed while the tears trickled down his nose.

"I didn't know what to do. I was at once horrified and disgusted, and yet I couldn't help feeling sorry. From time to time he gave a small harsh cry—the noise of a she-camel crying, or of some dreadful mechanical toy, perhaps. It was unlike anything I have seen or heard before or since. His trembling was communicated to me through the fringe of my gown which he held in two fingers.

" 'Get up' I said at last, and raising his head he croaked: 'I swear I did not mean to do it. It happened before I could think. She put her hand upon me, Clea, she made advances to me. Horrible. Nessim's own wife.'

"I did not know what to make of all this. Had he really harmed Justine? 'You just come upstairs' I said, keeping tight hold of my little pistol, for his expression was pretty frightening. 'Get up now.' He got up at once, quite obediently, and followed me back up the stairs, but leaning heavily against the wall and whispering something incoherently to himself, Justine's name, I think, though it sounded more like 'Justice'.

" 'Come in while I telephone' I said, and he followed me

slowly, half-blinded by the light. He stood by the door for a moment, accustoming himself to it, and then he saw the portrait. He exclaimed with great force: 'This Jewish fox has eaten my life,' and struck his fists against his thighs several times. Then he put his hands over his face and breathed deeply. We waited like this facing one another, while I thought what there was to be done. They had all gone to the Cervoni ball, I knew. I would telephone them to find out if there was any truth in this story.

"Meanwhile Narouz opened his fingers and peeped at me. He said: 'I only came to tell you I loved you before giving myself up to my brother.' Then he spread his hands in a hopeless gesture. 'That is all.'

"How disgusting, how unfair love is! Here I had been loved for goodness knows how long by a creature—I cannot say a fellow-creature—of whose very existence I had been unaware. Every breath I drew was unconsciously a form of his suffering, without my ever having been aware of it. How had this disaster come about? You will have to make room in your thoughts for this variety of the animal. I was furious, disgusted and wounded in one and the same moment. I felt almost as if I owed him an apology; and yet I also felt insulted by the intrusiveness of a love which I had never asked him to owe me.

"Narouz looked now as if he were in a high fever. His teeth chattered in his head and he was shaken by spasms of violent shivering. I gave him a glass of cognac which he drained at one gulp, and then another even larger one. Drinking it he sank slowly down to the carpet and doubled his legs under him like an Arab. 'It is better at last' he whispered, and looking sadly round him added: 'So this is where you live. I have wanted to see it for years. I have been imagining it all.' Then he frowned and coughed and combed his hair back with his fingers.

"I rang the Cervoni house and almost at once got hold of Nessim. I questioned him tactfully, without giving anything away. But there seemed nothing wrong, as far as could be judged, though he could not at that moment locate Justine. She was somewhere on the dance-floor. Narouz listened to all this with staring surprised eyes, incredulous. 'She is due to meet them in the hall in ten minutes' time. Finish your drink and wait until she rings up. Then you will know that there has been some mistake.' He closed his eyes and seemed to pray.

"I sat down opposite him on the sofa, not knowing quite what to say. 'What exactly happened?' I asked him. All of a sudden his eyes narrowed and grew small, suspicious-looking. Then he sighed and hung his head, tracing the design of the carpet with his finger. 'It is not for you to hear' he whispered, his lips trembling.

"We waited like this, and all of a sudden, to my intense embarrassment and disgust, he began to talk of his love for me, but in the tone of a man talking to himself. He seemed almost oblivious of me, never once looking up into my face. And I felt all the apologetic horror that comes over me when I am admired or desired and cannot reciprocate the feeling. I was somehow ashamed too, looking at that brutal tear-stained face, simply because I could not feel the slightest stirring of sympathy within my heart. He sat there on the carpet like some great brown toad, talking; like some story-book troglodyte. What the devil was I to do? 'When have you seen me?' I asked him. He had only seen me three times in his life, though frequently at night he passed through the street to see if my light was on. I swore under my breath. It was so unfair. I had done nothing to merit this grotesque passion.

"Then at last came a reprieve. The telephone rang, and he trembled all over like a hound as he heard the unmistakable hoarse tones of the woman he thought he had killed. There was nothing wrong that she knew of, and she was on her way home with Nessim. Everything was as it should be at the Cervoni house and the ball was still going on at full blast. As I said good night I felt Narouz clasp my slippers and begin kissing them with gratitude. 'Thank you. Thank you' he repeated over and over again.

" 'Come on. Get up. It's time to go home.' I was deathly tired by now. I advised him to go straight back home and to confide his story to nobody. 'Perhaps you have imagined the whole thing' I said, and he gave me a tired but brilliant smile.

"He walked slowly and heavily downstairs before me, still shaken by his experience, it was clear, but the hysteria had left him. I opened the front door, and he tried once more to express his incoherent gratitude and affection. He seized my hands and kissed them repeatedly with great wet hairy kisses. Ugh! I can feel them now. And then, before turning into the night, he said in a low voice, smiling: 'Clea, this is the happiest day of my life, to have seen and touched you and to have seen your little room.' "

Clea sipped her drink, nodding into the middle distance for a moment with a sad smile on her face. Then she looked at her own brown hands and gave a little shudder. "Ugh! The kisses" she said under her breath and with an involuntary movement began to rub her hands, palms upward, upon the red plush arm of the chair, as if to obliterate the kisses once and for all, to expunge the memory of them.

But now the band had begun to play a Paul Jones (perhaps the very dance in which Arnauti first met Justine?) and the warm lighted gallery of faces began to fan out once more from the centre of the darkness, the brilliance of flesh and cloth and jewels in the huge gaunt ballroom where the palms splintered themselves in the shivering mirrors: leaking through the windows to where the moonlight waited patiently among the deserted public gardens and highways, troubling the uneasy water of the outer harbour with its glittering heartless gestures. "Come," said Clea, "why do you never play a part in these things? Why do you prefer to sit apart and study us all?"

But I was thinking as I watched the circle of lovely faces move forward and reverse among the glitter of jewellery and the rustle of silks, of the Alexandrians to whom these great varieties of experience meant only one more addition to the sum of an infinite knowledge husbanded by their world-weariness. Round and round the floor we went, the women unconsciously following the motion of the stars, of the earth as it curved into space; and then suddenly like a declaration of war, like an expulsion from the womb, silence came, and a voice crying: "Take your partners please." And the lights throbbed down the spectrum to purple and a waltz began. For a brief moment at the far end of the darkness I caught a glimpse of Nessim and Justine dancing together, smiling into each other's eyes. The shapely hand on his shoulder still wore the great ring taken from the tomb of a Byzantine youth. Life is short, art long.

Clea's father was dancing with her, stiffly, happily, like a clockwork mouse; and he was kissing the gifted hand upon which the unwanted kisses of Narouz had fallen on that forgotten evening. A daughter is closer than a wife.

"At first" writes Pursewarden, "we seek to supplement the emptiness of our individuality through love, and for a brief moment enjoy the illusion of completeness. But it is only an illusion. For this strange creature, which we thought would join us to the body of the world, succeeds at last in separating us most thoroughly from it. Love joins and then divides. How else would we be growing?"

How else indeed? But relieved to find myself once more partnerless I have already groped my way back to my dark corner where the empty chairs of the revellers stand like barren ears of corn.

o   o   o   o   o

XIV

In the early summer I received a letter from Clea with which this brief memorial to Alexandria may well be brought to a close. It was unexpected.

"*Tashkent Syria*

"Your letter, so unexpected after a silence which I feared might endure all through life, followed me out of Persia to this small house perched high on a hillside among the cedars and pines. I have taken it for six months in order to try my hand and brush on these odd mountains—rocks bursting with fresh water and Mediterranean flowers. Turtle doves by day and nightingales by night. What a relief after the dust. How long is it—two years or more perhaps? Ah, my dear friend, I trembled a little as I slit open the envelope. Why? I was afraid that what you might have to say would drag me back by the hair to old places and scenes long since abandoned; the old stations and sites of the personality which belonged to the Alexandrian Clea you knew—not to me any longer, or at any rate, not wholly. I've changed. A new woman, certainly a new painter is emerging, still a bit tender and shy like the horns of a snail—but new. A whole new world of experience stands between us. . . . How could you know all this? You would perhaps be writing to Clea, the old Clea; what would I find to say to you in reply? I put off reading your letter until to-night. It touched me and reply I must: so here it is—my own letter written at odd times, between painting sessions, or at night when I light the stove and make my dinner. To-day is a good day to begin it for it is raining—and the whole mountain side under the hush of the rain and the noise of swollen springs. The trees are alive with giant snails.

"So Balthazar has been disturbing you with his troublesome new information? I am not sure that I approve. It may be good for you, but surely not for your book or books which must, I suppose, put us all in a very special position regarding reality. I mean as 'characters' rather than human beings. No? And why, you ask me, did I never tell you a tithe of the things you know now? One never does, you know, one never does. As a spectator standing equidistant between two friends or lovers one is always torn by friendship to intervene, to interfere—but one never does. Rightly. How could I tell you what I knew of Justine—or for that matter what I felt about your neglect of Melissa? The very range of my sympathies for the three of you precluded it. As for love, it is so paradoxical a creature and so satisfying in itself that it would not have been much altered by the intervention of truths from outside. I am sure now, if you analyse your feelings, you will find you love Justine *better* because she betrayed you! The whore is man's true darling, as I once told you, and we are born to love those who most wound us. Tell me, wise one, am I wrong? Besides, my own affection for you lay in another quarter. I was jealous of you as a writer —and as a writer I wanted you to myself and did so keep you. Do you see?

"There is nothing I can do to help you now—I mean help your book. You will either have to ignore the data which Balthazar has so wickedly supplied, or to 'rework reality' as you put it.

"And you say you were unjust to Pursewarden; yes, but it is not important. He was equally unjust to you. Unknown to either of you, you joined hands in me! As writers. My only regret is that he did not manage to finish the last volume of *God is a Humorist* according to plan. It is a loss—though it cannot detract from his achievement. You, I surmise, will soon be coming into the same degree of self-possession—perhaps through this cursed city of ours, Alexandria, to which we most belong when we most hate it. By the way, I have a letter from Pursewarden about the missing volume which I have carried around with me among my papers for ages, like a talisman. It helps not only to revive the man himself a bit, but to revive me also when I fall into a depression about my work. (I must go to the village to buy eggs. I shall copy it out to-night for you.)

"Later. Here is the letter I spoke about, harsh and crabbed if you like, but none the less typical of our friend. Don't take his remarks about you too seriously. He admired you and believed in you—so he once told me. Perhaps he was lying. Anyway."

Mount Vulture Hotel
Alexandria

'My dear Clea:

'A surprise and delight to find your letter waiting for me. Clement reader thank you—not for the blame or praise (one shrinks from both equally) but for being there, devoted and watchful, a true reader between the lines—where all real writing is done! I have just come hotfoot from the Café al Aktar after listening to a long discursion on "the novel" by old Lineaments and Keats and Pombal. They talk as if every novel wasn't *sui generis*—it is as meaningless to me as Pombal generalising about "les femmes" as a race; for after all it isn't the family relationship which really matters. Well, Lineaments was saying that Redemption and Original Sin were the new topics and that the writer of to-day. . . . Ouf! I fled, feeling like the writer of the day before yesterday, and unwilling to help them build this sort of mud-pie.

'I'm sure old Lineaments will do a lovely novel about Original Sin and score what I always privately call a suck-eggs *d'estime* (it means not covering one's advance). In fact, I was in such despair at the thought of his coming fame that I thought

I would go straight off to a brothel and expiate my unoriginal sense of sin right away. But the hour was early, and besides, I felt that I smelt of sweat for it has been a hot day. I therefore returned to the hotel for a shower and a change of shirt and so found your letter. There is a little gin in the bottle and as I don't know where I shall be later on I think I'll just sit down and answer you now as best I can until six when the brothels start to open.

'The questions you ask me, my dear Clea, are the very questions I am putting myself. I must get them a little clearer before adressing myself to the last volume in which I want above all to combine, resolve and harmonise the tensions so far created. I feel I want to sound a note of . . . affirmation— though not in the specific terms of a philosophy or religion. It should have the curvature of an embrace, the wordlessness of a lovers' code. It should convey some feeling that the world we live in is founded in something too simple to be over-described as cosmic law—but as easy to grasp as, say, an act of tenderness, simple tenderness in the primal relation between animal and plant, rain and soil, seed and trees, man and God. A relationship so delicate that it is all too easily broken by the inquiring mind and *conscience* in the French sense which of course has its own rights and its own field of deployment. I'd like to think of my work simply as a cradle in which philosophy could rock itself to sleep, thumb in mouth. What do you say to this? After all, this is not simply what we most need in the world, but really what describes the state of pure process in it. Keep silent awhile and you feel a comprehension of this act of tenderness—not power or glory: and certainly not Mercy, that vulgarity of the Jewish mind which can only imagine man as crouching under the whip. No, for the sort of tenderness I mean is utterly merciless! "A law unto itself" as we say. Of course, one must always remember that truth itself is always halved in utterance. Yet I must in this last book insist that there is hope for man, scope for man, within the boundaries of a simple law; and I seem to see mankind as gradually appropriating to itself the necessary information through mere attention, *not reason*, which may one day enable it to live within the terms of such an idea—the true meaning of "joy unconfined". How could joy be anything else? This new creature we artists are hunting for will not "live" so much as, like time itself simply "elapse". Damn, it's hard to say these things. Perhaps the key lies in laughter, in the Humorous God? It is after all the serious who disturb the peace of the heart with their antics –like Justine. (Wait. I must fix myself a ration of gin.)

'I think it better for us to steer clear of the big oblong words like Beauty and Truth and so on. Do you mind? We are all so silly and feeble-witted when it comes to living, but giants when it comes to pronouncing on the universe. *Sufflaminandus erat*. Like you, I have two problems which interconnect: my art and my life. Now in my life I am somewhat irresolute and shabby, but in my art I am free to be what I most desire to seem—someone who might bring resolution and harmony into the dying lives around me. In my art, indeed, through my art, I want really to achieve myself shedding the work, which is of *no importance*, as a snake sheds its skin. Perhaps that's why writers at heart want to be loved for their work rather than for themselves—do you think? But then this presupposes a new order of woman too. Where is she?

'These, my dear Clea, are some of the perplexities of your omniscient friend, the classical head and romantic heart of Ludwig Pursewarden.'

"Ouf! It is late and the oil in the lamp is low. I must leave this letter for to-night. To-morrow perhaps, if I am in the mood after my shopping, I shall write a little more; if not, not. Wise one, how much better it would be if we could *talk*. I feel

I have whole conversations stacked inside me, lying unused! I think it is perhaps the only real lack of which one is conscious in living alone; the mediating power of a friend's thoughts to place beside one's own, just to see if they match! The lonely become autocratic, as they must, and their judgments *ex cathedra* in the very nature of things: and perhaps this is not altogether good for the work. But here at least we will be well-matched, you on your island—which is only a sort of metaphor like Descartes' oven, isn't it?—and I in my fairy-tale hut among the mountains.

"Last week a man appeared among the trees, also a painter, and my heart began to beat unwontedly fast. I felt the sudden predisposition to fall in love—reasoning thus, I suppose: 'If one has gone so far from the world and one finds a man in that place, must he not be the one person destined to share one's solitude, brought to this very place by the invisible power of one's selfless longing and destined specially for oneself?' Dangerous self-delusive tricks the heart plays on itself, always tormented by the desire to be loved! Balthazar claimed once that he could induce love as a control-experiment by a simple action: namely telling each of two people who had never met that the other was dying to meet them, had never seen anyone so attractive, and so on. This was, he claimed, infallible as a means of making them fall in love: they always did. What do you say?

"At any rate, my own misgivings saved me from the youth who was, I will admit, handsome and indeed quite intelligent, and would have done me good, I think, as a lover—perhaps for a single summer. But when I saw his *paintings* I felt my soul grow hard and strong and separate again; through them I read his whole personality as one can read a handwriting or a face. I saw weakness and poverty of heart and a power to do mischief. So I said good-bye there and then. The poor youth kept repeating: 'Have I done anything to offend you, have I said

240

"No. No. The death of an artist is quite unassailable. One can only smile and bow.

"As for Scobie, you are right in what you say. I was terribly upset when Balthazar told me that he had fallen down those stairs at the central Quism and killed himself. Yes, I took his parrot, which by the way was inhabited by the old man's spirit for a long time afterwards. It reproduced with perfect fidelity the way he got up in the morning singing a snatch of '*Taisez-vous, petit babouin*' (do you remember?) and even managed to imitate the dismal cracking of the old man's bones as he got out of bed. But then the memory gradually wore out, like an old disc, and he seemed to do it less often and with less sureness of voice. It was like Scobie himself dying very gradually into silence: this is how I suppose one dies to one's friends and to the world, wearing out like an old dance tune or a memorable conversation with a philosopher under a cherry-tree. Being refunded into silence. And finally the bird itself went into a decline and died with its head under its wing. I was so sorry, yet so glad.

"For us, the living, the problem is of a totally different order: how to harness time in the cultivation of a style of heart —something like that? I am only trying to express it. Not to force time, as the weak do, for that spells self-injury and dismay, but to harness its rhythms and put them to our own use. Pursewarden used to say: 'God give us artists resolution and tact'; to which I myself would say a very hearty Amen.

"But by now you will think that I have simply become an opinionated old shrew. Perhaps I have. What does it matter, provided one can get a single idea across to oneself?

"There is so little time; with the news from Europe becoming worse every day I feel an autumnal quality in the days—as if they were settling towards an unpredictable future. And side by side with this feeling, I also feel the threads tightening in our sleeves, so to speak, drawing us slowly back towards the centre of the stage once more. Where could this be but to Alexandria? But perhaps it will prove to be a new city, different to the one which has for so long imposed itself on our dreams. I would like to think that, for the old one and all it symbolized is, if not dead, at least meaningless to the person I now feel myself to be. Perhaps you too have changed by the same token. Perhaps your book too has changed. Or perhaps you, more than any of us, need to see the city again, need to see us again. We, for our part, very much need to see you again and refresh the friendship which we hope exists the other side of the writing— if indeed an author can ever be just a friend to his 'characters'. I say 'we', writing in the Imperial Style as if I were a Queen, but you will guess that I mean, simply, both the old Clea and the new—for both have need of you in a future which. . . ."

There are a few more lines and then the affectionate superscription.

CONSEQUENTIAL DATA

o   o   o

Some shorthand notes of Keats's, recording the Obiter Dicta of Pursewarden in fragmentary fashion:

(a)

"*I know my prose is touched with plum pudding, but then all the prose belonging to the poetic continuum is; it is intended to give a stereoscopic effect to character. And events aren't in serial form but collect here and there like quanta, like real life.*"

(b)

"*Nessim hasn't got the resources we Anglo-Saxons have; all our women are nurses at heart. In order to secure the lifelong devotion of an Anglo-Saxon woman one has only to get one's legs cut off above the waist. I've always thought Lady Chatterley weak in symbolism from this point of view. Nothing should have earned the devotion of his wife more surely than Clifford's illness. Anglo-Saxons may not be interested in love like other Europeans but they can get just as ill. Characteristically, it is to his English Kate that Laforgue cries out: 'Une Garde-malade pour l'amour de l'art!' He detected the nurse.*"

(c)

"*The classical in art is what marches by intention with the cosmology of the age.*"

(d)

"*A state-imposed metaphysic or religion should be opposed, if necessary at pistol-point. We must fight for variety if we fight at all. The uniform is as dull as a sculptured egg.*"

Of Da Capo: "Gamblers and lovers really play to lose."

"Art like life is an open secret."

"Science is the poetry of the intellect and poetry the science of the heart's affections."

"Truth is independent of fact. It does not mind being disproved. It is already dispossessed in utterance."

"I love the French edition with its uncut pages. I would not want a reader too lazy to use a knife on me."

In a book of poems: "One to be taken from time to time as needed and allowed to dissolve in the mind."

"We must always defend Plato to Aristotle and vice versa because if they should lose touch with each other we should be lost. The dimorphism of the psyche produced them both."

"To the medieval world-picture of the World, the Flesh and the Devil (each worth a book) we moderns have added Time: a fourth dimension."

"New critical apparatus: le roman bifteck, guignol *or* cafard.*"*

(n)

"The real ruins of Europe are its great men."

(o)

"I have always believed in letting my reader sink or skim."

(p)

On reading a long review of God is a Humorist: *"Good God! At last they are beginning to take me seriously. This imposes a terrible burden on me. I must redouble my laughter."*

(q)

"Why do I always choose an epigraph from de Sade? Because he demonstrates pure rationalism—the ages of sweet reason we have lived through in Europe since Descartes. He is the final flower of reason, and the typic of European behaviour. I hope to live to see him translated into Chinese. His books would bring the house down and would read as pure humour. But his spirit has already brought the house down around our ears."

(r)

"Europe: a Logical Positivist trying to prove to himself by logical deduction that he exists."

(s)

"My objects in the novels? To interrogate human values through an honest representation of the human passions. A desirable end, perhaps a hopeless objective."

(t)

"My unkindest critics maintain that I am making lampshades out of human skin. This puzzles me. Perhaps at the bottom of the Anglo-Saxon soul there is a still small voice forever whispering: 'Is this Quaite Naice?' and my books never seem to pass the test."

SCOBIE'S COMMON USAGE

Expressions noted from Scobie's quaint conversation, his use of certain words, as:

Vivid, meaning "angry", ex.: "Don't be so vivid, old man."

Mauve, meaning "silly", ex.: "He was just plain mauve when it came to, etc."

Spoof, meaning "trick", ex.: "Don't spoof me, old boy."

Ritual, meaning "habit, form", ex.: "We all wear them. It's ritual for the police."

Squalid, meaning "very elated", ex.: "Toby was squalid with joy when the news came."

Septic, meaning "unspeakable", ex.: "What septic weather to-day!"

Saffron Walden, meaning "male brothel", ex.: "He was caught in a Saffron Walden, old man, covered in jam."

Cloud Cuckoo, meaning "male prostitute", ex.: "Budgie says there's not a cloud cuckoo in the whole of Horsham. He's advertised."

WORKPOINTS

"How many lovers since Pygmalion have been able to build their beloved's face out of flesh, as Amaril has?" asked Clea. The great folio of noses so lovingly copied for him to choose from—Nefertiti to Cleopatra. The readings in a darkened room.

o   o   o

Narouz always held in the back of his consciousness the memory of the moonlit room; his father sitting in the wheelchair at the mirror, repeating the one phrase over and over again as he pointed the pistol at the looking-glass.

o   o   o

Mountolive was swayed by the dangerous illusion that now at last he was free to conceive and act—the one misjudgement which decides the fate of a diplomat.

o   o   o

Nessim said sadly: "All motive is mixed. You see, from the moment I married her, a Jewess, all their reservations disappeared and they ceased to suspect me. I do not say it was the only reason. Love is a wonderfully luxuriant plant, but unclassifiable really, fading as it does into mysticism on the one side and naked cupidity on the other."

o   o   o

This now explained something to me which had hitherto puzzled me; namely that after his death Da Capo's huge library was moved over to Smyrna, book by book. Balthazar did the packing and posting.

NOTES

* *Page 131*

From Eugène Marais's *The Soul of The White Ant.*